Streethearts

Greg Herriges

Streethearts

Greg Herriges

SERVING HOUSE BOOKS

Streethearts

ISBN: 978-0-9858495-4-2

Cover design by Michelle Everst

Author photo by Carmen Perez

Serving House Books logo by Barry Lereng Wilmont

The author wishes to thank the following individuals for their support and kindness: Thomas E. Kennedy, Duff Brenna, R.A. Rycaft, Walter Cummins, Derek Alger, Tony Romano, Mark Breyer, Rick Vittenson.

Special thanks to Ileana LaBoy-Perez and Michael Perez for Spanish language consultation.

Published by Serving House Books, LLC
Copenhagen, Denmark and Florham Park, NJ

www.servinghousebooks.com

First Serving House Books Edition 2013

For my wife, my love,
Carmen Perez

Also by Greg Herriges:

Someplace Safe

Secondary Attachments

The Winter Dance Party Murders

JD: A Memoir of a Time and a Journey

The Bay of Marseilles and Other Stories

Lennon and Me

A Song of Innocence

"All alone, all alone.
Oh, what a joy to be all alone.
I'm happy alone, don't you see.
I've convinced you, now how about me?
All alone."

—**Lenny Bruce**

1

For starters, the alarm went off and the news station came on and the announcer said that a woman and her five children had been found murdered in their home in Sioux City, Iowa. A Ukrainian immigrant in California had confessed to killing his wife, his son, and four other relatives, said that they'd been trying to poison him. A Chicago cop was in the hospital in critical condition with a bullet in his brain. Ford was laying off another five thousand people. We were going to have to set the clock radio to a different station.

Marlyn lay next to me, asleep, or semi-asleep, stirred, made moaning sounds. She wore a chiffon nightgown and was as beautiful as the day we married, sixteen years ago, my former student, my wife. I wondered where sixteen years could have slipped away to so effortlessly. It occurred to me that we had not had much to do with one another lately.

First day of the fall semester. There was the spray of the shower, sting of the razor, and a thousand aches and pains that I had never known when I began teaching twenty-two years ago. Ten years away from early retirement and ten past giving much of a damn anymore, about any of it. I burned the toast and threw it away and stood drinking my coffee, looking out the vertical blinds at all the fallen acorns on the front lawn. You'd think the squirrels would recognize a windfall when they saw one. The raccoon had gotten the garbage again last night. A pale, full moon was melting in cobalt and I found myself looking for reasons to call in sick, then realized that this was not a good attitude. What the hell. Nobody had promised life would be fun.

Back upstairs I grabbed a sport coat from the closet and leaned over to kiss Marlyn's forehead. She mumbled a goodbye without opening her eyes, Spanish eyes. Out in the hallway I nudged open Jason's bedroom door. It looked like a bomb had gone off in there. Undershirts and Jockeys on the floor, blue jean shorts lying on his desk, football pads and jersey and pants thrown in piles upon other piles, rap CDs stacked carelessly on his dresser next to the retainer that he was supposed to be wearing to preserve the effects of three thousand dollars' worth of orthodontia. My boy was a slob, but I knew how lucky I was to have him, whether he could find the laundry hamper or not. I took a twenty dollar bill out of my pants pocket and inserted it in his wallet and left it on his desk.

On my way out the door, I tripped over Marlyn's gym bag where she had left it on the mat after working out the night before. She was a psychiatric nurse and would be working a double today. *That should be fun,* I thought, considering some of the patients she had complained of lately—the obese woman who thought she was going to give birth to John The Baptist, for instance, or the old man who urinated on the Martians under his bed. And a full moon to boot. I stooped, picked up the bag, took it down to the utility room, and stopped short of starting the washer. Funny. Her workout clothes were clean and folded. I thought she had said she'd been at the health club last night, but I must have been mistaken. This is what came of trying to be helpful.

I backed the old Jeep out of the garage and took Deerfield Road to the Edens Expressway. I had come full circle in the past decade and a half, having made the conversion from suburbanite to city dweller, and now here I was again in underground-sprinkler land. Every day I experienced the kind of culture shock that would send my neighbors to the Zoloft bottle, only now it didn't shock me anymore. I had been teaching at the same inner city high school for over two decades, and had the blank stare to prove it. When I was young and new at the game, it was the most exciting thing I had ever done, teaching kids who had grown up in the barrio and who knew very little about the world outside of its borders.

I wasn't young anymore.

I exited at North Avenue and stopped at a diner at the corner for coffee and a bag of doughnuts. The waitress knew me and said *hola* and asked me in Spanish how I was doing. "*Asi asi,*" I said. She was a pretty thing of about twenty-three with bright eyes and I wondered if she had plans to do anything else with her life other than tend counter. It was

10

none of my business, of course. It was more or less the kind of thing educators were trained to think, as if *we* had it so good. On the way back to the Jeep I saw a man in a parked car stick a hypodermic needle directly into his neck and push the plunger down. He rolled his head back and forth for a while and then lay still. Good morning.

Puerto Rican Town sprawled up against Ukrainian Village. You had your Caribbean restaurants (both of them excellent), salsa dance clubs, salsa CD shops, bars, a florist, two tattoo parlors, a *dentista*, the Caballeros de San Juan Credit Union, the Armory for the local Army Reserve, a local alderman's office, and rising eight stories into the air in the center of Humboldt Park, José Julián Acosta High School. It had originally been named after Freddie Prinze—but some neighborhood political forces thought perhaps that had been in bad taste, so now it took the name of the island's greatest abolitionist of the 19th century, a journalist. Taste is taste, I guess. It hadn't bothered me, either way. I had always liked Freddie, and Acosta had been a great man.

The place had run down pretty badly over the years. There were many reasons for this. Educating and handling 2,500 kids a year takes its toll, and upkeep is something that the school board never funded adequately. Also, the lower floor lobby windows were made of plastic, and the janitorial staff had not known that the solvent they used to clean them would melt the surface, rendering them opaque. Add to that graffiti, weather wear, crumbling concrete, and there you have it— an aging eyesore in the middle of the most gang-infested area in the nation.

Either my cell phone or my keys set off the metal detector alarm. Oscar, a security guard to whom I had said good morning every day for the past twelve years, grabbed my arm and made me go through it again. I said, "Oh, come on, Oscar. You know I haven't got a gun, for Christ's sake."

"I no care. Rules are rules. I have my orders."

Oscar knew all about rules and orders. I removed from my pockets the phone, the keys, a pen in my shirt pocket, and placed them in a tray by the side of the metal detector. I walked through once more and the alarm did not activate.

"You see?" Oscar said to me.

I saw, all right. Twelve years.

I was lucky enough to get on the elevator with Martha Ballinger, the principal. Martha was fifty-four, built something like a sack of Idaho potatoes, and she wore makeup badly. But at least she made the effort. She looked down at my loafers and slowly raised her eyes to mine.

"You might want to wear socks to work tomorrow, Mr. Spector. We do have a dress code, you know."

The lid on my coffee cup was loose and I accidentally scalded my hand. I said, "Does it seem at all odd to you, Martha, advising me how to dress? I'll be forty-five next year."

"I know," she said as the elevator doors pulled open. "You'd think you'd know better."

And there you have it—the bad boy who'd never grown up. Even when I'd been a high school student I upset the administrators. Nothing had changed, except that now they paid me for it. I thought this over as the doors closed and I rode up to the eighth floor, to Vince Arcelli's office. Actually it was a closet, Vince's office. Vince taught physics, and the physics program needed a closet, and I guess he figured he was harder to find this way. I fumbled my coffee and the bag of doughnuts into one hand and rapped three times upon the door. "Mr. Arcelli? Time to come out of the closet."

The door sprung open. Vince was sitting at his desk building a model rocket next to framed photos of his three kids. "You know, there are those among us who would consider that remark politically incorrect."

"Vince, I can't tell you how that worries me. You want a doughnut?"

"You've got doughnuts?"

I said, "Do school administrators have poor judgment?"

I liked Vince. A tall Italian with an olive complexion and a ready grin, Vince had been raised on the South Side and mangled English grammar as a sideline. We'd been friends for eighteen years, and I supposed anyone who could put up with me for that length of time was someone I should value. His wife and my wife hit it off and we saw each other socially. I said, "Going to put a mouse into orbit?"

He stood the rocket on its fins and regarded it thoughtfully. "The company that makes these things donated a hundred kits to my science classes. I'm gonna have the kids put 'em together and take 'em out on the baseball field next spring and launch 'em all at once. Whattaya think?"

"I don't think Martha will give you permission for that."

"I know she won't. That's why I'm not gonna ask her." He took a doughnut and dunked it into my coffee. "Besides, word has it that Martha might be put out to pasture."

Now, there was an apt idiom. For a moment I had a mental image of Martha grazing on a farm in those god-awful pumps of hers. "Oh? A shake up in the works?"

"A pretty serious one, Johnny. Murphy is the faculty representative on the Community Council."

"I know he is. He's also an idiot. So what?"

"That idiot sold out to the activists who've been trying to get control of the school and voted with 'em to replace Ballinger. The result—he now has release time and an extra ten thousand a year to take home from the work program."

"Tell me you're kidding."

Vince had a powdered sugar mustache on his mustache. He shook his head as he chewed his doughnut. "Wait—it gets more interesting than that. There is now a paid position for a community liaison, complete with a office next to Ballinger's and faculty overseeing responsibilities."

"An," I said.

"What?"

"You said 'a office.' You meant *an* office."

Vince stood up and put on his sport coat. "You goddamn English teachers. Did you just hear anything I just said?"

"I did. I'm just not surprised."

"You will be when you find out who got the job." He looked at me and waited for dramatic effect. "Isabelle Villachez."

That was not good news. Isabelle Villachez was suspected of having ties to the militant FALN terrorist organization, and had wanted some position of school authority for a good year and a half. The FALN, or the *Fuerzas Armadas de Liberación Nacional* (Armed Forces of National Liberation) were about twenty or so Castro-inspired revolutionaries who wanted independence for Puerto Rico and had in the past claimed responsibility for one hundred bombings, resulting in the deaths of five people and the injury of another seventy. We'd had political uprisings in the community before, and in the school as well, but we'd always had a fairly objective administration, no matter how fundamentally inept it had been. I did not exactly look forward to a guerrilla presence on the faculty.

I said, "Why do we need a liaison? That's what the community council is for."

13

Vince uncapped a thermos and poured steaming, black coffee into his mug. "It's not about what we need. It's about what *Isabelle* needs. Isabelle needs money. And power."

"I think I'm too old for this, Vince."

"You're too old for a lot of things, Johnny. Do what I do. Don't start counting 'em up." He slapped my back. "Come on. We've got a meeting to go to."

The first day of school is split in two sections. First there is an all-faculty meeting, then we pick up our record books and class assignments and run the students through an attenuated schedule. It's something like organized mass chaos. Vince and I took seats in the back row of the auditorium, and I spotted some new faces in the crowd.

I said, "This group doesn't look like the same group I remember from June."

"It's not. Sullivan transferred to Senn, Booker went to Taft, and I think Reynolds quit altogether. Either that or she retired."

"Reynolds is too young to retire."

Vince said, "Then she just quit."

I thought for a moment what a shame that was. Audrey Reynolds was a good teacher, and it wasn't as though we had enough of those to start giving them away. "Does a certain trend seem to suggest itself to you?"

Vince nodded and sipped from his mug of coffee. The mug said, *Getting old ain't for sissies.* "The rats know the ship is taking on water."

Martha Ballinger walked across the stage and tapped the microphone. She said, "Testing." I knew the routine by heart. First she would welcome us back with some cornball anecdote that was supposed to simulate warmth. Then she would list the successes of the past year—attendance statistics and things like that, numbers. The Chicago Board of Education loved numbers. That's why they had so many people downtown to count them. Next we would be introduced to the new faculty members who would stand one at a time and then we would all applaud politely.

Vince said, "Why do we come to these goddamn things?"

"You were the one who told me to come."

"Why do you listen to me?"

This year, however, Ballinger had a few new twists. First, we were to not only turn in lesson plans weekly, but also outcomes. Those were little analyses of how each lesson flew. If it hadn't worked, we were supposed to explain why and then fix it. These outcomes were expected to be on Martha's desk every Friday, no later than noon. Students couldn't fail anymore. Only the teachers could fail. And then this: Martha had made a commitment to diversity and sensitive handling of diverse issues. We would each of us be expected to attend mandatory sensitivity training sessions after school twice a week, beginning today. Youth Services, an independent organization operating within the school, would conduct these, and they would take attendance.

I whispered to Vince, "That's a violation of our contract. They can't give an outside group authority over the faculty."

Vince said, "You just need to be more sensitive."

"I'm serious, Vince. I'm going to talk to Jamel Saunders." Jamel Saunders was our union representative. She frequently had to fight to maintain the few rights we had left as a group.

I stood in line outside the records office for close to twenty minutes before being issued the standard green attendance book, rosters, and class assignments. These could have been put in our mailboxes ahead of time, but that way the administration couldn't demean us by making us stand and wait like obedient children. It was the educational equivalent of roll call in the military, a demonstration of just how rigid and unwieldy the bureaucracy had become.

Mike Parnell, an assistant principal, handed me my packet without so much as a nod. I opened it and immediately found two errors. According to my schedule, I'd lost AP English and had been assigned a student teacher.

"Mike, we've got a problem."

Mike said, "No, Johnny. *I* have a problem. I have seventy more packets to distribute and someone is holding up the line."

I handed him my schedule sheet. "I'm supposed to have AP English, and I never volunteered to accept a student teacher."

He perused the schedule brusquely and then shoved it back to me. "AP English rotates. Murphy has it."

Murphy. He certainly had a lot of perks suddenly. I said, "Mike, you know and I know that it rotates every two years, and this is my second."

Parnell had graying hair, wore suspenders, and was high-strung. I was just another dilemma winding his rubber band. "We changed the rotation period."

"You can't do that."

"Well, we did it. Johnny, this year's program assignments come from on high."

I said, "Don't tell me you've found religion."

Mike took a deep breath, rolled his eyes toward the ceiling, and for a moment I expected him to explode. "Is that all, Mr. Spector?"

"No. What about the student teacher?"

He picked up a packet and handed it to Louise Denning, an art teacher who had been waiting in line behind me. It was his way of dismissing me. "We ran out of volunteers and had to make the assignments. It's as simple as that."

Twenty-two years. "I'll grieve this, Mike."

"Fine. Grieve it all you want, but do it someplace else."

If it hadn't been for Louise waiting there, I would have made more of it. But Louise was a sweet lady with not much of a life, other than a terminally ill mother back in Pennsylvania or Ohio. Ohio, I think. She didn't need any more grief.

I took my packet back to my office and threw it on my desk. I wanted a cigarette. I had quit smoking five years ago and *still* I wanted a cigarette. I would not have been surprised to learn that the urge continued even beyond death.

I met with my sophomore homeroom class, which in Chicago's school system is known as *division*. Only seventeen out of twenty-six kids showed up, typical for a first day. I would have to make out an attendance report and nine individual absence slips. Then I would have to call the homes of each missing student—about forty-five minutes of wasted time in my teaching day. Though this was a returning group, there were five brand new transferees, and for each of these I needed to create a new file. But that could wait. I introduced myself, listed the ground rules for homeroom on the blackboard, and then asked the kids to tell us something about themselves. I asked Fernando Morales to go first.

"Oh, shit, Johnny. We all know who we is, and we only got twelve minutes." Fernando was a Dragon and his nickname was Undertaker. He wore one gray and one purple sock—the Dragons' colors—and had no patience for the trappings of civility.

"Then do it quickly."

16

Fernando shook his head and fidgeted his body in his chair as though it were constraining him. "Whatever. I'm Fernando, and I'm Folks and you don't wanna mess with me. Next."

Folks was an umbrella term for a legion of gangs. No matter what gang you were in, you were either affiliated with Folks or People, and the distinction determined who your allies and adversaries were. I tried to keep the business of gangs out of the classrooms, but it was like trying to keep humidity out of the air. It was everywhere.

Next was Kirk Douglas Perez. Kirk's mother was a big movie fan, and guess who her favorite star was. Kirk was a D, or a Disciple, a shy, slight kid with boyish good looks and a soft side that made him an easy target for some of the street toughs. He reminded me of my own boy, and I tried to look after him the best I could. Known as Hollywood in the hood, he told us how he looked up to his big brother, how he emulated everything he did.

"He cool, my brother. He gets respect in the hood, and everything he done, he done on his own. He taught me how to take care of myself, and how to stick with family. You stick with family and you never alone."

This was going to be trouble. I knew Kirk's brother. His name was Guiso, and I'd had him as a student before he dropped out and climbed the Disciples' hierarchy. Guiso was a junkie.

And there was Lucy and Daisy and Hilda and Jorgé and Nelson and all the rest of the kids I'd had last year. Hilda worried me because her boyfriend was brutal, though she seemed oblivious to this. I'd once seen him twist her arm behind her back in the hallway when he found her talking to another boy. I tried to keep it strictly professional with them all, but I wasn't much good at that. I was a pushover, and they knew it, or sensed it. I'd always liked street kids, a fact that drove my wife to distraction. She had come from their ranks, had grown up within this neighborhood. As far as she was concerned, I was a sucker and the kids took advantage. She even had a term for them, called them my *streethearts*.

"One of my dreams is to be a fashion designer." This was Hilda. The girls took the sharing activities more seriously than did the boys. They didn't have to wear game faces. "I always wanted to be a fashion designer since I was a little kid. I used to dress up in my mother's clothes. You know, I'd go up to her room and try her stuff on and look in the mirror."

17

"That's what Jorgé likes to do, too," Fernando said.

Jorgé, small and intense, sprang forward in his desk and said, "Fuck you, motherfucker."

"You wanna try, faggot?"

Hilda said, "Mr. Spector—it was my turn!"

And just like that in the midst of this hurricane we hit the eye. The voices went silent and everyone turned to the doorway. A very tall, exceptionally thin Latino boy stood there as if petrified, a book bag in one hand, papers in the other. He had mocha-colored skin and rabbit-scared eyes—handsome enough to get picked on, immediately.

"Damn," Fernando said, "*Que gran pato.*"

The room burst into laughter, not the kind I could do much about until it had run its course. I approached the boy and over the din said, "Are you looking for your division?"

He didn't answer. His eyes alternately scanned the faces in the room and telegraphed his fear. When he spoke, he occasionally broke into a stutter. "The man said come here, and I came here. That's just what I did, only I'm late. They made me fill out forms. See, I-I-I-I was with my counselor from the home."

"What home?" I said.

"Group home."

He waved the papers in front of my face, enrollment forms. His name was Lico Pacheco, it said. Under *parent name* were the letters DCFS—Department of Children and Family Services. The kid had no mom or dad. Someone named Jim Jarret had signed as responsible party.

I ushered him over to my desk to record his personal information in my green book, but even his movements spoke of some quiet hysteria, and they were not missed by the other students. I talked to him quietly under the running murmur in the room.

"It says here that you went to Orr High School last year."

"Right, right."

Orr was tough. Of course, so were we.

"But your transcripts haven't arrived."

"No, sir."

When Kirk Douglas Perez heard him call me *sir,* he howled. Fernando said, "Johnny, you'd better send this boy back to whatever home he escaped from."

For the second time in as many minutes an expectant hush fell over the classroom. A tall Asian boy wearing a backward baseball cap and baggy khaki pants knocked on the open door.

I said, "Come in."

He trudged in holding out a program to me. He did not look at the other students, just at me, with unflinching gravity. I took the paper from him and read his name. Phuoc Koc. Oh, brother.

"How do you pronounce your name?"

What he said sounded exactly like *Fuck Cock.*

And there went the room again, explosions of wild laughter. As it settled down, Fernando said, "Fuck Cock? I think I know your brother, Suck."

My division room had become a zoo. When you lose order on a scale that grand, sometimes the best thing to do is just leave it alone. I ushered Phuoc out to the hallway and said, "Look, this must happen to you all the time."

"Only in America."

"Yeah, Phuoc, but that's where you are, now. Don't you have a nickname or anything?"

He slowly and solemnly shook his head. I didn't want to damage the kid's sense of ethnic identity, but I also didn't want him to associate himself with a vulgar reference to a sexual act.

"How about from now on we call you Phil?"

"Phil?"

"Yeah. Phil Koch. Just in division—for roll call purposes. What do you say?"

"My name Phil Koch?"

"There you go. You've got it already."

What the hell. The world's first Vietnamese Jew.

The tone sounded and the kids stampeded out of the room, everyone except for Lico. I sized him up. He was articulate, well-mannered, and petrified.

I said, "Can you tell me something, Lico? Why the change in schools?"

His eyes went back and forth, as though looking for cover. "I-I-I-I was in a foster home."

No parents, then you have foster parents, then you lose them too. Nice system. If the kids aren't damaged enough, leave it to us.

"It must be difficult for you," I said.

"Not really. Not really. I've been in five foster homes since I was nine. Five of them. Moved around a lot. Been to a lot of schools. I'm pretty used to change. I'm good at it. I don't mind."

Like hell he didn't.

According to his schedule he would be in my sophomore English class. I thought that this might not be a bad idea, that maybe I could help him clear a few hurdles. I jotted down his group home counselor's name and signed his papers. "I'll see you tomorrow, kiddo."

He nodded as if confirming something to himself. "Oh, and Mr. Spector? I promise I won't be late. I promise."

I fought an inclination to slap him on the back. In the old days I would have done it. Now you weren't supposed to touch students, for fear of assault charges, sexual or otherwise. I simply replied, "I believe you, Lico."

By noon I had met with two of my classes, had them give me writing samples, distributed syllabi, filled out Federal ethnicity forms, and had a fairly good idea that this was going to be another semester I'd rather have done with. It was my hall guard period. Forty-four years old and I was sitting at a student desk in a dim hallway checking passes and trying not to go catatonic. I thought about Marlyn's unworn gym clothes, about the woman and her five children lying dead in their home in Sioux City. I'd been there once. It's a nice little town.

I riffled the one-paragraph student essays and found one by a girl named Blanca Ortega. She wrote in neat, square script and had even bothered to put my name in the upper left hand corner under hers.

Even though I like school last year I didn't do so good.

I got pregnant and had a beautiful baby girl. Her name is Ruth after my Mother she has the most gorgous big brown eyes as my Mother too. My boyfriend he didnt stick around. He dogged me and abdoned my baby and don't evenpay child suport. Says it ain't his kid, but he lies. He just scared is all. I work everyday after school at the Jewel store. I'm a casheer. My Mother watches Ruth. I do my home work during my dinner brake. It's not so bad but I wish my baby she had a father. Please don't get mad at me senor Spector if I get sleepy during class some times cause I dontget home till 12.

Thank you.

It's funny how a paragraph could tell you so many things. Blanca, aside from dealing with more hardships than a sixteen year old deserved, had a pretty good sense of sentence structure, tone, and logical sequencing. This paper, believe it or not, was above average. There was something to work with here, at least, and I would read her papers closely as they came in. I'd also have to have a talk with her about DNA testing.

"Hey, good looking."

I looked up at Nydia Velazquez. Nydia was Puerto Rican and had grown up in this neighborhood—a real American success story. She taught drama, took in kids who needed a temporary place to stay, and even owned her own business. We had known each other since college, and I guess you could say she was like family.

I said, "You better get your vision checked. There's nobody here but me."

She leaned over and kissed my cheek and messed up my hair. "I know what I see and I like what I see."

"Cut it out. We'll get arrested."

"Good. We can mess around in the back of the paddy wagon."

"I think they handcuff you," I said.

"It's sounding better all the time."

Nydia was petite and dark and had a pair of lethal hips. Some of the other Latin teachers resented her because she eschewed their socialist ideology and was an outspoken supporter of statehood for the island. There was some talk that she once had a thing going with one of her male students, but I didn't know if this was true, and I was no one to judge.

"Johnny, sweetheart, how would you like to do me a favor?"

"I'm in the middle of a stack of scintillating essays, but I'll bet I could work it in."

Nydia pinched my ear. "No, I don't mean right now. I know a young newspaper writer who has an idea for a story, and he needs to interview an inner city teacher."

"And?"

"And I thought of you."

For Christ's sake. That's just what I needed—to be featured in a news story because my life and career were going so well. "Honey, for you I'd go to the moon, but I'm going to have to beg off of this one."

"Oh, Johnny—why?"

"Well, for that matter, why not *you*? He's your friend, the reporter, right?"

"Because you're good at these things. The kids love you. You wrote two books. When he heard about the books, he said you'd be perfect."

That had been fifteen years ago, the books. I gave a shit, back then. I'd had the fire, and now I couldn't get so much as a spark going.

I said, "You know, I'd rather not go back to all that."

"He just wants to know about the day-to-day life of a city teacher, the regular stuff you do every day."

"I write attendance reports and sit in dark hallways. You see a story there?"

"Sweetheart, please, for me. Do it for me."

I remembered the first time I saw Nydia. It was in an American literature class at the University of Illinois, when we'd both been twenty-one, and she was bubbling over, showing off her engagement ring to her envious girlfriends. She just looked so *happy*. Now she was divorced and raising a kid by herself. Tough deal. *The nuclear family*, I thought. *Boom*.

I said, "What could it hurt, right?"

She rubbed my shoulders and said, "Thank you, thank you, thank you!"

"I'm doing this for you. You're going to owe me big time, afterward."

She blew me a kiss. "Lover, anything you want. How's your beautiful wife and your handsome kid?"

I really had no idea how Marlyn was. I couldn't remember the last time we had gone out or just stayed home together and watched TV. "Fine, I guess. Jason's getting big, Nydia. You wouldn't know him if you saw him."

"Sure I would. He'd look just like you."

"You know something?" I said. "They grow up and they grow away from you."

Nydia waved this remark away with her hand. "That's just temporary."

"It is, huh? Well, maybe we'll hang out together again when he turns thirty."

I watched her hips as she walked away, thought of her all that time ago, thought of how we'd already lived most of our lives. Now, how could that be?

§

At three o'clock the tone sounded and roughly 2,100 kids rode the escalators down to the first floor and became a sea of faces in the park. I was signing out in the main office when someone grabbed my arm.

"Hey, *profesor*—not staying for our first sensitivity session?"

It was Marco Gonzalez of Youth Services. Marco used to be a counselor here at Acosta High , but he was ambitious and organized and now ran the entire network of the parent organization. He was one of those guys who became more handsome with age—full head of hair, trimmed and grayed, and he'd shaved his mustache.

I said, "Marco, if I get any more sensitive, I'll break into tears."

"You're still one of the best teachers we have, Johnny. But there's always room for improvement."

I did not want to insult him, but that was a two-way street. "Sometimes if you try to improve something, you just end up lousing it up."

He flashed a smile at me—all those little nacreous, even teeth. "Stick around, Johnny. Learn something about multiculturalism."

I said, "Marco, I'm Hungarian and German. My wife is Puerto Rican. My kid is all of those. Try to find someone more multicultural than I am."

He laughed and slapped me on the back, but still you could tell he was miffed that I wouldn't be staying around.

I ran into Dave Volmer on my way out to the park. Dave had once been a very effective counselor and now he was just a counselor. Fifty-four years old, divorced, two grown kids. I wondered what he did when he went home alone to his apartment.

"Spector. You look like a man who could use a drink. What say we head over to Grandma's?"

"I don't know, Dave. I was thinking about watching my kid's football practice."

"One drink. What's the big deal?"

On the perimeter of the park near Sacramento stood Tony Calderon, a former student, and now a higher-up in the Disciples. He had a pit bull on a leash and kept pulling it taut, choking the dog as he did so. "Hey, Spector!" he called, waving at me. I waved tentatively. I did not like Tony. He had a vicious streak and was not particularly bright. He once confided in me that he owned the drug dealing corner of North and Cortez, that he made over two thousand dollars a week. Pit bulls were his trademark. He used to brag about how he beat them in the face to make them mean. He'd thought it was funny.

"Friend of yours?" Dave asked.

Standing beside him was Guiso Perez, Kirk Douglas' brother. Guiso was sucking on a cigarette and alternately rubbing his face. Junkie mannerisms. "Former students. Dealers."

"You know the nicest people."

"There's only one reason they're hanging around here. It's bold, even for them."

"I guess we could stand around and reminisce about our alumni, or we could go have that drink."

A drink sounded good. Lately a drink always sounded good.

Grandma's was an old bar on Western Avenue, right on the border of the old Ukrainian Village, just around the block from a Byzantine cathedral. It wasn't really *called* Grandma's. I don't know what its name was. It was dark and it was dank and was run by an old woman who Dave referred to as Grandma. There were some sad looking characters in old clothes sitting at the far end of the bar, looking into their drinks as if trying to commune with them. Next to the draft pulls was a jar of pickled pigs feet. It had been there for ten years, and I had never seen the contents changed.

"Hello, boys!" the old woman said, wiping the bar surface in front of us with a rag. "What can I get you?"

Dave said, "I'll have two of whatever he's having."

"Smirnoff on the rocks," I said. I used to like vodka tonics, and then somewhere along the way the tonic became superfluous.

I watched as she upended the bottle, splashing vodka generously over crackling ice cubes. The television flickered mutely in the corner. Dave pulled a previously smoked cigar from his shirt pocket and let it droop from his mouth, unlit.

"Ten months, eleven days. How does that sound?"

I said, "Like a long pregnancy."

He pulled the cigar from his mouth and sipped his drink. "It is. It's the gestation period of my retirement."

I remembered going to that bar with Dave fifteen years ago. Back then we'd talked about women, our jobs, our students, the Cubs, women.

24

Now there was only one subject.

Grandma dropped a coin in the jukebox and pressed a button. A few seconds later a polka band went into an orchestra, then rollicked double time.

"Which one of you boys is going to be my dancing partner?" Grandma called out, smacking the palms of her hands together.

Dave said, "It'll have to be Spector. I'm still waiting for my hip replacement operation."

"Oh!" Grandma said, making a face. "You're younger than that!"

"I used to be younger than *something*, but I can't remember what, anymore."

So I danced with her. She was a plump little lady with dyed orange hair and she took off her apron before tripping the light fantastic. There was a black and white photo of a dark-haired beauty tucked in the frame of the mirror behind the bar, and I wondered if this had been she once upon a time, perhaps in the old country. She spun me around, laughed at my clumsiness, told me to watch her feet.

I said, "You'd better watch mine instead. They're dangerous."

She was surprisingly proficient, and at her age. Afterward Dave applauded and she bowed. I sat back down on my stool next to Dave, trying to catch my breath.

"What the hell was that—the 'Two Left Feet Polka'?"

"I never said I could dance," I said.

"And now we all know why."

Then drinks were on the house and I said no, I shouldn't, but Dave overruled me, said there was no such thing as one drink, that I should know better. I saw us in the reflection of the mirror behind the bar, behind bottles of Rémy and Stolichnaya and Glenfiddich, looking as if we were two other people in another world where people actually did something constructive. Then out came an envelope from Dave's back pocket, and he began to explain that at the beginning of his retirement, he would make over one hundred thousand dollars a year.

I said, "Do you know that for the past six months all you've been able to talk about is retirement?"

He gave me a funny little frozen expression. "Is that so? And what would you rather have me do, talk about wet nursing gangsters, like someone else I know?"

Dave could get like that. "I don't wet-nurse anyone."

25

"The hell you don't. You listen to their sob stories, pat them on the head, drive them home, marry them. How *is* the lovely wife, anyway?"

My first impulse was to coldcock him, right there at the bar. But I'd been through this with him before, and knew that his bitterness was just a result of what life had done to him. I tilted my glass up, polished off the drink, and set it back down hard on the counter. I took a five out of my wallet and left it as a tip.

"You know, I've got to go."

As I walked out of the bar I could hear Dave call something after me, though I didn't know what, nor did I care.

It was a hazy, green leaf-flecked afternoon and I watched from behind a chain link fence as the Deerfield Warriors practiced on the back 440 field, mottled shadows on a September lawn. My kid was number 87, a starting wide receiver for the sophomore team. They ran routes—faked option tosses, sprinted and rolled. The booze had made me sleepy and the air smelled the same way it had at back-to-school time when I had been his age. Jason and his teammates high-fived one another, chest-butted, slapped each other's butts, boys coming together to be boys, following the natural inclination to form a group. The coach blew his whistle and bellowed angry directions at them. They nodded and took it, wanted so badly to please him. The approval factor. Who didn't need approval? I thought of Fernando and Lico, all those lost kids on the ragged streets of Chicago, and what might have happened differently in their lives if they could have been part of this. They say you're not supposed to take your work home with you. They say a lot of things.

Jason launched, spun in a circle to avoid an imaginary adversary, sped on long legs to the end zone, and pulled a forty-yard pass out of the air as though it were nothing but the wind, just reached up, and for a moment it looked like he was hanging from the ball. Sometimes you just want to grab someone by the arm and say, *That's my kid*, but there was nobody there but me. It would have been nice if Marlyn had seen it.

I went home to have dinner and found the garage empty. Five-thirty and Marlyn was still not home from work. I went inside and checked the voicemail. Nothing. Her gym bag was in the utility room where I had left it. I tried dialing her cell phone number, but a digital voice informed me that the customer I had called was unavailable. I already knew that. In the kitchen I got some ice and put it in a highball glass and filled it with vodka right up to the rim. The mail was all ads and bills and one of those fliers with two missing people on it and the dates that they were last seen. Outside the sun was squeezing itself into the horizon behind the treetops, and I just stood there watching it, thinking about missing people, and where they all go.

2

It was Tuesday of the following week and there was a note in my mailbox from Martha Ballinger informing me that my absence from the sensitivity sessions had been noticed. This meant that Marco Gonzalez's Youth Services people had overstepped their authority and had reported me to my own principal. I took the elevator up to the third floor and estimated how much teaching I could get done if people would just leave me alone.

Through a wire mesh reinforced window, I saw Marco in the Youth Services office, swathed in sterile, white fluorescent light. He had his suit coat off and was sitting with his Oxford shoes up on his desk, talking to a young male in a black leather jacket, a Disciple, given the blue-black wrist bands he was wearing. The kid had a scar above one eye, shiny, slicked-back hair, and acne. I walked in, held the door open, knocked deliberately on it.

Marco said, "Johnny—I'm in a counseling session right now."

I said, "I can see that," and held out the note from Ballinger to him. He took it, read it, flipped it over, and handed it back.

He shrugged. "I told you that we're intent on getting one hundred percent cooperation with the sensitivity project."

"You did not. You didn't tell me that, Marco. You said you'd like me to stop by, and I told you I couldn't."

"Well, I don't know what you want me to say. I have my projects, and you have yours, and we ought to cooperate with one another. Don't you think?"

"What I think is that we ought not to step on one another's toes. You've known me a long time, and you know I don't need any kids with shiny new B.A.s in social work telling me how to teach."

Marco took his feet off the desk and straightened his tie. "I'm in a session, Johnny."

I said, "Fine. I'll respect that. But I'd appreciate it if next time you come talk to me first, instead of sending one of your staff to tattle on me." I walked out and shut the door harder than I had intended.

We all used to be friends at this place and now everything had changed. Everyone wanted control. It didn't make any sense to me. It was a *high school*. What kind of power could you hope to amass? Corner the market on blackboard erasers?

At Acosta High , except for the ground-level main lobby, each floor looked identical to the others, with two stainless steel escalators cutting through the center. So to keep students and faculty oriented, the number of the floor appeared in giant red numbers in the carpet. I watched the 3 fade away as I inclinated and remembered all those years ago when I first saw Marlyn in these hallways, and what it had done to me. Two kids riding the *down* escalator began pushing and shoving each other against the black handrails, stole me out of my daydream.

"Knock it off," I said.

"Fuck you, asshole," one of them said back to me.

And what was I going to do? Jump the escalator and chase him?

"Miguel Cabrera," a voice said behind me. It was Fernando.

I said, "What?"

"The kid who just said that to you. He's Miguel Cabrera, division three forty-five. You wanna write him up, don'tcha?"

When I had been younger, I might have. But now the impact of a *fuck you* lasted about three point seven seconds, and then disappeared altogether. "I've got better things to do."

Fernando and I rode up to the seventh floor to division together. He had tight, curly hair (always perfectly groomed), and stylish slacks. Someone at home was taking good care of him. You noticed things like this. You just wondered why that same someone couldn't keep him out of street gangs.

"Listen, Johnny. You better be havin' a talk with your home boy, Hollywood. Know what I mean?"

"I haven't got the faintest idea of what you mean."

He looked behind him. Stainless steel steps folded into the fifth floor, the big 5 disappearing behind us. "He be bringin' shit into the neighborhood, tryin' to get our peewees strung out. It's his brother make him do it, Ratman. You know Ratman?"

Ratman was Kirk Douglas Perez's brother Guiso. I knew him, all right.

I said, "I've seen Guiso in the park with Tony, and I know Guiso's a junkie."

"So's Hollywood."

I shook my head. "Not Hollywood, Fernando. I know him."

"You don't know shit, Jack."

I grabbed hold of his arm, put a little pressure on it. "Now, what was that I just heard?"

He went into a nodding routine, held both his hands up as we stepped off at the seventh floor. "All right, all right. That's not respectful. You know what I mean; I was just sayin'. But that boy strung out, and it's 'cause he's underage that the D's are sendin' him into our hood. If Ratman gets busted one more time, his parole officer gonna haul his ass back to Stateville. If Hollywood goes down—what's he gonna get—six months probation?"

"Your boys aren't thinking of taking him out?" I said.

He raised his hands and fluttered his eyelids at me. "I'm just sayin'. Dragons are cool. We don't want no trouble."

"Uh-huh."

"But we ain't gonna 'low no one to come in an' fuck-up the peewees an' shit."

The peewees were pledges, the junior members anywhere from seven to eleven years old, sort of like what Cub Scouts are to Boy Scouts. Kirk had always been a good student, a good kid, and I didn't know how much of Fernando's story had to do with personal antagonism and jealousy. Gangsters liked to be one up on the competition, and everyone was potential competition, especially if they were smart or good looking, and Kirk Douglas Perez was both of these. On the other hand, I knew too well the kind of changes a sixteen-year-old boy could go through, the overnight mutability that was always possible. I thought of Jason, my own boy, wondered what new secret corners of his soul he kept hidden from me.

Mercury must have been in retrograde. When I got to my division room everyone had a problem. Jorgé kept shoving a yellow program change in my face, telling me that Mike Parnell had given him a course he had already had last year. Maria Negron had received a cut slip from a study hall that she swore she attended. "That *maricón* just can't

30

see, man. The old fart is blind, is all." And hands on her cute little hips, Daisy stood tapping the toe of one of her new Pumas on the floor, snapping her gum, annoyed with me. Just when was I going to check with her counselor about the work program she'd applied for, she wanted to know.

In one of those sloping, peripheral moments of awareness that sometimes present themselves in the midst of utter disorder, I felt Lico sidle into the room and beeline for the back row. He sat down and looked toward me, his big brown eyes seeking something in the worst way—comfort, direction, love. What had someone done to him? And how dare they? I wanted to know, but I didn't want to know. A kid by the name of Nelson had no notion I was watching, and he went to work on him immediately. He lurked around his desk with his hands in his pockets, head tilted in inquiry, eyes squinted. "The home let you out again, boy?"

Lico could not meet his gaze directly, but kept his face slightly averted, eyes darting back and forth. "It-it-it-it's not that kind of home. It's a group home. It's a place for wards."

"For *what?*"

"Wards. Wards of the state. I'm a ward of the state."

If I had run to his defense, I would have risked exacerbating the intimidation when I wasn't around. I took attendance, noticed Hilda wasn't there. This was the second day in a row she had been absent. Nelson put a sneaker on the seat of Lico's chair, pushed it a little.

"You one spooky dude, you know that?"

"My name's Lico. They call me Lico. I'm glad to meet you. What's your name?"

Nelson gave the chair another little push. "From now on you Twilight Zone. You understand? When I say, 'Hey, Twilight Zone,' you answer. You hear?"

I'd heard enough. I said, "Nelson? May I see you a minute?"

"What?" he said. "I didn't do nothin'."

"Out in the hall, please."

He breathed an explosive "Damn!" and slunk into the hallway.

Daisy said, "Johnny, I expect you to find out about that work program *today.* Not tomorrow. *Today.* Do you hear me?"

The whole seventh floor had heard her.

Out in the hall I closed the door slightly and leaned on one arm

31

against the wall, crowding Nelson, so close he could feel my breath.

"Hey-hey-hey. Why so close? Whaz the problem?"

I backed off. Gangsters do not enjoy infringements on their personal space. Then I leaned in on him again. Nelson wasn't a bad kid; he was just acting according to the urban laws of territoriality. "Don't tell me," I said. "All the tough kids you usually pick on are absent today, and so you had to try and scare a cream puff."

"Come on, Johnny. I was just gettin' to know him."

"Twilight Zone?"

Nelson cracked up. "Oh, man. You got to admit, the dude is *weird*."

"We're all a little weird, Nelson. But lay off. The kid's got no family."

"Yeah—what's his story?"

"I don't know yet. But I'll make you a deal."

Nelson cocked his head, crossed his arms. "What kinda deal?"

I said, "You leave him alone, and I promise I won't knock your head in."

He high-fived me. "All right, Johnny. My bad. I be cool."

The period tone sounded and the halls filled and swelled with young bodies, young energy. It was only eleven and I was exhausted. When I returned to the room I found Kirk Douglas Perez asleep on his desk, his head upon his arms. I nudged his shoulder, twice, and he slowly raised his head, covered by the hood of his sweatshirt.

"Get to bed kind of late, did you?" I asked.

He looked at me as if he were trying to remember who I was. Slowly he got to his feet, rubbed his eyes with his fist. "I stayed up doin' a project for biology."

Kirk had slightly sandy hair and chipmunk cheeks. There was a shyness about him that caused his eyes to drift away from yours in mid-sentence.

"What kind of project, buddy?"

"Tadpoles. I've got to feed them different amounts and measure them every two days."

I said, "Must be hard getting them to stay still for the tape measure."

He gave a half-hearted chuckle. "I gave them both names."

"Yeah? What are they?"

"Moe and Larry."

"Sounds like you're missing one."

"Curly died," he said.

The funny ones always go first. "Kirk—would you do me a favor?"

"What?"

"If something's not right, if you need some help—you'll let me know, okay?"

He picked up his book bag and said, "Sure, Johnny. See ya." I watched him stumble into the river of students.

§

By seventh period I saw the world through eyes that made everything look mosaic. After class, and just before my hall guard duty, I stepped into a men's room and ran cold water in a sink and splashed it on my face. I dried myself with gray recycled paper towels from a dispensing machine and wondered if I looked as bad and swollen as the mirror attested. On my way to the escalator I came across Jamel Saunders, our union representative. Jamel was a youthful looking African American woman with an aloof air of professionalism. She held the world at bay with this, but for some reason she had a soft spot for me.

I said, "I'm sure glad to see you."

Jamel raised an eyebrow. "Darling, everybody's always glad to see me. It's the height of their day. What kind of trouble are you in now?"

"Did you know Marco's Youth Service people are taking attendance records at these sensitivity things and turning them over to Ballinger?"

Jamel tucked a manila folder between the sleeve and torso of a tailored gray business suit. "If you would care for a word of advice, I would tread softly in, on, and around anything that has to do with diversity and sensitivity, if I were you, which I certainly am not, Mr. Spector, praise the Lord, and thank the stars."

"No fooling, Jamel. It's a violation of our contract and—"

"No fooling, Johnny, there are certain power alliances that are forming in the least subtle of ways. If one keeps one's ear to the ground, one may come to the unsettling realization that we are embarking on a new day with new, unspoken rules."

I put my hand in my trouser pocket, played with a paper receipt. "Let me see if I get this—do you mean to tell me that even the *union's* afraid of this PC bullshit they're trying to pull on us?"

"If I say yes, I'll bet I could save a lot of aggravation."

"But give me the lowdown—why?"

She raised her gaze to the ceiling for a moment and inhaled impatiently. "Two words: Community Council."

I said, "But we've always had a Community Council."

"Not one with plans as politically ambitious as this one. Note who your new assistant principal is."

The new assistant principal was Elizabeth Mojica. I said, "Help me along here. I'm a little slow today."

"You must be. Please tell me you've noticed her *ideological leanings*, if you follow the euphemism. Add that together with two facts: one, she is exclusively responsible for setting up the content of the diversity training sessions, and two, the rumor has it our new principal will be none other than the infamous Danny Velez."

Mojica was an outspoken supporter of communist regimes in Latin America, and Danny Velez was—well, Danny Velez. His sister Dalia was an FALN member who had received a fifty year sentence for bombings in New York, and Danny himself had been busted once for armed robbery.

I said, "They can't make Danny a principal."

Jamel touched a perfectly lacquered fingernail along the lapel of my sport coat. "I'm sure someone once told the Wright Brothers that they'd never get off the ground in Kitty Hawk. Now, I'm trying to give you a warning here, Mr. Spector, and you're doing everything in your power to not hear it. Look over your shoulder, and then go about your business."

I did just that. In the assistant principal's office at the end of the hall I could see Elizabeth Mojica, staring at us intently.

Jamel was already stepping on the *down* escalator by the time I looked back at her. *And so is that the future of this place*, I wondered, *a training camp for revolutionaries?*

It was four-thirty by the time I got home. It was becoming a regular event to find it empty. I went to the refrigerator and took out a tray of ice and poured a cocktail for myself. In the mail there was a cable television bill, a credit card bill, a request for a donation from some animal league that Marlyn belonged to, and two more missing people printed in blue on a white slip of paper. They were mother and daughter, and both had last been seen on October 27, 2010. The little girl would be fourteen by now.

The phone rang. I left the slip of paper there on the top of the stack and walked to the kitchen and lifted the receiver. I said, "Hello?"

There was a moment of silence, and then a click. I replaced the receiver in the cradle and thought about this. Well, wrong numbers happen.

I was out on the deck on my second vodka when I heard Marlyn's car pull in the garage. Marlyn Spector, nee Valentin, had been a student back when the school was still known as Freddie Prinze High. She had been eighteen and I was twenty-nine when we fell in love. We married the following year when she was a freshman at Loyola, and we had raised all those eyebrows. *Unprofessional* was the word I kept hearing whispered behind my back, and still that stigma lingered somewhat, like a shadow of something large and felt, but unseen. We had Jason the following year—neither of us knowing at first much about taking care of a baby. But we learned—boy, did we learn. It was difficult for Marlyn, no mother to help or advise her, just her father. And when it came to child rearing, he was about as useful as an exterminator. I wouldn't say he was cold, but warmth didn't enter into the picture, either. I'd stolen his daughter. He'd never forgiven me for that. We got along mostly by not having much to do with each other—an unwritten truce. And then somehow all those years had gone by, and now here we were.

The sliding screen door to the deck opened and Marlyn stepped out, sorting through the mail in her hands. Long auburn hair, smart skirt outfit from Bloomingdale's. "Anything important here?" she asked, shuffling the envelopes.

I kissed her cheek. "I missed you, too," I said.

She looked up at me, and then at my cocktail. "Starting kind of early, aren't you?"

"No," I said. "I started kind of early about forty-five minutes ago. Any idea where you want to go to dinner?"

She shook her head. "You pick."

"All right. How was work?"

"Don't ask."

If someone had shot this scene with a home video recorder and then gone back in the past to show us what married life would be like sixteen years later, I wonder if we ever would have tied the knot.

I said, "One of our oak trees is looking a little droopy."

Marlyn was opening envelopes and sorting their contents on the glass deck table in two piles—keep and discard. Very systematic. I didn't know if she had heard me.

"I hope it isn't dying."

She kept the cable bill and the animal welfare league brochure and the credit card bill and tossed everything else. The blue-white mother-daughter photo lay crumpled on the table.

We took Marlyn's Camry because she hated riding in my Jeep—hard ride. Washington Gardens was an Italian place in Highwood, one of my favorites—dimly lit bar, the best chef in town. I held her chair out for her, but was dismissed with a curt, "I've got it."

A young waitress with sweet eyes took our drink orders. I had a Bombay Sapphire gin martini and Marlyn had a Diet Coke. She kept her eyes rigidly to her menu and I started talking about my day.

"I've got a girl in my division who's been out for two days now. Girl named Hilda. I called her home, but the line's been disconnected."

"What are you having?" Marlyn asked.

"I thought I'd go with the salmon," I said. Her fingertips were thin and pretty, freshly manicured. "I guess you don't want to talk about work."

She folded her menu and placed it on the table. "Not very much, no."

If I had still smoked, I would have stepped outside to have a cigarette.

"Fine. So how's your father?"

"You don't have to try for my sake, Johnny."

Now, what was this all about? I hadn't forgotten an anniversary, and I hadn't stayed out all night with the boys. "On the other hand, it might get a little awkward, the two of us sitting here with nothing to say."

"Maybe we should have thought about that before we went out."

The waitress with the sweet eyes brought us our drinks and took our orders. I considered how much she must mean to some parent, and then I remembered the missing mother and daughter on the mailer.

When she left the table, I sipped some of my martini. Then I said, "I thought maybe we'd have a nice night."

Marlyn gave a lackluster little smile. "I'm sorry. This just isn't what I'd bargained for, I guess."

"We could have gone someplace else."

She shook her head, eyes trained on her water glass. "I didn't mean the restaurant."

"What *did* you mean, then?"

"Any of this."

I gave my silverware a little nudge and said, "Why am I having trouble getting the point here?"

"I don't know, Johnny," Marlyn said. "Why are you?" She gave a little sigh, looked away, and then looked back at me. "When we were first married, you were going to be a writer. You don't write anymore. You didn't drink. And now—"

"I think I see where this is going," I said.

"Do you? Do you know how sick I am of hearing about that place, about the administration, about all the trouble you're always getting into, about every delinquent's problems?"

It was not my favorite dinner. Getting through it was sort of like trying to light matches under water. When the check came I realized I'd left my wallet at home. Marlyn had to pay using one of her credit cards. She excused herself from the table as I filled in the dollar amount of the tip. I gave the girl five dollars more than the twenty percent, and then a funny thing happened. When I went to put Marlyn's Visa card back in her purse, I found a little greeting card in there. It read: *You're not just something, you're everything.* It was signed *With love, Bruce.* What do you know.

There was an early autumn chill in the air and the car ride home was all misty windows and the hum of the defroster. I let Marlyn out before putting the car in the garage, and afterward I did not go back in the house right away, but stood out on the lawn under a star-sprinkled sky, feeling a bit queasy. Two headlights floated up the driveway, and Jason jumped out of an old beater and slammed the door, back from football practice. He did not see me standing there, and I did not feel like announcing myself. I watched him walk up the drive carrying his athletic bag, and suddenly everything in my life seemed different.

§

Seven stories above Humboldt Park, from the relative obscurity of the teachers lunch room, I looked out upon Sacramento, at the shabby brownstones that lined the street in formation, as if they were ganging up on it. I drank some cafeteria coffee, terrible stuff, but it had caffeine, and caffeine was what I needed. The phone company had a service by which you could get a printout of all the calls that were made from your line over the previous three months. I knew this because I had just talked to a service representative who further informed me that I could have the records mailed to my place of work. Perfect. And then I wondered why I even wanted to see them.

"If you're curious about how fast you'd fall before you'd hit the sidewalk, I can tell you that all objects fall at the same speed."

Vince and the law of gravity. He placed a bowl of fruit cocktail and a cup of coffee on the table and sat down.

I turned away from the window and sat down across from him. "Did you hear about Danny Velez?"

Vince looked at me blank-faced. "What about Danny Velez?"

I said, "Meet your new principal."

"Get out of here." He dropped his spoon in the bowl of fruit cocktail and just stared at me like that. "His sister has a life sentence for terrorism. He's a petty criminal."

"I'll bet it doesn't say all that on his vitae."

He turned his coffee cup around and around on the table, deep in thought. "They've got a self-proclaimed Marxist as an assistant principal, Isabelle the FALN groupie as liaison, and now Velez as principal. What the hell is going on around here?"

But I'd lost interest in the topic as soon as I'd raised it. "What's the deal with private detectives, Vince?"

He had been about to make another attempt at his fruit cocktail, but dropped the spoon again. "Where the hell did that come from?"

I shrugged. "I just wondered how you went about getting one."

"This isn't about the marriage," he said.

"I hope you're not a betting man."

He blinked behind his lenses, once, twice, staring at me as though I were a specimen. "Jesus Christ, Johnny. I'm sorry."

I said, "Well, don't be sorry. I'm the one who's supposed to be sorry." I looked back out the window, at all those yellow and orange treetops. For some reason the idea of losing Marlyn hurt more because it was autumn. "I guess you just look in the yellow pages under 'Private Detectives,' right? But how do you know which ones are any good?"

"I had a friend who hired one." He spooned a grape and two orange slices into his mouth. He left all the pineapple.

"Was he good?"

Vince said, "I guess he must've been. Caught his wife doing a guy in a motel by O'Hare Airport."

Christ, I thought. *It's like paying someone to break your heart.*

"Are either of you Mr. Spector?"

We both turned our heads toward the open door of the lunchroom, toward the pretty young blond woman with a shoulder bag who had just bustled in. The bag was from Abercrombie, and she looked a little as though she might have been, too—khaki-colored trench coat, tweed skirt. Vince and I just stared.

She walked in, set her bag on a chair and began to push stuff around inside of it, in search of something. "If either of you are him, I'd appreciate it if you'd just tell me. This is my first day and I missed my train and I'm supposed to start in about fifteen minutes."

I said, "I'm John Spector. What is it you're supposed to start?"

She found what she had been looking for, a set of papers stapled in the corner. These she slid before me on the table. "Teaching," she said. "I'm Tracy Singer. I'm your new student teacher."

Vince's spoon was stuck once again in midair, between the bowl and his mouth. I took a sip from my cup. The coffee had gone cold, though that didn't make it any worse. Nothing could have made it any worse. Vince introduced himself, said that he taught physics. They shook hands. She was from DePaul University. She lived in Bucktown. Bucktown was a neighborhood about two miles away that used to be fairly gang-infested, but now was undergoing regentrification. All the up-and-coming young people lived there.

Tracy Singer. She *looked* like a Tracy Singer.

Next she removed a green notebook from her bag. It was a regular filing cabinet, that bag. She placed the notebook on the table squarely in front of me. "I didn't want to be rushed like this on my first day," she said. She ran both of her hands through her hair and then leaned over the table toward me. "I thought I'd start off by introducing myself to the students and then give them a little talk about different teen peer groups. The greasers, the soshes, you know."

I said, "The what?"

"Greasers, soshes—the preps. Then I have this—" Out of the

bag came a DVD, *The Outsiders*. She placed it down next to the green notebook. "I figure I'll show them one or two of the opening scenes, and then we can read the first chapter together."

There was no denying that she was enthusiastic, but she was also a little too much in charge. I hadn't wanted a student teacher in the first place, and now I had one and she was a Type A personality.

I said, "Look, Ms. Singer—"

"Call me Tracy."

No, I wasn't going to do that. "Ms. Singer, please sit down." She tucked some loose strands of hair behind one ear and then struggled to remove her trench coat. Vince, the gallant bastard, was on his feet in no time to help her with the coat. "Let's slow down a little, all right? I'm afraid there's been some sort of misunderstanding here."

"Misunderstanding?" Incredulity.

"Yes. In the first place, you won't be teaching today."

"But it's my first day."

She had gone to college and now she knew everything, and here I was standing in her way. "That's my point. Why don't you sit in on the class, get to know the students, the curriculum—"

"But I know the curriculum. Look," she said, opening the green notebook. I had known that she would get around to the notebook sooner or later. "I have complete lesson plans for every day of the semester. It took me a month to put them together." Each page was in a transparent laminated protective cover, the text laser printed. It was all very neat and probably would get her an A in some education class.

I closed the book. "I don't want to see your lesson plans, Ms. Singer."

She reached out toward the notebook with trembling fingers, a tremble that continued until it reached her voice. "But you're my supervising teacher."

"Then what do you say we let me supervise. Now, you won't be giving my students any talks about soshes and preps, and they're not going to read *The Outsiders*. They'd laugh you out of the classroom."

She looked at Vince as if for help. "But it's in the curriculum guide."

"Good," I said, "leave it there. Nobody reads that, anyway."

She sat up a little straighter now, an attempt to assert herself. "And why, may I ask, would I be laughed out of the classroom?"

"Vince—you want to tell her, or should I?"

Vince stood up and said, "I was just leaving. But let's do this again sometime, kids. It's been swell." He looked over his shoulder at me when he reached the door and shook his head.

Tracy Singer pressed her lips tightly together and mustered a brave little look of indignation. "Will you please tell me?"

I backed up my chair and stood. "Yeah—I'll tell you." I sipped the last of my coffee, crumpled the cup, and shot it at the trash basket. "Because the Disciples and the Kings and the Dragons have to hustle just to find dinner. They duck bullets on the way to school and again on the way home, and they hope that their parents don't get laid off, if they even have jobs, and they watch their friends die of bullet wounds and drug overdoses. I don't know what high school you thought you were coming to, but we don't have any preps. Your little S.E. Hinton novel will seem like a 'Brady Bunch' episode to them. Tell a kid named Undertaker about a teenager named Soda Pop and see if he can keep a straight fucking face."

She gathered up the green notebook from the table and then just sat there looking at it. Not at me, at it. "All right," she said. "All right. And would you mind telling me which book the students *will* be reading?"

"You'll start out with something that rings cultural bells, some Rosario Ferre, or Esmerelda Santiago—*When I Was Puerto Rican*."

"But I don't know those writers."

"So you'll learn about them. Sophomore English concentrates on American Lit, so we'll start with some poetry and work our way back to *Huckleberry Finn*."

Her eyes widened. "What? I can't teach that novel!"

"Certainly you can. And you will."

She shook her head and laughed an empty laugh. "Look—I don't know if you're aware of what's going on in English education these days, but—"

"And Ms. Singer?" I said. "When you first walked in here, you said, 'If either of you are *him*.' It's supposed to be *he*, subjective pronoun, because it's a predicate nominative."

She blushed, became flustered. "Of course. I know that. I didn't think you were going to pull apart every little—"

"If you're going to teach English, you need to use it properly. Especially if you're going to teach *my* English classes."

41

She likely wanted to kill me, and I had two thoughts just then. First, I didn't care, and second—well, the second thing wasn't important. I knew I probably should have been a little more gentle with her, but the business about detectives and the way Vince left all the pineapple in his fruit cocktail had me on edge. The remark about knowing what was going on in English education sent me *over* the edge. In any case, during class she sat quietly at the back of the classroom as I gave a lecture about Judith Ortiz Cofer and the legend of the Black Virgin, and I sent her home with a stack of narrative essays to grade. When she left, she did not say goodbye.

"Johnny? Message from your boss." I was signing out in the main office when Shirley, an office secretary, handed me a note. It was from Marlyn. I was supposed to stop at her father's house and pick up a batch of *pasteles* he made for us. *Pasteles* are a Puerto Rican dish, my favorite, in fact—*carne* or *pollo* encased in a batter made out of *platanos* and then cooked in boiling water. That was all well and fine, but I was not in the mood to see her father. I'd been married to his daughter for sixteen years and he still called me *maestro*—Spanish for "teacher." As I turned to leave, I saw Isabelle Villachez moving into her new office next to Martha Ballinger's. With her was our new assistant principal— Elizabeth Mojica. The only dealings I'd had with her was when she once told me I shouldn't teach *For Whom the Bell Tolls* because Hemingway was a racist. When I asked her what her proof was, she simply told me to read the book.

Miguel Valentin, my father-in-law, lived in an old gray house on North Francisco. Red front door, white shutters, he kept the place up nicely, but he was getting on in years and had slowed down recently. There was some chipped paint around the gutters, some weather stripping dangling from the garage's second story loft windows. There was an apartment up there which had been renovated just last year. Two rectangular windows glared down at me sternly. I found him out in the back yard in his garden. Retired now, he loved to plant vegetables and flowers, and he'd learned to tolerate the very un-macho craft of cooking, out of necessity, when his wife died, leaving him to raise a little girl all by himself. I would have liked to have had the opportunity to know him better, but I always had the uneasy feeling that he, like the garage, didn't like me very much.

I walked up behind him as he trowled the earth around his pepper plants. "You're either pampering your peppers or burying the evidence. Which is it?"

He turned a very straight face to me. It was a good face—tanned and lined, and he had a gray mustache. But I couldn't get him to smile to save my life.

"*Mi hija* called and said you come by."

"And you stuck around anyway?"

He got to his feet and removed his gardening gloves. "How is my grandson?"

"He's fine. Best wide receiver you ever saw."

"If ever I get to see him."

"You know how it is. The team practices every day."

He stood there looking critically at his peppers. When he spoke to me, he rarely made eye contact. "And how are you and my daughter?"

"I don't see your daughter very much these days, I'm afraid."

Now he looked at me, appraised me, stared until he seemed to come to some conclusion which he kept to himself. "Is there problem?"

I looked at his peppers. "I don't know," I said. "I don't know what it is."

He hummed some Spanish song to himself, bent, pulled out a weed with his bare hand. He had big veins in his hand. "I remember when you were so sure about everything, *maestro*."

"Yeah, well—so do I. Now I'm not sure about anything. The older I get—"

"Uncertainty does not come with age."

Always the opposition. He was going to argue with me about one subject or another. I thought that it might as well be this one.

"I'm fairly certain it does."

"No. Uncertainty is the child of misunderstanding, or from lack of study—how you say, examine."

"Examination," I said.

"Yes. Examination."

I said, "Why do I get the feeling I'm the horse and you know where the water is?"

"You are funny, *maestro*. You have always been very funny. Perhaps that is part of the problem."

There you go. At least we had established that I had a problem. I wondered how much he knew about our lives, about Marlyn's life. Did she confide in him? "Do you want me to say, 'Go on'?"

He turned toward me inquiringly. "You feel like?"

I shrugged. "Sure. Go on."

Now he turned again toward his pepper plants, rows of them extending to the back wall of his gray, weather-worn garage. In the corner of the lot, in the shade of the garage roof overhang, sat a concrete sun dial. "Look at that."

"At what?"

"At the way the peppers grow taller when they are not planted so close together. Last year I no know why they grew so poorly. Then I saw my friend Manuel's garden. His peppers were a good six inch taller than mine, so big he had to stake them up. At first I'm too proud to ask him how he did it. Then I'm no proud no more. When I ask, he laugh and tell me to look closely. Did I see any difference in the way he planted them, he ask. I saw at once—more space. They needed more space."

Now, there was a lesson here, somewhere. He turned and nailed me with his eyes. He would not turn away or take them from me. I grew uncomfortable.

"Okay," I said. "Call me *estupido*."

He slapped my back hard. "Come in house," he said. "I have *pasteles* for you all."

He moved slowly, señor Valentin did. He threw his gardening gloves on the seat of a kitchen chair and busied himself at the stove, pouring me a cup of Bustelo, strong Cuban coffee. I took the cup and thanked him. The house smelled of cooking and cleanser. On the hallway wall were framed photographs of Marlyn as a girl, and of our boy, Jason. There was even one of me with Marlyn—our wedding day. It was like looking at a museum of our lives. *It must be lonely living here alone*, I thought.

Almost as if answering me, Marlyn's father said, "Cooking keep me busy. It's important to be busy, no, *maestro*?"

"I guess so," I said.

"Yes." He packed a plastic grocery store bag fully of *pasteles*, each wrapped in some kind of leaves. "Most important. Work. Good for soul. Tell *mi hija* I made hers with corned beef, the way she like. I mark them with a 'C'. *Mira*."

"I see. Thank you."

"*De nada.*"

I stood, lost in the vapors of my coffee cup. All those years, and you can't get them back. Maybe Marlyn was right, and I should have left that school, those kids, years ago. Too late now. What had happened had happened. I wondered if I had taken my job too seriously, or if perhaps I had not taken the rest of my life, my family, seriously enough. Half full, half empty, who the hell knew?

When I came out of those thoughts, out of the coffee cup, señor Valentin was looking at me. I apologized and felt foolish. He handed me the bag of *pasteles*, for which I was grateful. He didn't have to do that for us, but he wanted to.

"Maybe we should have gotten to know each other better," I said.

He said nothing, only looked at me. On the counter behind him was a pair of salt and pepper shakers shaped like fish, and a small painting of Christ with a glowing red heart, which he indicated to the viewer poignantly with his forefinger.

At last he said, "Go home, *maestro.* "Go home and look at your peppers."

He picked up his work gloves and walked out the back yard to his garden, leaving me alone with Jesus and his irredescent heart.

3

I had gone to the records office to see about Daisy's work program schedule change, but I found the door locked. The door was never locked. Then I noticed that the mini-blinds were drawn. I knocked and someone inside said, "Jesus Christ. Tell whoever it is to come back later." There were blood stains on the carpet. I was standing in the middle of a syllogism, but I was too hung over to put its parts together.

And that's when the door burst open, cracked deafeningly against the metal wall. Two paramedics rolled a stretcher toward the elevator, Martha Ballinger following close behind. On the stretcher was a dark-skinned boy with an oxygen mask over his face. His eyes were shut. The paramedics made a jostling sound when they ran—all that equipment. Out the second-story window I saw two Chicago Police cars pulled up onto the curb. Two officers were leading a handcuffed boy to the rear door of one of the squad cars. Mike Parnell said, "Get rid of him," to Judy Santiago, his secretary, and then slammed the door of his inner sanctum.

I said good morning to Judy. She put her hand to her forehead as if to steady herself, and then merely asked me if I wanted a cup of coffee. Her hands were shaking. Whatever had happened to that kid had gotten to her.

"Coffee's fine. But that's no way to get rid of me."

"It's Mike who wants to get rid of you."

She got up from her desk and pulled a cardboard cup from a dispenser and poured coffee from a Silex pot unsteadily. Judy was twenty-seven and reminded me of Rita Moreno in her early days. She was wearing a brown and white paisley blouse that did very nice things for her caramel skin tone. Sometimes I wondered why I didn't spend more time around the records office—but then I always remembered. Mike Parnell.

"You look tired, Johnny," Judy said, handing me the coffee cup.

"All those restless nights, thinking about you."

"You're so full of shit." She tried to smile, but couldn't quite pull it off.

I handed her Daisy's schedule change. "Look, I know this is a hell of a time, but do you suppose you can take care of this? The poor kid's program was botched by someone we all know."

She glossed over the forms and said, "Of course. Did she fill out the application last semester?"

"Yep. Helped her myself."

Judy went over to a filing cabinet, opened it, flicked manila folders until she found the right one. "It's right here," she said. "I'll make sure she has the change by noon."

I thanked her and then leaned on the counter there in the office, reluctant to leave.

There were some damned nice people in this school yet, and maybe that's why I'd stuck around. "I don't mean to wear out my welcome—" I said.

"You couldn't possibly." Bright eyes. Some guy was awfully lucky. And then I thought of Marlyn and me, the way we used to be.

"Judy," I said, "that kid they rolled out of here—"

She stepped closer and whispered so Mike wouldn't hear. "Disciple. Stabbed by a Dragon. Lost close to a liter of blood. They dragged him in here so no one would see."

"They're not going to report it?"

"You know how it is. It never happened."

This sort of thing was more common than anyone would believe. We frequently found kids in school with guns, and the school received on average four bomb threats a week. None of this made its way to a written document, and the media were certainly never informed. There were two realities, the one we all lived, and the one the administrators of José Julián Acosta High School endorsed.

Judy leaned toward me again and added, "I think there's a turf war starting, Johnny."

Goddamn it. Fernando had warned me. I wondered if Tony and Guiso had anything to do with this, and then I worried about Kirk Douglas Perez. For the rest of the morning I found myself recalling the face of that poor kid on the stretcher. A liter of blood, for God's sake.

"Look—you don't have to come. I'm perfectly capable of doing this by myself. She's my division student, after all."

"She's my English student," Tracy Singer insisted. "And I don't mind going. I just don't see why we have to walk there instead of driving."

Today she'd taught her first class, and it had gone fairly well. The boys had certainly paid attention. But at times she had more *chutzpah* than I had the patience to tolerate. "No reason, really—other than it's September, and a beautiful day, and she only lives half a mile away, and this way I can be late for hall guard duty. If you want, you can take your car and wait till I catch up to you."

Her heels clipped-clopped on the sidewalk and I supposed that's why she minded walking so much—those dumb shoes. For an inner city teacher she dressed like a model from Saks.

We were going on a visit to Hilda's home. Four days out of school and a disconnected phone line. I could have left the whole matter to the truant officers—but they were backed up for close to a month, and to be frank, I was worried about her. She'd never pulled a stunt like this before.

Tracy Singer said, "You know, if there's something personal that you hold against me, you can just say so and I'll request a different supervising teacher." I stopped and she took two steps before she noticed, and then spun around, her blond hair whipping against her shoulder. "What?" she wanted to know.

"Why do you take everything personally? Why can't you just accept the fact that some people have been doing this longer than you have, and have learned a thing or two in the process?"

"I accept that," she said. "I just don't think *Huckleberry Finn* is appropriate reading material for fifteen year old children."

I suddenly wanted a cigarette so bad I considered sprinting to a drug store. "Tracy?" I said. It was the first time I had called her by her first name, and it felt strange, saying it. "Let me tell you something they should have taught you in your literature courses. *Huckleberry Finn* is one of the greatest novels ever written. End of debate."

"But it has the *N* word."

I said, "Oh, grow up. Of course it has the *N* word. Your students hear that word twelve times before breakfast. It's despicable and it's offensive, but they have to read that novel so they know *why* it's offensive. And they're not *children* anymore at the age of fifteen. Not here. This isn't Winnetka, or Lake Forest, or wherever you're from, for Christ's sake, and you're not at Radcliffe. Look where you are. Look." I extended my arm, swept it around, 180 degrees. Graffiti scrawled garages. Boarded up tenements. "And for your information, Twain wasn't a racist. Twain was the opposite of a racist. Don't you understand that book? It might be the trend to revise history these days, but not in my class. You start changing history, and you stop learning from it."

I always felt foolish after blowing up at Tracy. I didn't know why I even cared what she thought. I began walking again and turned west on North Avenue. She remained silent, kept her distance, several steps behind me. We passed Disco Salsa CDs and a tire shop. There at the corner stood a beaten building, the trim of which had once been painted green, but now was faded and splintered. There was a foyer and an inner door. I walked in and held the door open for Tracy, who would not look me in the eye. She hesitated.

"Come on in," I said. "This'll be a learning experience for you."

The floor was littered with food wrappers, junk mail advertisers, cigarette butts. Mounted on the wall was a set of apartment buzzers—only some of which were labeled. I found Hilda's—*Feliciano, 2C*. I pressed the button—could actually hear the buzzer go off upstairs. A door squeaked opened, there was some shuffling, but no one came down to let us in.

Tracy said, "Maybe she's not home."

"But you heard that, didn't you—the door opening?"

I pressed the button several more times. This time I heard the indistinct sonority of a male voice. Tracy said, "Maybe we should go."

She looked so out of place in that dingy foyer—Sandra Dee in the ghetto.

All at once two children, a boy and a girl, came running down the stairs. They pushed open the locked door and tried to rush past us, but I grabbed the boy's coat and held the door open.

"*Mira,*" I said, "*dile a Hilda que la necesito ver inmediatamente.*"

The little boy looked up at me with big brown suspicious eyes. "*¿Es usted un estranjero?*"

"*No. Soy el maestro de ella.*"

The little girl who was with the boy looked up at Tracy, at her clothes, her blond hair.

The boy told his sister—they were brother and sister, it turned out—to wait, and he ran back up the stairs. I heard him talking to someone but once again I could not make out the words. When he returned, fairly breathless, he said, "*Hilda no puede bajar—porque su novio lo dijo—*" and then shot out the front door, pulling his sister along with him.

Tracy said, "What did he say?"

I'd been afraid of something like this. "He told me Hilda can't come down, that her boyfriend says so."

"What are you going to do?" she asked.

"We're going to go upstairs and tell him differently."

The banister was loose and wobbled and the stairs groaned under our weight. Tracy kept whispering sibilantly behind me that maybe we should leave, but I ignored her. There had once been a carpet on the second story hallway floor; there were still remnants of it, carpet tack holes near the baseboard. I found apartment 2C and knocked on the door. There was some muffled talking inside and then the door pulled to and I recognized Hilda's boyfriend—pockmarked complexion, buzz haircut. When he saw me he tried to slam the door in my face, but I shoved, and I shoved hard, knocking him over with the follow-through. Without thought I dove on him, pinned his arms to the floor and sat on his chest.

"Hilda?" I shouted. "Get out here." To her boyfriend I said, "Someone ought to teach you how to be hospitable to guests. You don't slam the door on them. You don't want them to get annoyed and sit on you, do you? Of course not." I could have easily killed the little motherfucker.

From the kitchen, Hilda stepped around the corner holding a bloody Kleenex to her nose.

"Mr. Spector," she said. Her face was tear-streaked. "He didn't do nothing, I promise. I just got allergies, is all."

I was still sitting on her boyfriend. He had stopped struggling, so I eased up a little to allow him to catch his breath. I said, "Hilda, if that's so, they're the first allergies I've ever heard of that cause bruised noses."

"I promise, Mr. Spector. That's why I haven't been to school."

"You'd better be in school tomorrow, or I'm going to file a police report against your *novio*, here." I bounced on him for good measure. "You understand that, pal?"

He would not answer. His face was red with rage, the hate in his eyes hot and large.

"Hilda," I said, "I'd like you to meet our new student English teacher, Ms. Singer."

Tracy stepped awkwardly around the boyfriend and me on the floor as if she believed there might be land mines buried beneath her feet, and shook hands with Hilda. "Nice to meet you, Hilda," she said.

I told her boyfriend that I was going to let him up, but that when I did, he was to leave the apartment and not come back, and if he ever, ever hurt Hilda again, he would face me *and* the police. I asked him if he understood, and he nodded. Then I asked him if he was *sure* he understood. Once more—a brief, reddened little nod. I got up and he scurried to his feet and ran out the door and bolted down the stairs. I heard the front door rattle and slam and echo below.

"Where are your parents?" I asked Hilda.

"Just me and my mom. She's at work."

There was a black and white photograph of a man on the wall, palm trees behind him. "When does she get home?"

"Around seven."

Her boyfriend had left his gang sweater on an old threadbare couch. Black and blue. A Disciple. I was not making friends with D's these days.

"I want you to keep him out of here, do you hear?"

"Yes, Mr. Spector. I promise. I *want* to come to school. It's Tito who tells me I can't."

Call me old fashioned, but I remembered a time when you didn't need your boyfriend's permission to attend school. "You have your mother call me at school tomorrow."

"We got no phone."

"Tell her to call me from work. They have phones where she works, right?"

"Okay, Mr. Spector."

The blood on her nose had begun to dry. I gave her shoulder a little squeeze (against my better judgment—couldn't help it), and then told her to lock the door behind us. Out on the landing, Tracy said, "Oh, my God."

"You see how it is, now."

"How many live like this?" she asked.

"Too many."

"You could've gotten yourself killed up there."

I said, "Want to stop for some coffee?"

You would not find a Starbucks in that section of town. We had Bustelo at a little diner called Orlando's. Tracy slid out of her trench coat in the booth and stirred cream into her cup. Her fingers were slender and perfectly manicured a shade of mauve. She had small, delicate ears and wore silver earrings.

"I don't think," she said, "that when I become certified that I will be making house calls like that."

I said, "Well, if it's any consolation, it's not exactly standard procedure."

"Why do you do it, then?"

"You saw her nose, didn't you?" I played with a sugar pack and then tossed it limply upon the table. "To be honest with you, I don't know. The other teachers will tell you that I'm just crazy. My wife will tell you that I've gone native, that I'm a street kid enjoying his second adolescence."

"Who would be right?" she wondered.

I said, "All of them, probably."

"Do you like what you do—teaching?"

I gave a little involuntary laugh. "I used to love it."

She sipped her coffee, her lip leaving a trace of lipstick on the green plastic cup. "And now?"

I said, "Let's talk about you."

Tracy said, "Every time we talk about me, I end up getting yelled at."

Once more I had to laugh. "I'm sorry about that."

"Why is it?" she said.

"Do you have any idea how many cups of coffee I drink every day?"

"You don't think I'm a lousy teacher?" She waited expectantly for my reply.

Gray cashmere sweater, silver necklace. "No. I think you're a fine teacher."

She held her coffee cup with two hands just below her mouth, which formed a smile at the news.

"You're just square, is all."

She lowered her cup to its saucer. "I am *not* square."

"Squares never know they're square."

She stood up, began putting her trench coat back on. "I'm going back to school."

All I said was, "Jesus Christ, not again."

When I got back to school I stopped in the main office to check my mailbox. I pulled out several envelopes and an ad from a textbook publisher. One of the envelopes was from the phone company—my home calling records. I slid a finger under the flap and tore the envelope open.

"Johnny—Martha's looking for you." Shirley had followed me into the mailroom and spoke so that she would not be overheard. Understandable. She was employed by the adversary.

I said, "Well—make sure she doesn't find me, okay?"

"She wants to know why you weren't on hall guard duty."

I slapped my forehead with the envelope. "Please don't tell me she went around checking up on me."

"She did, and you weren't there. I can head her off, if you tell me what to say."

The administration of the Chicago Public Schools preferred to have me confined to a hallway looking at walls rather than checking up on a traumatized, truant student. And on top of that I had to justify my actions to someone who was actively engaged in ignoring logic.

I said, "Tell her I had to see my drug dealer."

"I'm afraid she'll believe that."

Boy, would she. "I was on a home visit, Shirley. Girl who's being abused by her boyfriend."

She put her hand on my arm and patted it. "I'll sign out and in for you. You fill out a visitation report and leave it on my desk. Pronto."

Shirley—oversized bifocals, red hair, and the heart of a saint. I would have been finished years ago if it weren't for Shirley.

They run in columns, the phone numbers on calling records, beginning with area codes, separated by dates and times. One number stood out, had been called every other day or night for nearly a month—847 555 9086. I dialed it from my office and was greeted by a tape recording of a voice that belonged to someone named Bruce. I thought back to the card I'd found in Marlyn's purse—*You're not just something, you're everything. Love, Bruce.* There is a service provided by the phone company called reverse search. You dial a number and enter the number you're trying to identify, and if it's listed, they give you the full name and the address.

Bruce Campbell. 2512 McCormick in Elgin. One of us at home had called him fifteen times during the month of August. I knew for a fact I hadn't.

I had been twenty-nine years old. Everyone had told me that I couldn't marry an eighteen year old, that the idea was crazy. What would we talk about? Marlyn and I had been so in love that we locked out the rest of the world. Her father had forbade her to go to college, preferred that she marry an older man, a friend of the family, preferred that she move back to the island. We defied convention, parental commands, the disbelief of our friends. She was bright beyond her years, read voraciously. On weekend mornings we had champagne brunches and later visited museums, took carriage rides, came home, made love. In the summers we went up to Lake Geneva, rented motor boats, swam. In the winters we took Jason sledding in Lincoln Park, watched orange sunsets behind the stark limbs of trees exalting in still dance. It was like living inside a remarkable dream.

For the life of me, I couldn't tell you what happened to change all that. We had four family photo albums on a shelf that bore testimony to those years, and that was about it. Time reduced to color prints.

I found Vince in the physics closet making a parachute for a rocket. I sat down on a chair with a torn, ugly green leather seat and held a piece of chalk between my fingers, cigarette style. I wanted one so bad.

Vince said, "What do you think about an autumn baseball league?"

I just looked at him and puffed invisible smoke from my piece of chalk. "What are you talking about?"

He put a little sticker on a piece of parachute string to hold it in place. "For the kids, an autumn baseball league after school. Keep 'em off the streets, you know."

I said, "You've been using that model glue again, haven't you?"

"Think about it, Johnny. Each of us coaches a team. At the end of the season, the winning team gets a free dinner from the losers."

Vince did not come up with ideas like this. There was an ulterior motive lurking, somewhere.

"I'm not coaching any intramural sports."

"Or," he offered, "we could get a six pack, pick up a couple of chicks, go to the beach." That had become our motto. We'd been saying it to each other for sixteen years.

"You have a dangerous mind, Vince. I hope you plan on leaving it to science."

"The Smithsonian," he said. "They're gonna put it right next to LBJ's ears."

There was a vacuum chamber on the counter that followed the perimeter of the closet. Turn it on and you drop a feather and a lead ball and they'd land together. Next to this was a fulcrum and weights. Slide rules. Pyramids with removable walls. All of these devices to explain the workings of universal laws, and there I was without a clue about what to do with my life in the next twenty-four hours.

"Your shirt's torn," Vince said.

He was right. The sleeve was separating at the shoulder.

I said, "I just got back from a student's place. Had a little trouble."

Vince shook his head. "I'm not even going to ask." He folded the parachute carefully into a perfect triangle, and tucked it into the cylinder that was the body of the rocket. To this he attached the nose cone, and soon he had the rocket standing vertically on its fins. "Presto. Move over, Captain Kirk."

Bruce Campbell. I wondered if he was bigger than I was.

"Johnny?"

"Hm?"

"Whadaya think?"

I said, "It's a very nice rocket, Vince."

"No—I meant about you and Marlyn."

I let out a burst of air involuntarily and rubbed my eyes. They burned, felt weary. "I wish you'd ask me about something I knew something about."

He looked at me in precisely the way people look at very ill puppies. "You still want that detective's name?"

Detective. I guess that was the next step. "Sure," I said.

He reached into his back pocket for his wallet, skimmed past the plastic photo protectors. I saw them all, his kids. Rocco, Jasmine, and Theresa. Nice kids.

"Here ya go."

He handed me a gray embossed business card. *Tiff McCulloch, Private Investigator.*

I said, "Tiff, for Christ's sake."

§

"Go out for a long one," I said.

"Can you throw a long one?"

"Don't be a smart ass, Jason. I still haven't given you your allowance."

We were in the back yard. My boy shot out along the shrubs and I hurled the ball up and out. He spun, saw that he had outrun the pass, and then sprinted back up and let it drop right in the crook of his arm. He'd come home early from team practice—there was a parents football meeting that night—and I'd been on my first cocktail. I'd said let's throw the ball, and he'd said okay, even though I could tell his heart wasn't in it. Twelve years later and the little boy who used to hold my hand when he crossed the street was six feet tall, shaved, and patronized his old man.

I said, "Given any thought to which college you want to apply?"

"Yeah. Someplace warm. Maybe Arizona."

He threw the ball back to me and I dropped it.

"That's what you base an educational decision on? Climate?"

"Nice hands, Dad."

"Never mind my hands." I arced a gentle one to him, up nice and easy, and he picked it off with one hand. "Arizona State, or University of?"

"Arizona State. Right near the Phoenix Airport."

He aligned his fingertips with the laces and shot a perfect spiral at me. Stung to catch. We didn't do this kind of thing often enough and now he was getting ready to leave home and we'd never do it again.

"I saw your *abuelo* the other day. He asked about you."

"You did? How is *Abuelo*?"

The two of them adored each other and I thought that was nice. I'd never had that kind of relationship with my grandfather. My grandfather shook hands when we met and never smiled.

I fired the ball back to him and said, "He's lonely, I think. You should come with your mother and me the next time we visit him."

Jason spun the ball between both hands. "Are you and Mom doing that kind of thing together?"

Well—there it was. Even he'd noticed it.

"I don't know," I said.

"What is it with you two lately?"

He stood next to a baby pine we'd planted the year he'd turned four. "I don't know that, either."

The sophomore parents football meeting was pretty much the same as the freshman parents football meeting the previous year, except now we all knew each other and there was a new coach. He was a nice guy with a flattop and he said "Tell you what—" at the beginning of each new response. As I sat and listened to him talk about the training staff, I looked at Marlyn and tried to imagine her with someone else. It was impossible. I don't mean that it was impossible for it to happen—it was simply impossible for me to imagine it. Those eyes were the most lovely eyes in the world. How could they conceal a thing like an affair, an office romance?

The coach had our boys' best interest at heart, he said. They were a group, a family. Tell you what.

"So how was your day?"

Marlyn and I were in her car together and I thought it would be nice to stop off and have some pie and coffee before we went home. It was the kind of thing we used to do, and I was surprised when she agreed to it.

I said, "My day? My day was swell. The principal caught me missing at my hall guard assignment, I beat up a seventeen year old in his girlfriend's apartment, and I sat in a closet with a forty-three year old man who was making a rocket. How was your day?"

"I know you too well to think that you made any of that up."

She had the pecan caramel pie and I had the apple. It had been a slow day at the hospital, she said—low census, down to five patients. She might have some extra time off soon, if that continued. "Which would be fine by me," she said. "I could use it."

She was pleasant, and I was pleasant, and it dawned on me that I would have no way of knowing if she actually went to work or not on any given day. I was not in the habit of calling her there. Maybe I should have been.

"Plying pretty young girls with pie. That's about what I expected of you, Spector." Barry Levine, and his wife Bonnie. Barry was a corporate attorney and lived in a house that had once belonged to God, and his boy Jerry played on the football team with Jason.

I said, "Barry, Bonnie. The pie isn't working. I was about to try scotch."

"Come back to our place," Bonnie said. "Barry just had his new bar put in." Bonnie was nice and motherly and you always had the impression that she had forgotten to put on her makeup.

Marlyn said, "Oh—we can't."

Barry said, "Of course you can. The boys will all end up there, anyway. Besides—you can't get any scotch in a pie place."

On the ride over to Barry and Bonnie's, Marlyn checked her watch and seemed to have become irritable. "You could have just made up some excuse, school night or something."

"It's just one drink. It's the polite thing to do."

Marlyn said, "It's the drink, Johnny. You know you're not polite."

I tapped the accelerator and the car jumped. I wondered if everyone out there was fighting a war on two fronts, or if it was just me.

I said, "You might let me in on just what the hell it is you're so upset about."

Marlyn began to hum. Whenever she was angry she hummed. It was an odd habit. Then she stopped humming and said, "I'm upset about the same thing I was upset about fourteen years ago, when you said you'd give up your gangsters for Jason and me."

I had not been ready for a flashback, but here it was. "I said that?"

She hummed.

"Marlyn, I might've said I'd spend more time with the family, but I can't give up my work. How could I do that?"

"Do you know how long it's been since we've had a vacation?"

I took a mental look back and got as far as six years ago. "If it's about a vacation—"

"Forget it, Johnny. It's not about a vacation. I stopped waiting for you about the same time I stopped believing you."

I did not know what I was supposed to say to that.

The Levines' home had been built in the late sixties and had been renovated several times since then, which gave it a sort of eclectic look. Tennis courts, indoor pool, rec room that was half video arcade, half night club. Sure enough, Jason and most of the offensive line were already over there. I sat on a bar stool and watched the kids as they shot lasers at one another's virtual men. Bonnie sat down next to me and said, "Johnny, if you need a refresher, just give a holler."

"Just started, Bonnie," I said. "Give me a second or two."

Barry was showing Marlyn his new skis. They were yellow and black, secured in a rack that was attached to the wall. Marlyn knew nothing about skiing. I knew nothing about skiing. In fact, the minute I noticed the skis, the first thing that came to mind was the Latin Kings. Yellow and black were their colors. I was probably the only guy in suburbia whose mind worked like this.

Some of the boys were showing Marlyn how their games worked. Jason draped his arm around his mom's shoulder proudly, affectionately. They were both beautiful, and she was the hit of the party; people were naturally drawn to her, to her equanimity, her openness. I had been, too.

"Strange," Bonnie said.

I sipped some of my scotch and said, "What's that?"

"The way they get so big so fast." She looked at the bar as she spoke.

I said, "I thought I was the only one going through that."

She shook her head. "Is Jason an only child?"

"Yes."

"Jerry too. I think that makes it harder."

I finished off my drink and the ice cubes rattled. "Naw. It just makes the inevitable more obvious. If you have two or three, then you can fool yourself for a few years and think that it will last."

"You know, Johnny—you and Marlyn are young enough to start over again, have another child."

Oh, yeah. That was just what we needed. I said, "Bonnie?"

"Yes?"

I pointed at my glass. "Holler."

§

It was a pancake house in Morton Grove, a northern suburb of Chicago—Saturday afternoon. I had asked Tiff McCulloch, my private detective, how I would know him, and he'd said not to worry, that he'd know me when he saw me. I thought, *Damn, he* must *be good.* I parked the Jeep and wondered if I should lock the door. It was nine years old and rusting. I figured that if somebody was that desperate, then they ought to just take it. The hostess asked, "Table for one?" and I told her I was waiting for somebody. I was brought coffee in a pitcher and sat listening to the background buzz of indistinct conversation. People—we sure liked talking. It didn't matter if what we were saying was important or not. We just liked talking, liked the company.

"John Spector?"

I looked up into the face of a solid-looking guy of about fifty-five—graying curly hair, glasses. Plaid shirt, down vest. Tiff McCulloch.

I shook hands with him and he slid into the booth across from me. I said, "I must look like the kind of guy whose wife plays around on him."

Tiff turned his coffee cup right-side-up and poured himself some steaming coffee. "It's not too tough to tell who's waiting for someone. They're usually alone."

The waitress asked if we'd like to order. Neither of us was hungry.

"So tell me the story," Tiff said.

I said, "Well, there isn't much of a story, I'm afraid. We've been distant from each other lately, my wife and I. I found a card in her purse signed by some guy, and I had the phone records sent out. Lots of calls to someone with the same name as the guy who sent the card." I played absently with the fork at my place setting. "I could just be paranoid."

"How old is she?"

"Thirty-five."

"What did the card say?"

I told him. He said I wasn't paranoid.

I said, "You think she's having an affair?"

He shrugged. "That's what we're going to find out. How about you—you holding up all right?"

I was beginning to like this guy. He hadn't even asked for the money yet and he wanted to know how I was doing. "I've had better times."

Tiff nodded. "If I catch her with him—and that's what we're talking about here, I hope you understand that—what are you going to do?"

I hadn't even thought about that. I said, "Jesus, I don't know."

Tiff spooned some sugar into his coffee, stirred it slowly. "You going to get a divorce?"

I'd been divorced once in my life, but that had been different. That had been my choice. Marlyn had been a part of my life for so long, I couldn't see living without her.

"I really don't know what to tell you. I don't know what I'll do."

"You still love her," Tiff inferred.

This time I nodded.

He sipped his coffee and assessed me with his eyes over the rim of his cup. When he returned the cup to its saucer, he said, "Used to fight some, did you?"

"What do you mean?"

"That nose, it's been broken."

I never thought people noticed a thing like that. "I've had some scrapes."

He smiled. He just sat there looking at me, smiling. Made me feel awkward.

"I brought what you asked for." From my leather jacket's breast pocket I took a photograph of Marlyn and laid it on the table before him. He looked at it, held it up. From the side pocket I retrieved an envelope that held five hundred dollars in cash. This I put down next to where the picture had been.

"Pretty girl," he said.

I began to understand just what was happening here. I was watching the unfolding of my life with Marlyn. It was a little bit like a funeral.

"Any children?" Tiff wanted to know.

"One—my son. He's nearly grown."

"That's too bad. I always hate when there are kids involved." He put the photo of Marlyn down on the table next to the money. I remembered the day that picture was taken, two years before. We had just returned from a birthday dinner with Vince and his wife Terri. She looked so happy at the moment it was taken. You would have never thought that that expression, that summer evening, would have ended up on a table in front of a private detective and next to five hundred dollars. "Now, John—is it all right if I call you John?"

I said of course it was. He would follow her from work, he said, and see what we have. He wanted to know if there was a number other than my home number at which he could contact me, and I said he could call my cell phone, I'd have it on.

"If we get lucky, we'll catch her on the first day."

Lucky, I thought.

"Then we'll see if we can catch them sleeping together. Usually takes a few times. Once you have that, you have some leverage in property settlement discussions."

I was beginning to feel numb, sitting there having reality explained to me as if I were a cretin, or a child. But I hadn't expected any of this, hadn't expected it because I hadn't wanted to believe it.

"Say," Tiff said, "are you all right?"

On our wedding night we had stayed at the Whitehall Hotel, stayed up till two sipping champagne at the bar, whispering to one another. "Sure—I'm fine. It's all a little new to me, is all."

He stood up, gathered the envelope, the photo. "Listen—my wife and I are having some friends over this afternoon. Barbecuing some steaks. Why don't you come back to our place? Make you a steak this thick." He held his forefinger apart from his thumb.

I said that it was kind of him, but that I couldn't. I just couldn't. He shook my hand again, told me to take care of myself. I sat there for a while listening to the hum of conversation, people talking to people. There had been the champagne till two and then the Georgian furniture of our room, the click of the door closing.

"Is everything fine here?" the waitress asked.

That first night together. "Yes," I heard myself say. "Everything is fine."

4

The opening of school had been delayed an hour so that the faculty could have a special meeting about curriculum. I was late to the meeting and hung over as I sneaked in the auditorium door. Nydia Velazquez said, "Psssst!" and motioned me over. I sat down next to her in the back row and she laid her arm across my shoulders. On her other side was Javier Acosta, a house assistant principal. House assistants were not the same as actual assistant principals. They took care of discipline and attendance on a given floor, but did not have much authority beyond that. Javier was good with the kids. He understood that they needed direction, not jail sentences.

The world came at me as if out of a box stuffed with cotton. I felt dizzy—still drunk from the night before. There was something about the look of this meeting that did not seem right. Martha Ballinger was nowhere to be found. On the stage were Isabelle Villachez and Elizabeth Mojica. They were introducing a man and a woman seated panel-style behind a table, as though they were holding a news conference. The woman was tiny and stoic and possessed the general demeanor of a military guard. The man was gray and balding and appeared bewildered. They were educational experts from the island, Elizabeth informed us, where they worked for the liberation of their people from the oppressive, imperialistic forces of the United States government. Standing at the left side of the stage was an American flag, and it had been pushed aside against the curtain as if it were an appurtenance. I wondered how they could miss the irony of this.

Our curriculum, Isabelle, added, was robbing young Puerto Rican children of their Latin culture, by supplanting it with Anglo culture. The Dr.s Cardoñas—they were a husband-wife team—had years of experience in designing culture-friendly curriculum for Latino students.

Because we were a neighborhood academy, our new curriculum would be custom-written, after the Curriculum Committee determined the special needs of our Acosta students. The members of the Curriculum Committee were then identified as none other than Isabelle, Elizabeth, the Cardoñas, and our brand new principal, Danny Velez.

With that announcement, the curtains parted, and out walked Danny Velez himself, with more than a fair amount of conspicuous drama. He was greeted by less than enthusiastic applause that rippled through the auditorium and soon died away.

Javier leaned forward and said to me—"You ready for the revolution?"

I said, "I don't know. I'm still trying to get used to being an imperialist."

Nydia's face became cold and set. She shook her head and said, "I can't believe this."

I said, "What exactly can't you believe?"

"That they think they can get away with taking over the school."

I had been willing to listen if they thought they had something that could improve our kids' education. But what I heard next was disquieting. Danny Velez spoke in revolutionary political jargon. I heard about the evils of globalism, and the liberation of political prisoners who were considered martyrs back on the island. The prisoners he spoke of included his sister, the bomb maker. I did not hear much about curriculum, except that ours was racist. Twice he referred to the non-Hispanic teachers as *Anglos*. I wasn't insulted, as I didn't feel any different from my Latin American friends. I was embarrassed—for Danny himself. He was a divisive force, and the way this new administration was shaping up, I assumed we would all of us come under close scrutiny. Buy the company line or else.

Javier stood up before the proceedings were over. "I've heard enough. What's wrong with you Johnny, teaching those kids all that capitalistic crap?"

"I'm just not sensitive, Javier."

When the lights went up, faculty members, joined in predictable cliques, climbed up the auditorium steps to the doors, some of them looking stunned, others just resigned. Nydia and I exited the auditorium together and rode the escalator up to the second floor.

"They're FALN," she said, "hardcore. You heard the rhetoric. I don't know how much they're getting or where the money's coming from, but I can sure as hell tell you where it's going."

"A conspiracy? Are you kidding?"

She whispered, "Shhh."

Isabelle was standing at the entrance of the main office as we reached the second floor. She shot an icy glance at Nydia, and then at me. When we walked further down the corridor, I said, "What was that all about?"

"She can't stand me. My father's the most successful Puerto Rican businessman in the neighborhood, and we both support statehood for the island. She's a leftist, an *independentista* As far as she's concerned, I'm delaying the revolution."

"She didn't look too happy with me, either."

Nydia tickled my ribs. "Lover, you're so naïve. You're with me, in the first place, *and* you married a Puerto Rican girl. Stole her from the neighborhood."

Funny. I'd always thought that would make me closer to the culture, not further away from it. I couldn't understand that at all. Neither did I know if Nydia's suspicion about the money was valid, or an exaggeration. But I didn't have time to think of any of that. When I got to my office the kids were at the door in a nervous huddle, gesticulating, murmuring. When they saw me, Daisy called out, "*Mira*, Johnny! Let us in. We gotta talk to you."

I said, "What the hell's going on here?"

When I got the door open, they stormed in past me before I could get the key out of the lock. Fernando leaned his back against a file cabinet. Nelson sat in a chair in the corner. Daisy tapped her foot on the carpet and stared at me with her hands in her hip pockets. They all smelled as if they'd just smoked a pack of cigarettes in a telephone booth.

I said, "Would somebody please tell me what's going on?"

Daisy kicked my door shut with her shoe. "I'll tell you what's going on. Hollywood fucked up and now the D's are gonna take Fernando down."

Nelson said, "Tell him about the kid. The kid they took outa here on a stretcher."

Fernando looked sick. His face was visible only as a shadow under the peak of a cabbie's cap.

I said, "What about the kid on the stretcher?"

Fernando started speaking somberly as if to himself without looking at anyone in particular. "Hollywood been sellin' shit in the neighborhood again, got my little cousin strung out on the stuff, and he's only twelve. His brother, Flaco—one of my boys—is the one who sliced him. Sliced him on accounta what Hollywood done. The D's want to take him out for revenge, but they can't, 'cause he went back to the island. Lives in Isabela. So they're comin' after me. They're gonna get me."

The pieces weren't exactly falling into place. "If your cousin has an issue with Kirk, how come he didn't come after Kirk?"

"'Cause he didn't know who it was that sold the shit, then. Only that it was the D's. He was all pissed and shit and he wasn't thinkin'."

I still could not feature Kirk Douglas Perez as a heroin dealer. "You sure it's Hollywood and not his brother?"

Fernando half-laughed, half-sighed. "Man, I know you like him, but you gotta face facts."

Daisy slapped my arm. "You gotta do something, Johnny. Fernando can't even go home. They see him try to get out of the park, they gonna shoot his ass."

I said, "Me? What am I supposed to do? Take their guns away?"

Daisy said, "Who's the teacher here?"

I slumped into my chair. I wondered if I should inform Daisy that they hadn't covered student assassinations in my education classes.

"Who's got a square?"

Nelson reached into his jacket and pulled out a crush-proof box of Newports. "Didn't know you smoked."

I said, "I don't. I just want to hold it." Sometimes if I held one between my fingers the old craving went away. Sometimes. I thought about calling the police—but what would they do—give Fernando an escort home? Not likely. And even after they'd gone, he had to come out sometime. He couldn't hide forever. What this school needed was a gang member protection program. What we had was the promise of a new curriculum at the expense of the canon.

"Let me ask you this—why you? Why not any member of the Dragons?"

"'Cause we blood, man. Ain't no other Dragon be blood to Flaco."

I thought vaguely of the Montagues and the Capulets. "When is your cousin coming back from the island?"

"Maybe never."

You couldn't blame him.

"*Damn*, Johnny. What you gonna do?" This from Daisy.

I looked at them all, Nelson sprawled in the chair; Fernando slumped and fearing his own mortality; cute little Daisy who ought to be more concerned about who to ask to turnabout, if we still had dances. (Parents were too afraid to let their kids come into the park at night.) *What are you gonna do, Johnny?* I thought.

"Come home to my place tonight," I said, and then I imagined the hell I'd catch from Marlyn.

"What?" Fernando said. "You crazy?"

I stood up and handed the cigarette back to Nelson, who stuck it behind his ear. "Just listen to me. You come back to my place for a night or two, till the neighborhood cools down, and we'll take it from there."

"But what about my mother when I don't come home? She'll be worried. And I ain't got no clothes or shit."

Slinging guns at the age of fifteen and he was worried about what to tell his mother. "I'll call her, okay? I'll work everything out with her. You can borrow some of my boy's clothes. But you make sure you're here in my office the minute ninth period is over. You understand?"

The guys slapped my hand before they left, and Daisy squeezed my shoulder. "You're doin' the right thing," she said.

I felt like asking her if she'd explain that to my wife. I looked at my watch. Nine-thirty. Nine-thirty and I needed a drink.

Up in the cafeteria I grabbed a cup of coffee and ran into Dave Volmer. I noticed that the collar of his button-down shirt was frayed. Dave had been wearing that shirt for over ten years.

"What do you say we stop in on Grandma's after school?" he asked me.

"Can't," I said. "Got a student emergency."

Dave shook his head as he walked away. "For Christ's sake, Spector. Your *life* is a student emergency."

I stopped by the supply room and picked out two red pens and an overhead transparency marker. It was about all that was left. We were underfunded, hadn't even the basic tools we needed. There was always talk of improvement down at the board of education, but it was just talk. When I walked into the classroom, Tracy Singer had been waiting to spring at me.

67

"We need to speak," she said.

Tracy—the walking overreaction. I said, "Can't it wait till after class?"

The answer was a resounding no, so I followed her out into the hall and she slipped a student essay in my hands. "Read this—all of it, and don't say anything until you've finished."

It was Lico Pacheco's narrative assignment. I had brought handouts of poems by Judith Ortiz Cofer from *Terms of Survival* and wanted to distribute them to students before they had a chance to get bored and out of control, and now this. I read the first three or four sentences. The standard my-earliest-memory routine, but soon there was a dark turn. Lico's mother had been a drunk and a drug abuser and often left him and his brothers and sisters alone for days at a time. No food, no clean clothing, no hot water. Then came an even darker turn. His stepfather used to lift him up from the soiled mattress he slept on at night and take him to his bed. He had been abandoned and then taken in by DCFS. His mother had recently been given visitation rights, and when she failed to show up, sometimes he would go to Union Station on Canal Street and sit in the Amtrack waiting room and scan the faces of passengers, on the off chance that she might be among them. The rest was too awful to finish.

"Go on," Tracy said. "Read the rest of it."

My stomach turned and I needed to sit down. "I don't want to finish it."

Tracy had clear green eyes that she used at times like searchlights. "What are we going to do?" she wanted to know.

All right. What are we going to do? I thought. *Well, we could always kill ourselves.*

I had not even had a chance to set down my coffee, and now I didn't want it. "Let's just teach the class, and think about this afterward."

Her mouth opened in wonder. "You mean, you can just forget about this?"

"No. I can't forget about it. But I think it would be a good thing for everyone if we just go in there and teach for now."

It was awkward at first, when we walked in the classroom, neither of us knowing how to make the transition from reading that essay to teaching. But we went through the motions and soon things moved along smoothly enough. Tracy had worked out an activity whereby students read the poems aloud to each other in small groups, and then paraphrased one stanza at a time. She went from group to group and encouraged the timid kids to take a turn reading. Afterward, she had the groups all get together and each student read a paraphrased section. She explained what figurative language was, and alliteration, and I looked at Lico, wondered how he had made it this far. That stutter. Those roaming eyes, seeking cover. Where had he found the courage to write about this? Or maybe it wasn't courage at all, but desperation. And if Marlyn was having an affair, how would I keep from killing Bruce? The son of a bitch.

Tracy had done quite a nice job. When the tone sounded she collected the papers, reminded the kids about homework, and then closed the door when they were all gone.

"Well?" she said.

I loosened my tie and opened my collar button. "Mark the paper like an ordinary paper. Show him his run-on sentences and tense inconsistencies. Then make a remark to show that it touched you. You know. Words to the effect that it must have been difficult, and would he like to talk about it with someone."

"Is that all?"

I leaned over the podium, thinking. "No—we'll make an appointment with Marco Gonzalez and let him in on it. Marco usually knows what to do with this sort of thing."

"You've read papers like this before?"

I nodded. "Unfortunately. Life's a bitch."

Those clear, green Tracy Singer eyes—open and astonished. "Is that it? Life's a bitch, too bad?"

I had a brief but very distinct mental picture of a Smirnoff bottle. It was open, next to a highball glass filled with three ice cubes. "I'm not a therapist, Tracy. I have to get though my day, just like everybody else."

She stuffed the papers in her Abercrombie bag and mumbled, "Maybe years of teaching hardens people."

"Maybe. You did a great job today, by the way."

She looked up suddenly, as if she wanted to say something, but then didn't. It was nearly eleven and we were both late for division.

You didn't want to be late to division. Things tended to happen, like the brawl we walked in on. You could hear the shouting all the way down by the escalators. I had to push my way into the room past bodies

69

of kids who didn't even belong there. Flying fists, curses. Fernando was beating Kirk Douglas Perez to pulp, pounding his head, spit flying from his mouth as he shouted, "*Motherfucker junkie bastard!*"

He hadn't meant to, but as he cocked his fist once more, it caught me on the lip and knocked my head backward. I'd jumped between them to break up the fight, and we'd all gone down on the floor. Kirk was hurt and trying to keep from getting pummeled, with little success. His face was a smear of blood, and one sleeve of his sweatshirt had been torn away, exposing rows of dark welts—track marks. I rolled over on Fernando and put him in a bear hug to restrain him.

"Stop, now. Take it easy. Slow down."

"I'll fuckin *kill* the motherfucker." I could feel his chest pounding on my chest, his face darkened from the flush of blood pumping through his veins and arteries. I heard someone speaking over a walkie-talkie and looked up to see Elizabeth Mojica and two security guards clearing out the room.

"Get outa here, now!" ordered a short, husky guard with black hair and a mustache, as he shoved kids out the doorway.

"But this is my division!" Daisy. He'd picked on the wrong girl.

"That's all right. She belongs here," Tracy said, holding Daisy by the shoulders. She still had that crazy bag slung over her shoulder, and looked frightened to death.

As Fernando and I struggled to get up, I whispered, "Go with them. Be cool. I'll take care of everything later."

The taller guard put his arm on Fernando's back and guided him out the door. I'd seen it at the last second, the sparkle. The kid had had tears in his eyes. Mr. Tough Guy.

Elizabeth Mojica was a rather short woman with hair piled on her head in a neat bun. She had to look up when she spoke to me. "How did you lose control of the situation, Mr. Spector?"

I thought, *Oh, no. Not in front of my students, you don't.* "Well, I'll tell you Elizabeth. I didn't lose control of the situation. I *took* control of the situation."

"It didn't look like you had control of it to me."

"Thankfully I don't have to worry about the way things look to you. I just have to do my job, and my job is to teach."

"Your job is also to maintain order."

I'd had my masters degree before she'd even entered college.

"Elizabeth? If it were a perfect world, I guess our jobs would be a lot easier."

I started picking up overturned desks from the floor and setting them in rows. I hadn't seen what had happened to Kirk, but I imagined the other security guard had escorted him down to Martha's office—which was now Danny Velez's office, presumably. I wondered how long he'd been using, thought about how he was always dozing off lately. Hooked by his own brother, the son of a bitch. It was going to be the Disciples against the Dragons—out-and-out war between my own kids. Now, how do you take sides on a thing like that?

§

"How come everybody in your town is white?"

I'd just driven home with Fernando. We stopped at the local Walgreens to pick up some sundries for him, toothbrush, razor and such, when he made this blunt and mostly accurate sociological observation.

I said, "People here are from all different ethnic backgrounds."

"They all look white to me."

It was all about color, his world. Racial colors, gang colors. I picked out a shaving bag for him, something to keep his things in. I knew from experience how a teenager needs to feel he has his own belongings.

I had not wanted a confrontation with Danny Velez on his first day as principal. After ninth period I'd stopped in the main office to pick up Fernando, and Shirley informed me that he had been taken to the detention room until Mike Parnell had time to write a suspension. I went to Parnell on Fernando's behalf, but he told me he had orders from Velez—zero tolerance for anyone involved in a fist fight.

I'd said, "Lack of tolerance is what creates these situations, Mike. It doesn't prevent them."

And he'd said he wasn't about to go up against Velez's orders. So I had to.

I'd found him in his office, which, it seemed to me, was unusually dimly lit. He was seated on his sofa, talking to Isabelle Villachez. He must have seen me standing there just outside his doorway, though he managed to ignore me for ten or so minutes before lifting his head in an annoyed manner and saying, "Yes?"

71

Danny Velez was handsome in a hoodish way—shiny, combed-back black hair, one slightly lazy eye. His suit was copper-colored and didn't seem to fit, was too long at the sleeves and hem of the jacket. He remained seated next to Isabelle during our entire exchange, which was brief. I told him I'd come to talk about Fernando, and asked him to reconsider the suspension.

"Zero tolerance," he'd said.

I explained that suspensions were a bad idea when it came to these two, as they were members of rival gangs, and too much time on the streets would give them a greater opportunity to kill each other.

"Zero tolerance," he'd said again. He spoke in fragments.

Marco Gonzalez had appeared behind me a few seconds earlier to wait his turn to enter Danny's court, and he'd overheard our conversation. He spoke right up and told Danny that I had it right, that the situation on the streets could only be made worse if we turned kids loose on them. Danny turned to Isabelle, said something I didn't catch, and then nodded.

"All right," he'd said to me. "This one time. But more trouble with these two again, out." He shook his index finger at me as he delivered this last line, as though I were the one being threatened with suspension.

I slapped Marco on the back before I left, and thanked him. He pulled me aside and spoke in murmurs so as not to be overheard. "There's talk of a war out there. How's he getting home?"

And I said, "He's not going home. I'm taking him back to my place."

He looked into my eyes a long moment, a very long moment, as if he were trying to determine something about me, and then said, "You get too involved, Johnny. You get too close."

"What the hell, Marco. First you want me to go to sensitivity sessions, and the next thing I know, I'm too involved."

"They're not the same thing. I'm talking about being a professional."

He stood there in his navy blue pinstripe suit with his hand clasped around my arm, lecturing to me about professionalism. I pulled my arm free from his grasp. "Okay," I said. "Let's be *real* professional. Let's not get involved at all."

§

I led Fernando upstairs to the computer room and made up the couch as a bed—pillow, quilt. I put his shaving bag and supplies on an end table. "It's not exactly the Ritz, but I think you'll be comfortable. By the way, when I spoke to your mother, I promised you'd call her tonight."

Fernando sized up the room, looked inside the closet. "Yeah, later." He pulled a package of Newports from his jacket pocket.

I said, "You'll have to smoke that thing outside."

"Aw, come on, Johnny. Be cool."

"I'm too old to be cool. Go out on the deck and I'll join you in a second."

He shook his head, breathed labored breaths of disgust, and slunk down the stairs. I led him to the sliding glass doors and then stopped in the kitchen to pour a drink—three fingers of Stoli. The ice cubes cracked and misted in the glass. The first sip did the trick—welcome numbing. Four-fifteen. I thought of Marlyn, pictured Tiff surreptitiously eyeing her from his parked car as she left the hospital. Maybe it had been a mistake, hiring a detective. In any case, I felt guilty about it, setting her up. If you had to do these things in a marriage, wouldn't it be more dignified just to pack your things and call it a day? But the uncertainty—that was the trouble. It would pack itself along with your belongings and follow you wherever you went.

Out on the deck, Fernando paced the wooden planks in his Nikes and looked out at the trees in the back yard. "Damn, man. Why it's so quiet?"

I said, "That's the way I like it. I get enough noise during my days."

"Don't you get bored to death?"

"No. I also don't get shot to death."

Fernando took a deep drag on his cigarette. "Where's your O.G?"

O.G. was *old girl*. He meant my wife. It was anybody's guess. "She'll be home soon."

"They say you married one of your students."

I sipped some more of the Stoli, pinpricks upon the tongue. "I married a woman who used to be one of my students."

"Same thing," he said. "How come they didn't fire you?"

We had been so thrilled, dating, sneaking around the city together, looking for out-of-the-way places where we wouldn't be seen.

"Well, buddy—for one thing, I didn't break any laws."

"She Rican, right?"

"Yes."

"*Chingar*, Johnny. Didn't her folks get pissed an' shit?"

"Her mother's dead. Her father wasn't thrilled."

"Damn, man. You too much."

Well, I used to be.

"How about you?" I asked. "What's your story?"

"I ain't got no story."

"Everybody's got a story. What's it like at home?"

Fernando flicked his cigarette into the back yard. "It's all right. Ain't no thang. You know. It's me and my ma. My old man, he come around sometimes." He walked to the railing, looked up at the sky as though he were challenging it. "He got a girlfriend. Lives with her."

"You miss him?"

He turned to face me and frowned. "Naw. The Dragons, they my family. They my brothers. We look out for each other—take care of the block."

A blue-black *D* had been etched into the brown skin of his forearm—a homemade tattoo job. I knew the story, had heard it a thousand times. Sociologists can list for you all the reasons kids create gangs and honor their colors and symbols, their rituals and myths. Lack of guidance at home. Acceptance. Safety. Loneliness. Need for a support system. They just can't tell you how to get them out before they get killed.

I had worried about how my son and Fernando would hit it off, but I needn't have. There was the initial social awkwardness that comes whenever two teenagers from different worlds meet, but Fernando was Fernando and he broke the ice in his style. He'd said to Jason, "You sure you Rican? You look *white*."

And Jason had laughed as they slapped palms, saying, "I'm both. Whattup?"

I ordered a pizza for the boys while they went out back to shoot baskets. When they tired of that, they got out the fielder mitts and played catch. What I had not known was that Fernando was an expert pitcher. Jason had had to switch to a catcher's mitt because Fernando's fast ball had such sizzle. The kid must have been throwing at over ninety miles an hour. When I asked him where he'd learned to pitch like that, he told me it was back when he was on the island. There was a baseball camp that many young kids dreamed of attending, and his uncle had paid the tuition.

Six o'clock, no Marlyn. I carried my cell phone in my shirt pocket, waiting for a call from Tiff. Outside the sun had become a pink and orange flare at the horizon beyond a ridge of trees to the west, and I sipped another vodka on the rocks, trying to remember what it had been like to be fifteen. At fifteen I think I possessed a fair amount of judgment, had a realistic sense of what was going on around me, but just below the skin there had been an incendiary emotional lining that could, from one moment to the next, blaze up, move me to anger, fear, sadness. It was still there, I guessed, though dulled, calmed. Adults tend to forget. That was part of the problem.

I was still sitting on a leather chair in the living room when the door shoved open and Marlyn walked in. She did not see me at first, and when she did, her face took on a forced insouciance that masked anything she might have been thinking.

She said, "What are you doing sitting in the dark?"

"Watching a sunset, trying to remember what it was like being a teenager."

"That shouldn't be too difficult, for you." After she hung up her jacket, she turned on a light on an end table and saw the drink in my hand. "Oh—here we go down memory lane. I see."

She did not see, but I wasn't going to explain it to her.

I said, "Out kind of late, aren't you?"

She went through the mail on the coffee table and did not look at me. "We had a unit meeting and then a few of us decided to go out for dinner."

I said, "A phone call would have been nice."

She set down the mail and straightened some tchotchkes on the bookcase. "Why should I call? We don't have anything to say even when we're together."

"Still," I said, "basic consideration."

She gave a short laugh. "Basic consideration is what you should have showed your family years ago, instead of crusading for gangsters, Johnny. Don't talk to me about basic consideration."

With that, as if I could use any more dilemmas, the back door opened and slammed shut. Jason and Fernando, raucous, laughing, stormed through the room. I stood up and said, "Honey, I meant to tell you—we have a house guest, tonight. I'd like you to meet Fernando."

Fernando had been about to run up the stairs, but stopped short, turned and walked back toward Marlyn. He looked sheepish, did not know whether to extend his hand or not. In the end he held it out and said, "Whattup?"

Marlyn took his hand in hers, and I noted her eyes as they registered the tattoo, the diamond earring. She said a polite hello, and then Jason and Fernando headed up the stairs together, arguing over who had the baddest hook shot in the NBA.

Cold, knowing—that stare. It was Marlyn's I've-had-enough stare. "And so now you're bringing them home."

"It's just for one night," I said.

I might have been wrong about the stare. It might have been her You're-utterly-impossible stare. They're similar. "I will not have my home turned into a halfway house for Disciples."

I said, "He's not a Disciple."

"I saw the D on his arm, Johnny. You're not fooling any—"

"He's a Dragon."

Marlyn took a deep breath, held it in a second or two, and then deflated. I'd done it again—exasperated her in no time, without even trying. It's a talent, I guess. A few minutes later I heard our bedroom door slam and I knew I would be spending the night on the couch.

§

"Here's the story. Do you want to hear the story?"

Tracy Singer at seven-thirty in the morning. She'd cornered me in a classroom and made me sit down at a student desk. I could barely get my eyes open past a squint and it felt like my brain was leaking out my ears. "I'm sick of stories. All I ever hear is stories."

She would not be put off. Today she was in a white pant suit and black sandals. She looked like the spokesperson in a furniture commercial. "I sat down with Lico and got him to talk about his mother. Did you know he hasn't seen her since he was six years old?"

I did not know that. I wanted coffee. "The way he wrote about it made it sound like it was just a few years ago."

"That's what *I* thought. She left the family with nothing—I mean *nothing*, when he was in kindergarten. The kids waited for days before they realized she wasn't coming home."

"What about the stepfather?"

"I don't know. Apparently he was out of the picture by then—and they'd never really gotten married. They were just living together. Anyway—since then, he's been in seven different foster homes. *Seven.* Now he's in a group home. It's sort of like a townhouse, with a live-in counselor."

The fluorescent lights of the classroom were an assault on my sensibilities. "What about his brothers and sisters? In the essay he talks about three or four, doesn't he?"

She stood above me as though she were giving a lesson. She had a little mole on one of her ears and I remember thinking it was a nice touch. "One sister, two brothers. He talks to one of the brothers every few weeks—the others are in Michigan, and they're not in touch."

In my shirt pocket was my cell phone. It was like being on high alert, waiting to hear from Tiff. And now all this about Lico—what was I supposed to do about it? I said, "Look, Tracy—I'll give all this information to Marco and we'll have a meeting, okay?"

I did not know what kind of reaction she had wanted, but she looked somehow disappointed. "But is this not the *most* incredible story you've ever heard?"

I thought back across twenty-two years of teaching in this neighborhood. "No," I said. "It's not."

Up in the breakfast line I poured some miserable steaming coffee into a paper cup and waited to hand a buck to the cashier. The girl behind me—pretty hair all scrunched up and held in place by one of those scrunchy things—had a milk carton on her tray. There was a child on the milk carton, Sylvia Cortez. She was four feet, eight inches tall, eleven years old and had not been seen since February of 2008. All of that was listed there, right next to the fat content of the milk, number of ounces, and the added vitamins. Facts are facts.

There was a crowd in the teachers lunchroom, more teachers than I had remembered that we had. There was Murphy, the sellout, and Betty Frycus, Jamel Saunders, and Ira Hirsch, the head of the English Department, a nice guy who was afraid of his own shadow, but he could quote from Spenser. At the back of the room at a round table sat Vince Arcelli, blowing on his coffee. I sat down beside him and waited for the room to steady.

"What a gruesome sight," he said.

"You know, Vince, I'm sure other people have told you this, but I like you better when you're blowing."

He sipped his coffee and looked over the rim of his mug. This mug said, *I'm out of sick days*. "I take it we had a hard night last night."

Over at the other table Murphy was asking Ira Hirsch which Greek play he should teach the advanced placement English class. This was not just his notion of morning badinage. Murphy was stupid. He really needed somebody to tell him what to teach. I looked up at Vince. His aviator lenses were reflecting enough fluorescent light to illuminate the Merchandise Mart. I said, "You know that idea you had about an autumn baseball league?"

"Yeah—I know. You think it's dumb."

I forced some coffee down and wiped my mouth with the back of my hand. "No, I've been thinking about it. I think maybe you were on to something."

"Really? But you said—"

"Forget what I said. What the hell do I know? It's worth a try. What was that you said about the winners?"

"The losers buy dinner for the winners at the end of the season. We could keep a record of wins and losses—maybe get the kids a trophy or somethin'. I'm not talking about a serious level of play. Just for fun."

"Sure."

"What changed your mind, anyway?"

I turned one palm up in a who-knows gesture. "It's like you said. It sounds like fun. Maybe we could up the stakes a little, too."

Vince set his coffee cup down and regarded me carefully. "Whattaya mean?"

I said, "I don't know. Maybe add on a little something, you know. Bottle of scotch."

"You think your team'll be better than my team?"

"Maybe a case of scotch."

From the other table Murphy called out, "Hey, Spector—you know that advanced placement class I'm teaching?"

Patrick Murphy—red complexion, dandruff and suspenders. His victory was not complete unless he could rub it in. I turned around slowly and said, "You mean the one you stole from me?"

The lunchroom fell silent. Murphy was impervious. He knew

he was a mercenary. Everyone knew. "Don't be jealous, Spector. I was wondering which Greek play you think I should teach."

I said, "Why don't you try *Lysistrata*, Murph."

He began to jot the title down. "That a good one?"

"Uh-huh. Right up your alley. None of those guys were getting any, either."

Murphy didn't laugh. He thought Aristophanes was someone who used to be married to Jackie Kennedy.

A staccato little ring went off in my shirt pocket—my cell phone. I got up and walked out of the lunchroom before answering it.

"Spector here."

A static-ridden voice on the other end said, "John? Tiff McCulloch."

I said, "Hello, Tiff. I was expecting to hear from you last night."

"I know you were. I never call my clients at night."

"Why is that?"

"Because I don't want them to do anything stupid to their spouses when they're home. You sitting down?"

"Yes," I lied.

"Well, your wife's got herself a boyfriend. Guy by the name of Campbell, Bruce Campbell."

Now I sat down. There was a hall monitor desk in the seventh floor corridor, and I sort of slumped into it. I said, "Are you sure?"

"I'm sure, all right. Followed them out to Grant Park. They parked and swapped spit for nearly an hour."

They swapped spit. When you talked to Tiff you always felt like you were on a fishing trip with your uncle from Georgia. He told me to finish the day at work, and to think twice before going home, but I barely heard him. I was gazing out the big cafeteria windows into the lonely milk-white sky over Humboldt Park, a sky so blank and dense it threatened to swallow me up. I had wanted certainty. Now that I had it, I wasn't certain I wanted it at all.

5

It was as if someone had clicked on a switch that operated my brain, and it sputtered into action before I could even open my eyes. The first thing I was aware of was a piercing pain in my shoulder that continued, freeway style, all the way down my spine to my lower back. And I was cold, so cold my fingers had lost sensation. At first I did not know what I was looking at, only that it was dark and gray and rectangular. A floor mat—the passenger floor mat in my Jeep. I'd slept in my car. I sat upright and my stomach lurched after me. To the east the sky was a muted pink-and-gold eruption of light. I checked my watch—eight o'clock. My mouth tasted like old shoe leather and my clothes smelled like stale cigarette smoke. I had not gone home last night, this much was clear, and then somewhere beyond the throbbing pain in my head, the recollection of what had happened presented itself like unexpected fanfare. Marlyn had someone else.

From there the pieces fell together slowly, painfully. I had finished my day at work, walked vacuously through lessons and study hall. Fernando informed me that he would be moving in with his father and his father's girlfriend, and on my way out of the building Dave Volmer suggested a drink. I needed little convincing, thought that perhaps I could fill the hole in my heart, or at least anesthetize it, with a pint of vodka. We had started at Grandma's and then ended up at a Puerto Rican bar where we drank exotic rum-somethings. They put them in a shaker and the next thing you know you see palm trees. I remembered that Dave had got a little looped and stepped on some guy's shoe accidentally, and tried to excuse his gaucherie in broken Spanish.

"No era mi intencion de mearme encima de tus lentes."

And the guy, a big, burly man with thick sideburns, had looked at him wide-eyed, before sidling down to the other end of the bar. I'd said,

"Where the hell did you learn Spanish?"

Dave said, "Why? What did I say?"

"You just told him you didn't mean to pee on his glasses."

"Christ, and here I thought I'd only stepped on his shoe."

Then there were some blurry impressions—we shared a bag of peanuts for dinner, played a few rounds of poker with someone—and not much else.

Out the windshield I saw a street sign at the next corner, but I was not close enough to read it. I pushed open the driver's door, stumbled into the street, walking past a boarded up tenement with a rusted bicycle frame in the front yard. Just the frame, no wheels. Campbell Street. What do you know about that. I was not more than a mile from school, but I had no idea how I'd ended up here. Back in the Jeep I considered my situation. I could not go in and teach like this. The authorities would call the authorities. In the rearview mirror my eyes appeared to be little red slits. Open them too wide and I'd bleed to death. Marlyn and Jason would be frantic about my not having come home. At least Jason might be, I thought. I reached for my cell phone but it was not in my shirt pocket. I checked my sport coat, pants—nothing. It was lying on the floor of the Jeep, I discovered, after minutes of frantic searching. It had been on all night and was nearly out of power.

The phone rang several times before Mike Parnell answered it. I told him I was taking a sick day, and I had to listen to his feeble attempts at humor.

Playing hooky, huh? Going to catch up on the soap operas, right?

I slumped over the steering wheel and said, "Mike, would you just get a sub for me?"

I did not need a substitute for the full day, he informed me, since I had a student teacher. He would schedule class coverage only from noon on.

I said, "What are you going to do—pay some poor sub for half a day? They already make nothing at all."

Mike said, "Got to watch the public's money."

Sure. Tell that to Murphy, who was paid $90,000 a year to teach one class and monitor a work program.

A Gonnella bread truck swooshed suddenly past, gears groaning, making me think of bread, fresh bread. A little tabby cat with three legs hobbled down an alleyway, stopped, looked up at me, and then limped away. At last the sun had risen above the skyline and brought the morning to life on Campbell Street. Little droplets of condensation on the windshield caught the light, celebrated. Presently I started the Jeep, turned on the heater, and sat shivering, wondering what the hell it was that I was supposed to do.

Odd to be driving in the opposite direction in the morning. The southbound lanes of the Edens were at a standstill. I thought, *Here is something I won't have to worry about anymore, commuting.* The thing to do was to get an apartment in the city. Live alone again. Plenty of people did it. They survived.

I had not expected Marlyn to be home, but her car was in the driveway. If Bruce was in there with her, he was going to have to beat himself up. I was in no condition to do it. An ocean of oak leaves rustled as I made my way up the walk. The sky was break-your-heart autumn blue, no help at all. I remembered how we used to take Jason to a pumpkin farm in Marengo every year at this time when he was small, pick our own pumpkin. Get on a cart filled with hay bales and a tractor would pull us into the field. Marlyn and I took turns snapping photographs. You wanted to save moments like those.

The television was on in the family room. I could hear the insipid sales cooing of two middle-aged housewives all the way from the front door.

"Did you ever see beauty like this?"

"Never!"

"Do you see the baguettes? Cut and polished in Italy."

"To *die* for!"

"You put this on and you'll think you've died and gone to heaven."

That's not where they were going.

The suitcases were in the basement. I had a matched set of black fabric cases that had grown dusty under boxes of Christmas and Chanukah decorations. I moved some of the boxes and inadvertently knocked over a roasting pan that hadn't been used in years. I might as well have set off an alarm and announced myself.

"Hello?" Marlyn called from the top of the stairs, a timorous edge to her voice. "Who's down there?"

I chose a fold-over suit bag and the large suitcase and started up the stairs. I said, "Relax. It's just me."

"Johnny? Where in God's name have you been?"

82

When I reached the top of the staircase, I walked around her to the living room stairs and climbed them. I tossed the bags on the bed and began throwing clothes from the closet on top of them. Shirts, slacks, sport coats. Marlyn appeared at the door and looked at me quizzically.

I said, "Just pretend I'm not here. That's what I'm doing."

Marlyn said, "You were drunk, weren't you?"

"I wasn't just drunk," I said. "I was absolutely shit-faced. And you've been cheating. There's enough blame to go around, if that's what you want to do." Socks. I almost forgot to pack socks.

"Oh, God—now you're paranoid."

I said, "Maybe I am, but my private detective isn't."

"You don't have a private detective."

I threw a few neckties in the suitcase. I don't know why. I almost never wore them. "Do you really want to have this discussion now, Marlyn?"

"I don't want to have any discussion with you at all, Johnny. I just would like an explanation. I think your son deserves one, too. He worried about you all night."

I sat down on the bed and began folding the ties, absently. I hadn't wanted my boy involved, but what can you do? This thing touched us all. "His name is Tiff McCulloch," I said.

"Whose is?"

"My private detective. He phoned me during sixth period yesterday, said he'd followed you and Bruce Campbell to Grant Park two days ago—where, as Tiff tells it, you swapped spit for an hour or so."

Marlyn said not a word, just looked at me in quiet defiance.

"Tiff talks like that," I said. "It's a hell of a thing to do to somebody—set a detective on them. But so is what you're doing to me."

"I'm not doing anything to you, Johnny."

"Yeah, well—I don't suppose the husband ever sees it the way the wife does, when this kind of a thing happens."

"Where will you go?"

No admission, no excuse, just that one question. That one question said it all.

I stood up and zipped the suitcase, the suit bag. "I guess I'll get a motel room until I can find a place of my own. That's what I did the last time I got divorced."

Marlyn turned her back to me, pretended to arrange perfume

bottles on the dresser. "No one's asking you to move out."

I said, "It's a little crowded in this relationship, don't you think?"

I could see her face in the dresser mirror, but her eyes were half-lidded, veiled. I couldn't read her thoughts as I was normally able to. "It hasn't been a relationship, between you and I. Not for some time."

"Between you and *me*," I said.

I picked up the bags and for a moment stood behind her. It was a peculiar arrangement; I loved her even when I couldn't stand her. My old student. My wife. The silence was becoming unbearable, and since I couldn't think of anything else to say, I walked out—out of the room, down the hall, and out of the house. Momentum—it didn't give you any answers, but it kept you going.

§

"Sh-she lives on the South Side, my mother. At least she did till last summer. Last summer they told me she moved, but nobody knows where."

I was having a heart-to-heart with Lico out in the hallway while Tracy taught class. We were both seated in identical student desks. His eyes were doing ninety as he spoke.

I said, "What about your brothers and sisters? Do you ever see them?"

"My sister, yeah. I get to see my sister. She has a foster family in Cicero. She comes to visit me on weekends and we go out together, you know. She has an SUV. Sometimes we go to the movies."

"And your brothers?"

"I don't get to see them so much. M-my brother Robert, we talk on the phone. Maybe once a week. He lives in Washington, DC. He's got a job and he's going to night school to be an engineer. We talk."

Lico was wearing nice, freshly-laundered clothes—a sign that he was being cared for. But there was something about the desultory path of his narrative that hinted at fabrication. I didn't buy it. Either he was making it up as he went along, or he was editing out huge chunks of the story.

I said, "You play baseball?"

His head twitched in surprise. He knew a non sequitur when he heard one. "No, sir. I know how, but I don't."

"Want to play baseball after school with the division?"

"I'll have to ask my counselor at the home."

"You do that. Tell him your teacher wants you to, all right?"

"All right. I'm not much good, though."

"It's not about being good, Lico. It's about having fun."

I sent him back into the classroom and remained seated at the desk. Something in my stomach told me I had fallen out of orbit and was in free fall. For so many years I'd had something to go home to, and now I didn't even have a home. I supposed I should get a lawyer. Who knew? Maybe Marlyn would snap out of it and we'd get together again. But did I really want a woman who didn't want me? And how could I murder Bruce without getting caught?

"How'd it go?" Tracy Singer was standing over me as the halls filled up. I'd lost track of the time.

I said, "He's got a story, but it doesn't sound like the one he told you."

"It's not easy to get him to warm up. He keeps moving around—you know, revelation avoidance."

I held up my hand to stop her. "Revelation *what?*

"Avoidance."

"Don't tell me there really is such a term."

She didn't understand. "Why, of course—"

"Never mind. Has he told you anything else, when he hasn't been avoiding revelation?"

She was flustered. She shook her head and all this blond hair went this way and that. "He keeps changing the details. *Now* he says he visits his mother on weekends, sometimes by himself, sometimes with his brother."

"He told you that?"

"Yes. Like I said, it's kind of hard to get him started—"

"For Christ's sake," I said, standing up. "Get your stuff."

"Where are we going?"

"To see Marco—about bullshit avoidance."

In the Youth Services office we were greeted by a young counselor with hair that was waxed straight up—about six inches from his scalp. He said that Marco was busy, but that he would take care of us.

I said, "No, you won't. Marco will."

The kid said, "But I just told you. He's busy."

"So we'll wait for him."

Tracy nudged my arm out of embarrassment. "Be nice," she whispered.

"You don't understand," I whispered back to her. "You get one of these little bleeding hearts straight out of sociology school and they want to sit down and *feel* for the kid. They believe everything they say, and all that does is enable them to keep lying."

I caught Marco's attention through the glass panel of his door. He was talking to someone, but raised his finger a moment and stepped outside.

"Johnny—" he said, and then held a hand out to Tracy. "I don't believe I've had the pleasure."

"Marco, I'd like you to meet my student teacher, Tracy Singer."

"Ms. Singer," he said. His eyes seemed to twinkle when he looked at Tracy. I didn't know why, but this irritated me.

I said, "Look—I know you're busy, but we have a kid who needs help."

Marco turned his hundred-watt smile on me. "That's very interesting, Johnny. I ask one little favor of you, and you refuse, but the minute you need one—"

"Cut the crap, Marco. This isn't about either of us. It's about a kid. His name is Lico Pacheco—has a history of abuse. We can't get a straight story out of him. Something's not kosher."

"And what would you have me do?"

"We thought you could get all his teachers together for a round table—compare notes. He's got a counselor at a group home. Guy by the name of Jim Jarret. Maybe you could give him a call."

Marco nodded. "All right. I can do that. Can you stick around and fill out the paperwork?"

"Tracy can do that, can't you, Tracy?"

Tracy said, "Why, yes. Yes, of course."

Marco said, "Now, see how smoothly that went, Johnny? The polite thing would be to reciprocate. We have a sensitivity session scheduled for this afternoon."

"That's swell. If I'm not there on time, feel free to start without me."

The period tone sounded, an electronic bleep that triggered classroom doors to burst open and streams of kids to overflow into the corridors. I wanted to go down to my office, but both escalators were moving upwards. This confused me.

"Brilliant, isn't it?"

I turned around and found Javier Acosta there. "What the hell is going on?"

"Danny Velez's answer to the increased number of cuts in afternoon classes. He figures if you run all the escalators up, it's harder for kids to leave the building."

I had never heard of anything so stupid in my life. The kids were as confounded as I was. Several of them tried to run down the moving escalators—it had turned into something of a game.

I said, "Javier—you have a master's degree in administration. Why aren't you running this place?"

"Because I want to stay healthy. You know who's running this place."

He was not kidding.

"Come on," I said. "You're not really afraid of them, are you?"

No smile, not a hint of irony. If Javier was intimidated by the new regime, that said something.

I had a free period and decided to stop in on Vince. On my way up to the science floor I ran into Fernando and Daisy. The way I got it, Fernando was not crazy about his new living arrangement, but it kept him safe. Daisy said she had finally gotten into the work program, but that Mr. Murphy had not been able to find her a job. If I knew Murphy, he wasn't even trying.

I said, "I'll talk to him, sweetheart. You wouldn't have a cigarette, would you?"

"In my book bag. Open the zipper."

She had an army green bag strapped to her back, and I zipped open the little pocket and extracted a Newport from a box.

"Thanks. You know you ought to quit."

"Don't rag on me, Johnny. I'm having a lousy month."

Fernando said, "Month? Shit, I'm having a lousy *life*."

I told them to hang in there, that things would turn around. I don't know if they believed me, but I didn't have anything else to tell them. When I walked in the physics closet, I found Vince on the floor, assembling a plastic contraption that looked a little like the Eiffel Tower.

"Hell of a thing, isn't it? They gave me a hundred free rockets, but only one launcher. Where the hell am I going to get the money for ninety-nine launchers?"

I put Daisy's cigarette in my mouth, tasted the menthol. Oh, for the guts to light a match. "Your problems are staggering, Vince. Want to trade them for mine?"

Vince dropped a rubber washer on the launcher and sat up. "The marriage?"

"I guess you could say that. The wife, the kid, the house, the whole works. You can put them all in the ex-category."

He stood up now, dusted off the knees of his slacks, and walked over to the counter, where he poured some coffee from his thermos into a mug. This one said, *I love cats; they taste just like chicken.* "You caught her?"

"Not me, but my detective. If you don't mind, I'd kind of like not to go over the details."

Vince took a sip of his coffee and walked over and slapped me on the shoulder. "I'm really sorry about this, Johnny. If there's anything you need—"

There was a little silver gyroscope behind him on a shelf. Give you balance. "I'm all right. I've done this before."

"Where're you staying?"

"The Heart 'O' Chicago Motel. Lovely place. I've got a bed and a bath and a parking space. What more could a man want?"

Last night had been kind of lonely. The sheets of my bed smelled foreign and the orange no-vacancy neon sign buzzed right outside my window and I could not stop thinking of my boy. Maybe tonight would be better.

Vince said, "If you want, I could stop by. We could buy a six pack, pick up a couple of chicks—"

"Go to the beach?"

He nodded. "Something like that."

"Too cold at the beach." I drew on the unlit cigarette, held it between two fingers.

"You want me to light that for you?" Vince asked.

"Naw. There's a crummy nobility in denying myself."

He sat on a lecture stool, the kind with a back, and cradled his mug in his lap. He wore gray chinos, a St. Christopher's medal, and a gold ID bracelet. You could have ordered him from Macy's catalogue under

"I" for Italian. "I suppose you seen the escalators."

I said yes, I had seen them, that Danny Velez was living up to all of my expectations.

"It's a violation of the fire code. I called it in myself."

I said, "You did? And they're going to cite him?"

Vince shrugged. "Who knows? They'll probably just tell him to run the goddamn *down* escalators down again and cover it up. The fun part was reporting him. But get ready for this. I was walking past Hafka's history class today and I heard something very interesting."

Anatole Hafka was a nervous little sweaty guy who wore his communist ideology on his shirt sleeves. I'd always thought he was harmless. He was such a nut, no one ever listened to him.

I said, "And how is Comrade Hafka?"

"It's no joke, Johnny. He was showing the kids addresses of websites that give directions on how to make bombs, and others that are terrorist links. He had it all on the overhead—said that the real patriots were fighting to overturn the U.S. military establishment."

"He'll never win the Golden Apple talking like that." The Golden Apple was an award for teaching excellence. I had never known anyone who had won it. The way I saw it, all the really good teachers were too busy to bother with awards and banquets.

"Let's add up what we got here," Vince said, setting his coffee mug down on a shelf next to a Van de Graaf generator. "Danny, our principal—with a police record and a sister jailed for life as a terrorist. Elizabeth Mojica and Isabelle Villachez, both with FALN ties. Anatole, who is teaching Introduction to Revolution, and two curriculum writers who want to liberate convicted terrorists from U.S. imperialists."

I said, "That's what we've got. I just asked Javier why he didn't have a more central role in the administration. He as much as told me he's afraid for his life."

Vince said, "Maybe I should have called the FBI instead of the fire chief."

"No one would ever believe you, Vince. A ring of terrorists who've taken over a high school in Chicago? It's too fantastic, your word against theirs. You need proof."

Vince was far away in his thoughts, spoke distantly to himself. "There's got to be a way," he said.

I thought maybe I'd go to the cafeteria and try to put something solid in my stomach, see if it would stay there. "It's not worth it. It would mean a fight, and I'm not up to a fight. I don't think you are, either."

Vince said, "Okay, but don't blame me if next week they got you teaching Chairman Mao's *Little Red Book*."

There was a bar just two blocks away from the motel, which meant I could have one too many and still get back to my room without having to kill innocent people or get a DUI, or both. It was just the way I liked bars to be, dark, and the gin was cold. I took Daisy's cigarette out of my pocket, straightened it, and held it between my fingers. Kirk Douglas Perez had not shown up today. I didn't know if that was because he was afraid of facing down Fernando, or if he had been hurt worse than I had estimated. I thought of his arm—all those tracks, bruises like little purple flowers, and then I hoped he wasn't sharing needles with anyone. Teachers are not supposed to admit to this kind of thing, but when I'd had his brother Guiso in class, I disliked him. I disliked him immensely. You could see the set coldness in his eyes, the utter disregard for other people. Kirk was not like him at all, but he could be, I knew, given enough time, enough dope.

I had the newspaper rental ads folded in front of me. Nothing under fourteen hundred bucks a month if you wanted to live in Lincoln Park. If what I'd heard was correct, I could count on twenty percent of my income going to child support. Maybe I could get a paper route.

Someone had left a rumpled copy of the *Enquirer* on the bar next to a bowl of peanuts. Julia Roberts was devastated because she had thought she was pregnant until her doctor told her otherwise. Mariah Carey was having another breakdown in Barbados.

Maybe nobody was happy, and everyone was keeping it a secret except for the *Enquirer*. I ordered another martini and asked for blue cheese olives, but the bartender—a fellow who looked like Ozzy Osbourne before dissipation had set in—said he didn't have any. What kind of a world was I living in—no blue cheese olives?

"Hello?"

"Jason—how are you?"

"Fine, Pop. Where are you?"

I'm missing in action, kid, missing in action. Someone had selected a Frank Sinatra number on the juke box and I had to bring my cell phone over near the men's room to hear.

"I'm in a noisy bar in Chicago. How was school today?"

"Okay."

"And football practice?"

"Fine. I caught everything they threw me."

"That's my boy. I just thought I'd give you a call since—well, you know."

Silence. Frank was telling Joe to set 'em up, that he had a little story he wanted him to know. "So how long do you think this is going to go on?" Jason asked me.

"What—this Sinatra song? About three minutes."

"You know what I mean."

I did indeed. "I don't know, buddy. But you take care of yourself, okay? I'll be at your game on Saturday."

He said, "Okay, Pop," and was off the line. I don't know where he'd picked up that Pop stuff, but it was very funny. Not funny enough to make me laugh, but funny just the same. I went back to my seat at the bar and contemplated my martini. It looked so empty.

"I've got the kind with pimento, if you like." Ozzy was back.

"Okay," I said. He speared two on a tooth pick and sank them in my glass, but it just wasn't the same. They looked like little green fish, the glass, an aquarium. Time for bed.

Señor Valentin kept many varieties of plants on either side of the steps to his house, plants with red, orange, and glaucous leaves, and I couldn't name any of them. I was a lawn man, myself, or at least I had been, up till a few days ago. I felt that I owed him some explanation about the break up, but I hadn't wanted to do it over the phone. When the front door pulled to and he appeared at the screen door, his face was rigid, eyes informed. I got the feeling he had recently spoken to his daughter and knew the score.

"*Maestro, venga aca.*"

At once I could smell the richness of coffee. I followed him inside and down the narrow hallway, past Marlyn's wall of fame—Marlyn on roller skates aged nine; Marlyn graduating eighth grade; Marlyn as a senior, Marlyn's wedding photo with a guest appearance by yours truly. She was beautiful in each, but I could have lived without the tour. It didn't do much for my resolve. In the kitchen señor Valentin took a cup and saucer from a cabinet, placed a spoon upon the saucer, and lifted the stainless steel pot. "You have much on your mind, *sí*?"

In fact I did. Once again Kirk had not turned up at school. Danny Velez had dropped a nasty note in my mail box about lesson plans. A kid named Angel in my freshman comp class had been shot in the park the previous night, and his condition was serious. And there was always the crumbling of my marriage. I said, "My mind is a messy place right now, señor. Too many problems, not enough gin."

"The answer is not always in a bottle. Sometimes a bottle come between a man and his wife."

He placed the coffee on the kitchen table. I pulled out one of the vinyl upholstered chairs and sat down. Steam rode over the cup. "Sometimes a lot more than a bottle comes between them."

He stood, leaning his back against the kitchen sink. "So you no live at home anymore."

I said, "Why don't you have a seat, señor?"

He remained standing. "Where will you live?"

The coffee was hot and burned my tongue. "Right now I have a motel room. I'm looking for an apartment."

I wished to Christ he would sit down, but he just stood there, looking down at me. At last he picked up a dishrag and wiped the counter. He straightened the fish-shaped salt and pepper shakers. As if thinking aloud he said, "A family cannot be a family and live apart. No good for the boy."

"It's not good for any of us, but it's kind of out of my hands."

"Young people sometime no see answers when answers stand right in front of them. Too much other things get in the way. Look at you. So smart. You have education, but you no see."

I played with my spoon in the coffee, stirred little cumulus clouds out of it. "Look, I don't know if your daughter has told you what this is all about or not—"

He waved a dismissive hand at me. "How you say—essence. Make it the essence."

I said, "You mean, essentials?"

"Yes. *Essentials.* When everything grow too big, too crowded in a man's life, he must throw out everything but essentials."

I said, "Yeah, well—that's about what I'll have left after the divorce."

Señor Valentin grunted out of frustration with me. "So smart, so blind. Like talking to a log. *Mira*, come with me."

What the hell is he going to show me now? I thought. I rather preferred not to be likened to a log, but I understood that there were gaps between us, generational, cultural, and I supposed a man of his age had earned the right to be annoyed with younger people and their untidy lives. Perhaps when you got to be his age, essentials were all that mattered, and that was what he had tried to explain to me. Still—a *log*.

I followed him out the back door and across his garden. There were some lovely shrubs there, turning fiery yellow, their leaves scattering like confetti in the breeze. He went right up the whitewashed steps of the garage to the little loft apartment, and once again I obediently fell in behind him. The lock gave him a little trouble, but soon the door swung open and he clicked on a light switch.

Except for a small kitchen and a bathroom, it was all one room. It had some cheap furnishings, an end table, for instance, a television. "You stay here," he said flatly. "Fifty dollars a month."

I walked inside—four steps and you'd seen it all. "Here? You want me to live *here*?"

"You family. You want to live with strangers?"

It was *essential*, all right, about the most essential place I had ever seen. It was, however, only a mile from school, and had the added benefit of affordability. But my father-in-law as a landlord? "Look," I said, "this is awfully kind of you, señor, but I just don't think it would be healthy."

"No, no. Very clean."

"That's not what I meant. I meant you and me—seeing each other every day."

"I leave you alone. You come and go like you please."

I didn't know how not to acquiesce, but the arrangement left me with an uncomfortable feeling, something like when your socks are falling down and there's nothing you can do about it.

This would be one for the legal journals. My wife gets the house in the suburbs and I get her father.

It was no way to start a day. Tracy Singer sat in a chair in my office with her legs crossed under her flannel plaid skirt, and I tried like hell to ignore them while we discussed how to teach kids about poetry. She wanted to go down a list of poems by different poets and select the ones she liked, and I told her she was going about it in an inverted fashion. She didn't know what I meant.

I said, "Look, if you have a particular poet in mind, consider what it is that the poet has to say that you want to transfer over to the kids. Take Whitman, for example. If you want the student to take something specifically Whitmanesque away from a poem—his passion for life, the acceptance of the beauty and sorrow of primal yearning and loss—well, you might skip over 'To A Locomotive in Winter' and 'A Noiseless, Patient Spider' and go directly to 'Out of The Cradle, Endlessly Rocking.' Otherwise, if you just go down a list, it's like selecting a song from a juke box. You haven't put any thought into what it is you want to teach, and why."

Tracy sat looking at me with that half-bemused, impatient expression of hers. She re-crossed her legs. "I don't see why I can't just pick out the poems I like."

I said, "You can do it that way, if you want. There's no reason to think that maybe I've discovered a few things after two decades of teaching."

"Now you're getting defensive again."

There was a sudden pounding on my door followed by someone saying, "Yo, Johnny."

I rolled my chair over and flicked the doorknob. Nelson, Jorgé and Daisy came in and shut the door behind them. Daisy took a cigarette from a pack of Newports and handed it to me.

I said, "Thanks."

Daisy said, "You're gonna need it."

"Word, Johnny." Jorgé stood before me, short, fierce, and out of breath. "You know that kid, Maniac?"

"I know a lot of maniacs."

"No, dude. The kid from your freshman class, the one who got shot in the park two nights ago."

"You mean Angel," I said.

"Yeah. He died last night. He was a Spanish Cobra, man, and it was a Disciple who shot him. Everybody's pissed at the D's and theys gonna be trouble. Theys gonna be big trouble, man."

Another kid gone. There would be no acknowledgment on behalf of the school, no ceremony, not a word. I thought about the empty desk in my classroom during eighth period. Angel.

I said, "Jorgé, why'd they shoot him?"

"I think he was buyin' shit. The deal fucked up, or he owed them some money."

Tracy cleared her throat uneasily and raised her eyebrows at me. "Perhaps I should come back later," she said.

"No—stick around. This is good for you." I put the cigarette in my mouth and put my feet up on my desk. "Where's Fernando?" I asked this of Nelson. Nelson had been standing quietly by the door, letting Jorgé do the talking. Pecking order.

"He be layin' low. He comes to school when there's a crowd at the last minute. His old man drops him off and he just go right in the crowd, you know."

"That's a good thing for him to do," I said.

Tracy said, "What about that poor boy, Angel?"

The kids and I all looked at each other. "Well, Tracy—they'll bury him."

"No, but I mean, shouldn't we find out about the wake, maybe go?"

I glanced at each of them in turn. Daisy nodded. Jorgé shrugged. Nelson deferred to Jorgé.

I said, "Good. Daisy, you find out which funeral home and get the day and time. We'll all go together."

When the period tone sounded I got up and walked the kids out into the hall. I took Jorgé and Nelson aside and told them that I was going to need some help moving into the city the following week, and that if either of them could lend a hand, I'd certainly appreciate it.

Nelson said, "You and your family movin' back here?"

"Not my family, just me."

Jorgé looked concerned. "Yeah? Damn, Johnny. You gettin' a divorce?"

I held my finger to my lips. "Let's not send out any press releases, okay?"

They both gave me their word, and when I went back into the office, Tracy was standing, arranging the papers in her shoulder bag. "You let them call you by your first name, I've noticed." She spoke without looking at me.

The first-name approach bothered many people, especially people with parochial views about education. I'd never understood people with parochial views about anything.

"It seems like a natural thing to do."

"You don't find it somehow unprofessional?"

She was going to fit right in with the Chicago Board of Education. I said, "Tracy, do you know what's unprofessional? Caring more about etiquette than about the kids."

She stood up, hoisted her overly full bag, and walked to the doorway. I thought perhaps I had offended her, that she would simply walk away, but she lingered in the hallway just outside my office. "I think Frost," she said.

"Beg pardon?"

"I was thinking about Frost's isolation and loneliness, and decided on 'Bereft' as the first poem. Just following somebody's advice."

I said that was a fine choice, and she regarded me in silence for some time.

"I'm sorry about your divorce," she said, finally. "I wish you would have felt as though you could have told me."

That had been a nice thing for her to say. I stood there looking out into the hallway long after she had left, thinking about Frost's poet narrator on his front porch, facing the sea, alone.

On my way to division I was stopped by Isabelle Villachez in front of the main office. She said she wanted to speak to me about something, but I told her I was already late, that perhaps it could wait until later.

Then she had this to say: "You don't seem to have time for any of your duties, Mr. Spector."

Isabelle Villachez—gray hair, black, chilly eyes, and the habit of standing with her arms stationary at her sides, like an unposed mannequin. Though I did not approve of her tactics, she had done some good things for the people in the neighborhood. That was her bit—the acquisition and preservation of power. However, she had no official title, no college degrees, for that matter. And she certainly had no authority over teachers. I said, "I'm not aware that I have postponed any duties. I'm also not aware of what concern my duties are to you."

"I have not seen you at one of our sensitivity sessions. I hope this is not a sign of any disrespect."

I'd been sucker punched. All I had wanted to do was go to my division room, and now this insinuation. "I'll tell you, something, Ms. Villachez. You're making me late to my homeroom. I hope *that's* not a sign of any disrespect."

I hopped on the *up* escalator—they were all *up* escalators now—without excusing myself. Through the wire mesh windows of the main office I saw Murphy sitting in Isabelle's office. I could have sworn he was smirking at me.

Lucy was openly weeping when I walked into my division classroom and Daisy had her arm encircled around her. Tracy stood by, offering warm words of comfort. What the hell was it now?

"Mr. Spector," Lucy said, choking back sobs, "Mrs. Anderson won't let me in gym class 'cause I don't got my gym fee. She said she's gonna flunk me 'cause each day I ain't got it is a cut."

Mona Anderson—girls gym teacher. She had all the humanity of a Patton tank and looked like Patton's brother. "Sweetheart—no one's going to flunk anyone. How much is the gym fee?"

"Three-three-three"—the poor kid couldn't catch her breath, she was so shaken. "Three-fifty. My mother lost her job and-and-and the unemployment check hasn't come yet and we don't got the money."

One thing this job did for me—it kept things in perspective. Here I'd thought *I* had it rough. I tried to imagine what must go on inside the heart of an adult who could do this to a kid.

Not much.

I got down on one knee in front of Lucy, who was busy gurgling into a Kleenex. She was an extremely sensitive kid, unlike Daisy, who would have just given the teacher a right uppercut if she found herself in a similar situation. "Lucy—listen to me. I'm going to talk to Ms. Anderson right now. You won't have any cuts charged to you, and you won't have to worry about the gym fee. We can waive it."

"But she-she-she said—"

I got up and told Tracy to take care of division attendance and marched right out into the hall and down to Javier Acosta's office. He had two sullen-looking kids sitting in chairs before him, their photo ID cards on his desk. Bad dudes. I asked if I could use his phone, and he held out his hand graciously. "*Mi teléfono es su teléfono,*" he said.

When Mona Anderson came on the line she barked her last name at me. "Anderson."

I said, "Mona—Johnny Spector. I have a girl in my division named Lucy Arroyo who's having a nervous breakdown because you apparently can't live without three dollars and fifty cents, and she hasn't got it."

"She's playing you for a fool, Spector. These kids can buy designer clothes but they can't pay gym fees. And you're stupid enough to believe 'em."

"Mona—I'm not stupid, and she hasn't got any designer clothes. As a matter of fact, she hasn't got much of anything, including the self respect you managed to rob her of. Her mother lost her job."

"Then what's she do with her welfare check?"

"She's not on welfare, Mona. She's on unemployment, the same as you'd be if you lost your job, God forbid."

"Rules are rules. She owes three-fifty to the department before she can attend class."

"You can't do that. It's against the law to deprive a kid of education."

"Watch me."

What could you do with a person like this—I mean other than what would get you ten to twenty? I said, "Mona—don't go anywhere. I'll be right there. I'm going to give you the goddamn three-fifty myself."

"Don't you use obscenities with me!"

I hung up. Mona didn't know the difference between *obscenity* and *profanity*. Mona didn't know a lot of things.

Javier had his elbow poised on his desk, his chin in his hand. "Johnny, it's not even eleven o'clock and you're already doing battle. It won't be long before you're at war with the entire faculty."

"I'd rather fight them than join them, Javier."

He gave me a patient smile. "Well, don't let Mona bend you out of shape. She lacks the milk of human kindness."

"Oh, she has it—it's just two percent milk, is all."

The two boys sat with their hands clasped in front of them, slouched forward, looks of dejection etched on their faces. I said, "What did you guys do to get busted?"

Javier said, "Caught 'em smoking reefer in the bathroom."

Dejection of Coleridgean proportions. I said, "Reefer, huh?"

They had eyes only for the carpet.

I said, "Got any more?"

"Get out of here, Spector! You'll lose my certificate for me."

I opened the door, walked out, and then stuck my head back inside and said, "I'd be doing you a favor."

Tracy handled the sophomore English class by herself; she was more than able. Kirk had been on my mind. I couldn't shake the feeling that he was in trouble and needed help. Only fifteen and shooting dope—the world must seem like a pretty lonely place. I called his number several times from the main office, but there was no answer, no answering machine. Out the office windows to the west, beyond a curtain of yellow and orange leaves, the sun kissed the white concrete of St. Mary's hospital, and beyond that, the buildings that were the Loop skyline stood at attention.

"Call for you, Johnny. Line three." Shirley pushed a hold button on her telephone and replaced the receiver.

"Can't you tell whoever it is that I retired or something?"

"He sounds official."

Wouldn't want to miss an official phone call. I hit line three and said, "Spector here."

A gruff, bass voice greeted me. "Mr. Spector, this is Mitchell Arnoff, of Arnoff, Bloom and Kimball. I'm your wife's attorney."

I slowly sat down in a secretary's chair, felt as though somebody had let all the air out of me. And how had Kimball gotten into that lineup?

Up until a second ago there had still been hope for this day. I said, "And what can I do for you, Mr. Arnoff?"

"Mr. Spector, on behalf of your wife, I have filed a petition for divorce with the Lake County court system. At this time are you represented by an attorney?"

Nydia Velazquez bounced into the office with a young, bespectacled fellow who could have been a string bean with clothes on. She motioned with her hand that I should hang up the phone and go with her.

"No," I said. "No, I'm not."

"Johnny!" Nydia whispered.

"Well, Mr. Spector—you might want to arrange for representation as soon as possible. Your wife—my client—will want to discuss terms, dispersal of property, child support, visitation rights, and she'll want to do that soon."

I said all right and looked around for a pen. My hand shook as I scrawled down Mitchell Arnoff's phone number. I wondered how you went about finding an attorney for yourself. When I got off the line I felt damp around the collar, my legs, rubbery. I looked up into Nydia's expectant face.

She said, "Johnny, this is Brian Podhorst, the reporter I told you about. He's come to interview you for the paper."

All I knew was that I had woken up that morning inside the Heart 'O' Chicago Motel, and then everything had gone straight to hell, and now somebody wanted an interview.

6

Marlyn and I had closed on the house nearly ten years earlier, and that winter we enjoyed having our own place, a yard. We made big, shapeless snowmen with Jason, went sledding at the local sledding hill. The whole family shoveled the driveway together, an effort that always degenerated into a snowball fight, wild screeches, frigid cold of January snow against raw cheeks. Later we warmed ourselves by the fireplace as the logs crackled, and I thought our lives would always be like that.

I drove into Deerfield, into reality, that Saturday for Jason's football game. I did not know if Marlyn would be there or not, but if so, it would be awkward sitting on different ends of the same spectator stands. How the hell were we supposed to explain it to all the other parents? *Here we are, ladies and gentlemen, the Spectors, slightly fragmented.*

I thought of the interview I had given the reporter, what's-his-name, the human string bean, and about how far over the line I had gone, taking out all my morning's frustrations on the Chicago Board of Education. To begin with, he had asked very needling questions, managed to push all my hostility buttons. I had built up quite a backlog of resentment for the board over twenty years—having witnessed more than just a little incompetence, hypocrisy, inflexibility, corruption, and then he came along after I had heard about Angel's death and had spoken to Marlyn's lawyer. I didn't recall just then, as I pulled into the high school parking lot, if I'd called the superintendent a supreme horse's ass, but there was that distinct possibility. I *had* sounded off about the leftist propaganda that had made its way to the classroom, the politicization of the school's programs, and that alone would trip Isabelle and Elizabeth's switches. And I'd made a few wisecracks about Danny Velez's checkered past—his brushes with the law and his sister, the terrorist. *Need a robber and someone good with a fuse?* What the

101

hell—it was all true. What could they do to you for telling the truth?

It was a brisk autumn morning and the air was chilly, so I bought a Warriors sweatshirt near the concession stand and pulled it on right over my shirt. The aroma of hot dogs and popcorn surfed upon the breeze, and the marching band played random, discordant notes. I took a seat nine rows up at about the fifty yard line. Beyond the athletic field, the tops of trees ran together like the bristles of orange and yellow brushes set on end. If you squinted, you would have thought the world had been invented by Monet. Down on the field the sophomore Warrior team warmed up, stretched, in their red and gray uniforms. I found Jason, number 87, not so much with the aid of the numerals on his jersey, but by his wiry legs and his white cleats. He was the only team member with white shoes. How he loved those shoes, ordered them special on the Internet. I watched him run out for a long pass, pick it off one-handed, tuck it, halt, reverse. The kid was pumped. My kid.

"Hey—Mr. Johnny Spector. I'd sit down next to you, but I'm waiting for your wife. Where is she?"

Barry Levine. He shook my hand and beamed his big, friendly grin and accidentally spilled some popcorn from a bag he carried in the crook of his arm.

"She'll be along soon, I guess, Barry. How's the boy?"

He turned and looked down at the players' benches. "Got a sore knee. We debated whether he should wear an elastic brace or not. Decided not to. It's like drawing a target on his weak spot. I see your boy's catching miracles down there."

"We epoxy his hands for him."

"Well, it's working. Hey! There's Aaron Gold! I'll see you later, Johnny."

Sooner or later either Marlyn or I, or both of us, would have to own up to the divorce, and that's when the awkward moments of silence would begin, the little blank expressions of surprise, embarrassment. *Oh, I'm so sorry to hear that.* And then. just like that, we'd be instant social outcasts. People would break their necks running away from us. There was no place for singles in a community of married parents. You'd be more popular if you had a good case of the clap.

Today we were playing Glenbrook North—sort of a grudge match, as they'd ruined our homecoming a year ago. Advance word was that their quarterback could throw the long ball, but their defense was weak.

They came running onto the field as the band went into "Go Big Red" and the crowd cheered our boys in response.

My head throbbed mildly at the temples—and therein lies one of the differences between a scotch hangover and a vodka hangover. Scotch will give you less collateral damage the next morning—just fatigue and a slight headache. Vodka will kill you. In every way. Blurry vision, dizziness, dry mouth, high blood pressure, nausea. Still, I preferred vodka. It took you to the next level, kept the world at bay, and that was the whole idea.

The Warriors won the coin toss and opted to kick. They had an average kicker and you had to pray that he wouldn't accidentally pooch the ball. In the stands down below I spotted Marlyn sitting alone. My heart slid out of place, and I imagined that it would never be easy to see her like that without me. She was wearing a red sweatshirt and had her hair pulled up and looked much younger than her thirty-five years. Alan Gross found her as he was climbing up the aisle. Alan sold outerwear, a slightly balding guy with a closely-cropped black beard that made him look somehow canine. He stopped and chatted with her, laughed and chatted, bent down low to hear her as the crowd roared at a Warrior interception on the Glenbrook forty yard line. *Get lost, Alan*, I thought. *Horny bastard.*

The interception turned the psychological tide. Glenbrook's timing was off and the Warriors capitalized, completing a fifteen-yard pass to the other receiver. Jason had been in the clear and I thought the ball should've been his, but we'd made the play.

Carl Davis—broad chest, full head of blond hair—stopped to talk with Marlyn now. She was a regular husband magnet—other women's husbands. He turned on the charm, laid his hand on her arm, Carl, the old raconteur. There was a sudden explosion of laughter over something he had said. Then he inclined earnestly toward her, made a point with sincere eyes, and then laughed again at his own wit, all those white teeth. Who had teeth that white? They looked like they'd been painted, for Christ's sake.

No one had expected it. Jimmy Jesser, our quarterback, faked a handoff, optioned the ball to Jason, who swung around and ran it down the perimeter for a touchdown. I shot to my feet, cheered wildly. That was my boy, my boy, and Carl Davis was hugging my wife, the bastard. I was tempted to go down there and—and what? What could I do to Carl Davis?

The Warriors were up 13 to 0 at halftime. I thought I'd go say hello to Marlyn, at least be polite and face the difficulty of the situation, but Monica Corbett stopped by and gave me one of those fake embraces that acquaintances at football games think is mandatory. Her oldest son, she said, was at Cornell. He'd just been awarded a scholarship for something or other, and her summer home in Indiana was being renovated. I thought of Lucy, who could not pay her three dollar and fifty cent gym fee, of Fernando, who had to slink his way into and out of school, who could no longer even live with his mother in his own neighborhood. And I thought of poor Lico, who had been so badly hurt that he could no longer tell the truth about it. Monica had traded in her BMW SUV for a Mercedes, she said, and I told her that was great, just great.

The marching band took to the field and I noticed that Marlyn had left the stands. Jeannie Adams waved at me from down below and was now headed my way. Cute hourglass figure, shades, and a silly straw hat. Only Jeannie could get away with that hat.

"Johnny—" fake kiss, just a little smacking sound near my ear. "Jason's wonderful today."

"Thank you, Jeannie. Your Eric has been making great return runs."

She looked at the empty space beside me. "Where's Marlyn? I have to tell her about this great nail place in Niles that does silk-wrap manicures. They're all Vietnamese men, can you believe it?"

"We sort of got separated. I saw her sitting down there, by the stairs."

"Well, when you find her again, tell her I have to talk to her."

"I certainly will. Bye, Jeannie." Fake kiss. Smack.

I supposed a girl needed a place to get a good silk-wrap manicure, but talk like this was making me feel more like an outsider every minute, as if I'd had my suburban visa revoked. Cornell, summer homes, BMWs, and I had to go to a fifteen year old's wake tonight in Logan Square.

Glenbrook came back stronger in the third quarter. They scored on their third play, a pass that could have easily been deflected. We were playing more conservatively, running the ball up the middle, two yards here, three there. It called to mind Achilles' Aegis, the moving illustrations of struggle and strife, acquisition and loss. I spotted Marlyn—she had reappeared at the side of Morrie Rubloff, an investment banker. Morrie was extremely animated, had a perennial tan, and wore a Ralph Lauren sweater on his back, the sleeves tied around his neck. His hands painted the text of some silent anecdote in his private brand of sign language, while Marlyn listened, captivated.

The passing of victory. You know you need a drink when a high school football game turns into a metaphor for your life.

The Warriors won 16-7. I waited for Jason down at the chain link fence that separated the viewing area from the field. The coach always kept them in a huddle after every game, highlighting their strengths and weaknesses. The last I saw of Marlyn, she had been swept out with the crowd, and I remember feeling distinctly alone, on the field, in this town, on the planet. North Shore existentialism. It's just a more expensive brand of detachment.

It looked like war paint, the black smudges under Jason's eyes. His hair was damp with perspiration, his forehead reddened by the pads of his helmet. We slapped our palms together in a high-five that lingered, grew into a victory clench.

I said, "Nice game."

"Thanks, Pop."

"The touchdown was terrific. Nice crack blocking, too."

"I could've had another score. I was open in the end zone in the fourth quarter, but Jimmy didn't see me."

"They had him surrounded, buddy. It wasn't his fault." Six feet tall. Built like one of those brick houses you always heard about. When we'd made those snowmen together, he came up to my waist and weighed forty-eight pounds. "You want me to stick around—give you a ride home?"

"Sure. Where's Mom?"

I looked toward the parking lot, held my hand out in that direction. "I guess she left."

He nodded as if to himself, eyes to the ground. I put my hand on his shoulder and we stood there for a moment like that, on either side of the steel fence, spectator, player.

There was a green Dodge Neon parked in our driveway. I didn't know anybody with a green Dodge Neon.

"I wonder whose car that is," I said to Jason.

"It's Bruce's," Jason mumbled.

They call it blind rage, but the truth was, I could see just fine. For an instant, I believed I could pick up that car and hurl it into the street. When Bruce exited the front door with Marlyn, I decided to throw him instead. I pulled my arm back to take a swing at him, but Jason jumped in front of me.

"Dad—you don't want to do that."

"Let him," Bruce said. "Let's see what the old guy's got."

Jason turned on him next. "You don't talk to my father that way— not in front of me."

Protected by my own son. It was easily one of the most painfully humiliating moments of my life. I looked into Marlyn's eyes as she stood beside Bruce, and what I saw there was an enigma. I suddenly felt as though I had never known her at all. Yes, I drank too much, spent too much time with the kids, no question. But this was unnecessary. We had the ingredients for creating a good life together. There was no reason to throw it all away. I walked back to the Jeep, a long walk, and drove off, away from my wife, my son, my home. I drove myself right out of my life.

§

"I didn't know what to wear. Do you suppose this will be all right?"

Tracy had opened the passenger door and stood there outside the Jeep in gray herringbone slacks, matching gray wool sweater, black jacket, and black beret. I said, "If *Cosmo* covers gang wakes, you'll get a rave review."

"You don't have to always be so sarcastic," Tracy said, as she climbed in and slammed the door.

"I'm sorry," I said. "I just met my almost ex-wife's new boyfriend and I have a slight inclination toward murder. It'll go away soon."

"God, I'm sorry. What kind of guy is he?"

Now, there was a question I hadn't even considered. I'd only wanted to kill him, not get to know him. "I have no idea. He looks like a guy you'd call to check your furnace. I don't know what she sees in him."

"What did she see in you?"

I pulled a U-turn. I would take Armitage to Ashland and Ashland to Division Street, I decided. "I don't know that, either. I was a teacher. She was a student."

You could hear Tracy's jaw drop. "At Acosta High ?"

"Yeah. I think at first she admired me before she got sick of me. Something about hanging out with gangsters bothered her."

"I can't believe it."

"Can't believe what?"

"That you married one of your students."

I had come to a stop at a red light. I turned to Tracy and said, "She was in college when I married her. It's not like I abducted her from prom or something."

"Even so—"

"People *do* fall in love, you know, Tracy. They don't stop first to see if everyone else thinks it's a fine idea or not. We had a normal life, for a while. We raised a beautiful kid."

"Did you really love her—or was it just because she was young?"

Somebody behind me honked. The light had turned green, and I'd missed it. "What kind of a question is that? Of *course* I loved her. I loved her from the first time I saw her. And if you'd care to know—not that it's any of your business—I *still* love her. If that's all right with you, that is."

She clicked her seat belt into place. "It's just that it's unusual, is all. You don't hear about teachers marrying their students every day."

"Sure, you do. People just don't go around announcing it. You know Louise Denning, the art teacher?"

"Yes."

"She married her teacher."

"Get out—Louise did?"

"Yes, she did."

"But she's in her fifties."

"She was young, once. And Mike Parnell married one of his former students."

"The assistant principal?"

"Unless you know another Mike Parnell." Tracy was exceptionally bright, but so naïve, so overly protected from the world. "Anyway, I don't feel like it's anything I have to apologize for. I didn't use her. I didn't run out on her. We've been married for sixteen years."

A Volkswagen cut in front of me from a side street and I hit the brakes. When I turned to Tracy again, I found that she had been staring at me. "I can see how it might happen," she said.

"How what might happen?"

"How you could fall in love with one of your students. You're so close to them—it's as though they're no different than you are."

A bus stopped in front of us and I couldn't get around it. "Tracy—don't you *get* it? They *are* no different than I am, or you, for that matter. They're the same."

"But they're students."

"They're *people*."

Daisy called me on my cell phone to give me directions to the funeral home and to ask for a ride. I picked her up on North Francisco, not more than two blocks away from my father-in-law's place. We'd soon be neighbors. Every time the conversation experienced a weak spot and I had a moment or two to think to myself, I saw Bruce walking out of my house with Marlyn. I was by myself now, I realized, and might be by myself for the rest of my life. No plan, nothing to shoot for, just one day following another. I'd turned into Eleanor Rigby.

Amintello's Funeral Home was on Diversey just west of Logan Square. The parking lot was already crowded. I knew what to expect inside and I knew I wasn't going to like it—I'd never had much tolerance for wakes in general—but it seemed to me that if you died at fifteen, people who'd known you ought to at least show up. Tracy waited for me to come around and open her door. I wasn't surprised; that was part of who Tracy was. Doors had been opened for her all her life.

"Latch is right here," I said, pulling the handle to demonstrate for her. "You just pull it and you can let yourself out. Won't have to wait."

"That's all right," she said. "You need the practice."

"Practice for what?"

"Being polite."

Daisy hopped out of the back seat. She was wearing a beige windbreaker and jeans, and she snapped her bubble gum every few seconds. "Wonder where Fernando and the guys are?" she asked.

I said, "Is it safe for him to come here?"

"I don't think there's gonna be any D's around here tonight." She snapped her gum again.

Tracy said, "Daisy, maybe you ought not to chew gum inside."

"Huh? Oh." She pulled her gum out and stuck it on the wall of the funeral home. It looked like a little pink squid on the brickwork.

Inside the lights were dim and yellowish and the room was stuffy.

Angel's wake was well attended, crowds of people in the front lobby and the adjoining rooms both left and right. We had not brought a card for the family, and that omission came as a late regret, but I went ahead and signed the guest registry.

"Where's Angel?" Daisy asked.

"I imagine he's around here somewhere," I said. "Why don't you try that room over there."

I was in no hurry to find him. What embalmers did to corpses upset me—the waxy complexion, sewed lips in unnatural positions. But I couldn't avoid the inevitable for long, and soon I was beside his coffin, a brown metal one, shiny brass trim, pale blue silk interior. Angel looked like he was sleeping, except his chest did not move. Across it had been laid his Spanish Cobras sweater, green and black. A young, pretty Puerto Rican girl, no older than eleven, perhaps, stood at the head of the casket, crying silent tears. Her hair was long and black and her eyes, nose and chin resembled Angel's. I gathered that this was his little sister. I wanted to say something to her, to tell her that it would be all right—but I was no one to her, and it wouldn't have been true anyway. It was not going to be all right, and she would never have her big brother again.

In the back of the room two young Latin men held the arms of a plump lady who wailed so mournfully, it sent shivers down my back.

"The mother," Tracy whispered to me.

"That would be my guess."

Tracy pulled me by the wrist to follow her. "I have to step outside. Come with me."

I did not know if she felt faint or was just overcome with emotion, but something in the way she touched me, or the way she assumed we were together in this was appealing. Not appealing, really. Yes, appealing. *Tracy Singer*, I thought.

Outside the cool air was refreshing. Some young guys were standing around smoking, speaking lowly amongst themselves in Spanish.

Tracy said, "That was positively painful."

I said, "If it doesn't hurt, how do you know you're alive?"

She tucked some wisps of blond hair behind a pretty ear, the makings of a smile forming on her lips. "The tough Mr. Johnny Spector. You're not half the cynic you pretend to be."

"Oh, I wouldn't want to wager on that."

"Well, you're not, and I know you're not, even if you don't want to admit it. I couldn't figure that out about you, at first."

Down Diversey streams of headlights floated till they were inked out by the night. "Figure what out?"

"That you're soft and you just don't want anyone to know it."

"Is that so?" I said. "How would you know a thing like that?"

"The way you are with the kids, and how hurt you are about your wife."

I turned sharply toward her. "Who said I was hurt?"

"You didn't *have* to say it."

Fernando stepped out the front door of the funeral home; he'd been in there all the while. Behind him came a young Latin man with a thin mustache and perfectly groomed hair.

"This is Angel's *maestro, señor* Spector. Yo, Johnny. This here's Angel's *Tio* Aurelio."

The young man held out his hand to me, said it was good of me to come. Then he put his other hand on mine, and for a moment his eyes welled up and I thought perhaps he was going to break down, but that passed and soon he regained his composure. I introduced him to Tracy, and Tracy said how sorry she was.

"I didn't think the school, it would care," Aurelio said. For a moment I wanted to tell him the truth, that the school didn't, but that we did.

Jorgé and Nelson strolled up, two men about town, pounded knuckles together with Fernando in some kind of gangster greeting. They were always doing funny things with their hands. Jorgé had spiffed himself up, white shirt, black pants creased as sharply as a switchblade, and one of them had recently bathed in Old Spice. "How he look?" Jorgé asked.

Fernando tilted his head, then shook it. "He looks dead, brother."

Jorgé said, "They got snakes on the next block. We saw 'em from the bus, about eight of 'em, two on each corner. They representin'. They showin' the D's."

Snakes were Spanish Cobras.

Fernando shrugged. "They stayin' away, out of respect for the family. They'll be havin' their own wake tonight, later."

We went back in for a half hour or so, mingled, met some more of the relatives, who treated Tracy and me warmly, and with extreme propriety. The Latino community has great respect for learning, and for educators. If the board of education would keep the schools open at night for community functions, allow the local residents to feel at home within the facility, they would find this out firsthand. But nothing is that simple, and there were other problems in the neighborhoods, like trying not to get shot, or jumped. People feared for their safety.

I thought of Angel in class, thought of him lying motionless, being lowered into the ground. His little sister remained at the head of his casket, keeping diligent vigil amidst flickering candles and whispered Spanish prayers, unaware of the strange beauty of the scene. Suddenly there was a flash; someone had snapped a photograph of Angel lying in his casket. That was not a picture I would care to see.

I always know when it's time to leave.

"Johnny—why don't you and Ms. Singer come back to my crib? We got some family comin' over, you know."

Fernando had caught up to us as we were walking out, slapped me on the back. Tracy started to make apologies, when I said, "Why not? Tracy—"

"I'd better not John—Mr. Spector."

I leaned in toward her ear and whispered, "In their culture it is considered an insult to turn down hospitality when it is offered."

She reddened, looked from my face to Fernando's as if for help.

"A *terrible* insult," I whispered again.

That could have been true, though I didn't know for sure if it was.

We dropped Daisy off in the dark stillness of North Francisco. The street had already gone to sleep. From there the three of us drove on to Fernando's place. It was a three-story walk-up directly across from Humboldt Park on Sacramento. This was Dragon territory, had been for as long as I'd known about it. It was not my first time here. Fernando led us up the concrete steps and pushed a buzzer. The building was sore with age, but its original architecture was intriguing—convex windows on the first floor and behind these inner doors in the foyer. A slight, short woman with an apron appeared at the door and twisted open a lock for us. She was visibly agitated.

"¿Donde estabas? Tenias que haber llegado a casa hace una hora. ¡Estaba preocupadisima!"

Fernando hung his head. "Estaba en el velorio; ya te lo dije. Tengo invitados. ¡Portate bien!"

"*Me está convirtiendo en una vieja, Fernando, con tanta preocupaciones.*"

Mrs. Morales held the front door open and motioned us in lavishly. She was an attractive woman with a kind smile, and she nodded to us in greeting. She asked Fernando in Spanish if Tracy was my wife. Fernando got a kick out of that, and of course Tracy was completely unaware, just smiled and said, "*Gracias*," which I believe was the only Spanish word she knew.

Mrs. Morales sat us down in the dining room and insisted on serving us dinner, though it was nine o'clock at night.

"But I couldn't possibly," Tracy said. "I'm absolutely full."

I lifted an eyebrow at her, and she kicked me under the table.

The kitchen was pungent with the scent of sofrito, an indigenous spice that was used in the preparation of many dishes, including the ones we were having, *arroz con pollo* and *alcapurria*. Mrs. Morales would not allow either of us to help her, and so she hurried back and forth from the kitchen with plates and bowls and serving forks. At last she stood behind Fernando's chair, her forearms balanced on its back and watched us eat.

I said, "*¿No vas a comer, señora?*"

"No, no thank you," she said. "Already I have eaten. Is good?"

Tracy's mouth was full. She tried to speak and couldn't get anything out, just nodded extravagantly.

"It's good to have my boy home. Things bad. Things bad in the neighborhood. I work hard. Maybe we move."

Fernando grimaced under the weight of embarrassment. "Ma— *calléte, por favor.* Jesus."

I said, "Let your mother talk, Fernando. She's concerned about you, is all."

"He live with my husband now. I no see him so much. The streets—no good. I worry."

Fernando let out a silent, "Sheesh."

I said, "If it'll make you feel any better, Mrs. Morales, we're watching over him at school."

"*Gracias, señor.* A mother, she worries."

We were served coffee in the living room, where there was a bookcase. I stood up and examined the titles—the bible, an old encyclopedia, some issues of *Readers Digest*, and lo and behold, *Don Quixote*, in Spanish. It had a wonderful leather cover and had been well used. This made all the difference. Fernando had a swell home.

We shook hands with Mrs. Morales at the end of our visit and thanked her for dinner. Fernando led us out into the hallway as we said our goodbyes, but instead of leading us outside, he began climbing the stairs to the second floor.

"Yo, Johnny, Ms. Singer—up here. I want you to meet the family."

Tracy said to me, "I thought we *had* met the family."

Mrs. Morales called up the stairs after him. "Fernando, not too late!"

I knew what was going on now. It all depended on exactly who you considered family. I said, "You'd better hold on to your beret."

"Why? Where is he going?"

At the second floor landing Fernando took a right and knocked several times on a door marked 2B. There was salsa music blaring and the boisterous conversational sounds of a party. The door jerked open, revealing twenty or so young people—some dancing, some drinking. Hanging in the air was a gray sheen of smoke, cigarettes, cannabis. The young man at the door was tall and wore a full beard and a gray and purple sweater. He clenched Fernando's hand in a gang sign, and turned a wary eye toward us.

"Undertaker—who they?"

"They my teachers, man. Have some manners."

A wide grin spread across his face, exposing perfectly straight but slightly large teeth. I found out later that his nickname was Doggie. "Undertaker's teachers," he said. "Come in. Welcome. Hey everybody—look. Undertaker brought his teachers."

The music stopped. The place went still. I could feel Tracy falter under the weight of the combined examination. We were like space people. Several girls in tight jeans stood still, eyes on Tracy. They had dark aqua eye shadow, and thick black eyeliner. Most of the guys wore Dragon sweaters, cigarettes dangling from their lips, and someone said, "Who the babe?"

Out from the shadows in the back of the living room, a man in his thirties stepped forward into the yellow light of two shaded table lamps. His hair was combed straight back and rose to a high widow's peak, and his cheekbones were strong, narrow, descending to a jutting chin. He looked at me deeply and said in a slow manner, "Fuck-ing John-ny *Spector.*" He grabbed my arm, turned to face the rest of the gathering.

"This guy was *my* fucking teacher fourteen years ago! Johnny, don't you remember me?"

"Jesus Christ," I said, "Chilo, is that you?"

Chilo laughed a deep laugh and gave me a bear hug. Chilo Fuentes was one of the first Dragons I'd ever had in class. Or maybe not. Maybe I was just beginning to understand about gangs the year he was in my junior English class. Chilo had had it tough. His mother had died of breast cancer and he was left with a younger brother to support. He worked at the Jewel food store on Chicago Avenue and had joined the Dragons to keep from getting killed by the Latin Kings on his way back to the neighborhood.

"Let me get you a beer," Chilo said.

"I'm not stopping you."

"Jesus Christ, Johnny. How are you? Is this your wife?"

"Yes," I said. "Get her a beer, too."

Tracy looked at me in astonishment. "I am *not* his wife. I'm his student teacher."

The salsa music started up again and couples danced to thin Caribbean strains of trumpet over bass line piano notes. Chilo popped two Budweisers and handed them to us. "Well, I'll bet you don't have an attendance problem, lady. Johnny, did they give you the prettiest student teacher because you got seniority?"

Tracy blushed, stammered, said, "No, thank you. I don't drink beer."

Chilo handed her the can once more. "When you're here, you *must* drink beer."

She looked to me. "Is that true?"

"It's a rule," I said.

She raised the can to her lips and took a sip, made a face. Someone handed her a joint. It was stuck between her fingers before she realized what it was. "Oh—no. No, I don't—" but no one would take it back from her. She went off walking between dancing couples, swaying bodies, looking for an ashtray. In the corner of the room next to a sofa Fernando was dancing the merengue with one of the older boy's girlfriends. He was quite good, too, smooth, fluid, had all the right moves. One of the young men had caught Tracy by the hand and began to dance with her. I saw her shake her head in refusal, but he just dipped her, pulled the joint out of her hand, took a hit, and lifted her back up.

"She's something," Chilo said. "One of the job's perks. I'll bet your wife's not crazy about her."

"You remember my wife, don't you, Chilo?"

Chilo gulped down some of his beer and his Adam's apple bobbed and he nodded. "Oh, yeah. She was a senior when I was a sophomore. I remember she was beautiful. How is she?"

"We're getting a divorce."

He lowered the beer can to a big round table. "Johnny, I'm sorry to hear it. Damn—you got kids?"

"One. A boy. He's fifteen."

"That's how old I was when I had you. He must think you're the best."

"Chilo, these days I don't know what he thinks."

"He'll keep it together. You'll make sure he does. That's why I'm still with the Dragons, Johnny. See these kids? They're not on the street. They're here, safe."

On the table right beside him were five handguns—three thirty-eights and two nine millimeter specials. "Well, safe in a relative way, Chilo."

"What—the guns? Shit, Johnny—we gotta have guns. Do you know what's going on down there on Sacramento?"

I finished my beer and said that I had heard.

"Disciples are selling shit to our kids. They're taking our neighborhood away from us. Dealers on three corners just north of here. You know how it is, Johnny. Come on, now. Don't tell me you've become one of them."

"One of them what?"

"One of them straight motherfuckers that pretends everything's gonna get fixed if we wear a tie and vote. You know what I mean."

"Sure," I said. "I know." I looked around to see where I might throw out my beer can.

He slapped my arm. "I'll take that from you. Come with me."

He led me around the corner to the bathroom and turned on the light. Lining the walls straight up to the ceiling was a red-white-and-blue pyramid built out of empty Budweiser cans. There must have been three thousand of them. The handwritten sign on the door read: *One dollar for every can knocked over.* Chilo placed my can precariously on the brims of two others.

115

I said, "How does anybody relax enough to go in here?"

"If they're smart, they don't. We had one guy lose three hundred bucks last week."

"You enforce it?"

"Oh, yeah. Where do you think we get the money for the beer?"

It was good seeing Chilo again, knowing that he had made it safely out of adolescence. He told me that now he was the manager of that grocery store where he had started all those years ago, had a pension and a 401k. I was happy for him. I wondered what would become of all the kids out there in the living room, the kids with the nicknames and the sweaters and the guns. Would they get managerial jobs like Chilo, or die as Angel had died? I thought of Marlyn and me starting out, how impossible that dream had been, only we hadn't known it was impossible then. *All those years*, I thought.

At around eleven the music was turned off and we were instructed by a short, tough looking guy wearing a Dragon sweater to take a place at the big round table. They called him Blade, perhaps because he had a scarred cheek, and from what I gathered, he was the current leader. Tracy took the chair next to mine and whispered, "I think we'd better go now."

I put my mouth next to her ear and said, "Can't. It's the initiation."

"What initiation?"

A candle in the shape of a large *D* was lit in the middle of the table. Shot glasses were set in front of everyone. Around the table came Blade with a bottle of vodka. He filled each little glass to the top, careful not to spill a single drop. Behind him followed Doggie with a butane lighter, allowing the flame to skim the surface of everyone's drink. When the lights were shut off, little blue flickers floated above the shot glasses, forming a circular perimeter of light.

Blade said, "Family and friends, Folks to the end. May the circle never be severed, Dragons forever."

I wrote that pledge for them back in 1984. Unfortunately I'd had several shots of vodka first.

Blade picked up his shot glass and drained it, still lit. Everyone followed suit. Everyone, that is, except Tracy. I nudged her, said, "Go ahead."

"The damn thing's on fire, Johnny," she hissed at me."

Blade said, "We ask our new friend to join us."

Tracy lifted the glass from the table in tremulous fingers, closed her eyes, and then just kept it suspended there.

I said, "If you're waiting for a drum roll, I left my sticks at home."

"Do it quickly," Blade said.

Tracy opened one eye, regarded the little blue light.

Blade bellowed, "DO IT!"

With that she tipped the little glass back, swallowed, and went into a coughing fit. Everyone applauded.

Someone brought a glass of water for her, and she had a sip or two. "Is there a bathroom here? I need a bathroom."

One of the girls came over and went with her. I found my blazer and put it on, and as if in a reception line, each of the young kids came by and gave me the Dragon handshake, which was performed with an inverted grasping of the wrist after first raising your hand in the Dragon pose. I got better at it as I went along, but after a while it began to hurt. Getting old. It sucks.

I said goodbye to Chilo and told him to look me up for lunch sometime. He wished me good luck with the divorce and I thanked him. It was just polite talk, because after all, what good could come of it? Fernando told me he would catch a ride to his father's house with someone called Tank. I did not know what was keeping Tracy so long. She was extremely high maintenance, required twice the time to do anything than it took anyone else. I had pretty much made up my mind to go in after her when I heard a terrific crash and clatter from around the corner.

Doggie shouted, "We got beer money!"

Slowly the bathroom door opened. Back lit by the bathroom light, Tracy stepped out, sheepishly, over dozens and dozens of fallen cans, some of them still rolling. She moved over next to me and hid her face behind my shoulder.

I said, "Nice going."

"Get me out of here," she mumbled.

"One hundred and twenty-seven," Blade announced. "A hundred and twenty-seven bucks!"

There was raucous laughter and shouting, and of course Tracy wanted nothing so much as to die, immediately. She lifted her purse, opened it, and said, "Will you take a check?"

Which brought more laughter. They had no intention of making her pay. Chilo came over and put his arm around her. "This time you

117

get a pass, señorita, but next time you pay *double*."

"It wasn't that funny, you know."

Tracy sat beside me in the Jeep. I turned up the heat. "Relax. They loved you."

Headlights flickered through the windows, created shadows, and I caught her face in profile. Tracy was beautiful. There was no denying it. I just wished I wouldn't keep noticing it.

"Do you really think it's a good idea, Fernando being around the drinking, the marijuana?"

I turned on Armitage. There was a man on the corner holding on to a light pole for balance. The world was spinning a little too quickly for him. "No, I don't think it's a good idea. I just don't think there's much you can do about it, given reality. Given *his* reality."

"You seem to approve of it."

"Tracy, sometimes you have trouble making the distinction between what *is* and what *should be*." She had a point, though. Just having been there was a kind of implicit endorsement. "Still, we might try to encourage him to stay at home more often."

That profile again. Hell of a profile. She looked pleased.

"You agree with me, then."

I did, but I didn't want to say it.

"You wouldn't be happy if your son was doing that."

"You're right. I wouldn't."

"You have a double standard."

The shadows between lampposts passed like phantom railroad ties, hiding her face, then allowing the light to fall full upon it. "You need to hear me say it, don't you?"

"Yes, I do."

"All right. I have a double standard."

"Thank you."

As we approached Bucktown, the pedestrians became more plentiful, more fashionable, the residences regentrified. "It's not really *my* double standard, though. It's just that different worlds come with different rules. I try to play the game with whichever set they give me."

Tracy turned to me with a victor's smile. "That sounds like a cop out."

"I admit that it does, but I think it might be true."

118

I pulled the Jeep to the curb in front of her place and pulled up the parking brake. Tracy's seat belt cut diagonally into the soft fabric of her sweater. Under the stark lamplight she appeared colorless, as if in a black and white movie. I thought of Bogart and Bacall.

"Anyway," I said, "you sure know how to toss back a flaming drink."

"You could have warned me that was coming."

"It was more fun the other way."

We sat in silence. A bus roared past, and in the distance someone called out to someone else, "I see you!"

"Would you like to come upstairs? I mean—have a cup of coffee or something?"

I didn't know what was wrong with me, because I couldn't get a word out. I had been about to say something, but I didn't know what.

"I mean," she said, "it's probably pretty late and—"

"Yeah—yeah, it's late. Thanks. Some other time, maybe."

She smiled, but didn't move, just sat there. At first I didn't know what was going on, but then I remembered.

"Oh," I said, and got out and walked around and opened the door for her.

"Thanks," she said. "You're getting better."

I watched as she walked up the steps of her building and let herself in. She said good night, and I said good night, and then the door closed and I stood there a while on the street in the chill evening under the street lamp, wondering why some things happen they way they do.

7

Fernando rode shotgun in the U-Haul moving truck that I'd rented from a place on Fullerton. It was Saturday morning and today was the day I was moving out of my house. Jason had a football game and would not be there to see it, thankfully. That would have been awful, like watching your own general defect. The truck was about an eighteen-footer and every time we went over a bump, the dolly in back came down with a jarring crash upon the floor.

Earlier that morning I saw something terrible. As I stood waiting for the rental agency to open, two pigeons on the sidewalk were involved in what first looked like a dance, but soon I saw that one bird had the neck of the other in his beak and he was trying very hard to snap it. I shooed the bigger of the two away. The smaller one, I noted, was stunted, his wings too small, his head ravaged. He stumbled around in circles, breaking into a pathetic plea that sounded like *peep, peep, peep.* I knew the attack must have been going on for some time, because he was missing feathers and his back had been pecked into open wounds. Without warning, the instigator returned, swooping down upon the little bird once more, again wrenching the neck with his powerful beak. Now I found myself kicking at the larger bird until he spread his wings, rose into the air, and landed on the roof of a building across the street, where he sat and eyed us steadily. At that moment a man with a beard and a flannel shirt appeared inside the agency and opened the door with a ring of keys, allowing me in. The last I saw of the poor injured bird, he was staggering down the sidewalk on shaky legs. I was fairly certain of his fate. I could not stand out on the corner all day to protect him, but I couldn't stop thinking of him, either, of how there was no one in the world for him to turn to, no rescue anywhere at all.

"Your wife gonna be there?" Fernando asked.

"I'm pretty sure. She'll want to keep an eye on the family treasures."

"How do you know what stuff you're allowed to take?"

"We discussed it already. Everything she wants to throw out is mine."

"Did you have one of them agreements—what you call 'em?"

"A prenup? No."

"How come?"

"They cost more money than we had."

Fernando rolled down his window and lighted a cigarette. "Shit. I ain't never gettin' married."

I remembered having said that before and after my first marriage.

I pulled the truck into the driveway a bit too quickly and scraped the bottom on the concrete sidewalk. It was a clumsy vehicle and reverse was nearly impossible to find with that gear shift, but I managed to get the nose into the L portion of the drive and turn so the back end faced the garage. I might as well have rented a billboard for the neighbors that read: GUESS WHOSE MARRIAGE FAILED?

Fernando and I hopped out and stood around the truck like a couple of Teamsters. He was still finishing his cigarette.

"You gonna miss this place?"

Two big pines in the front. They looked pretty, snow-laden in the winter. The side yard where Jason and Marlyn and I played badminton every summer. The azaleas Marlyn planted every year along the front walkway. Strangely, though, the sadness would not come. It was as if someone had given my heart an injection of Novocain.

"Don't ask me questions like that. We'll never get the truck loaded. Come on."

I rang the bell and stood waiting on my own stoop for someone to let me in. Divorce means being reduced to the status of company. Fernando flicked his cigarette butt into the shrubs and Marlyn swung open the big front door. She was wearing a black pant suit and looked disarmingly elegant, a cross between Kate Middleton and Catherine Zeta-Jones. I looked down at my torn dungarees and dirty gym shoes, feeling like the hired help.

She said, "Johnny."

"Marlyn. You remember Fernando."

"Hello, Fernando."

"Whattup."

I wanted first to get the bed from the guest room, so I started for the stairs, but was stopped by Marlyn. "The bed is in the family room. I had it taken apart for you."

I was about to ask who had done that, but fell short when I realized I'd end up hearing Bruce's name again, and I didn't need that right now. Fernando and I carried first the box spring and then the mattress, and he hauled the metal frame to the truck by himself while I went to the kitchen for a glass of water. It's funny how a room can begin to look foreign to you after as little as a week or so. I'd never liked the wallpaper.

"Are you getting treatment?"

Marlyn had come into the room behind me. She was so beautiful.

"Uh . . . no. Do I need treatment?"

She gave a silent half-laugh. "It's not the kind of thing that would be a mistake to think about."

I set the glass down upon the counter. "Treatment for what, again?"

"For your drinking."

"Why would I want to do that?"

"Because, Johnny, you drink too much. You drink because of your job. You drink because of the marriage. You drink for almost any reason at all."

I said, "Cut it out. You're making me thirsty."

"You can joke about it, if you want. That's your other defense mechanism."

She had me all figured out. What I never understood about people who pointed out the defense mechanisms of others was why they would want anybody to go around defenseless.

"It's how I get by. When you teach all day at that place, you've got to have something. Drinks and jokes—they work for me."

"Why don't you apply for a full-time position at the college?"

I taught as a part timer at a small suburban college in June and July because there was no summer work with the board of education—English 101, Introduction to Literature, courses like that.

I said, "They've got all those young Ph.Ds. Why would they want an old, broken down high school teacher?"

"You've got experience."

Boy, did I.

I approached her, walked directly up to her until we were separated by only inches and I could smell the familiar smell of her perfume. "I know I have a lot of faults, but I still love you."

She gave me a smirk. "And I love you, but I will not watch you destroy yourself."

"So that's why you went out and got Bruce."

She crossed her arms in front of her. "No one went out and got anybody."

"What do you see in that guy, Marlyn?"

She narrowed her eyes and the smirk turned into an artificial grin. I couldn't say which I disliked more. "Would you like to know? Bruce gives me flowers. Do you know the last time you brought me flowers? Nineteen-*ninety-nine*. Bruce brings me flowers, Johnny."

I thought I must be hearing wrong. "Flowers? *Flowers*, for Christ's sake?"

"That's right, flowers."

"Well, let me tell you something. He might bring you *flowers*, but I pay for your goddamn health insurance. Try checking into a hospital with a goddamn *chrysanthemum*."

What a stupid thing to say. Even now I can't believe I said something so stupid. I had not wanted a fight, not during the last time we'd be together in that house, but I couldn't help myself. I couldn't think about Bruce at all without wanting to kill him. Fernando just stood in the hallway gaping at us like he was one of our own kids.

Marlyn stalked out of the kitchen to the staircase. "That's enough. Take your things and get out." She climbed up the stairs and I watched her till she disappeared behind the bedroom door, which she slammed, an act of physical punctuation. Fernando continued to stare with the uneasy demeanor of an unwilling spectator.

And somewhere a baby pigeon was being pecked to death. The world—it's not a pretty place.

"I didn't think teachers and their wives fought like that. It was like listenin' to my old man and my ma. 'Cept they do it in Spanish."

We were back in the truck, headed for the city, to my new home, and Marlyn's former one. "Yeah, well—it doesn't matter what you do for a living. It's all about men and women."

"Sounds better in Spanish. Got more soul. You ought to try it next time you guys have a fight. Just say, *'¡Cállete, carajo!'*"

"Chances are, Fernando, there won't be a next time."

"Oh, sure there will." Fernando blew a trail of smoke out and studied his cigarette thoughtfully. "She got another dude and shit?"

I adjusted my sunglasses and kept my eyes trained on the road. I did not answer him.

123

He took another drag of his cigarette and French-inhaled. "That's a bitch, man." He wore a sweatshirt with cut off sleeves, proudly displaying the blue D on his arm. "Me and my boys, we could fuck him up, if you want."

"No. Thanks for the offer, though." I did not want to discuss Bruce with Fernando. I did not want to discuss Bruce with anyone.

"No kidding, Johnny. We could really fuck him up good."

He was already fucked up. I said, "Did you do your homework yet this weekend?"

"Homework? *Chingar*—it's only Saturday, man! I got all day tomorrow." He turned suddenly to look at two pretty Latin girls in a black Camaro to our right. "Damn, Johnny! Look!"

I honked the horn and the girls looked up at us and laughed. The driver was stunning—there were copper-colored streaks in her hair and silver bracelets on her wrist. Fernando hung out the window, slapping the side of the door with an open palm, saying, "Oh, mama, you so fine, girl!"

I said, "See? This is how it starts. One minute you're salivating on her in her car, and the next thing you know, you're carrying an old bed out to your truck."

North Francisco Street. Daisy, Nelson and Jorgé were camped out on the front steps of señor Valentin's house—the welcoming committee. Jorgé played with something silver in his hand that reflected sunlight in a bright flash. A stiletto. I was going to have to have a talk with that boy. Señor Valentin's face appeared in the living room window as he separated the curtains. I remembered that that was how I had first seen him years ago when I brought Marlyn back home from one of our surreptitious dates. Gray hair at the temples, pencil thin mustache. I thought of how lonely it must have been for him then—his wife gone, his daughter growing up and leaving home, how lonely it must be for him now. Perhaps that was why he had wanted me to move in.

I stepped out on the ledge of the truck and jumped to the driveway. Fernando walked around from the other side and lifted the back panel. Daisy ran up and held on to one of my arms with both of hers. She had her hair braided and pinned up and she smelled of bubble gum. "I can't believe you're movin' into the hood, Johnny. Damn! We can hang out."

I said, "Yeah. We can start our own gang. The Insane Neighbors."

Nelson looked back at the house. "You movin' in there?"

"Nope. Out back, over the garage."

"The penthouse," Jorgé said.

I worked my arm free of Daisy and slapped Jorgé on the back, and then quickly fished my hand into his pocket and pulled the knife out. It was an outrageous weapon—black pearl handle, polished steel blade that shot straight out when the button was pressed.

He looked up into my face with those intense black eyes of his and said, "Son of a bitch! How'd that get there?"

And I said, "I'm going to kick your ass." I palmed the stiletto and carefully dropped it into my windbreaker pocket.

There was the sudden thud of a car door closing. Daisy gave a little frown and said, "What's *she* doin' here?"

"Hey, Ms. Singer!" Nelson called, and ran out to the curb where her white BMW was parked. She had her hair tied back and was wearing faded jeans and a sweatshirt. A white Beemer, for Christ's sake. I thought, *Gidget Goes Slumming*.

She walked up the drive, or rather she bounced up the drive, all perky smile and innocent wonder. "You look like someone who could use some help," she said, standing with her hands in her jeans pockets.

I said, "And you look like someone who should be home grading papers."

"That's what Sundays are for."

We walked out back through the garden toward the outdoor stairway that led to my new apartment. I said, "No kidding, Tracy. How did you know I was here?"

"Informants," she said. "They're everywhere."

Daisy snapped her gum so loudly it startled me. She was right behind us, glowering at Tracy's back as though she were an intruder.

While the kids moved what little I had brought—the bed, a few chairs, a tree lamp, my clothes—and while Tracy obsessively-compulsively folded my bath and hand towels for the bathroom (several hundred times, it seemed), señor Valentin walked me up to the apartment and proudly demonstrated the new shelving system that he had had installed in the closet. "Good use of space," he said. "All you need. Eh?"

The little place started to shape up. It could have used some bookshelves and a painting, but other than that it was fine. There was an old-fashioned toaster on the kitchen counter, a waffle iron, in case I ever decided I wanted to learn how to make waffles, and a crucifix over the sink. If I got lonely, I could invite some friends over and say Mass.

At around one o'clock Nydia Velazquez climbed up the wooden steps with a basket full of sandwiches for the kids. My moving day had turned into a party. I didn't mind, but I would have liked to have known who'd set it up. Nydia gave me a big hug out on the landing.

"How did you know where to find me?" I asked her.

"Lover, I could find you in a haystack. As a matter of fact, there's an idea."

While everyone talked and ate, I looked out the window at the pale orange leaves falling from the oak branches in the yard, at the aged bungalows, and at señor Valentin's garden. It wasn't home, but it was going to have to be. I wondered if Jason's team had won. I wondered if late at night when the house was silent and dark, he ever thought of me, and if he did, what he thought. The rental truck sat parked down below, its rear door retracted, a ramp running diagonally to the ground. In big orange letters on its side it sagely announced to the world at large, *Adventure in Moving.* Just what I needed.

Tracy gave Jorgé and Nelson explicit directions to move the bed. It had to face north, she said. She'd read it in a book on karma, so with some mumbled complaints in Spanish, they picked it up, and lined it up against the other wall. Nydia was filling the refrigerator with sodas, and gave me a funny little smile, and then looked at Tracy.

I said, "What?"

She leaned toward me and whispered, "Now your karma's all adjusted."

I said, "It's a good thing, too, because it was beginning to feel tangled."

"Just face north. She'll tell you which way it is." Then she winked at me.

Out on the steps, Fernando and Daisy were sitting, smoking cigarettes. Daisy was still wearing a grudge mask, for whatever reason. "You didn't happen to have anything to do with inviting our two teacher friends over today, did you Daisy?"

She flicked her cigarette butt down to the garden, exhaled an angry blast of smoke, and stood up. "Shit, no. If I did, that *traga* wouldn't be here." She climbed hurriedly down the steps, back out around to the truck.

I sat down next to Fernando, who was looking off toward infinity somewhere. "It's Tracy she means, isn't it?"

Fernando shrugged. "Women. Who knows?"

"Why is she so angry at her?"

"I dunno that, either."

And then it dawned on me. "It was you, wasn't it?"

Fernando said, "Me what?"

"You told Ms. Singer and Ms. Velazquez to come here."

He crushed his cigarette out on the step and would not make eye contact with me. "Thought you was gonna need some help, is all. Ain't no thang."

It was a damned thoughtful thing for a kid to do, making sure I had friends around on the day that I moved out. It made me think about how close we'd become in such a short time. Of course he couldn't take my thanks, or even look at me. Men did not do these things. I held my hand out. Fernando slapped it, eyes still trained on the sky and beyond.

Later that night after everyone had gone and I realized I hadn't even made arrangements for a telephone, I found a cardboard box in the closet that I at first thought must have been neglected. When I opened it up, there was a child's stuffed horse, a photo of Marlyn's mother with Marlyn in her arms—a collection of broken dreams. I did not know how the box had got there, but I remembered with a bent sense of irony the remark señor Valentin had made earlier about that closet—*good use of space.*

§

"I know some of you have classes to get to, so I'll make this just as quick as I can." It was Monday morning and Marco Gonzalez had gathered several teachers together at a round table in an inner office of the Youth Services complex. There was Betty Frycas, a history teacher who I think had been in the Revolutionary War, Jamel Saunders, Nydia Velazquez, and seated directly beside me, Tracy. I had not known that Lico was one of Nydia's students, or I would have talked to her about him much sooner.

"Mr. Spector and Ms. Singer have brought it to my attention that a student you have in common, a sophomore named Lico Pacheco, has a troubled background and is offering conflicting stories about his home circumstances. Johnny—tell me if I'm right, but I gather Lico seems to have some personal problems?" Then to the others he explained, "Lico

127

has opened up to Mr. Spector, as many of our more troubled youth do."

Jamel Saunders said, "Saint Spector—same old song. Save those kids."

She had not meant this in any but a joking manner, which was her way. Nonetheless I felt Tracy bristle. She sat more upright at my side.

I said, "You're right, Marco. And Jamel, I think this kid is worth the trouble. I've read a very disturbing narrative he wrote about his upbringing. He was abused in just about every way a kid can be abused, and now he's lying to his teachers about his home life. To me that raises red flags. I thought we ought to look into the matter."

Betty Frycas lifted her hand as if she had to be called on. Marco said, "Betty?"

Betty put both her elbows on the table and folded her hands beside her chin. The skin of her neck folded in pleats. "How do you know he's lying?"

Tracy spoke up. "You need to know something about Lico first. He was abandoned by his mother when he was six years old—after having been repeatedly raped by his stepfather. He was turned over to DCFS and was shipped to foster home after foster home. Every time he gets close to someone, he loses them. Right now he has no one at all. He lives in a group home with a counselor."

Betty said, "Is this necessary? Do I have to hear about a boy being raped?"

Betty lived in a world that did not have sex or violence.

Marco said, "Betty, yes—I think you might have to. Ms. Singer, maybe you could give us an example of the inconsistent stories you've heard from Lico."

Tracy wore a white business suit this morning and looked like a TV anchorwoman. She doodled on a yellow legal pad while she itemized examples for the group. Lico hadn't seen his mother since she left him when he was boy. Lico's mother was living in Georgia. He didn't know where his mother was. He does not know where his siblings are. He had a sister who lived in Cicero. A brother who was an engineering student in Washington, DC.

"I didn't know any of this Johnny." Nydia said. "Lico's in my theater class and my dance troupe. He told me that he sees his mother on weekends, that his brother drives him down to visit her every weekend in Crown Point, Indiana. But I had a feeling about him. The first thing I noticed was his terrible stutter, that, and the fact that he sometimes asks to borrow money and says he'll pay me back. He hasn't so far."

Jamel said, "What we've got here is a troubled kid who's misrepresenting himself. I don't know a thing about his personal life, because unlike Mr. Spector, I only try to teach my students, not raise them."

Tracy flushed. "Ms. Saunders—I think we need to consider the well-being of our students as well their progress in our classes."

Jamel furrowed her forehead and said, "I'm sorry Miss—and you are *who* again?"

"All right, people," Marco broke in. "The point is, we've established that Lico is not telling us the truth about his family. It could be as simple as a lonely boy fabricating a missing family—or it could be much worse. He could be very disturbed, perhaps borderline personality disorder, or perhaps even worse than that."

I said, "Have you got a hold of that counselor of Lico's—Jim Jarret?"

"We had a short conversation last Thursday," Marco said. "And that's why I'm a bit worried that Lico might be more troubled than we at first thought. Lico's had some trouble with the law. Did any of you know that?"

No one did.

"He seems like such a sweet boy," Tracy said.

Jamel blew compressed air through her lips. "Always look out for the sweet ones."

Marco stood up, signaling an end to the meeting. "In any case, thank you all for being here today. I'll meet with Mr. Jarret later this week and see if we can't get to the bottom of this. In the meantime, I'd appreciate it if you would keep all this information confidential. Lico is a minor."

Everyone got up and began to file out. Jamel gave Tracy a raised eyebrow and turned and walked away, her purse flung over her shoulder.

"She hates me," Tracy whispered.

"You have to understand about Jamel. She knows the ropes, and you're a young upstart."

Betty Frycas gathered up her notebook and said, "Everything is sex, sex, sex these days. The world's gone mad."

Marco was walking back to his own office when I caught up to him. "Well, *profesor*," he said. "I thought that went well."

I said, "What was the arrest for?"

"Three arrests in Chicago alone. Vandalism, theft, and the other one you don't want to know about. It's because of that last one I didn't list the offenses. I didn't want to prejudice his teachers against him— some of them are not the broadest minded people. And I didn't want to give Betty a heart attack."

"Jesus," I said. "You think you know somebody."

"Come on, Johnny. I thought you were hard-boiled."

"Not me," I said. "I'm over easy."

Marco's hands were in his suit pants pockets. He rattled his change. "Still haven't seen you at our sensitivity sessions."

He was an elegant dresser, imported black brogues, black Italian suit. He was a success and he wanted the world to know it. I said, "Have I told you I'm going through a divorce?"

He looked genuinely concerned to hear it. "Why, no Johnny, you haven't. Would you like to talk about it?"

"No. Not everybody in the world needs therapy, Marco."

"And not all of those who do know it."

I found Nydia and Tracy talking to one another in the Youth Services waiting room. There were three or four kids sitting in chairs against the wall, waiting for counseling sessions, kids with scars on their knuckles, kids with body piercings. When I walked in, Nydia wrapped her arm in mine and said, "So our boy is not who we thought he was."

Tracy said, "I'm just sick about it."

I said, "Well, get better fast. Are we still on for lunch?"

"Twelve sharp. Maggiano's. You're driving."

She said goodbye to Nydia before leaving and Nydia just stood there staring directly into my eyes, wearing a suspicious wrinkle of a smile that would not go away.

I said, "Either you're trying to hypnotize me, or you've finally run out of things to say."

"Do you see what's going on here?"

I looked around. "Yeah. I'm standing next to a beautiful Latin woman whose arm is flagrantly intertwined with mine."

Nydia said, "She's in love with you."

"Who is?"

"Your little student teacher."

I said, "There's a psychologist in the next room, if you'd like to see one, and I think you should."

She pulled me out into the hallway where there was such a between-classes racket that we couldn't be overheard, even by the CIA. With an open hand she hit me in the chest. "Don't you see what's going on? This girl has fallen for you, and she's fallen hard. My God, she can't even look at you without broadcasting it." She stopped, put her hands on her hips, squinted her eyes, and tilted her head. "Wait a minute—is something going on between you two?"

"No."

"Are you sure?"

"Of course I'm sure. I think you're crazy, altogether."

"Then why go to Maggiano's? Why not the cafeteria?"

"Because the food in the cafeteria has been eaten once before."

She pointed her index finger at me, told me to mark her words. I watched the pendulum of her hips as she walked away and got on the escalator and slowly descended into the mass of student bodies. Tracy Singer was only twenty-five and had been invented by Neiman Marcus. She could not be in love with me.

When I got to my office I found Brian, the human string bean reporter, loitering outside the door. He was wearing a long trench coat that must have been in style once and had a large, tan floppy satchel, which rested on the floor beside him.

"Mr. Spector—I didn't know what your schedule was and I—"

"Brian," I said. "Come on in. I only have a second, but let's sit down."

I opened the door and drew up a chair next to my desk. Brian sat down and lifted the satchel to his lap. He opened it, withdrew a manuscript held together by a black clip, and threw it down in front of me on my desk.

Inside the Inner City Teacher;
A Veteran Educator Lets Loose
by Brian Podhorst

That title wasn't going to win him a Pulitzer. The first page was all introduction and gave a semi-accurate account of who I was—". . . a hardened professional who's seen it all." The kid's narrative read like a script from one of those true-life cable TV police shows. As I flipped through the pages, two things became crystal: first, I had given an over-the-top interview, and next, Brian was completely unfamiliar with sensitive ethnic issues and protocol.

I said, "Are you going to leave this with me?"

"Yes. It's your copy. I want to know what you think of it."

"Well, Brian, I can't finish it now, but I can tell you that I was in a pretty foul mood when you talked to me that day."

"You were hysterical. You should see some of the lines you came up with. My editor cracked up."

Danny Velez would not crack up when he read it. He would have me burned at the stake, just as sure as anything.

I said, "Humor aside, I think it should be toned down some."

"But this is what you told me."

Christ. Brian Podhorst and journalistic integrity. "And another thing," I said, "you don't refer to Puerto Ricans as *Spanish* people. They are *Hispanics*. Go through it again and make sure you correct each case in which you refer to them that way."

Brian wrote this down on his own copy of the manuscript that was still inside his satchel. There was a remarkable vehemence about him; you could almost feel him cross his t's. He wore industrial steel glasses frames and had hair so straight it would not lie down, but rather hung at angles off the sides of his head.

"Will you contact me—I mean, after you've read the interview?"

"Sure," I said, standing up and opening the door for him. "Nydia's got your number, right?"

"I've got a card here, somewhere." He fished inside his bag, pulled out a notebook, stuck the notebook back, and with a quivering hand pulled a wallet from his back pocket. The period tone sounded and the hallways filled up. After another few minutes of furious hunting, Brian left a bent and frayed business card on my desk and shook my hand vigorously with a very damp palm. Jimmy Olsen came to mind.

I went to the main office to check my mail, though I knew better. Every time I looked in my mailbox, there were five more things for me to do than I had time for. Shirley was at her desk and beckoned for me with her finger.

I walked behind the counter up against the far wall, making sure I could not be seen from Danny Velez's office window. I said, "What is it now? The warden order a lockdown?"

132

"I just typed up a memo to you about your outcomes. You haven't submitted any."

"Shirley, there's a good reason for that," I said. "I haven't *written* any."

She took her glasses off and let them hang from a cord around her neck. "He's watching you, Johnny. Just a friendly warning."

"I know," I said. "Thanks, Shirley."

Danny Velez had ties to a terrorist group and he was worried about my goddamn outcomes. There you go—priorities.

"And Johnny? I want you to keep this to yourself for right now, but there are funny things going on with the accounting books."

That was interesting. "What kind of funny things?"

She looked over my shoulder toward Danny's office, then back toward Mary O'Hare, another secretary, who at the moment was busy at the copy machine. "The year book account has been emptied, and the poverty funds for after school tutoring are being drained."

"Drained where?"

"That's a good question. I don't know. I don't get to see the actual checks, but they're being requisitioned by Mike Parnell."

Mike Parnell was an assistant principal, and assistant principals were not in charge of fiscal management. I said, "Isn't that supposed to be Danny's responsibility?"

Shirley retrieved her glasses from around her neck and put them back on. "It's supposed to be."

The yearbook account couldn't have had more than five thousand dollars in it—but the poverty funds totaled over one hundred thousand a year. Maybe they were legitimate expenses. But wouldn't Shirley have known if they were?

"Johnny, *mira!* It's Hilda. She's hurt bad."

I'd just walked outside the main office as Daisy and Lucy ran up and grabbed me.

I said, "What happened? Where is she?"

"She's in the bathroom. It's her mouth. Tito punched her."

That little son of a bitch. I had known something like this was going to happen. I ran between kids who were passing in groups through the second floor fire doors to the entrance of the girls washroom. I called for Hilda to come out, but got no response.

I said to Daisy, "Are you sure she's still in there?"

"I'll go get her," she said.

Lucy was not naturally as gutsy or determined as Daisy, and remained just outside the entrance with me, biting at her fingernails. I could hear Daisy coaxing Hilda, but she was saying no, she couldn't. I said, "What the hell," and walked in after them. Hilda stood hunched over a sink holding a wet paper towel to her mouth. The water ran in the sink as Daisy comforted her, arms around her shoulders.

I crouched before Hilda to meet her at eye level and said, "Let me see, sweetheart. Hold the paper away."

She was crying, mouth etched in a frown, and when she pulled the paper away I felt faint. Her upper lip was three times its normal size, and one of her front teeth had been loosened. A thin stream of blood trickled from her gums.

"All right," I said. "Here's what we're going to do. We're going to take you to the nurse's office—"

"No!" Hilda cried. "Tito'll get in trouble."

Tito was already in trouble, only he didn't know it yet. I was going to kill him.

"No, he won't, sweetheart. We're going to take care of you. The nurse has ice. You need to put ice on this."

"But I look so ugly."

"No, you don't. You just look swollen. You put ice on this and the swelling will come down. I promise."

Hilda made hiccupping sounds as she tried to catch her breath between sobs. I recalled the time my boy Jason had fallen off a slide on the playground at school and tore a hole in his face, how I pretended to be calm. I missed my boy. I missed him very much.

"You w-w-walk next to me," Hilda pleaded. "Don't let nobody see me, Johnny."

"Okay," I said. "That's a good idea. Daisy, you take the other side. We'll keep our arms around you like this. How's that?"

"Fine," she said.

We sort of huddle-walked her between us to the nurse's office through the crowds of curious onlookers as she held the paper towel in place to conceal her battered mouth, and Lucy timidly followed. Fran Melnavicz was the school nurse, a wiry, white-haired lady who was a professional mother. If you were hurt, Fran was your lady. She saw us approaching through the nurse's office windows and left a seated kid with a thermometer in his mouth to meet us at the door.

"What have we here? Come inside, honey. Just sit down." She turned to me and said, "Is it her mouth?"

"Swollen lip, loose tooth."

"Did you fall, honey?" Fran asked.

Hilda looked up at me with terrified eyes. I said, "Fran—the less said about it, the better. Can you take care of her while I get her mother's work phone number in the records office?"

"Of course. There, there, sweetie. I'll get you some ice."

The records office was directly next door. When I ran in, Judy Santiago was already standing at the counter. She'd seen us walking Hilda.

"What happened, Johnny?"

"Boyfriend punched her. I need her mother's work number—Hilda Feliciano, my division, number four-o-two."

Sometimes I make good decisions, and then there are other times. I told Mrs. Feliciano that I would drive Hilda to the Wood Street Police Station to fill out a complaint against her boyfriend, and that she should meet us there, that we needed an adult signature as well. I took Daisy with us because I couldn't keep Hilda calm by myself. Mistake number two. I had taken two students—female students, mind you—out of class and off campus in a vehicle without parental or administrative permission. The only thing I could say in my own defense was, *You should have seen her lip.* It was not much of a defense, but I could think of little else other than getting Tito arrested.

Tito punched her because he didn't like the blouse she had worn that day.

On the way to the station Daisy attempted to convince Hilda to sign a complaint against Tito, but Hilda wasn't having any part of it. The desk sergeant was a patient guy with thinning blond hair who told me he'd seen this kind of thing again and again. A girl gets beaten by her boyfriend, and then defending *him* becomes more important than defending *herself.* He tapped the eraser end of his pencil on his desk blotter as Daisy said, "Don't be stupid, Hilda. He don't care about you, girl."

When Mrs. Feliciano showed up and saw her daughter's beaten mouth, she threw her arms around her and wailed. Soon they were both crying and swaying back and forth, moaning, lamenting. This went on for some time. I finally sat down in one of the chairs in the station house and waited for the storm to pass. When it did, Mrs. Feliciano also refused to sign a complaint. Her reason? She said she was afraid Tito might hurt her daughter if she did. Daisy once again tried to explain the patently obvious, that Tito had *already* hurt her daughter. But that didn't matter.

I looked at my watch—1:30 p.m. And that's when I remembered my lunch date with Tracy.

8

I had never met my attorney. His name was Arnold Gluck and he came recommended by the teacher's union referral hot line. I wasn't certain about any of this business. All I knew was that we all—Marlyn and her attorney and Arnold and I—would meet in a conference room on the second floor of the Waukegan court building to discuss terms. I was lucky enough to get a parking spot on the street, but two guards made me empty my pockets and take off my belt as soon as I entered the building. They put these through the x-ray machine. The female of the pair told me that last week they had caught someone smuggling a razor blade in his belt.

I said, "Imagine that," as I collected my change from the plastic tray and put my belt back on.

The second floor was crowded and hot and I'd never seen so many briefcases and trench coats in my life. There were courtrooms with trials ongoing. Every once in a while a door would open and someone would slip out and for a moment you could hear a lawyer say, "Your Honor—" and then the door would close.

When I got dressed that morning I could not button my collar. For the past twenty years I'd worn a fifteen-and-a-half-inch collar, and then I woke up one morning with a sixteen-inch neck.

For my first divorce I hadn't even had to show up at court. Of course that was because I let Shelly, my ex-wife, have everything, and we didn't have children. This time it was different. This time I actually had something to lose—my kid, my house, my pension and 401k, Marlyn. I was surprised that she was pushing things along so quickly. For a while there I thought we might have had a chance, but no. She said she wanted to get this over with, as if it were a trip to the dentist to have something removed. There was nothing to do now but watch all

137

the lawyers assure their tense looking clients, and I had plenty of time to think about all the things I would have rather not thought about—mostly the future, which from my vantage point looked something like a big, blank space straight ahead. Forty-four years old and everything up in the air. And a fat neck.

"Hello, Johnny."

I turned and found Marlyn beside me. She was wearing a long black leather coat and a navy slacks outfit. Behind her was her attorney who was not introduced to me. He was a tall man with a face like an eagle's and a comb-over. He wore a gray pinstripe suit and cowboy boots.

"Is your lawyer here?" Marlyn asked.

"He could be. I've never met him."

Cowboy boots.

Marlyn's attorney said, "Come this way," and escorted her, encircling his arm around her, to an empty conference room. Things were getting off to a bad start. There was nothing else for me to do but follow them. So far divorce court felt like the first day of sixth grade in a new school.

It was a small room with one imitation mahogany table and six chairs spread around it. Marlyn's lawyer let his valise fall upon the table with a thud. He opened the locks and withdrew several copies of a paper-clipped document and slid one toward me. I had not even sat down yet.

"I'm Mitchell Arnoff and I represent Mrs. Spector in this divorce action against John Spector. I assume that you are John Spector and that you've secured counsel."

As I've grown older I've tried to resist forming hasty first impressions of others, however a couple words did come to mind. I sat down. I crossed my legs. "Yes," I said.

Mitchell Arnoff looked at his watch. "Well, I hope he'll be here soon. I have a three-thirty court appearance and I can't be late." He slid a chair out for Marlyn and she thanked him. "Not at all," he said. Then to me: "What's your attorney's name?"

I did not want to answer that question, because when I did, it would sound like *Arnold Gluck.* So I said, "I've engaged the Feldstein-Rebner firm. I'm not certain who they're sending over."

"Never heard of them."

One of the words that had come to mind just a while ago was *arrogant*.

Marlyn removed some lint from the sleeve of her suit. Mitchell Arnoff looked at his watch again and sighed. We sat there like that for a good several minutes.

Presently a short man with red hair and a worn, unwieldy briefcase knocked on the open door and said in a surprisingly high-pitched voice, "Spector vs. Spector?"

Spector vs. Spector, I thought. That was really what this was all about. It sounded like the title of a very domestic wrestling bout, our marriage, our entire relationship, reduced to the jargon of the WWF.

The short man set his briefcase down on a chair, struggled a moment or two with his trench coat, and announced what I had been afraid of. He was Arnold Gluck. He extended his hand to Mitchell Arnoff and said, "Mr. Spector?"

I raised my hand. "Over here," I said.

When the initial confusion was settled, Gluck sat down beside me and opened his battered case, which still sat upon a chair. He extracted a manila folder and placed it to his right upon the table. From his front breast pocket he took a pair of black-rimmed eyeglasses and ran his finger down the first page of the Arnoff papers. Occasionally he said to himself, "Uh-huh. Uh-huh."

Arnoff said, "I'm sure you'll find the court papers in order. Following are a list of assets held in common, and following that you'll find our demands on behalf of Mrs. Spector."

Arnold turned the page and ran his finger down that one, too. Then the next. He nodded. At last he took off his glasses and threw them on the table. He reached for his manila folder and removed from it yet another set of papers. This he slid across the table to Arnoff, who had remained standing all this time. Arnoff skimmed the first page, the second, while Gluck rubbed his eyelids with his fingertips.

"I've just submitted to Mr. Arnoff our counterproposal, Mr. Spector. Your wife is asking for sole ownership of the house, along with thirty percent of your income, fifty percent of your retirement funds, and in addition she wants you to pay for her attorney's fees and your son's college education. I'm assuming you'll find this unacceptable."

Marlyn was a lot of things, but she was not a thief. I knew her lawyer must have talked her into playing hardball.

I said, "Marlyn, is that true? Is that what you think is fair?"

Arnoff got to his feet and snapped, "You will direct your questions to me, Mr. Spector."

"Like hell, I will. Marlyn? Is that really what you want?"

Arnoff said, "Counsel, please advise your client to address his questions to me, or I'm afraid we're leaving."

Gluck said, "Mr. Spector—"

I got up and walked over to Arnoff, stood face to face with him, looked him up and down. Then I smiled and said, "Why don't you take a fucking hike, Tex."

His face reddened and his jaw clenched tight; for a moment I believed he was going to take a swing at me, but instead he snapped shut his briefcase, lifted it off the table, and said to Marlyn, "Come on, Mrs. Spector."

Marlyn got up, shaking her head. A few seconds later Arnoff bounced back into the room just long enough to say, "I'll see *you* in court, you son of a bitch." The door slammed shut.

Gluck just sat there looking at me. His hair was mussed up and his feet barely touched the ground. He looked as though he was going to bar mitzvah practice. At last he said, "That was very nice, Mr. Spector. Very nice."

"He must be sensitive about his boots," I said.

§

The next morning at school I set the metal detector off again when I went through it. Oscar, the security guard, told me to empty my pockets and I said it was just my cell phone. But when I stuck my hand in my windbreaker pocket, out came Fernando's goddamn stiletto.

I said, "I'll be damned. How did that get there?"

"Come, you know the rules." Oscar grabbed me by the arm and began escorting me up the escalator. He was a short man, but he had a well-developed upper body and a hell of a grip.

I pulled my arm away from him. "What rules?" I said.

"Any weapons, we call police."

I said, "For Christ's sake, Oscar. Do you really think I intended to sneak a knife into school?"

"Rules are rules."

No wonder teenagers hated us.

Danny Velez's office had been newly furnished. No more plaid fabric upholstery. Now there was a teal leather couch, a contemporary Italian chair, and an ultra-contemporary Italian coffee table/settee. He did not use the industrial fluorescent light fixtures, but preferred a shaded table lamp and art deco floor lamp. It occurred to me that his vistas were widening rapidly.

He walked into his office wearing a stern expression and another suit that was too large for him. This one was steel blue. He shut the door with a flourish and then made a big production out of staring at me with what I supposed was disapproval.

"You are in big trouble, Mr. Spector."

Story of my life. I crossed my legs. My jeans were more wrinkled than I had realized. I'd taken a personal business day yesterday, and when court was finished I spent the rest of the afternoon in my new digs with a bottle of Johnnie Walker Red. After that, who cared if their jeans were wrinkled?

I said, "I'm a little old to be listening to lectures, and you're too young to give me one, so why don't you just throw the book at me and be done with it."

He pulled the stiletto out of the breast pocket of his suit coat. For a second I thought maybe we were going to have a knife fight. He threw it on his desk. I'm certain he hadn't meant for it to, but it popped open, and when it did, he gave a little jump.

"May I ask why an Acosta teacher needs to carry an illegal weapon to school?"

I said, "I forgot that it was in my pocket. I confiscated it from a kid last week."

Danny's eyes widened. "You confiscated a weapon from a student at school and did not report it or turn it in?"

"Not at school. At my apartment."

"You have students in your apartment? This is not permitted, Mr. Spector." He wagged a stern and foreboding finger at me. "But I can't say I'm surprised, not after what you did yesterday."

I said, "Look, the kid was helping me move. Don't try to make it sound like that. And what do you mean, what I did yesterday?"

He was pacing dramatically back and forth behind his desk. He wore pointy black shoes (the kids called them *roach killers*) and I noticed his feet were very small. "You took two young girls off campus and drove them in your car. Is that not right?"

I said, "How do you know that?"

He stopped pacing abruptly and grabbed the back of his chair tightly with both hands. "The mother. She called. She wanted to be sure we did not report the boy to the police."

I was going to have to thank Mrs. Feliciano for that. I said, "Well, he should be reported to the police. If we were doing our jobs—"

"Doing our jobs! If you'd been doing *your* job you would not have taken two girls out of class, off campus and into your car without permission." He was now pounding a fist into his open hand as he enumerated my transgressions.

"Danny, you make it sound like we were having a party. The girl had been punched by her boyfriend. Her mouth was swollen and bleeding. I got her medical attention first and then tried to get a warrant sworn out against the offender. I did what any parent would have done in that situation."

He spun toward me and bent over his desk. "Are you her parent? Are you?"

I'd once had Johnnie Walker Blue Label—it's a fine scotch, very smooth, but it's two hundred dollars a bottle. If I'd had that last night, maybe my hangover wouldn't have been so severe, and then it wouldn't hurt so much to listen to Danny's harangue.

"No, Danny," I said, "we both know I'm not her parent. But I'll tell you something—if I were, I'd want a teacher to do for her just what I did, to hell with the rules."

Danny was now examining one of his cufflinks. It was polished silver and it held in place a cuff starched as taut as a priest's collar. "Mr. Spector, do you know what I could do to you because of your reckless actions?"

"I have a pretty good idea, yeah."

He was pacing again, but now he had his hands clenched behind his back, like a prosecuting attorney putting the screws to a guilty defendant. "I could have you arrested right now—one call to the police. That's all it would take. I could report you to the district superintendent and have you removed from the classroom, suspended indefinitely, or else sitting down at the district office, doing nothing."

That didn't sound like such a bad gig. But that's not what I said.

What I said was, "What the hell. It's your call, Danny."

Now he came around to the front of his desk, slowly, and looked down at me inquiringly. "Do you do these things deliberately? Do you *want* to be taken out of here?"

I said, "Why would I want a thing like that?"

"Exactly. Why?" He sat on the edge of his desk now, and I saw that he wore transparent blue silk socks. He had little or no hair on his legs. "And from now on, Mr. Spector, I want you to address me as *Mister Velez*. Is that understood?"

My cue to leave. "Sure," I said, standing. "But I still think that anyone who is a parent would have done exactly what I did."

A little vein stood out on the side of his forehead. He ran a hand back through his hair and rubbed the back of his neck. "I know what you think. Please, get out of here now."

This was not just about taking Hilda and Daisy off campus. It was about falling in line with the new political agenda, and I knew it all the more when I opened the door to leave and discovered Isabelle Villachez standing outside her office door, watching me like a sentry. I turned back for a moment and pointed at the stiletto. "Hey," I said. "Be careful with that thing. You could hurt yourself."

§

"You're not supposed to close your eyes when you're trying to catch the goddamn ball," Jorgé instructed Lucy. He'd been hitting pop-ups to her, and so far she had not managed to catch one.

Lucy strutted off the field in a fury. "You tell him to talk to me with respect, Johnny, or I ain't playing."

Jorgé let the bat fall to the ground in disgust. I walked over to him and slapped him on the back. "Look, have a little patience. Go show her how to do it."

"Shit, man. If we put her in the field, we gonna lose, brother. She couldn't catch a cold."

"We've only got eight players, Jorgé. Go over and make up with her and show her how to do it. And be nice."

Jorgé said a dirty word and went off to talk to Lucy.

We were on the baseball diamond on the south end of the park, Vince's team along the first base line, and mine on the third base line. It was a pretty sad little field, but you couldn't have asked for a nicer October day—sixty-seven degrees, a sky that looked like the ocean. I had Nelson and Phil warming up as pitchers because I didn't want Vince to see the kind of dynamite Fernando could throw, not at first, anyway. I'd drafted all my regulars, and at the last minute I gathered some of my English students, Alfredo Munoz, Pedro Ruiz, Chico Martinez. Chico was a half-black, half-Puerto Rican power hitter, and the others weren't bad either, though I'd had to bribe them all by promising to show a movie in class at the end of the week. And I had Tracy as assistant coach. She'd insisted, in fact. She knew absolutely nothing about baseball, and nobody seemed to care. I watched as she played catch with Lico, and thought about what a difference she seemed to make in his life. She'd devoted herself to him, and I think that's what made me certain that she would become a good teacher. She had it.

"After my team wins the game, maybe you and I could pick up a couple of chicks, buy a six pack, and go to the beach." Good old Vince. He'd walked over to scout out my players, especially one of them. Tracy fired a ball wide to Lico, and he went running after it. Vince pulled his green visor lower on his forehead and shook his head. "Man—I don't know how you get any teaching done with her in the classroom."

"Vince," I said, "I'm a professional."

"A professional liar. And it's an unfair advantage—having an assistant coach."

"Yeah, but she throws like a girl."

"Boy, she sure does."

A breeze stirred and brought a flurry of golden leaves our way. Deep autumn. I thought of my boy at football practice, and of the empty space in bed beside me last night. My old life seemed so far away now, and at times I had to fight the sensation that I was sliding downhill.

"How are the wife and kids, Vince?"

He turned his head toward me and squinted under the visor. "They're fine. You seen Jason?"

I shook my head. "Not much. I saw Marlyn yesterday, though."

"Yeah?"

"Yep—in divorce court. Met her lawyer, too. He's quite a prick." That was the other word that had come to mind.

"Well, he's a lawyer, after all. Whadaya say we have a drink after the game?"

"I'd like to, Vince, but I'm giving Tracy a ride home."

I could feel his eyes on me. He let the silence stretch and then: "You know, sometimes I can't tell if you're a credit to mankind, or a low down dirty dog."

Tracy took public transportation because she didn't like to leave her BMW in Humboldt Park, where it was an advertisement for free spare parts. I had said I would give her a ride. But this is not what Vince wanted to hear or believe, so I just gave him a shot to the shoulder and told him to get ready to have his team's collective ass kicked.

We lost the coin flip and took to the field. Vince had some little Pentecostal girl with long hair and an even longer dress keeping score. She asked me as I stood on the sidelines what the name of our team was.

"We have to have a name?"

"Si. Señor Arcelli's team, they're called the Comets."

"He must have stayed up all night to come up with that one." I thought about it, and nothing much came to mind, except what I'd had for breakfast, so I told her we were the Flying Bagels.

"*Bagels?*" she said, because of course she'd never heard of bagels before.

And I said, "That's right, and we're damned proud of it."

I probably shouldn't have said *damned*—she cringed when I did— and I thought about how odd it was to worry about a thing like mild profanity when you lived so close to dangers that could *really* hurt you.

Daisy could shag ground balls like nobody's business. I put her in at shortstop and she did a swell job. But Vince's Comets had some heavy hitters, and by the end of the first inning, they were up two to nothing.

"When you gonna put me in, Johnny? We gonna lose the damn game if we don't get some strikeouts." Fernando—who at first had not really cared too much about after-school games—was hooked. His sense of competition had kicked in, as I had hoped it would.

"Strategy, Fernando. We're going to give Mr. Arcelli the fourth inning surprise of his life."

"Fourth inning! Shit, Johnny—we'll be fuckin' *toast* by then."

"Just take a look at his face after your first pitch. And do me a favor, will you?"

"What?"

"Watch your fuckin' language."

145

Fernando chuckled, gave me a low-five, and I looked around to make sure that the Pentecostal girl was out of hearing range. I didn't want to send her into apoplexy.

Lucy struck out, but Daisy knocked a double into right field. That brought up Chico, and the best hope for a two run score that we'd seen yet.

"This was a very good idea," a voice at my side said.

Tracy. She was wearing a white, short-sleeved knit turtleneck and a pair of Levis. She stood so that her shoulder touched my arm.

"It was Vince's idea," I said. "I can't take any credit for it."

"You like Vince, don't you?"

"Sure," I said. "Vince is a great guy."

"Tell me about him," she said.

Where do you start? I said, "Well, he cares about his kids, and his kids at home. He's got a sense of humor. He knows which parts of this job are bullshit, and which really count."

The wind blew her hair onto her forehead and she brushed it back with her hand. "You don't respect most teachers."

"No," I said.

"Why is that?"

I don't know what it was called, but I remembered her perfume from the night of Angel's wake. My Jeep had smelled of it for a day afterward. I hadn't minded. Not in the least. "Think back," I said. "How many teachers did you respect when you were in high school?"

She looked up as though she were trying to remember something, and once again smoothed some fine blond strands of hair back. "I don't know. Most, I think."

I smiled. "You were some little honors snot, I'll bet."

"And what's wrong with that?" She rubbed the toe of one of her Keds absently against the ground.

"Nothing," I said. It just figures."

"You judge people," she said. "You judge them awfully harshly."

"Yes, I do. You spend enough years with people and it becomes obvious who came into this job with natural talent, and who should be working in a hardware store somewhere."

"I'll bet," she said, her eyes glinting in the sun, "that you think most of them *shouldn't* be here."

"Since when do you know what it is I think?"

Just then Chico knocked the ball almost literally out of the park, and my Flying Bagels cheered him around the bases, just like kids anywhere else, my kids. Tracy jumped up and down beside me, clapping her hands together, and then she turned and threw her arms around me.

"Oh, my God," she said, letting go, backing up. "I'm sorry."

She glanced up at me and smiled and then looked back at Chico crossing home plate. Her fingers were intertwined with the chain link backstop, and when seen from profile, each of her facial features competed for most valuable player. I did not want to think about her beauty, but for a moment I found it difficult to think about anything else.

There was the rest of the universe, and then there was Tracy Singer. *Somebody buy me a drink,* I thought.

At the end of the inning, despite Fernando's protests, I put Nelson in once again as pitcher. The idea was to keep Fernando a secret as long as possible, let the Comets become overconfident, but by the end of the second inning, we were down by three runs. Daisy picked up her fielder's mitt and pulled me, literally by my arm, aside.

"We ain't gonna win this game unless you let Fernando pitch—*now.*" She was in her Daisy stance—hands on both hips, head tilted at me menacingly.

I said, "Is that your professional opinion, Slugger?"

She pushed me backward with both hands and popped her gum. "Yeah—and I got another professional opinion for you. Stay away from her," she said, nodding toward the sidelines, where Tracy stood.

"Stay away from who?"

"You know who. She's tryin' to play you, Johnny. Don't be a fool."

She marched onto the field and I thought, *How do you like that?*

I put Fernando in, because honestly, I was afraid not to. He struck out the first two batters and nailed the third by catching a high pop-up. Vince made a beeline toward me from across the field. You could almost see smoke in his wake.

"What the hell did you do—hire a major leaguer?"

"Vince—I swear. I didn't even know the kid could pitch. My other pitcher blew out his arm, is all. What are the chances?"

He tugged at his visor and jabbed at the air with his forefinger. "You're a low-down, dirty, lying son-of-a-bitch dog, Spector."

I said, "How many cases of scotch did we decide on?"

147

I'd never seen Vince that angry before. He turned and walked heatedly back to his players, saying, "The game ain't over yet."

Yes, it was—and he knew it. The rest of it was just a formality. Lucy was the starting batter, and I was huddled over her, trying to explain how to bunt, when Tracy said, "Johnny—isn't that Kirk?"

I straightened up. On the far corner near Sacramento and some side street stood Kirk Douglas Perez, talking to the driver of a parked, late-model black Mustang. Kirk had never returned to school after his fight with Fernando, and now he turned up on that corner where Tony Calderon made his livelihood. Jorgé called to me, asking where I was going, but I paid no attention. I passed a pocket of Disciples—you couldn't miss the black-blue sweaters—and walked alongside a small lake. I remembered a story about a kid who dove into that lake drunk, how he hit bottom and broke his neck and became paralyzed. The park had a lot of stories. As I came nearer, the Mustang took off, burned rubber. Perhaps they thought I was an undercover cop.

"Hello, Kirk."

He looked at me out of glazed eyes, raised his chin somewhat. "Johnny. What're you doin' here?"

Guiso stepped out of the gangway of a three-story apartment building. He wore a long coat, a do-rag, and had both his hands in his pockets. "Yo, teach. Whatup?"

Ratman. You didn't have to guess how he'd gotten that name. I said, "Hello, Guiso. I wanted to talk to your brother."

"Yeah? What about?"

I said, "Well—I'll just tell him, if that's all right with you."

Guiso was big and imposing and walked slowly toward me. "Anything you got to say to my brother, you can say to me."

Wasn't that funny, I thought, *he sounds just like Marlyn's attorney.*

I stepped around him and faced Kirk. "When are you thinking of coming back to school?"

Guiso said, "I told you—"

"Stay out of this, Guiso. This is between me and your brother." Kirk was rubbing his face with his hand. I turned back to him. "Kirk— you're still on the books. I can talk to the teachers of the classes you've missed, make sure you can still pass the semester."

Guiso reached his hand toward me and I spun away from him. "Man—" he said.

"You touch me and I'll have you busted so fast your fuckin' head'll spin for a week. You understand me, Guiso?"

"You got no business comin' here, talkin' shit to my brother."

He was high; they both were. That far-away zombie stare in Kirk's eyes was about enough to break my heart. Guiso. That son of a bitch.

I said, "Your brother is fifteen years old—too young to drop out of high school. I've got every right in the world to come and bring my students back to school. You're breaking the law, keeping him out. That's something else I can get you busted for."

"You get the *fuck* outa here," Guiso shouted, "or I'll get my boys and we'll just *see* who gets busted 'round here."

Kirk stepped in front of him and held out his hands. He said, "Guiso, please."

I stared Guiso down. It was imperative. You flinch and a gangster will do just what he promises to. "You picked a fine role model, Kirk. Now you can grow up and be a junkie, just like your brother."

"You get your fuckin' white ass outa here," Guiso said, flailing his hands in gang signs. "Nobody wants you here, motherfucker."

You win some, you lose some. Lately it seemed like I lost a lot more than I won. I turned around and walked back to the park while Guiso hurled obscenities at me, one after another. *White faggot motherfucker. Dick face.* Once again, what first looked like a good idea turned out to be something else.

When I got back to the diamond, the game had stopped and Vince was talking to Ed Faber, the head of the PE department. *What is it now?* I wondered. The kids were standing around looking on earnestly while Ed poked an index finger against Vince's polo shirt.

Tracy said, "It's just a game, Mr. Faber."

"I don't care about that, missy. This field is not to be used for organized school functions unless they are cleared with the department first. I want you all outa here now."

As I came walking up behind him I said, "What's the problem, Ed?"

Ed had never liked me. We had gotten into it my first year of teaching—something about making his star hitter stay after school to make up a test. He was John Wayne. He wasn't going to let that happen.

He folded his arms against his chest. "Spector. It figures. Get these kids outa here now. I already gave my explanation to your gumba here, Arcelli. I'm not goin' over it again with you."

I looked over at Vince, saw him bristle. I said, "Ed, the field wasn't booked for anything else. We're not hurting anything here."

Ed had wispy gray hair, a flabby middle, and big pores across his nose. I could remember when he used to intimidate me. Now he was just pathetic. "If you don't do what I say, I'll go to Velez."

I said, "You can do that if you like, Ed. But I wish you'd reconsider and just let us finish our game."

He stared at me, then at Vince, then back at me, as if he were suddenly confused. "Do any of you people understand what rules are? In order to use this field, you gotta fill out a requisition, and the requisition has to be approved."

Lucy stood in left field, looking worried. Fernando and Jorgé were just behind Ed on the mound, laughing behind their mitts. Jorgé said, "*Pendejo.*"

Ed snapped around when he heard that and said, "What did he say?"

He had picked up no Spanish in all his years at Acosta High . "He just said *pendejo*, Ed, which means, It's a shame we can't finish our game. It sure is a *pendejo*, all right."

To this Fernando added, "*Gran cabron.*"

I said, "Yes, and it's a *gran cabron* as well—big disappointment. It's a *pendejo* and a *gran cabron*. Come on, Ed. What do you say? We'll be out of here in half an hour. I'll fill out the paperwork next time. You have my word."

The big old man rubbed the stubble on his chin and frowned. He had wanted to tangle with someone and blow some hot air, was all. His lower lip quivered the way old people's do sometimes when they're confounded, and he said, "One half hour, that's all." He looked at each of us again in that bewildered manner of his, and then trudged back to the PE building on knees that had no bounce. It was painful to watch him walk.

Vince said, "How do you like the nerve of that guy? Now I'm a gumba."

I said, "You've always been a gumba, Vince. Now, how about we play some ball?"

The afternoon waned as the sun sank below the roofs of buildings, battered buildings that stretched out to the west side of town, and melted in a gray autumn haze at the horizon. Strident voices filled the air with delight and derision, my streethearts, rounding the bases, feet pounding the leaf-thick ground. Out of habit I estimated the rush hour traffic back to Deerfield at this late hour, until I remembered that I didn't live there anymore. That awful empty room waiting for me.

"Vince will get over it, won't he? I mean, he won't stay mad at you." Tracy and I were walking through the park to my car in the soupy twilight and I wished we might just stay there for a while together.

"Vince hasn't got an angry bone in his body. He just doesn't like losing."

Fourteen to six. He wouldn't speak to me for a week.

Tracy said, "What's wrong with that Mr. Faber?"

I said, "Got an hour or two?"

Two Spanish Cobras stood together near a park bench sharing a joint. You could identify them by their colors—black and green. One of them played the bench like a conga, his hands a blur above the bare boards. The smell of marijuana rode the air, and I thought about all the years I had spent at that school, and all the kids I'd taught. Where had they all gone?

"Anyway," Tracy said, "you handled it well. I was surprised you didn't get into a fight with him."

"You've got to choose your fights," I said, as we entered the parking lot. "You can't fight with Ed. It wouldn't be fair—like playing chess with an idiot, or arm wrestling an amputee. Hey, how would you like to—"

We had come to my Jeep, but I lost the rest of my thought. Something was wrong here, though it took me several moments to process what it was. No wheels. My Jeep had no wheels. It stood on rows of bricks, balanced the long way. If you sneezed, it would topple over.

"Son of a bitch," I said, circling the vehicle. "They even took the spare." There was a gaping empty circular space above the rear bumper. Still I struggled to comprehend. It looked so . . . so *stationary*. All set to go nowhere.

Tracy said, "I can't believe they did it in broad daylight."

"Son of a bitch," I said again.

I called a service station from my cell phone, but they said they couldn't do anything until the morning. By that time, they wouldn't have to do anything—there'd be nothing left. I took a long last look at my old ride. Bricks, for Christ's sake.

"You don't have to do this, Johnny. I can get home by myself."

I'd walked Tracy to North Avenue, and we'd taken the Western Avenue bus. Across the aisle from us sat a woman with Native American features and a nylon scarf over her head. She stared gravely before her and never turned her head, seemingly never blinked. At Armitage we passed the Cole Taylor Bank, where my father had once worked, and Margie's Candies, where I'd once had lunch with an old English teacher of mine, before I discovered he was gay. He'd said to me, "Anal intercourse is a gas," and still I didn't get it. So young. So naïve.

I said, "I'm not going to let you go home by yourself at night."

"But you'll have to come all the way back again."

"You're doing me a favor. Otherwise I'd be cooped up in that little apartment, all night, bumping into things."

Tracy grasped my hand. I did not try to pull it free. "You're sweet," she said.

"Don't let me fool you."

What I'd begun to ask her before the sight of my wheelless Jeep stopped me was if she'd like to have dinner with me. As we'd walked down North Avenue and I was a little less stymied, I got the full question out this time, and she'd said, yes, she'd love to. We rode the Western bus through the October night, through that battered part of town, past St. Elizabeth Hospital, and got off at Division Street. I figured we'd take the Division Street bus straight down to Rush Street and have our pick of trendy restaurants, filled with trendy people. The temperature had fallen. Tracy wore only a nylon shell jacket over her short-sleeve top and she shivered slightly with her arms wrapped around herself as we stood under the transparent plastic bus shelter. I remembered why I hated taking public transportation. It was because of the relentless hope that every pair of approaching headlights belonged to your bus.

"Do you want my jacket?" I asked her.

"No. I don't want you to be cold. Is that our bus?"

I'm far-sighted, which meant that my hope was dashed a good block sooner than hers was. "No. That's a minivan."

She said, "Did you see how well Lico was getting along with the others?"

I said, "Yeah. He's really coming along. You've done very well with him."

"I can't stand to think of what they did to him, is all."

"I know," I said.

"Fernando too," she said. "He's not as angry as he was. He looks up to you, you know—kind of like a father."

I thought of Jason. It used to be so comforting at night to know he was just down the hall in his room, safe, either studying or playing video games.

Another pair of headlights drifted toward us—not a bus, either, a car, a rusted, gold Buick. It slowed. I thought perhaps somebody was going to ask for directions. I did, that is, until I saw the passenger, both his arms extended out the window, muscled, dark, a gun aimed directly at us, his face half-concealed in shadow. All this in what felt like slow motion, or a dream.

"Down!" I said, but there was no time. Already the gun blasts exploded around us. I threw myself at Tracy, brought her down hard upon the cement, held her beneath me as the blasts continued, three, four, five of them, the plastic shelter shattering, fragments of broken plastic showering upon us. I could feel Tracy's breaths rise, her lungs pumping spasmodically. For a moment, I was too afraid to move, too afraid even to open my eyes. There was the sound of tires squealing against tarmac as the car sped off, and the eerie stillness that followed.

9

The first snow of the season. It sprinkled out of dark clouds as I closed the front door of Tracy's apartment building behind me. 5:30 a.m. I could not go to school in the same clothes, and I needed a shower. I calculated that if I stopped at home first, I could still get to school by 7:45.

And then I thought, *Home*.

Quite a night. By all rights, we should have been dead. The only thing that had saved us was the fact that most gang members are incredibly poor shots. Of course there was always the possibility that Tito had meant only to scare us, and if that was the case, he succeeded wildly.

It had been Tito. I'd only seen his eyes and the wide bridge of his nose, but I knew. And I knew too the measure of his brutality. In order to miss two targets at close range, he'd *still* have to be exceptionally good with a handgun.

One question still mystified me: How did he know I would be there?

I'd made the emergency call on my cell phone, and a squad car had arrived on the scene within minutes. After we'd filled out the police report (once again at the Wood Street station—those guys were beginning to feel like family) we took a cab to Rush Street and had two drinks before dinner. One of Tracy's elbows had been scraped in her fall, and she left the station with a bandage, which half the police force willingly volunteered to apply.

Tracy lifted her second glass of Merlot to her lips. Her hand still trembled slightly as she placed it over mine on the bar. "You could have been killed," she said.

I said, "We both could have." Johnnie Walker on the rocks. I thought about having a third, but after what had happened, I worried that I might collapse out of sheer exhaustion.

"You risked your life for me."

I said, "Don't make me out to be so gallant. I just felt like jumping on you."

She slapped my arm. "Thank you," she said.

I spent the night on her couch. She said it was too late for me to try to get home, that I should get some sleep. That's what she was going to do. We talked for a while in front of a muted TV. She had changed into flannel pajamas and her hair was tied in a pony tail. Her feet were bare and exceptionally pretty. She looked like she was going to a slumber party.

"What are you going to do? After the divorce and everything, I mean."

I said, "Am I supposed to do something?"

She gave a little shrug. "I don't know. When people's lives change, sometimes they make other changes. Are you going to stay at Campos?"

She was starting to sound like Marlyn. "What else would I do?"

"Anything's possible," she said.

And I thought, *Not when you're forty-four, it's not.*

She said, "Use your imagination. You could go to Arizona, be a painter."

"When I try to paint something, it ends up looking like something Pollock threw up on."

"Or—you like helping people; you could join the Peace Corps."

"Yeah—I hear they pay real well."

"It's not all about money."

I said, "It is when you have a kid who's going to college in three years."

Then she looked at me, a long look, and I wondered what it was she was thinking. "You miss him," she said, finally, "don't you?"

I nodded. "Of course. He's my boy."

After she had fixed up the sofa as a quasi-bed and left the room so I could get undressed and slip under the covers, she returned with a glass of milk and placed it on the coffee table.

"What the hell is that?" I said.

"I warmed some milk for you. Help you sleep."

Warm milk would not help me sleep. If you put warm milk into my body, my liver would reject it, just on principle. And then without

155

ceremony or any build up whatsoever, she leaned down and kissed my mouth. It lingered, the kiss, and then she touched the side of my face and said, "Good night, Johnny."

I didn't sleep much, that night.

And now the snow was coming down harder at a northern tilt as I waited on the corner of Armitage for a bus that was taking its goddamn sweet time, the flakes cold against my forehead, wind slashing at my throat. I had a car on bricks, a job on the edge, a former family, and a twenty-five-year-old student teacher who brought me warm milk and even warmer kisses before I went to sleep on her couch. I squinted through sheets of wet snow. Was that my bus?

My insurance covered one hundred percent of the expense for new wheels because there is no deductible for vandalism. That was the good news. The bad news was that during the night someone had ripped the dashboard apart and stolen my CD player. The car would be in the shop for two days, during which time I would be a reluctant pedestrian.

Before class I stopped in the records office to check a student's schedule—kid named Jaime Soto. Betty Frycas kept sending him cut slips and he claimed he didn't know a Betty Frycas. While I was in there, Judy Santiago showed me photos of her new German Shepherd, and Mike Parnell complained about his ulcer. I told him that someone with a job as soft as his had no business having an ulcer, and he must have missed the humor.

"You have no idea of what goes on around here, Spector. Absolutely *nada.*"

My wheels and stereo get stolen and someone tries to kill me at a bus stop, and he thought *he* had problems.

I found Jaime's schedule. He wasn't even in Betty's class. Betty was writing cut-slip fiction. I closed the file drawer and told Mike to keep both his chins up, and he told me to go to hell.

From the back row I watched Tracy teach a sophomore English class. I had a notebook of outcomes assessments on my desk, but I couldn't concentrate on them. At odd moments her eye would catch mine, tarry a moment, as though we held a mutual secret, and then we would both look away. She was twenty-five years old. I needed my head examined. Then Tito popped up and pointed a gun at me and I heard the percussion of each of those shots all over again. When I opened my

156

eyes I was back in the classroom. If this wasn't excuse enough to smoke, what was?

I stood up and slipped out of the classroom, closing the door behind me quietly. I took an elevator down to the lower level where the auto shop was. José DeLaTorre was the auto shop teacher, and he smoked. I found him under a raised Pontiac G6, a grease mark on one cheek. José was around thirty-five, wore black sideburns, and liked the Three Stooges. When I asked him for a cigarette, he said, "You moochers in English. I thought you quit?"

I said, "I did, and I'm going to quit again, right after I have this one."

He gave me a Marlboro and a package of matches with an ad that said, *You can change your life today!* and I lighted up near one of the ground floor exits inside a dim, cold stairwell. I almost choked on the first puff. *These goddamn things should be illegal,* I thought. I grew dizzy in no time. I heard the click of someone's heels coming down the stairs and was about to flick the cigarette away, until I saw that it was Nydia Velazquez.

She greeted me by saying, "Lover, I need to talk to you." She zeroed in on the cigarette. "What do you think you're doing?"

I said, "You'd probably call it smoking, but I like to think of it as *inhalation therapy.* Don't scold me. I had a horrible night, last night."

Of course she wanted to know all the details, but it was a long story, and I'd only borrowed one cigarette. I painted the events in broad brushstrokes, till the cigarette burned down to the filter, and I flicked it away. I left out the part about sleeping at Tracy's place. I also did not tell her about señor Valentin catching me sneak in at six-thirty in the morning. We'd met in the back yard, where the apartment windows glared down at me in familiar disapprobation. I'd mentioned something to him about having car trouble, about having slept at a friend's house, but I don't think he bought it. "You a grown man," he'd said. "You no have to explain to me." But I could see what he was thinking, because his eyebrow would not un-arch.

Nydia said, "What was Tracy doing with you at the bus stop?"

I said, "I had no car. I couldn't let her go home alone."

The door was cracked open a few inches and outside a big delivery truck was backing up to the shipping dock. Two kids dressed in green and black strolled by, one carrying a boombox blaring salsa, a Celia Cruz song. Nydia said, "You're going through a divorce, Johnny, and you're vulnerable. You make a wrong move now, you may regret it for the rest of your life."

I said, "I'm a big boy, Nydia."

"She's twenty-five, Johnny."

"I know what she is. How come you're more worried about her than the kid who tried to kill me?"

Nydia said, "Being dead isn't a problem. Being in a bad relationship is." She tickled my ribs as she said this. "Now, do you want to hear my news or not?"

Some news. According to Nydia, Isabelle Villachez and Elizabeth Mojica were bringing in two leftist activists for an all-school show. They were being billed as motivational speakers, but the message was revolution. Nydia had asked questions when Elizabeth contacted her about booking the auditorium. Nydia was the stage director and all the auditorium business went through her.

"I pretended to be very interested to see how much more I could learn, but Elizabeth wasn't exactly forthcoming. I know that the speakers are being paid, and I'll bet it's going straight into the pockets of the FALN, or the sister group on the island—the *Macheteros*."

I remembered what Shirley had told me about the books—how Mike Parnell was requisitioning checks. I shared this with Nydia, and thought about what Mike had just said a few minutes before, about how I had no idea what goes on here. I supposed that funding revolutionary organizations with public money could be a very good reason for having an ulcer.

Nydia said, "If Mike's writing the checks, Danny stays clean."

I said, "What's in it for Mike, besides an ulcer?"

"Mike gets to keep his administrative post instead of being sent back to the classroom. He only has three years till retirement and two kids in college. His pension amount is based on the average salary of his last three years. An assistant principal makes about twenty grand more than a teacher."

Nydia was in the wrong field. She should have been a detective. Detectives made me think of Tiff, and Tiff made me think of Marlyn in a car with Bruce. A wave of loneliness washed over me as I remembered what it was like to have a family. It's funny, but when you're living your life, you never think the circumstances of it will change, and when they do—well. There you are.

I said, "Can Mike be that stupid?"

"He can be that *desperate*. How can we get a look at the books?"

I wasn't sure I wanted to make this kind of commitment. Whistle blowing was a risky business, and it required so much effort. "Shirley might let me see them. I don't want to get her in trouble, though."

"I'm going to look into the backgrounds of the individual speakers," Nydia said. "I still have friends on the island. See if you can get photocopies of the entries. And if you can, give them to me." She reached out and took both my hands in hers. "And Johnny?"

"What?"

"Be careful."

I gave her hands a squeeze and said that I would, that I wouldn't even try to see the books if I thought I couldn't get away with it, and she said, "I meant with Tracy."

During fifth period I was paged over the intercom system and told to come to the main office. I could just imagine what my colleagues were thinking—*Spector, busted again.* There was a phone call waiting for me, a Sergeant McLellen. They'd picked up Tito. Could Ms. Singer and I come down to the precinct station on Belmont for a lineup, he wanted to know.

I said, "Sure. When?"

And he said, "Now."

I had no car, and Tracy had left hers at home. There were still four periods left, so I had to arrange for a substitute. Normally a request for a sub would go through Danny or Mike. But they would want a reason, and I did not want to have to say, "**Well, you see, Tracy and I have been summoned by the police for a lineup because someone tried to shoot us last night when we were standing alone together in the dark at a bus stop three hours after school let out.**" Instead I asked Ira Hirsch to cover for me, and he agreed, though hesitantly.

"What if by chance Danny Velez walks in the classroom and wants to know where you are?" Poor Ira. He had more worries than I had problems.

"Tell him I'm out joy riding with coeds, or else he might get suspicious."

"I've never been to a lineup before. Do you think it's like it is on TV—two-way mirror and those height charts behind the suspects?"

It was midday, so the bus was not crowded. I folded my transfer and put it in my jacket pocket. "Look, Tracy—I don't like this. I don't like your name on the police complaint. Tito will have access to it. What if he decides to come after you?"

Tracy crossed her legs as she considered this. She was wearing a gray skirt and top and gray pantyhose. Today she looked as if she was in charge of a corporation. "He's already tried to kill me once. I could do nothing and he might try again anyway."

I said, "He's after *me*, not you."

"Yes, but I'm always with you these days. Aren't I?" She reached down and cupped my hand with hers. "Besides, I didn't really get all that good of a look when it happened. I was too busy freaking out. You're the one who's going to have to identify him, and you're the one he's going to be angry at."

There was a comforting thought. She laced her fingers with mine and we sat like that all the way to Belmont.

Sergeant McLellen was a tall man with slightly stooped shoulders and glasses. He had a file on our complaint that included the warrant for Tito's arrest and his rap sheet. *Tito Herrera: three robberies, four assaults, one case of breaking and entering, and two instances of disorderly conduct.* This was his first arrest for public discharge of a weapon and unlawful possession of a firearm.

I looked over the documents and said, "He didn't just discharge the gun. He kind of discharged it *at* us."

"Let's take one step at a time, all right, Mr. Spector?" the sergeant said. "Can I get either of you something to drink? Coffee?"

We both said no, thank you, and in a few minutes another officer led us down a tiled hall to a side room. Inside there were several rows of chairs, much like the TV set up Tracy had speculated about, and before the first row there sat a plainclothesman with a control panel and a microphone. On the floor in the corner I noticed cigarette butts and a crushed white Styrofoam coffee cup. We were directed to sit apart from each other on separate ends of the room.

When the suspects entered, the officer said, they would not be able to see us. We should examine each of them and then write down the number of one we might recognize in connection with the crime. He handed both of us a piece of paper and a stubby pencil. There were a few minutes of anxious waiting during which Tracy and I exchanged brief glances. She had one long leg crossed over the other, her foot bobbing up and down metronomically—all that gray nylon. I thought about the day she first stumbled into the cafeteria, disoriented, so square. And then I thought of last night.

When Sergeant McLellen walked in the room, the door was shut and the lights went on behind the two-way mirror. Several men shuffled into the room, each holding a piece of cardboard with a number on it. Tito was number four. He wore a navy blue Adidas t-shirt and stared defiantly straight ahead. My hand shook as I wrote the number down on the slip of paper and held it out to Sergeant McClellen.

"Take one more look at each of them," he instructed. "Just to be sure."

There was a white male with two day's growth of beard, a short, squat, bald Latin boy, a thin black man with sunken cheeks, and a Latin teenager with black hair. And then there was Tito, arrogant, angry at the world. I once again extended the slip of paper to McLellen. This time he took it.

Tracy shook her head. She couldn't identify any of them.

"That's all right," McLellen said. He then ordered the other officer to have the suspects led back to their cells. The lights in our gallery came up.

I asked what would happen next, and was told that they would document the positive identification and confer with the D.A.'s office. If the D.A. decided to upgrade the charges, they'd notify me. In the meantime Tito would be held until a final decision was made. Then, depending on the charge, bail would be set.

I said, "You mean, the guy who wants to kill me will get out?"

"If he can make bail."

"Well, are you going to give him my address so he knows where to come and shoot me, or are you going to make him look it up himself?"

"Mr. Spector," the sergeant said, "I didn't design the justice system. I just try to make it work."

"Try a little harder, will you?"

Tracy said, "Johnny," and pulled me by the arm toward the doorway while Sergeant McLellen just looked at me, his bored expression set in cement.

Once we were outside she said, "You don't want to go around burning your bridges."

I knew she was right, but it just seemed like such a dumb thing to do—let a guy out of jail, even though they knew he wanted to kill someone. I was going to be nothing more than a target.

I looked at my watch. "It doesn't make any sense to go back to school."

I suggested a drink. I meant just one, but of course there is no such thing, as Dave Volmer often reminded me. We took an 'L' train to the Loop and found a little bar tucked away in a corner on Jackson. It was a dark place with red leather stools, and I had a Bombay Sapphire martini and Tracy ordered a glass of Chablis. We toasted one another and she said, "What should we drink to?"

I said, "To not getting our heads blown off last night."

Then I had an Amstel Light and Tracy had another glass of Chablis. She began to tell me about her sister in New York. Her husband had a consulting business and they kept a horse on Long Island. She was going to visit her in springtime.

I said, "You mean there are more of you?"

"Nope," she said, "just one me."

That was a fact. I remember that for a long time we just looked into one another's eyes, and I thought that maybe something was beginning to happen between us, something special and almost imperceptible, or else we might have just been drunk. Somehow I got the crazy notion to go to the top of Willis Tower and look down on the rest of the city—see it from God's perspective. Twenty minutes later, on the observation deck, one hundred and some floors above the city of Chicago, we stood before floor-to-ceiling windows, gazing down at square patches of land below us. You could see four different states, the tour guide said. For the first time in a long while I felt free—of the high school, of that claustrophobic apartment, free in every sense of the word. It was like remembering how to breathe.

I caught a glimpse of Tracy after having explored the horizon as far as it stretched, and at that moment she looked so proximal in contrast, so immediately beautiful, that I took her in my arms and kissed her. It was a long kiss. And then we kissed again.

I was still holding her when she said, "I didn't know this was going to happen."

"That makes two of us."

A fresh crowd of sightseers spilled out of the elevator, and we suddenly stood apart from each other, as if we hadn't been making out shamelessly in public.

Tracy took my hand and we began strolling down the deck way. "Last night, and now this."

"Now this," I said.

"What exactly *is* this?"

"Hell if I know."

When I left her at the 'L', she kissed me once more and said, "Johnny, call me tonight, all right?"

Her hair blew in the wind as the train approached behind her, snaking its way between buildings. I said, "All right," and then skipped down the stairs to Wabash Street. There was a scruffy man with a beard there who was selling religious newspapers in the shadow of a skyscraper. He had a big cross around his neck, and said he could save me from damnation. I thought, *There's a trick I'd like to see.*

A few days later I got my Jeep back and I drove out to Bensenville after school on a Tuesday. Bensenville is a suburb that the city of Chicago was trying to buy, block-by-block, for the purpose of expanding O'Hare Airport. For some reason it has several gun shops. Leo's Gun Haven looked as promising as any of the others—big yellow sign with a bull's eye. The guy behind the counter was skinny, had a beard and wore a blue baseball cap. I did not know if he was Leo. He said, "What can I do you out of?"

"Looking for a gun," I said.

"Well, pal, you come to the right place."

I knew nothing about guns. Or next to nothing. I knew that if Tito had one and I didn't, odds were in his favor, and I was out to change that. The fellow with the baseball cap asked me what the gun was for. Protection, I said. He recommended a training program that the shop conducted in the shooting range out back, and I thought that was a good idea.

"Semi-automatic, or a revolver?"

I said, "Automatic," because revolvers looked so antiquated.

"Automatics sometimes get stuck."

"So show me one that won't."

He allowed me to handle several different models. I don't like guns and I never have, but the one that felt best was a Ruger .45 Decocker.

It was light—only thirty ounces or so—and the handle was very narrow. Pop in the clip and you were good for eight rounds. At just over seven and a half inches, you could conceal it easily. I knew that you were not supposed to—but tell that to Tito.

I filled out an application for a license and bought the Ruger—cost half a paycheck. There was a ten day waiting period, so I would have to come back to pick it up.

"That there gun could become your best friend," the guy who might have been Leo told me.

"It already is," I said.

A horse named Guilty Pleasures was running in the third race at Bay Meadows at eleven-to-one odds. I don't know why, but I had a feeling about this horse, and I always bet based upon my feelings. When I did this, I usually lost. Jason sat across the table from me at Trackside, a restaurant at the Arlington Park race track in Arlington Heights. He ran his finger down a racing form and checked the television monitor above us. Jason had been going to the races with me since he was just a boy, and was quite the handicapper.

I said, "Which ones look good to you, buddy?"

He sipped some of his Coke. "I'm looking at number four and number seven—Ariel Messenger and Kid Glove. They've run pretty consistently on wet tracks before."

"Want to box them?"

"Yeah. Just a two-dollar box."

I got up and walked to the cashier and bought a two-dollar box on four and seven, and a straight-up ten-dollar wager on Guilty Pleasures. There were still ten or so minutes before the race, so I ordered a scotch on the rocks.

Back at the table Jason was still poring over the race forms. "So tell me about this girlfriend of yours."

Marlyn had not been at home when I picked him up that Saturday, but she had told me when I had called earlier in the week to set this date up that Jason had his first steady girlfriend.

"Her name's Dee-Dee."

I waited, but apparently that was the extent of his response. I said, "And what kind of a girl is she?"

He looked up from the forms. "She's the female kind of girl, Pop."

"No, I mean personality, looks."

"She's got both."

Jason did not like to share personal details about his friends, especially when it came to girls.

A gaunt man with dark glasses and a green ascot sat at a table behind us. He had a tremor in his right arm that made his racing form flap as he held it, as though he were trying to fan a fire.

"So," I said, "is she a sophomore?"

He sucked on his straw till the glass was empty. "What is this, the Inquisition? She's a nice girl. That's the story."

My drink arrived. I ordered another Coke for Jason and sat there twirling the ice cubes with a swizzle stick. He was angry, and he had a right to be. I had not wanted my son to be raised in a broken family. Was that term even used anymore—*broken family*? I had been raised in one, and whenever I'd heard it referred to that way, I had the mental picture of a house with a jagged crack down the center.

"You know," I said, "this business between your mom and me. . ."

He jotted down some numbers. He would not look up. "Let's not talk about it."

To my immediate left was a hefty woman in her sixties with black nail polish and a gold and rhinestone cigarette case. She was reading a newspaper and licked her fingers before turning the pages.

I said, "Sometimes talking about it is good."

"This must be one of those other times, then."

That attitude—I knew where he'd learned it. I just never thought it would come back to haunt me.

The waitress came by with Jason's Coke, and he thanked her. The kid had good manners, was smart, and handsome. I was proud of him, but it was difficult to be locked out of his life like this. He was so distant, and I didn't know what to do to bridge the gap. *If Marlyn would just give me one more chance*, I thought, *or maybe if I got a different job.* But what would I do? What was I *qualified* to do, other than talk about Goethe or semicolons?

"I didn't mean for it to happen," I said, as if thinking aloud.

Watching the monitor, Jason said, "It's not your fault, Pop. Neither one of you can help being the way you are."

"No, I don't suppose we can."

When the race went off the place got noisy—gamblers encouraging their horses by yelling at the monitors. Guilty Pleasures wasted no time going to the back of the pack, but Jason's number four and number seven stayed neck-and-neck through most of the heat, despite the muddy track. Along the far turn, though, number four was outrun by number nine, and number nine finished just behind number seven.

I said, "Well, you were close. You bet a good bet." He did not say anything to this, and I thought it was better for both of us to call off the day. "You'd rather be with your girlfriend, wouldn't you?"

He shrugged. "She asked me to come over. I can go later."

"I'll take you there now."

"No, really."

"Jason, it's all right. Hell, that's where I'd go, if I were you."

Marlyn's car was in the driveway when I drove past the house. I tried to see inside through the blinds, but it was too gray a day for much light to get through. Dee-Dee lived just a half mile away, on Carlisle Street. Big colonial house, three-car garage. Jason gave me a high-five before he got out of the car. "See you," he said. I watched him walk up the walkway. He was getting so big, almost a man, and I wouldn't be there for his last years at home. What I hated most about these awkward visits was that always the last thing I saw of him was his back as he moved away from me.

I had started with scotch and so I thought it would be a good idea to stick with it. I picked up a bottle on the way back to the city and then watched the neat suburban homes give way to warehouses and billboards and smokestacks and was soon swallowed by the urban jungle. The apartment proved too close, so I kept my leather jacket on and brought my cocktail glass out on the porch. It was only about four in the afternoon, not dark yet, but twilight was around the corner. Señor Valentin's back yard was a sad little dead place in November. The sundial sat uselessly off in its corner under bare tree limbs and masses of dark clouds. No time.

"Psst, Johnny!"

Down near the house was Daisy, standing in the driveway. I said, "What are you doing here?"

"*Mira*, I told you I live right down the street. Can I come up?"

I told her of course she could. She skipped up the steps and I slid over on the top one to make room for her.

"What're you doin' out here? Ain't you cold?"

166

Daisy wore a powder-blue nylon parka and jeans so tight they might have been a second skin. She sat down right beside me and snapped her gum once, twice.

I said, "It's a little cold, but inside it's a little small, you know? Too small."

"I came by before, but you weren't home." She tied one of her sneakers and followed this up with, "Where you been?"

I thought it was amusing that she was keeping tabs on me. "Visiting my boy."

"Oh," she said. "That's nice. I'll bet you're a good father, huh?"

I wished people would quit saying that to me. "I'll bet I could be a better one. What's up with you?"

She chewed some on her gum. "I'm bored. Nothin's happening. I called Lucy, but her mom won't let her out."

"Why not?"

She rolled her eyes. "I dunno. Her mother treats her like she's five."

Daisy—woman of the world. I had some of my drink and then asked her if she'd like something.

"Naw. It's cold enough out here. What're you drinkin'?"

"Scotch."

She made a face. "I don't know how you can stand that stuff."

"I'm giving it my best try."

She shivered and drew her hands inside the sleeves of her coat. "Wanna go inside?"

"I don't think that's such a good idea, sweetheart."

"Why? Oh—you mean 'cause of what people might say?"

"Something like that."

"I'm not afraid of no *bochinché*." *Bochinché* is gossip. "Beside—you ought to hear what they're saying about you and Miss Singer."

This was news to me. "Oh? What exactly are they saying?"

"Plenty, brother. They sayin' you two are hookin' up."

I said, "That sounds like what railroad cars do."

"It ain't funny, Johnny." She pouted a bit and concentrated on scraping off some pink polish from one of her fingernails. "Well, are you?"

"Am I what?"

"Hookin' up."

167

I sipped my drink. "Honey, I'm the most unhooked guy in Chicago."

She gave a little snap of approval on her gum. "When she's finished being a student teacher, does she stay at Acosta and be a real teacher?"

I said, "Ms. Singer? No. That's not how it works. She'll apply to other schools, depending on where she wants to teach, and she'll go on interviews if they have openings."

"Good." She had made a little pile of pink flakes on the second step and whisked it away with a brush of her hand. "I don't know what the hell I'm going to be. I'll probably be a hairdresser like my mother."

"You can, if that's what you want."

She looked up at me with big, brown kid eyes. "What else could I do?"

"You can do anything you want to do, Daisy."

"Like what—you think I could be a doctor or somethin' like that?"

I swirled my scotch around the inside of the glass. "You don't do something like that just for something to do. You do it because you want to do it so much, you can't *not* do it. You make plans toward it. You fight for it. Anything you want to do that bad, you can do."

The night had crept up on us, and now we sat together on the top of the steps in the dark that was broken only by cones of yellow light that shone from the street lamps of North Francisco. "What happened with you and your wife, Johnny?"

Marlyn's face swept across my mind. This was the very house she had lived in when we fell in love.

I said, "Damned if I know, kid."

"She was Rican, right, a student of yours?"

I nodded. "Yep. She sure was."

"Man, that's romantic. Nothing romantic ever happens to me."

"Romance is overrated. What you ought to be thinking about is college."

A burst of air shot out of her mouth and she said, "*Col*-lege. Like I'll be goin'. I don't even know how to apply, and my family ain't got no money for college."

Daisy lowered her head. Her right ear was pierced, had two silver hoops. I'd never seen them from behind before. "Hasn't anyone ever sat down and talked to you about college?"

"Nobody talks to me about *noth*ing."

That was probably true, and it could explain her in-your-face attitude, the constant desire for attention. "Well, you and I are going to have a couple of college sessions every week from now on. Teach you all you need to know. What do you say?"

She shrugged. "I guess so."

"Sure. We can get some catalogues from Ms. Ramirez, the college counselor, and look through them, see which schools you might like to apply to. If your family doesn't have money for education, that doesn't matter. You can get grants and scholarships."

"But I don't even know what I want to *do* yet."

I said, "Most young people don't. We'll talk about that, too."

Daisy played distractedly with one of her shoelaces. She had sweet looking hands and a ring on almost every finger, even her thumb. "You think maybe I could be a teacher, like you?"

God help her. I said, "Well, I think you'd be a fine teacher—but I hope not one like me."

We sat there like that, she turning her rings occasionally, me holding my glass, until she unexpectedly kissed my cheek and sprang to her feet. "Thanks, Johnny."

She took the steps two at a time, turning to wave when she reached the bottom. Then she disappeared down the driveway into the nighttime that falls so hard in that part of the city. I touched the sticky spot on my cheek. Bubble gum kiss. I thought of Jason's back when he'd walked away from me earlier that day. My glass suddenly needed a refresher.

"I put in a request with Ed Faber so we could have the field after school today." Vince was entering grades in his standard issue Board of Education green book. Before him was a coffee mug I had not seen before. It had a graph on it, numbered from one to ten, and beneath this were the words, *You just scored a two on my give-a-shit meter.*

"Oh? And is he going to honor our request, or have us run off by the National Guard?"

"He wasn't too happy. He told me he'd just learned what *pendejo* meant."

I said, "Well—now if he ever visits San Juan, he'll know what the locals think of him. Is the game on?"

He was totaling up points with a hand calculator. "My fourth period science class is bad news. This kid has a twenty-eight percent so far. Hm? Oh—yeah. The game's on. I gave Ed a rocket for his grandson. He couldn't seem ungrateful."

"Good. I hope the kid aims it at Ed's ass."

Vince said, "But did you hear what I said about my fourth period class? I'm not kiddin', Johnny. These kids are tough stuff. One white kid hit a black kid in the forehead with brass knuckles, cracked his skull open. Did it right in front of me."

I said, "Vince, what can I say? You're talking to someone who was shot at five times at close range. This is the inner city. Did you have a little lapse? Do you remember where you work, now?"

Vince stood up and walked to the counter and opened his thermos. "I caught a kid in that same class trying to put something into my coffee cup yesterday. I'd turned my back for a moment—"

"You can't do that," I said. "If you bring a drink into a classroom, you can't let it out of your sight for one second."

The coffee steamed from his thermos into his mug. "I know that. I spaced out, is all. You can't be on guard all the time."

I had a pen in my hand and I sat at his little makeshift desk doodling on a yellow legal tablet. "The kid who shot at us may be out on bail next week."

"Yeah? What are you going to do?"

I began drawing little pistols on the lines paper. "I bought a gun, Vince."

"Shit. I don't think I want to hear the rest of this."

"See, the thing is, Vince, you *do* have to be on guard all of the time."

Vince lifted his mug to his lips and then changed his mind and set it on his desk. "Maybe we really have been here too long. Do you ever think of that?"

I said, "I think I've mentioned that to you several times every week for the past fifty-two weeks."

Vince sat staring into his invisible future. "What would we do instead?"

I thought that over. "The way I see it, we could buy a six pack, pick up a couple chicks, and go to the beach."

There was a knock at the door. Vince called out, "Yeah?"

"Vince, is Johnny in there?" It was Shirley. She sounded slightly piqued and out of breath. If she had come all the way up there to find me, something must have been very wrong. I jumped up and opened the door.

"Shirley—what the hell?"

"There's a boy on the phone downstairs for you. He's at the police lock up at Twenty-sixth and California. At first I thought that he was kidding me when he told me his name—Kirk Douglas Perez."

I said, "For Christ's sake."

"You go ahead," she said, fanning her face. "I'm going to wait for my breath to come back."

The elevator took forever. While I was waiting I wondered what they'd nabbed Kirk for. Maybe it was for something minor—driving without insurance. When the elevator door slowly retracted on the second floor, I ran to the main office and called out to the other secretaries in general, asking them which line was for me. Nobody seemed to know, or care, so I started pushing lighted buttons on Shirley's phone.

"Hello?

"Yo, Johnny? It's Kirk. I been busted, man."

"What are the charges?"

There was static on the line and he was mumbling, so it was very difficult to hear him. "Something about a controlled substance, carrying a concealed weapon. Possession of an unlicensed firearm. Shit—they say they're gonna send me to a youth detention facility. You think—you think you can get me out, or call my ma?"

I said, "Listen to me, Kirk. When did they bust you?"

"When?"

"Yes, when. Was it this morning?"

"No, man. I think it was last night. They kept me sitting in the tank, and they kept asking me all these—questions. All kinds of questions, you know?"

The kid was fifteen years old. He was scared and lonely, and he was higher than the Hubble Telescope.

I said, "What kind of questions are they asking you, Kirk?"

"What?"

"I say, What kind of questions? What do they want to know?"

He exhaled a great amount of air in the mouthpiece. "They wannna know where I got the shit. They keep asking about my brother. They want to nail my brother."

171

I thought, *They* ought *to nail the bastard, and then let him hang out to dry.*

"I'll try to do something for you, buddy, but it's going to take some time. You've got to hang in there, all right?"

"I'm gonna get sick, Johnny."

He was going to be the worst kind of sick, withdrawal. "I know. I know you are, but they kind of won't let me bring you a fix, you know?"

"Could you hurry?"

Could I hurry. "I'll do my best, kiddo."

There was a long gap in the conversation. And then he said, "Call my ma, Johnny."

"Sure."

"Tell her not to worry."

"I will," I said, and then without a goodbye, the line went dead.

10

It was crowded and noisy and packed with suits—the lunchtime scene at The Berghoff in Chicago's Loop. I was the only guy in the place with sneakers and a leather jacket, and was generally regarded the way street musicians are on city streets. Everybody was trying to be heard above the general babble, and cute, slinky waitresses in little black skirts zipped in and out of crowds of bodies, as though they were doing some kind of dance.

"Johnny—how are you?"

Glberto Marquez squeezed through the throng and extended an open hand to me. I made an attempt to get up, but my chair was backed up against a wall, and so I simply grabbed his hand and shook it.

I said, "You look terrific, Gilberto."

"I *feel* terrific," he said.

Gilberto had been a student of mine fourteen years ago, an up-and-coming skyrocket of success—honors student throughout high school and college, law school graduate. He'd joined a prestigious law firm, and now he was a district judge. He was half-Mexican, half-Puerto Rican, and maintained close ties to the community. No one could have been prouder of him than I was—except for his parents.

A waitress said something to us I couldn't hear, and Gilberto held out two fingers and said, "Beer."

I said, "You goddamned lawyers. You're with each other all day— you'd think you'd spread out during lunch."

"It's not that we want to be together. We just make most of our deals here where the senior partners can't hear us. So—I take it you've got another kid who's in a jam."

"A bad one, I'm afraid. His older brother runs heroin for the Disciples and uses him as the drop-off because he's fifteen."

Gilberto bit into a breadstick, saying, "He should beat it if he's that young."

"There's more. They caught him with twenty-five thousand dollars' worth of smack and a concealed handgun. Sold some shit to an undercover agent." This is what I'd learned when I'd spoken to Kirk's mother.

"Has his case been assigned yet?"

I said, "I don't think so. They've got him in some youth detention center."

Gilberto reached into the breast pocket of his suit and pulled out a card and a pen.

"You must see something in this kid."

"Yeah, Gilberto, I do. He's really a terrific young man. It's his brother who's got him into this. I'd like to kill the son of a bitch."

"Give me his name, Johnny."

"Kirk Douglas Perez."

Gilberto did not write it down, but just looked up at me.

"His mother is a big movie fan," I said.

"She must be." Our beers arrived and Gilberto had a long pull at his. "I'll see what I can do. You willing to testify on his behalf, character witness, that kind of thing?"

"You bet. Whatever it takes."

I took a moment to look over the menu. Gliberto had it memorized. He ordered a Reuben sandwich and I asked for a burger, medium, and another beer. "I remember when I needed *your* help, once upon a time," Gilberto said, loosening his tie, and unbuttoning his collar button. "I still appreciate it, Johnny."

"What—that? That was nothing."

"Maybe nothing to you, but it helped save my ass, and my career."

Gilberto had gotten into some trouble in college, a misunderstanding. I'd written a letter for him, was all. Apparently it had worked. In any case, he believed he owed me something, although more and more throughout the years it seemed to me it was I who owed him.

I knew he would ask it sooner or later.

"How's your beautiful wife?"

I put my beer glass down and said. "She's about to become my beautiful ex-wife."

"Oh, shit, Johnny. Do you feel like talking about it?"

"I do not. I feel like drinking about it."

"Go easy, *maestro*. The last thing I need is you appearing before my bench for a DUI command appearance."

I said, "I took public transportation here. If I fall down, the most they can get me for is illegal dumping."

The guy at the table next to us said to his companion that they needed someone who could think outside of the box regarding exisiting statutes.

I said, "You guys all use the same script."

"It's all about precedent. They teach us in law school that you can't do anything that hasn't already been done, but if it has, you can do it. Eventually we end up talking that way, too."

I asked Gilberto how life was, and he told me he had been investing in real estate and doing quite well at it. He gave me a tip on a neighborhood that was about to be regentrified—terrific bargains there.

When our lunch was placed before us I asked the waitress for a Johnnie Walker Black Label, and Gilberto gave me a funny look. "How's teaching, Johnny?"

"Damned if I know. I'm too busy getting divorced and keeping kids out of trouble to do any of that."

I noticed he hadn't touched his food, but was simply looking at me. I said, "What is it, Gilberto?"

He folded his hands on the table and I saw that he wore French cuffs with amethyst cufflinks. "Did you ever think of maybe getting away for a while?"

"Many times. Many times. But I've got a kid to put through college and two attorneys who are counting on me for their livelihood." The waitress put my scotch down on the table and I lifted it as in a toast. "Don't worry about me, Gilberto. I've got it all under control."

§

First week in November. It was the ninth inning and Vince's Comets were on top of the Flying Bagels six to five. Two outs and Jorgé was up to bat. The pitch came right over the plate and Jorgé swung *after* the ball was in the catcher's glove.

I said, "What the hell is *wrong* with him?"

Tracy put her hand on my arm and said, "It's just a game. Let them have fun."

"How can you have fun if you don't win?"

Vince's pitcher squinted toward the catcher to read a sign. He wound up, let go, and Jorgé smashed the ball into next week. What I saw next I couldn't believe.

He just stood there.

"*Run!*" I bellowed. The entire team was on their feet shouting at him. He took off at a sluggish trot—and this time he stopped at first base.

I thought I was going to lose my mind. "Don't stop, Jorgé! Run, for Christ's sake!"

So he ran, not to second base, though. He ran straight to the pitcher and tagged up on the mound.

I said, "What is it he's doing instead of playing baseball?"

Tracy just shook her head.

The center fielder lobbed in the ball and the pitcher tagged him out. Inning over. The other team came off the field, but Jorgé maintained his position on the mound. Fernando and Daisy ran out to him and gave him general hell.

"What you doin', man?" Fernando demanded.

Jorgé said, "What you yellin' at me for? You told me not to stay on first! You told me to run!"

"To second!" Daisy hissed. "You're supposed to run to second base!"

Jorgé looked at the angry faces surrounding him. He scratched his head. "Ain't this second base?"

I took one look at his bloodshot eyes and understood. Jorgé was stoned.

My kids were not used to losing. I kept them after the game for a few minutes, huddled in a circle off the first base line. I said, "I think we all learned something here today."

Daisy said, "Yeah, we learned that Jorgé is a fuckin' *pato*."

"Don't you be talking 'bout me like that, girl. I'll show you my *pato*."

"No, wait a minute." I put my arms out to keep them separated. When Daisy was pissed, she was not afraid to use her fists. "We're not going to turn on each other. We're a team."

176

Lucy said, "We're the Bagels, man."

I said, "That's right. We're Bagels. In the long run, if we work together, we'll come out on top. We made some terrific plays. Of course, it would be a good idea not to smoke a blunt before the game, Jorgé. But that was a terrific hit. You won't remember it in the morning, but it was a terrific hit. I'll see you guys tomorrow."

They scattered off into the darkness, heads lowered in defeat, all except for Fernando, who stayed behind with Tracy and me.

"Johnny," he began, "You s'pose I could get a ride?"

Tracy and I had a dinner date, which was not something I was anxious to share with the kids, but I said, "Sure. Any particular reason?"

He lifted his book bag from the ground, slung it over his shoulder. "D's. They're puttin' the heat on me again. It's hard to get home to my ma's crib. My old man, he's out of town visitin' his girlfriend's family."

Priorities. The old man was on vacation while his kid had to run for his life. So many times I wished I could do more for Fernando. When we got back to the Jeep I said, "Now, how does this work?"

"Miss Singer—I should probably ride shotgun, 'cause when we get to the end of my block, I can jump out and book. Johnny, you hit it. Do a U-turn, but don't go by any parked cars. And keep your heads down, both of you."

Tracy said, "My God, Fernando. Do you have to do this every day?"

"Not if I come home late. If I come home late, I can sneak in the back way."

The Jeep was drafty and I turned the heat up on high. There was not much traffic on the side streets, as we rode past the lighted front porches of bungalows and the gloomy gangways of apartment houses.

"Up there," Fernando indicated with his index finger pointed at the windshield. I noticed that he kept one hand on top of a zippered compartment of his book bag. "Shit," he said. "Stop, Johnny."

I pulled over to the curb. "What is it?" I asked.

"That Taurus. That's them. You got to turn around. Take me back to the next block and go down through the alley."

I couldn't make a clean U-turn, and I knew that the driver of the Taurus had seen us, because his lights went on. I backed the Jeep up, got it headed back down the street, and took a right turn on the next intersection. Fernando began to unzip the book bag pocket.

I said, "Are you carrying?"

Fernando took his hand away from the bag. "Johnny, you got to understand."

"No," I said. "*You*'ve got to understand. If you get stopped with a gun, there goes your future. No career, just a rap sheet. You leave that damned thing at home. You hear me?"

"All right, Johnny. All right. Take this alley to the right. That's it. When you get to the next street, don't stop, man. Just go right on through. I'll say *stop* when we get to my crib, and then you get out of here."

I wondered if I should kill the headlights, but decided that that would make us all the more conspicuous. For just a sliver of a second I caught Tracy's eyes in the rearview mirror. They looked like exclamation points.

We crossed the street and continued down the alley, but the Taurus left the curb and came after us.

"Stop! This is it," Fernando called out.

I hit the brakes. The passenger door flew open, and Fernando made a blind dash for his back yard. The headlights of the Taurus bobbed as it came down the alley after us. I shifted into first, second. He was gaining on me and there was nothing I could do. Two rapid, staccato gunshots echoed in the night.

"Keep your head down!" I shouted to Tracy.

"Johnny, they're fucking *shooting* at us!" she hollered back

We were going to die. I was certain of it, but I didn't want to frighten Tracy.

I said, "Why, Miss Singer—the way you talk."

"Shut up and get us out of here!"

The alley ended at the next block. I'd have to take a turn without braking, and the street was lined with parked cars on either side. Another gunshot was fired behind us, a dull crack. I sat down lower, hit the clutch, and made a sharp left. I could feel the wheels leave the pavement momentarily, and then the back passenger side of the Jeep smashed up against and ricocheted off of a parked car. Tracy screamed and I sped down Yates Street, past boarded up buildings, old empty lots. After a series of zigzag turns down alleys and still more side streets, I was fairly confident I had lost them. I pulled over and turned off the lights. There was quiet, except for the steady rattling of the engine. My heart threatened to pound itself right out of my ribcage as I looked over my shoulder at Tracy, sprawled across the back seat on her stomach. She struggled to get right-side up, breathing furiously.

I said, "So, are you more in the mood for seafood tonight, or we're you thinking maybe Italian?"

§

"This poem's too long, Mr. Spector. Shit—it's more like a novel."

Lashaun Matthews. He was an African American kid in my junior English class, the one class Tracy didn't teach. He was talking about Keats's "The Eve of St. Agnes." The students were to have read half of it for today's class, but only a few of them had, as it turned out.

"There's a reason for that, Lashaun. This is one hell of a sexy, romantic poem. It takes time to reach its intensity, you know?"

Alfredo Muñoz, one of my Bagel sluggers, said, "Johnny—I don't think Keats knew too much about romance. They got a picture of him in the book, and I got news for you, dude. He looks like a fag."

Uproar. I should have stuck to "Ode on a Grecian Urn."

I said, "You meant to say a gay man. Let me tell you something about Johnny Keats. He was a short little guy who learned to use his fists early, to protect himself and his little brother. His mom abandoned him and later died, and he carried the family through—became a doctor, and fell in love with a beautiful woman named Fanny. You take my word for it—Johnny Keats knew something about sex and romance."

Lashaun scratched his head with the eraser end of a pencil. "I read this, Mr. Spector, and I didn't see no sex."

At least we were talking about it. If they hadn't been interested, they would have closed their books and taken a nap. "Christ, Lashaun— it was eighteen-nineteen. Keats couldn't come out and blatantly write a sexual encounter—besides, that wouldn't be artistic, wouldn't have depth. He had to write it with subtlety."

"Yeah—whatever," he said.

"No—not *whatever*. Look at the set-up. It's very much like *Romeo and Juliet*. I never said Keats was above borrowing. Hell, even Shakespeare borrowed."

Alfredo said, "But that's plagiarism."

I said, "Yes it is—except when you do it as well as Shakespeare or Keats, then it's called *art*. Dig the plot. You've got a hottie named

Madeline who's fasted all day so that she can pray to St. Agnes for a vision of her future husband. That was the legend—that if you were a virgin, and you followed the steps, you'd go into a supernatural trance."

Alfredo interrupted. "I've put a few virgins into supernatural trances."

"We're talking about Keats's fantasies here, Alfredo, not yours." The room erupted in laughter and chaos and Alfredo gave me the angry sneer I probably deserved. "Now, you've got a poem with a beautiful virgin, you need a handsome romantic man—enter Porphyro."

Lashaun said—"Yeah—who is this guy Porphyro? All I got was that Madeline's family hates him. I didn't get that he was some handsome dude who be making it with the ladies."

I hopped off my desk and began pacing in front of the blackboard. I wrote *conflict* on it with a piece of chalk. "You're right. Madeline's family is having a big party this night—but they hate Porphyro because they have a feud going with his folks."

Someone in the back row yelled, "People!" Folks-People—the two gang alliances.

I said, "Yeah, yeah, yeah. Forget that shit and follow the plot. You'll have plenty of time to beat each other senseless after school. So—Porphyro is desperate for Madeline, and he comes knocking at the door. Angela, the old servant, tries to get rid of him, because she knows his ass is grass if Madeline's parents find him. They'll literally kill him, but he doesn't care. He's got his mind on other things." I pointed to the word *conflict* on the board. "You don't have a problem, you ain't got a story. Period. And, if you know anything about life, problems get worse before they get better. That's called the *complication*." I wrote this word on the board. "These are fiction terms, but they work with lyrical poetry sometimes, too. Keats was a wordsmith, but he was also a storyteller."

Ester Collazo, a thoughtful girl who took class seriously, raised her hand and I called on her. "But what's Madeline doing all this time? Mostly Keats focuses on Porphyro."

"Good. Yes—but go back to stanzas six, seven, and eight. That's where we see Madeline preparing to enter the trance. She's in her room; she can't even hear the music from her parents' party down the hall. 'Full of this whim was thoughtful Madeline / The music yearning like a God in pain / She scarcely heard: her maiden eyes divine / fixed on the floor'. She's out of it. Or, rather, she's just getting *into* it."

"I don't get it, man," Alfredo complained. "How do you know what those words mean?"

I said, "You have to read closely, over and over. It takes practice. The more you do it, the more you enjoy it. Look at those words—'yearning like a God in pain'. What is it about music that can be expressed that way? Yearning means desire, desire as intense as that of a God, a God who wants something so much it hurts. Jesus—that's hot stuff, but notice it's all outside of Madeline's door. *Inside* her bedroom, she's having a spiritual experience. There's another conflict—spiritual versus sexual. Madeline represents spiritual heights, Porphyro—physical or sexual intensity. Everything implies its opposite."

Ester raised her hand again.

"What is it, Ester?"

"What does that mean—everything implies its opposite?"

I shouldn't have gone there; I was losing them. I could hear notebooks closing, pens being clicked. "Well, think about it. Everything has an opposite. Life-death. Day-night. Order-chaos. Male-female. Everything eventually gives way to its opposite. There are moments of intense sexuality, and then there are other times of spiritual uplifting, which is anything but physical."

"But only after someone's married, right? Keats isn't saying virgins should have sex, is he?"

The Church. It ruined literature for kids.

"Keats doesn't say *should* or *shouldn't* about anything. He just gives us poetry and story. This isn't a moral lesson—it's *art.*"

Alfredo said, "How do you know Porphyro is all hot for this Madeline babe?"

I turned the page of my textbook and ran my finger down the column. "Go to stanza sixteen. Look where it reads, 'Sudden a thought came like a full-blown rose / Flushing his brow, and in his pained heart / Made purple riot'. Just before this, Angela has told Porphyro what Madeline is doing upstairs in her bedroom—you know, the whole supernatural thing. And he gets really turned on by the idea. His forehead turns red, he's flushed. In his heart is purple riot—my God. Purple is a symbol for passion, and its no small passion. There's a whole mob of it running around in there. This is hot stuff."

Some kids had their heads down on their arms, others daydreamed out the window. Lashaun looked confused. Ester raised her hand once more, and I called on her, hoping for the best.

"But don't they have sex and then Madeline runs away from her family with Porphyro?"

Miss Anticlimax. "Essentially, yes."

Alfredo said, "Shit—she ruined the plot!" and slammed shut his book.

"I don't think that's right, Mr. Spector," Ester said, looking distressed. "They should have waited until they were married."

I said—"Ester—they could never marry. Their parents hated each other."

"Well, then they shouldn't have seen each other and obeyed their parents."

I just stood there in utter defeat. I turned around, erased *conflict*, and then *complication*. "Okay," I said. "You just took away the conflict, the complication, and now we have no story. What the hell. Who needs literature?"

The tone sounded, saving me once again.

I closed my green book, collected my manila folders of overhead transparencies, and was about to leave when I looked up to see Tracy standing in the doorway. She had her hair tied back today and held several books in her arms in front of her like a school girl, a school girl who looked like Grace Kelly.

"Can I talk to you for a minute?"

She meant *may* she talk to me for a minute, but something in her face told me that this was not the time for a grammar lesson.

I sat on the desk and said, "Sure."

Tracy walked into the room and put her books down on a student desk. She remained standing.

"We were almost killed last night for the second time in two weeks. I was just wondering if you'd given that fact any thought."

I shrugged. "Just twice, huh? Well, you hit a slow period every once in a while. Things will pick up."

She shook her head and looked at the ground before addressing me again. "Being flip doesn't make it better, Johnny. This is not the kind of teacher I wanted to be. I'm starting to understand why the others think you're crazy."

I tossed a piece of chalk in the air and caught it several times. I really could have used a drink. "You don't have to be like me, Tracy. You also don't have to be *with* me. As I recall, it was your choice. I didn't hound you, or make a play for you."

She reddened. "Are you saying I've chased you? Is that what you're saying?"

"No. It's just a statement of fact. I haven't pursued you. If you aren't happy with my company, don't hang out with me. It's that simple."

"It's just that you do crazy *things*, is all. You go too far."

I stood up now and threw the piece of chalk at the blackboard where it hit with a *crack* and splintered onto the carpet. "What crazy thing did I do? Take a kid home so he'd be safe? Drive away from a lunatic who came after us? Did I tell the driver of that Taurus to shoot at us?"

Tracy was now openly shouting at me. "We didn't have to *be* in that neighborhood at that time of *night*."

"No—*we* didn't, but Fernando *did*. Is that it? I should let a kid fend for himself while gangsters try to kill him? I've got a flash for you, Tracy. Go teach at New Trier or Highland Park. You don't belong here. You want a nice, cushy school where you can sponsor the fucking local chapter of the Future Executives Club, a place more suitable for your wardrobe, for Christ's sake."

I picked up my books and began to walk out of the room. Before I got out she said, "How *dare* you?"

I spun around. I lost a little steam when I saw that she was crying. I said, "Don't give me that righteous indignation routine, all right? Spare me the drama."

She wiped her eyes with her fingertips and a black mascara streak ran all the way to her cheekbone. "What would you have done if that driver had caught up to us last night?"

She rubbed the other eye and now had two big swirls of mascara. It was like arguing with a raccoon. "What would I have done? Well, I guess I would have told him a few gangster jokes. You know how flip I can be. Or I would have reached inside my glove compartment for my gun."

Her mouth made a perfect "O" of astonishment. "You have a *gun*?"

"Certainly, I have a gun, and so should you."

"Why would *I* need a gun?"

"Because I know you. You're not going to New Trier or Highland

Park. You're going to stay here, no matter what you say. You *like* the danger—as much as I do. You like the kids, too. You just pretend you're horrified by the circumstances. Gives you an air of decorum. You don't approve, but you like."

"You *are* crazy."

Maybe I was, but I still needed that drink.

"Go fix your face," I said. "You look like Zorro."

I walked out of the classroom and took the stairs down to the second floor, because per usual, the escalators were all running up. I smelled marijuana coming from the boys bathroom and was tempted to stop in for a quick hit. When I got to my office I found Danny Velez standing in front of the door, peeking in through the window. *What does that horse's ass want?* I thought.

I said, "Anything interesting going on in there, Mr. Velez?"

He jumped back instantly, and I noticed he was holding a stack of fliers of some kind. "Mr. Spector, I was looking for you."

I inserted the key in the lock, shoved open the door, and said, "So I saw. After you, Mr. Velez."

He entered my office awkwardly, kept turning around toward me as if he were afraid I was going to hit him over the head with something. I would have loved to.

"I have come about your outcomes assessments," he said.

I rolled a chair over to him and sat down and put my feet up on my desk. I said, "What outcomes assessments? I haven't written any."

"That's why I'm here."

Danny was wearing a khaki-colored suit and it was November. He sat down and placed the stack of papers on his lap. His fingers tapped nervously upon the stack.

I said, "You mean, if I had written them, you wouldn't be here?"

"That's right."

"Well—if I'd known I could keep you away with a couple of assessments . . ."

"Let's not be funny, Mr. Spector."

"All right. Let's not."

He crossed his legs and unbuttoned his suit jacket. It was at least a size too big for him. "You are the only teacher in your department who has yet to turn in your outcomes assessments, and I would like an explanation. I would like an explanation right now."

He wanted an explanation and I still wanted that goddamn drink.

"Let me tell you where the term *outcomes assessments* comes from, Danny. It comes from a process practiced in colleges. A committee from each academic department works in conjunction with the office of research to try to find a rubric that professors can use to evaluate student performance in a given class. The purpose is to attempt to standardize, as much as possible, those evaluations. Now—someone here in the administration at Acosta High heard the term *outcomes assessment* and had no idea what it meant, so that person made up a process about reevaluating lessons plans that don't work. So now we have a mistakenly named, mandatory process that is a complete waste of time, and we use it to reevaluate another complete waste of time. And because I would rather teach than waste my time twice, you're sitting in my office wasting your time and mine."

Danny sat staring at me with no discernible expression. Then he said, "Don't you ever get sick of this, Mr. Spector?"

"Sick of what?"

He stood now and looked down at me. "Of these constant run-ins with authority."

"Hey," I said, "*you* came here to see *me*. This wasn't my idea."

He wanted to kill me. He didn't say so, but you could see it in his eyes. He pulled a flier from the stack and laid it upon my desk. "This is a schedule of English classes that will report to the auditorium on Thursday to hear our motivational speakers. I will expect you to follow it, and I will expect your outcomes assessments on my desk no later than noon on Friday. Is that clear?"

He had great expectations. I picked up the schedule and read it. The motivational group was called *Comrades of Liberation*—a socialist revolutionary group. I said, "This is very interesting, Danny. Does the central office downtown know about this?"

"Of course. They're funding it. And please, Mr. Spector. From now on address me as Mr. Velez."

He walked out and slammed the door after him. The entire office shook from the force.

I turned on my computer and logged on and began writing a letter.

Mr. Marshall Korman,
District Superintendent, Chicago Public Schools
Dear Mr. Korman:

Here is a flier that was just given to me by my Principal, Mr. Danny Velez. He has instructed me to bring three of my English classes to a presentation by a group he euphemistically refers to as *motivational speakers*. As you can probably see in an instant, this group has leftist political interests and has nothing to do with academic concerns.

Mr. Velez assures me that the Central Office knows about this presentation, and he further informs me that the Chicago Board of Education is financing the appearance by The Comrades of Liberation. I find this difficult to believe, but if it is a fact, perhaps you could explain to me how a speech by a revolutionary political organization is a better use of class time than a lesson on world poetry.

In the meantime I'm sure the administration of Acosta High will welcome an inspection of the accounting books, conducted by your offfice, to show where the funding of this presentation is truly coming from.

Sincerely,

John Spector

I picked up my phone and dialed Shirley's extension. Documents generated by my computer were printed in the main office, and this was one I preferred to keep private.

"Acosta High School," Shirley sing-songed.

"Shirley? Johnny. I'm about to print something that I'd like you to pick up right away. Can do?"

"Certainly, Johnny. I have a message here for you from a Mrs. Perez. Something about a boy named Kirk."

I said, "All right. I've got her number. One more thing, Shirley. That so-called motivational group—Comrades of Liberation. I take it they're being paid by one of our academic funds."

"Mm-hm. Mike requisitioned the check just two days ago."

Mike again. How could he let this happen? "Shirley, do you suppose you could photocopy the ledger page of that check for me?"

There was a long pause. "I don't know if that's possible."

I said, "I'll tell you what, Shirley. Think of it as insurance."

"Insurance?"

"If Mike and Danny get caught at this game, everyone who had anything to do with making it possible is going to be in hot water. Mike's name on the requisition will be sort of valuable. Better we can prove who set it up rather than have them point fingers at the little people. Know what I mean?"

"I hadn't thought of it that way."

"You'll try, though?"

"Sure, Johnny."

I hung up the phone and kept my hand on the receiver. If this backfired, I was going to be in it up to my neck. The way I saw it then, though—I was always in it, anyway. Might as well go out with noble intentions. I dialed Kirk's mother's number next, but there was no answer. I wondered what Tahiti was like this time of year, and why I hadn't thought of it sooner.

"I still think it was risky, both of us calling in sick. Do you think they'll put two and two together?"

I said, "If they do, they'll get five. Let them think what they want."

We were in Tracy's BMW heading for divorce court in Waukegan. She had offered to drive, and at first I didn't know what to make of that. Maybe she wanted to be sure I really *was* getting divorced. We'd had drinks after work the day of our spat, and we'd made up. Actually we'd made *out*—parked in the Jeep on the side of North Avenue, for about an hour. Afterward one of my legs was asleep and I had a crink in my neck. I hadn't done anything like that since high school. I was simultaneously appalled at and proud of myself.

"What's your wife like?"

She had both hands on the steering wheel and looked at me every now and then. She reminded me today of Tippi Hedren in *The Birds*. I said, "Keep your eyes on the road."

"Really, though. Does she have dark hair?"

I said, "Why did you want to come with me today?"

She took a deep breath, but did not answer right away. "It seems we both have lots of questions," she said.

The sun was out, but the sky was pale and it was only about thirty degrees. November sunshine was sad and weak and made me think of when I was a kid. I said, "Marlyn is stubborn and smart and very beautiful."

Tracy drove on, down Route 41 through Lake Forest, past bare fields and skeletal trees. "I was curious," she said, "about her. That's why I wanted to come along."

She was lovely, Tracy Singer was. There was something thrilling about her jealousy; it almost took away the pain of losing Marlyn. *Complex, these dances that we dance with one another*, I thought. And then I thought of Kirk, of how he must have suffered through withdrawal. I'd finally reached his mother last night. His court date was set for the end of the week, and though Gilberto would not be hearing the case, a friend of his would, and he had been spoken to. I was spending more time in court these days than I was in school.

I said, "See if you can't talk to Kirk's mother on Friday. I tried to tell her to keep Guiso away from Kirk, but she's in denial about what a bastard he is."

"He's her oldest son," Tracy said. "A mother always sees the best in her children."

"Talk to her, though. You have a way about you."

"Do I?"

"You're just looking for flattery."

"Girls can't get too much of that."

I said, "Some girls have had way too much of it."

She dropped me off in front of the court building and I told her she could wait at a coffee shop at the end of the block. As I got out of the car and leaned over to say goodbye, Marlyn said, "Hello, Johnny." She was standing right next to me on the sidewalk. I said, "What did they do—beam you down from the *Enterprise*?"

For just a moment, Tracy and Marlyn exchanged inquisitive looks, and then Tracy drove off and Marlyn and I walked in the courthouse together. It was very awkward and I didn't know how I felt—about any of it.

"I see you have a new friend," Marlyn said. We waited for an elevator along with two or three other people who looked like the kind of people who stand around inside of courthouses. She was removing her gloves and I noticed her fingers were shaking.

"You mean Tracy?"

Marlyn said, "Is that her name, Tracy?"

The elevator doors parted and the two or three people got on and we followed. Marlyn did not speak, just stared straight ahead at the elevator door. The second we were off, however, she asked, "How old is she?"

Before I could answer, Arnold Gluck and Mitchell Arnoff beckoned to us from down the hall. They were laughing together about something and seemed as though they had been trading family snapshots. Once again we were escorted into a little room where we sat at a table and looked over papers. The latest property settlement was much more reasonable. I would remain half-owner of the house, and Marlyn had the option of living in it for the next three years, after which time she could sell it if she so chose. We were both financially responsible for Jason's college expenses, and we would pay our own attorney's fees.

Mitchell Arnoff offered me a pen, and I took it, and I thought how strange it was to end a relationship with a document. "Looks like you covered everything," I said.

"Wasn't that complicated," Arnoff said. "You don't make that much."

The son of a bitch. I said, "Maybe not, but at least it's honest work."

Marlyn was next to sign. She glossed over the document, went to put her signature on the dotted line, and once again her fingers trembled. We were told that there would be just one court appearance, and I didn't have to attend unless I wanted to. I could not figure out why I would want to.

Arnold Gluck said, "Well, that's it folks. Quick and painless." For him, perhaps. He extended his hand to me. "Mr. Spector," he said. Then he shook Marlyn's hand. "Mrs. Spector."

Mitchell Arnoff did not offer his hand, but rather took Marlyn by the elbow and was about to usher her to the door until she said, "Mr. Spector and I have to discuss a few things."

He nodded uncertainly at her and gave me a final look of contempt.

When the door was shut, she said, "Who is she?"

It was Tracy. That was why her hands shook so. She was genuinely upset, and I felt terrible for her, and in an awful way I enjoyed it, too. She still cared.

I said, "Marlyn, we just signed a paper to dissolve our marriage. Does any part of this discussion seem at all odd to you?"

She dropped her purse on the table and placed her hand on her hip and said, "I know what we just did. Who is she?"

I looked at the carpet. It was teal. "She's a friend."

"And where did you meet this *friend*?"

I said, "She's my student teacher."

Marlyn's eyes hardened. She picked up her purse, said, "I *hate* you, Johnny," and marched out of the room.

"Mr. Spector—why do we got to go to an assembly about Puerto Rico?"

It was Lashaun. He and another African American kid, Duane Daniels, pulled me over to the corner in a stairwell. I had been a thousand miles away, daydreaming of Marlyn, about a cruise we had taken to the Bahamas, and she had worn that sensational gold bikini. She'd looked so beautiful on the beach, palm trees swaying behind her.

I said, "Because the principal said so."

"But we ain't Puerto Rican," Lashaun protested.

I said, "Neither am I. But a lot of students here are. Let's show them a little respect, all right?"

"This sucks," Lashaun concluded.

The auditorium was crowded and noisy. On the stage there was a podium and microphone and full-size Puerto Rican flags on either side. Salsa music played over the sound system and some kids danced in the aisles. Standing behind the very last row of seats in front of the projection booth were Nydia Velazquez, Marco Gonzalez, Javier Acosta, and Judy Santiago. I walked over and joined them.

"Lover," Nydia said, squeezing my hand. "Just when I needed a dancing partner."

I said, "You'd better dance with Marco. I have all the rhythm of a neurological patient."

Marco said, "I knew there was something peculiar about you."

Javier handed me a pamphlet. "Have you seen this? Your tax dollars at work."

It was a little blue and white pamphlet in Spanish and English that enumerated United States' policies that were culturally harmful to the people of Puerto Rico. One of them had to do with the Young Bill, and why statehood was not a viable option for the island.

Judy said, "If they want to have an assembly about Puerto Rico, they ought to give time to all the political options. Do you know how many people voted for independence in the last referendum? Four percent."

"They had three options," Nydia said, "to remain a commonwealth, to become a state, and to become independent. This group wants another referendum without commonwealth status on the ballot."

"So much for democracy," said Javier. "Limit the choices and they might pick up some votes."

Marco said, "Their point is that the island has been a colony since 1898, when we fought the Spanish-American War. Colonies are supposed to be a thing of the past."

"But face it, Marco," Nydia spoke up. "There are all kinds of options this group doesn't even acknowledge—like free association. That's the kind of relationship the U.S. has with Micronesia. The Comrades of Liberation—how much would you like to bet they're not Marxists looking for political power?"

Marco nudged his head in my direction. "What about you, Johnny? What do you make of this?"

I said, "Oh, no you don't. Don't get me involved in this. I think the Puerto Rican people should have exactly what they want."

Javier poked me in the ribs. "Spoken like a true coward."

"I just don't think Federal poverty funding ought to be skimmed and channeled to *independentista* groups like this one," I added.

Marco said, "That's a pretty strong charge, Johnny. Can you prove it?"

Nydia winked at me.

"Not yet," I said. "But when I can, will you still be interested?"

"Of course."

The lights went down, the music stopped, and two men walked onstage to cheers and applause. One of them held a picture of José Julián Acosta. He waved it from side to side, crying, "*Viva la liberación*," causing a fierce outcry of approval. Most of the presentation was in English and covered the history of US-Puerto Rican relations. However, when they switched to using Spanish, the rhetoric became more heated and politically charged. They called for revolution here within the United States, and referred to the jailed FALN bombers as heroes and political prisoners.

Nydia pinched my arm and whispered, "Did you get the photocopies of the books?"

I lowered my mouth to her ear. "Not yet. Shirley's working on it."

"Where's Barbie?" she asked. "I hardly recognized you without her."

"She's with her student teaching advisor."

She pinched me a second time. "What?" I said.

"Nothing. I just wanted you to whisper in my ear again. I like the way it feels."

When the assembly let out, some of the kids were worked up and went on a rampage through the lobby, overturning trophy display cabinets and cracking the wire-enforced windows of the stairwell. A group of twenty or thirty ran past me and dispersed through the exits. Oscar and another security guard went after them, but they couldn't keep up. We'd had full-fledged riots in the past, and this was nothing in comparison; however the flames were being fanned. Javier put it best as we righted one of the trophy cabinets together. "They're kids," he said. "They need to be taught, not provoked."

Kirk looked terrible at the court appearance. When they called his case and he was led out of the tank, his face was bruised, he had dark circles under his eyes, and he had lost weight. His mother could not have missed this either; she was sitting in the aisle across from me with Tracy, and gave a little cry when he appeared. His attorney, a thin, pale man in a worn suit, stood beside him in front of the judge's bench and listened to the charges and put in a plea of no contest.

We could not have gotten luckier with the judge. He was a young man of about thirty-six named Raphael Colon, and he had neatly trimmed black hair and a square jaw. He talked to Kirk about the seriousness of the charges, the possession of a firearm, the selling of heroin.

"No one wins that game, young man. Not with heroin. It's a dead end, and it only takes a short time to reach it. Do you know how I know this?"

Kirk was spiritless. In a muffled monotone he said, "No, Your Honor."

Judge Colon said, "I'll tell you how. I was right where you are once, before a judge, for the very same charge. I was a heroin addict.

I didn't care about anything except my next fix—not school, not my family, not even God. That's the way it is, isn't it, Kirk?"

Again— fatigued, hollow delivery. "Yes, Your Honor."

"The judge I faced did for me what I'm going to do for you. He gave me a second chance. I'm going to put you into substance abuse treatment and give you one year probation. In addition, you are to fulfill four hundred hours of community service under the direction of one of your teachers. Is there a Mr. John Spector here?"

Christ—just what I needed. More time looking out for my kids. I stood and said, "I'm John Spector, Your Honor."

"Mr. Spector, do you agree to monitor and mentor Kirk in some sort of after-school project once he has completed his treatment?"

"Certainly, Your Honor."

He put on a pair of black-rimmed glasses and looked over a paper. "I understand that you have a very high regard for this young man."

"I do, Your Honor."

He said that was very well, that because of Kirk's previously unblemished record, and because his teachers valued him as a young person of potential, that he was consigned for twenty-eight days of drug rehabilitation and one year of probation. He did not want to see Kirk before him again, he said, and he asked if Kirk understood that.

Kirk did.

The case was dismissed.

Mrs. Perez ran to her son, embracing him as he attempted to make his way down the aisle, causing him to stumble while his attorney held up the rear. Tracy and I followed the emotional scene as it spilled out into the lobby.

"*Mijo, gracias, Dios. Gracias.*"

Tracy searched her purse for some Kleenex. Kirk patted his mother's back and looked at me with haunted eyes.

"Well," his attorney said, smiling, "I'd like to thank you two teachers for coming here today." Turning to Tracy, he added, "I'm afraid I didn't catch your name."

"You were beaten, weren't you Kirk?" I said.

He slowly nodded.

I asked, "Who did it?"

"Kings. They put me in with Crowns."

Kings were People. Disciples were Folks. And never the twain

193

shall meet. You'd think the jail officials would know better by now.

The attorney said to Tracy, "Can I give you a lift somewhere?"

"No, that's quite all right," she said.

I noticed then two things—the attorney looked extremely uneasy, and there was yellow yarn wound around the handle of his briefcase. "Well, I'm glad I was able to get you off, Kirk," he said, congratulating himself.

He hadn't gotten him off. It was a done deal before he'd even walked into the courtroom. Of course, I couldn't say this, and it was irritating me that I couldn't.

Mrs. Perez was holding onto her son desperately now, sobbing quietly. My cell phone rang. I fished it out of my pocket, pressed the button.

"Spector here."

"Mr. Spector? This is Sergeant McLellen. I just thought I'd let you know that Tito Herrera just made bail."

My stars must have been crossed again. I said, "That's great, Sergeant. Now he can beat up his girlfriend and try to kill me again."

He sighed a long sigh on the other end of the line. "I know how you feel, Mr. Spector."

The court guards had given Kirk a few minutes with his mother, but now they came to take him to the treatment facility. It was going to take a crane to get Mrs. Perez to let go of him.

"No, you don't, Sergeant," I said into my phone. "You really don't know at all how I feel."

11

"I make the *masa* yesterday. More easier to use when it's cold."

It was Christmas break and I was getting a *pasteles* cooking lesson from señor Valentin in his kitchen. *Masa* is dough. We were preparing the meat stuffing this morning—a complicated process. There didn't seem to be any measuring involved at all. My father-in-law simply eyeballed the quantity of each ingredient, and there were plenty.

"*Mira, maestro.* The *relleno* we cook quickly for five minutes, and then let simmer for about twenty-five. But first we must add ingredients. You follow?"

"This pork here, you mean?"

"You chop pork, then I'll add onion, garlic, recao leaves, garbanzos, olives and a little *achiote* oil."

He demonstrated how to chop the meat finely with a wooden handled knife. His hands were weathered and knotted from years of toil, but they worked the food well, as if sensing what next to do. Then he handed the knife to me and I did not do as well.

"No, no, *maestro!* Cut it fine, with care."

I said, "You know, I'm probably not the best guy to ask to chop pork. When I was growing up, this stuff wasn't even allowed in the house."

He took the knife from me and showed me how to do it again.

"Maybe we could open up a Jewish-Puerto Rican restaurant," I said. "Serve pasteles and lox. Of course, our only customers would be Geraldo Rivera and my son."

"Enough jokes, *maestro.* Chop."

The garbanzos were skinned before they were included, and the chili peppers were crushed in a mortar. I watched snow fall out the kitchen window, and from the living room Caribbean Christmas music played—*musica de navidad*. Jason was spending the weekend with me, was, in fact, up in the apartment, sound asleep. The boy slept till noon and beyond on the weekends, if you let him. It was good to have him with me again, gave me a sense of well being. And I enjoyed the work with señor—but Marlyn's absence was conspicuous. We all felt it, but no one would acknowledge it.

I said, "How many will this make?"

He crushed three leaves that I later learned were *cilantro* leaves before answering, and mixed these with the meat filling. "*Yo no se*— perhaps twenty, twenty-four or so. You don't think about the end when you cook. You think only about what you do at the minute."

Sometimes he looked at me hard after giving me instructions, as if to see if his words had settled in, if they had any effect upon me.

"Is it ready to heat?"

"Almost." The pungent smell of the sofrito filled the very localized air of the kitchen. I would never have sinus problems again. "And so, have you talked to my daughter?"

One minute we were cooking, and the next we were in marriage counseling. I said, "Not since our last meeting in court."

"Turn up the fire, *por favor*." He put the pot on the circular blue-orange flame, stirred the contents, and then covered it. "Court," he said. "Ha. You two need sit down together, talk. Stop monkey business."

He opened the refrigerator and took out the *masa*. Then from the counter he took the plantain leaves and spread them out on the cutting board on the kitchen table.

I said, "I think your daughter has made it pretty clear what she wants, señor."

"Because the road, it is rough, that does not mean it ends. You young people so ready to quit. You want everything easy."

"Let me ask you something," I said. "When Marlyn and I fell in love and wanted to get married, you did everything you could to keep us apart. What exactly are you doing now?"

He had been washing the leaves at the sink when he suddenly stopped. He did not look at me when he spoke. "One way to know one is right is to say when one has been wrong in the past. *Sí?*"

That could not have been an easy admission for him. I said, "Yes, I guess so."

He nodded vigorously over the garbanzos. "Well, then."

Some people will cook their finished *pasteles* in aluminum foil. It's much easier to seal them that way. You just fold the edges and press them tightly. But we were more traditional. We folded them in plantain leaves and tied these with string—once the long way, and twice around the middle. When the filling was cooked, and the *masa* filled, we would put them in the big kettle of water and bring it to a boil and cook them for about an hour. Señor cleaned the counters and hummed along to the music. Presently he turned to me and said, "Call her."

I suddenly craved a cigarette. "She doesn't want to speak to me."

"A woman does not always mean what she says."

I said, "I don't understand your daughter, señor."

"Sometimes you no need to understand. Sometimes it is enough to accept. People are people. They make mistakes. Go upstairs, *maestro*, and call her."

Jesus sat on the counter with that swollen red heart of his, looking as though he could use a cardiologist. I went upstairs then, but I did not call Marlyn. I sat and watched Jason sleeping for about fifteen minutes. The eyebrows were mine, the mouth Marlyn's. Look what we'd done.

"Buddy?" I nudged his shoulder and he rolled onto his back, made a fist and rubbed his eye.

"Hm?"

"Time to get up. *Abuelo* has pasteles cooking."

He squinted at me and nodded and yawned. "Maybe I could call Fernando, we could do something."

"That's an idea. Have him come over to the house."

He sat up abruptly and stretched once more. "You know what, Dad?"

"What's that?"

"I was just thinking—it's going to be a really weird Christmas this year," he said.

As understatements went, that was a pretty good one. I felt a cold draft in the old apartment, and a chill raced up my spine. "I know," I said. "I know."

§

"I'd like to speak to Jason, please."

It was Marlyn. I had been watching TV down at my father-in-

197

law's place, and when the phone rang, I'd answered it out of reflex. Now I regretted having done it.

I said, "Hello, Marlyn. He's not in right now."

"Not in? May I ask where he is?"

"He's out with Fernando."

There was a slight pause on the other end. "Fer*nando*? You let him run around that part of the city at this time of night with a gangster?"

"You know, *you* grew up in this part of the city, too."

"Don't pretend you don't know how dangerous it is down there, Johnny. Jason isn't used to it. He doesn't know a thing about it."

"And he never will, unless you let him experience it. He's fine. Quit worrying."

"He'd better be. I want him to call me the minute he gets in."

"All right."

There was another pause, a slightly shorter one this time. "I'm surprised you're even home."

I said, "Oh? Why is that?"

"I would have thought you'd be out with your student teacher— giving her a few lessons."

It had really gotten to her. If I had known she would have reacted like that, I would have personally introduced the two of them weeks ago. "No. She's in New York, visiting her sister."

"Oh? That's too bad. I hope you don't get lonely."

Out the window snowflakes danced in the yellow glow of streetlights and a car drove through the slush. "So," I said, "when is the divorce official?"

"They haven't set the date yet. Can't wait, huh? Is she going to be the new Mrs. Spector?"

That was not why I had asked. I said, "I'll have Jason call you when he gets home, Marlyn," and then placed the receiver back in its cradle. I did not feel like fighting.

Señor Valentin and I sat on his couch watching *"Sábado Giganté."* Don Francisco was singing a song with the audience and two scantily dressed girls about a breakfast cereal, and I was sipping a scotch on the rocks. I wondered what would become of me. I imagined going back to my old house, flinging myself upon the front steps, begging Marlyn to take me back. No—that didn't look like reality. Then I had a little vision of moving into Tracy's apartment with her, two inner city teachers in a wild love affair. Late evenings in clubs, languorous Sunday mornings, breakfast in bed.

Naw. Tracy would get upset if her Nordstrom sheets got wrinkled.

The front door shoved open and Jason spilled into the foyer. Fernando was right behind him, kicking the snow from his shoes on the doormat.

"Hey, Pop—I'm home."

Something about the liquid timbre of his voice sounded funny. I got up from the sofa and went to meet them.

"Go ahead, show him," Fernando said. "Johnny, wait'll you see this."

Jason's eyes were glazed and he gave me a silly grin.

I said, "Show me what?"

He took off his jacket, rolled up the sleeve of his shirt, and proudly displayed a Dragons' *D* tattoo on his bicep.

"Ain't it dope?" Fernando said.

I said, "You'd better tell me that washes off, or I'm going to kick your ass."

Fernando slapped Jason's back and hung an arm around his shoulders. "Relax, Johnny. You gonna give yourself nerve problems. I used a ball point pen. He's an honorary Dragon now."

I said, "Oh, shit. You didn't give him the Dragon drink, did you?"

"Sure! The boy took it *con gana*. Just one shot, was all. I'm tellin' ya—you gonna give yourself a nerve condition if you don't relax, man."

"Quit worrying about my nerves, Fernando, and get the hell out of here. Don't you have a rumble to go to or something?"

"All right, Johnny," and then to Jason: "Yo—Li'l J—later."

The cold breath of night stole into the house as the door opened and closed. *Li'l J.* Just what every father wanted his son to be—an honorary Dragon. Jason just stood there looking at me with that dumb grin. He was a good kid; I knew he was. But maybe I was a lousier influence than I had realized. I told him to go wash that *D* off his arm and call his mother.

"Oh, and Jason?"

"Yeah?"

"It might not be a good idea to tell her about tonight, you know?"

"Sure, Pop."

199

§

It was her first time at a firing range, though you wouldn't have known it. Tracy blasted eight rounds, one after the other, and when the target came back, only one shot had missed.

She was wearing white denim jeans with a matching fitted white denim jacket. She said, "How do I look with a gun?"

I said, "The same way you look without one—dangerous."

It was my Christmas present to her, the Ruger Decocker. Now we had a matched set.

"Mike Parnell asked me to stay on at Acosta for the spring semester as a cadre sub."

A cadre sub was just that. Each school had a trusted pool of substitute teachers. "Oh? Why would you want to do that?"

"My student teaching advisor thinks it might be a good idea. Most schools do their hiring for the fall, and this way I can get teaching experience."

I put a new clip in my gun and fired eight rounds in rapid succession. Son of a bitch—three shots had missed entirely.

Tracy said, "What do you think?"

"I think I'm overcompensating to the right."

"No—I mean about my staying on for the spring semester."

I didn't know what to think. I had wondered what would happen to us when her student teaching term was over—had even worried about losing her. Now I was worried about *not* losing her, about falling in love.

When I didn't have a ready reply she said, "You don't think it's a good idea."

"No, I didn't say that. That's not it at all."

"What is it, then?"

I wasn't sure exactly what to say, so I kissed her. I had never kissed anyone holding a gun before. Her mouth was soft and warm, and when our lips parted, I looked into her eyes and tried to see a future there.

"I'm going to take that as a sign of approval," she said.

We drove back into the city. It looked good in the snow, as though it had dressed, and I thought it might be nice to have lunch downtown. We ate at The Cheesecake Factory in the Hancock Building, or rather I ate while Tracy told me about her visit with her sister Alice on Long Island. They had had a snowstorm and Alice was opening a new office for her husband's telecommunications consulting business. There had been a community theater play (*The Mikado*) and it had been really quite good, and Tracy had gone shopping and found the cutest velvet suit. There was a new Japanese restaurant in town. And she had run into her ex-fiancé at her sister's club.

"Wait, wait, wait," I said.

"What's the matter?"

I pushed my chair back from the table a few inches to make room for my surprise. "It's funny, but I don't remember ever having heard about any fiancé."

"*Ex*-fiancé. There's a difference. Ex, meaning former, and that's why you've never heard about him. Anyway, we were just going to the spa they have there, for a pedicure and a massage, you know, girl things, and of all the people to run into when I just wanted to visit with my sister—there he was. . .Woodrow."

"Woodrow?" I said.

"Woodrow Wilson. Oh, we were only engaged for six months. It's no big deal. He's a very sweet boy, but he's too rigid. He can't let go."

I said, "Tracy, Woodrow Wilson was a president."

"I know. That's who he was named after. It was very difficult for him as a child, having a name like that."

"I'll bet."

"His friends all call him Woody. Anyway, it was a lovely visit, except for that. I really miss my sister."

She had brought him up and now I couldn't stop thinking about him. Woodrow. Woody. It was almost as though he was sitting at the table with us. She began eating her pasta and I wanted to ask her what they had said to one another, why they had broken up, but that would have made me look silly, so I dropped it.

"So what happened while I was gone?" she asked.

"Nothing much. Had my boy over for a night."

"Oh, Johnny—that's good. Did you have a nice time?"

"He did. He became an honorary Dragon."

"No he *didn't*."

"Yeah—Fernando inducted him. If my wife finds out, she'll kill me."

She put her fork down discreetly, lifted her napkin to her mouth, looked up at me, and then down at her plate. "I've never heard you call her that before."

"What—*wife*? It's a temporary situation, you know."

She did not reply. She had some of her water and then excused herself from the table, to freshen up, she said.

Afterward we had drinks at the Deca at the Ritz, where a bartender named Carlo in a white jacket made a Long Island iced tea for Tracy and a gin martini for me.

"Top shelf?" he wondered, and I said yes, and Tracy gazed out the big window at the skyscrapers to the south.

"I love the city," she said. "I've always wanted to live in a penthouse of a tall building and have two dogs and take them for walks and have the doorman open the door for me and tip his hat. Doesn't that sound like a nice life?"

"That's not a life. That's an Audrey Hepburn movie," I said. "Besides, you're going to end up in the suburbs raising two children and driving a Volvo."

"I will not! I'm not the spoiled North Shore snob you think I am."

"Aren't you?"

"No. I live in the inner city, and I teach at an inner city school, and I carry a gun, so watch your step, buster."

During our second round of drinks Tracy brought her very pretty face up close to mine and said, "Johnny, are you having second thoughts about the divorce?"

I kissed her on the cheek. "Honey—I've had second, third and fourth thoughts about it. I'm way beyond second thoughts." A moment passed and then I said, "What does your ex do for a living?"

She pulled back and looked as if someone had just tickled her. "You're *jealous*, aren't you?"

"How could I be jealous of a guy named Woodrow?"

"You are, though," she said, and kissed the tip of my ear. "And I think it's wonderful."

He was a stockbroker, Woodrow. This I learned later in the afternoon in a bookstore on Michigan Avenue. Tracy was looking for magazines while I riffled through newspapers.

"We met at a party that a friend of Alice's threw. It was a crowd mostly Alice's age, and so when Woody and I were introduced, we naturally spent most of the evening together, talking. He's very intelligent and all, though the subject matter is always business. Finance. You know."

I did not believe my eyes.

"But it's nearly impossible maintaining a long distance relationship, no matter what anybody says, and . . . Johnny? Are you listening to me?"

It was in the feature section of *Chicagoland Today*. **"Inside The Inner City Teacher," by Brian Podhorst.** Not only had he not given me any warning about its publication date, but he included comments of mine that we'd agreed would be off the record—such as the fact that I had married a former student. The way he'd worded it, you would have thought it had happened last week, rather than sixteen years ago.

"I'm going to kill the son of a bitch."

Tracy was now reading over my shoulder. "Oh my God—you said *that*?"

"I distinctly told him not to print those comments. I got a little too smart-alecky—carried away. You know my hard-nosed routine, but it doesn't come across in print."

I'd made some throw-away remark about how we should have gang-color Fridays the way some offices have casual-dress Fridays. It was supposed to be a joke, but if you weren't a regular, it wasn't funny.

Worst of all, Brian had too literally taken my advice about changing the word *Spanish* to *Hispanic*. One of the questions was about teachers of Spanish, referring exclusively to the language. He wanted to know if I thought that my students should be taught by Spanish teachers in Spanish. And I'd replied that they would never learn English that way. But Brian had changed even this reference, and so now I was telling every *Chicagoland Today* reader that I didn't believe Hispanic teachers could teach English.

Oh, boy.

Tracy put her hand on my coat sleeve and said, "What are you going to do?"

"Funny, I was just wondering the same thing."

"Maybe you could get him to print a retraction."

"I was thinking more along the lines of bludgeoning."

We stopped for one more drink at a bar on Oak Street. I had switched to scotch, and I tried to reach Brian Podhorst on my cell phone, but he wasn't in. The drink was not doing the trick. I felt all sick inside.

"You can't let an article do this to you," Tracy said.

"No matter what you say, it's going to do this to me, so please don't say anything."

I drove her home, and she didn't speak the entire way, and neither did I. She let herself out of the Jeep, and I wished I would have kissed her, or done something, or said something, but I didn't have it in me, and then it was too late. The winter afternoon grew dark and everything felt like Sunday. I went home and paced and worried and cursed until I fell asleep.

§

"To get straight to the worst, he was tortured since he was four years old, perhaps even earlier."

Lico's home manager, Jim Jarret, sat in a Youth Services office with Marco and me. This was the meeting we'd wanted to have since October, but one thing or another always came up in one of our schedules, and then it had got pushed aside.

Marco said, "May I ask you to clarify that, Jim—torture?"

Jim Jarret was a man of medium build, somewhere in his early forties. He wore a sport coat with elbow patches and had an attentive face. One of his ears stuck out more than the other, giving him a lopsided look. "I assure you I'm not exaggerating when I use that word. Think of any of the ways a child could be tortured, and it was probably done to Lico. Physical, sexual, psychological."

Marco stood now, said, "Mr. Jarret, can I get you some coffee?"

"Yes, please. Black."

While Marco stepped just outside to the waiting room for the coffee pot, I grew curious. "Who did this to him?"

"His mother."

My stomach sank.

"What kind of a woman could do that to her own child?"

He said, "I don't know. All I can tell you is that she's a white woman from South Carolina, an intravenous drug abuser with HIV."

Marco returned with a cardboard cup of coffee and set it down on his desk before Jim Jarret, who thanked him and took a sip.

I said, "Mr. Jarret, would you please tell Marco what you just told me?"

"Certainly. Lico's mother was the source of the torture. She beat him so badly he had broken bones, infected welts, suffered sexual mutilation."

Marco's face fell. "What kind of sexual mutilation?"

"She attempted to cut the tip of his penis off with a scissors."

I felt myself leave my body momentarily, float somewhere up near the fluorescent tubes. Twenty-two years of this kind of thing—parents who set their kids on fire, hit them, starved them, raped them—but nothing like this, until now. A *scissors*, for God's sake.

Marco said, "Where is the mother?"

"Why, she's in prison, just outside of Wichita, serving a twenty-five year sentence. You see, Lico has four siblings. He wasn't the only victim."

I felt light-headed and my stomach was queasy. I leaned forward and folded my hands between my knees. "Mr. Jarret," I said, "Lico gives us different stories."

"He confabulates. He's been diagnosed as a borderline patient. It's a defense mechanism, or at least it started out that way. Now he routinely lies to manipulate people, to avoid responsibility. He's in therapy twice a week, and he has group sessions as well, but a borderline is a borderline."

Marco said, "He tells stories about visiting his mother, his siblings."

Jarret shook his head and folded his hand around his coffee cup. "No—he hasn't seen his mother or his siblings since he was five. He doesn't even know where they are. The kids didn't stay in touch. They were all so young."

Well, we had our answers about Lico, though I could have easily lived without them. Marco said, "Thank you for coming in, Mr. Jarret. If there's anything we can do on our end to support your efforts, don't hesitate to call me, or Mr. Spector."

"Just hold him accountable. If he lies to you, tell him you know it's a lie. Confront him with the truth. And if you need me for anything, you have my number."

"Of course," Marco said. We all stood, and Jarret shook hands first with Marco and then with me, and struggled a moment to free his overcoat from the coat tree in the corner of the office.

When he had left, Marco sat down again, lifted a pencil to his chin, and tapped it there a few times. He was in his shirtsleeves and wore what looked like a J. Garcia tie.

"What is it?" I said.

He threw the pencil down upon his desk and leaned back in his chair. "Given any good interviews lately?"

I said, "Oh, that."

Marco stood up and paced and put his hands in his pants pockets. "What the *fuck* were you thinking?"

"What can I tell you, Marco? The guy got me on a bad day and I was misquoted. It's not as though I'm happy about it."

"Hispanic teachers can't teach English?"

"I never said that. You know me better than that."

He stopped short and turned to me. "What about the people who *don't* know you better than that? Are you aware of the fact that right now, downstairs in Isabelle Villachez's office, there is a meeting to discuss having you fired because of racist comments?"

I gave a sort of half laugh and said, "For Christ's sake, Marco. I'm not a racist."

"You'd never be able to prove it by that article."

"The article was a mistake."

He nodded at me, forehead furrowed, as though he was deep in thought. "Likely the biggest mistake you've ever made."

I said, "What can they do to me? I have my first amendment rights, tenure."

"Don't be naïve, Johnny. Do you think Isabelle or Elizabeth Mojica or Danny Velez give a good goddamn about your First Amendment rights? They tried to get me to join a protest rally against you this afternoon in front of the school. They're calling a press conference about it."

This was not news I was happy to hear. "And you declined?"

"I did. You and I may disagree on your methods, but I don't turn on friends."

He put his hand on my shoulder and I felt suddenly sorry that I'd given him such a hard time about the sensitivity sessions. I said, "Thank you, Marco."

"I don't want your thanks, but you could do something else."

"Sure. What?"

"Get me proof that the *independentistas* have taken control of the school, that they're siphoning the federal poverty funds."

I said, "I thought you didn't believe that."

He lowered his head, looked up at me knowingly. "Let's just say I've overheard a few things lately."

We had just come off holiday break and I already felt as though I could use a vacation. After I left Marco's office, I took the escalators up to the eighth floor and noticed people looking at me funny, as though I had mismatched shoes or an open fly. I waved at Javier Acosta as I passed his office window, and he turned his back on me.

When I knocked on Vince's door, he called out, "What's the password?"

I said, "Open the door, Vince."

The door pulled open and Vince just stood there. "What the hell kind of a password is that?"

I stepped inside and then shut the door behind me. "Vince," I said, "I think I'm in trouble."

Vince went over to his desk and picked up his coffee mug. This one said, *Homo sapiens, the overrated species.* "Well, at least you've had experience in that area."

It was apparent that Vince had not seen the article. There was another knock at the door, and Nydia Velazquez asked if I was in there.

Vince said, "Make her say the password."

I let her in and she had the newspaper article with her. "They're going to hang you," she said.

I said, "Close the door. It's members only in here."

Vince's face was an advertisement for bewilderment. "What happened?"

"You haven't heard?" Nydia asked. "Your friend here gave an interview that's going to win him an office in the KKK." She turned to me and slapped the newspaper against my arm and said, "Johnny, what the hell happened?"

"Nydia, you've got to believe me. It was *your* friend, Brian, who distorted everything. He didn't do it on purpose, and he didn't do it out of spite. He's just not professional, is all."

"Let me see that," Vince said, taking the paper from Nydia.

"There's a small mob down in Isabelle's office, including an alderman and a state senator. Every revolutionary on the faculty is shmoozing them. Do you know what you've *done?*"

"What have I done?"

Vince had evidently gotten to the good part of the piece. He said, "Jesus fucking Christ."

Nydia said, "You've given them a platform. Now they can curry favor with local politicians and go on a witch hunt, solidify their power base."

That's what I had done, all right. It was a little much to take in all at once. Every other time I had been in a jam, I'd had some inkling of what to do about it. This time I had no idea.

Vince said, "You've got to phone this bastard reporter."

"I will," I said. "I think it's too late to do any good, though. Pandora's box, you know."

Nydia looked so disappointed, it made me feel terrible. There was nothing to say, and we all knew it, and so I left. I tried to get through my sophomore English class, but it was too much for me. I gave the kids a reading assignment and stood at the window looking out at the bare trees of the park, the jagged tops of the buildings down in the Loop, poking at the sky. Twenty-two years, down the drain.

A young, husky security guard appeared in the open doorway of my classroom and held a white envelope out to me. I walked over and said, "What's this about?"

"Open it," he said cryptically.

Inside there was a note from Isabelle Villachez, instructing me to go to her office immediately.

"I'll watch the class," the security guard said.

"No, you won't. You're not qualified." I reached in my shirt pocket for a pen and then wrote upon the note:

Sorry, Isabelle. I have a responsibility to my students. If you'd like to speak to me, you can make an appointment during my office hours.

I folded it, slipped it back inside the envelope, and held it out to the security guard. "There you go," I said.

"But I have instructions to stay here."

"Well, I've just changed them."

He stood there for a moment, looking back and forth between me and the envelope, and then he turned around and left.

There is a certain amount of freedom that comes along with being absolutely screwed.

"Mr. Spector, you gave that interview of your own free will. I did nothing to coerce you."

208

"Brian—listen to me, and listen to me carefully. You didn't make the distinction between a teacher of Spanish and a teacher of Hispanic descent. You asked me a question worded one way, and printed it worded another. That's either unethical or unprofessional, and the reading public needs to know it was your doing, not mine."

There was silence on the other end of the line. Then at last Brian spoke up. "Well, I don't know exactly if that's the case."

"That's exactly what happened, and you know it, goddamn it. You'd just rather leave me on the spot than take the heat yourself."

"I have another assignment I have to get to, Mr. Spector."

"Yeah, sure. Thanks, Brian. Thanks a hell of a lot."

I slammed the phone down and sat back in my office chair. The little bastard wouldn't even own up to his own mistake.

What the hell. It was my fault. I never should have talked to him in the first place.

There was a rap at my door. It opened a crack and Daisy peaked in.

"Johnny? Can I come in?"

I said, "Sure, kid."

She had her hair up and wore a gray hooded sweatshirt and stone-washed blue jeans. Her gum snapped in her mouth as she lowered her book bag to the other chair, but she remained standing.

"What is it?" I said

"Do you know what they're saying about you?"

I let out a sigh and hunched over my desk. "I know. I hope you don't believe any of it."

"Then why are they doing this to you?"

"Because they have the opportunity. I gave it to them. You know how I kind of don't do things according to the rules?"

"Yeah. 'Cause you're cool."

"Well, they finally found a way to make me pay for it."

Daisy slumped against the wall. "That bitch Mojica is with the news guys out in front of the school. I'll bet they're just waitin' for you to go to your car."

I said, "They're out there already?"

"Yeah. Me and Phil saw 'em just now from the second floor windows. There's gotta be a hundred people out there. Kids, too."

That's just swell, I thought. They must have spent the entire day organizing a protest. What I couldn't get over was how badly they wanted

209

to nail me. I must have angered a lot of people over a lot of years.

Daisy came over and put her hand on my back. "Let me get the boys for you."

I looked up at her. "The boys? Why?"

"To help get you to your car."

"I don't need them to get to my car."

Daisy chewed on her gum and gave me a worried look. "I'm tellin' you, Johnny. There's a crowd out there just waitin' for you."

"No, Daisy. All right? I'll be fine."

"Then can I come with you?"

"No."

She picked up her bag and left the office with a nasty little pout. I looked at my watch—ten minutes till the end of the school day. I was supposed to drive Tracy home, but there was no way she would be able to leave the building with me. I took the elevator to the seventh floor and ran into Anatole Hafka, our resident radical history teacher. Anatole was a tall, skinny guy who wore the same rumpled black suit every day. When he walked, it was always in a slightly diagonal fashion, as if one half of his body couldn't agree with the other as to which direction he should be moving. Anatole and I generally did not speak to one another, but as he passed me, he grinned and said, "See you after school, Mr. Spector."

Tracy was subbing for Murphy. I tapped on the glass of her classroom door to catch her attention; she looked surprised to see me. When she stepped out in the hall, I told her I couldn't take her home, and that I was sorry.

"I'm hearing terrible things," she said.

"They're all true."

"I'm not afraid to face it with you. To hell with them."

"They're after me, Trace. I don't want you to get mixed up in it."

She had chalk on her hands, and rubbed them together. "We do everything together."

"Not this. You don't want any part of this. I'll call you tonight."

She reached out for my hand, gave it a little squeeze. "Promise?"

"I promise."

The escalators were still all running up, so I took the stairs to the second floor to check my mailbox in the main office. When I walked in, every head turned, and people stopped doing whatever it was they had been doing. It reminded me of a "Twilight Zone" episode about living mannequins. I entered the mail room, found bulletins and surveys and an insurance ad in my mailbox, and walked back to the central part of the office, over near the windows. Daisy had miscalculated. Just below there was a throng of at least three hundred people. Two television news crew vans with satellite dishes were parked along the curb, and the technicians were unreeling cable.

Shirley walked over to me. "I'm sorry, Johnny. If there's anything I can do—"

"You could find those account books for me."

"I'm working on it."

When the final tone of the day sounded and the halls filled up, I just sat in my office. What if I just stayed there and they had to have the rally by themselves? Of course, they might camp out all night, and the custodians locked and chained the doors by five o'clock. No, this was no way to live.

My door opened and Fernando walked in. He had a toothpick hanging out of the corner of his mouth, and he was with a kid named Orlando who had been in my sophomore English class the year before. Orlando was a tough kid and had a reputation for being someone whose path you did not want to cross.

Fernando said, "Whatup?"

I said, "What are you doing here?"

"You seen what's goin' on outside?"

"Yeah, I've seen it. Did Daisy tell you to come here?"

"You want to make it out of here, don't you?"

"And what are you two going to do—beat up the mob for me?"

Fernando said, "Just wait."

They straggled in—one, two at a time. In the next five minutes I had half the Dragon's organization in my office. There was Tank and Turtle and Flaco and Jorgé and a kid named Miguel Melendez whose nickname I didn't know, but *Gigantor* might have worked. He stood close to seven feet and the top of his head barely cleared the doorway.

"You just close in around my man, Johnny," Fernando ordered, "and don't let nobody get to him."

I said, "This is ridiculous."

Fernando put his face directly up next to mine and chewed on his toothpick. "You wanna see somethin' ridiculous, you watch the news tonight if you go out there without us."

What I hated to admit was that he was probably right. "Okay—but I don't want any rough stuff," I said.

Jorgé was already worked up. He had his game face on, and he said, "Damn, Johnny. Someone push me and I'm gonna push him back."

"Listen to the man," Fernando said. "You hurt somebody, and Johnny's the one who'll get in trouble."

Jorgé said, "All right, but I ain't takin' no shit."

We rode down the escalator as a group. I had three men in front of me, two at each side, and two behind me, for all the good it would do. I saw immediately what we were up against through the windows of the first floor. There was a woman on a dais with a bullhorn in her hand. What do you know—it was Isabelle Villachez herself. I guessed that this is what happened if you turned down a request to come to her office.

Fernando said, "Holy shit. Look at 'em."

There were even people with placards. One said *"Racist Teacher Must Go."* I couldn't read the others, but I imagined that they didn't recommend me for Man of the Year. Two news crew vans were still there, and we would have to get past these just to go as far as the parking lot.

We stood at the exit watching the commotion. People were pressed up against the building, chanting something I couldn't make out. "How're we gonna do this?" Miguel asked.

I said, "Let's just do it."

Tank pushed the doors open and off we went into the surging crowd. Fernando and Miguel charged their way through bodies, and we made some progress, until Isabelle spotted me from the dais and began shouting something in Spanish over the bullhorn while pointing at me. We were pushed and jostled from all sides, became separated, and for a very frightening few seconds I thought we might very possibly be crushed to death. But Jorgé had had enough, and he belted two or three of the kids who were doing most of the shoving, and that opened up a path to the parking lot. A camera crew on the dais caught the whole thing on tape, and as we emerged from the crush of bodies, the chant suddenly became distinct: *"Fire Spector now!"*

Fernando called out, "Get in the Jeep, Johnny. Let's get out of here."

I opened the Jeep's doors and then turned to watch the spectacle, angry fists in the air, placards waving. All this time working with these kids, and now I was the enemy.

12

The next morning I parked the Jeep on the street rather than in the parking lot, for obvious reasons. I'd had a few cocktails, or a few too many the night before, and only now did that seem like a poor idea as I struggled up the icy pathway to the front entrance, my head throbbing. I did not pay them much attention at first, the purple fliers that were taped to the Plexiglas windows, their corners flapping in the cold January wind. But as I got closer, I saw they featured a photo of me that had been clipped from a yearbook of several years ago. This is what the fliers said:

John Spector, Racist

In a recent interview titled, "Inside The Inner City Teacher," which appeared in *Chicagoland Today*, John Spector revealed himself as a vicious racist who has been infecting our classrooms for the past twenty years. Spector stated that he believes Hispanic teachers cannot teach English, and he sarcastically recommended that Acosta High School should sponsor Gang Color Fridays, so lightly does he take his responsibilities, and with such contempt does he look down upon Latinos.

He is known to have wed a 19 year old Campos student—an act repulsive to the people of the community who entrust their children to the care of teachers whom they expect to conduct themselves professionally.

There is only one response we can have to the actions and the statements made by such a negligent, disreputable teacher—*SPECTOR MUST GO!*

In the bottom left hand corner, a group called the Committee Against Racial Hatred At Acosta High School took responsibility for the text. Interestingly, there were no individual names of the committee members. I tore five or six of the fliers down, but once I got inside the school, I saw that it was pretty much a futile gesture. They were everywhere—on walls and trophy cases, the stainless steel sides of the escalators. Isabelle must have stayed up all night running the photocopy machine.

I left my jacket and books in my office and took the escalators up to the cafeteria. I needed coffee. Coffee and a public relations firm. I guess what galled me was the fact that Isabelle and Elizabeth both knew that I harbored no racist ideas or feelings. They were inciting people to believe the worst about me so that they could create an issue around which to rally.

But how do you tell people that? Was I supposed to create fliers of my own, blame the revolutionary faculty members for having seized the school? Who cares about politics? It's so much easier to hate a racist.

I stood in line, waiting to pay for my coffee. By the time I got to the cashier, she pulled the dollar bills from my hand with a rude jerk and slammed my change down hard upon the counter. Even the kitchen staff hated me.

I found a table in the student section of the cafeteria and sat down. Only some of the fluorescent lights had been turned on, and I was relieved to be sitting in the shadows. Every now and then a few teachers would stand together holding coffee cups, speaking lowly, stealing glances in my direction. You'd think I had given birth to a bastard. This is how Hester Prynne must have felt.

A voice behind me said, "Well, your next ten years or so ought to be fun."

I turned around and saw Dave Volmer standing behind me. He was wearing an old ski jacket and had one of the fliers with him.

I said, "Hello, Dave. I'm not exactly having a stellar morning so far, and you're about what I expected next."

215

He pulled out a chair and sat down, setting his briefcase on the chair next to him. "Don't be so snippy. At least I'm still willing to be seen with you. Wait till you see how quickly you can clear out a room, just by showing up."

I went to lift my coffee cup and noticed that my hand quivered just from the simple act of trying to bring it to my mouth. I set it down without having taken a sip. "Is there something I can do for you, Dave? I was kind of hoping to have some time alone before classes."

"Oh, you'll have plenty of time alone." He struggled out of his jacket and folded it over the back of his chair. There were a few moth holes in his dirty beige crew neck sweater. "I just wanted to get the scoop on the interview. Were you drunk when you gave it?"

"No, but I've been pretty much drunk ever since it appeared."

Dave blew on the surface of his black coffee. "I take it the reporter missed the subtle humor of some of your responses."

"He mangled the goddamn piece, Dave."

"Have you thought about suing?"

My head was splitting on two sides. *Wouldn't it be something*, I thought, *if it just fell open on the table?* "It would be my word against his. He didn't use a tape recorder. Besides, I'm already suing my wife. I can't afford another lawyer."

Dave was not aging well. His cheeks were hollow and his hair looked as though it had been recently painted. "Want to go to Grandma's after school?"

I said, "I can't think of a more depressing place to go."

"Oh, yeah? Wait till you get to your apartment."

Touché. The son of a bitch was right, and I hated it when he was right.

"Can you think of what Elisa's chrysanthemums might represent in this story?"

It was my first period sophomore English class, and only fourteen kids had bothered to show up. Of those fourteen, seven had their books open to the correct page and the others might as well have been home asleep.

"All right," I said. "It's eight o'clock in the morning, and we're talking about a story by Steinbeck, and you'd rather be having a root canal. I know. I was a sophomore once, too. But humor me. Pretend you give a damn. We've got a woman here with not much of a marriage, and not much of anything else, either. Look at how she talks about her flowers to the wandering man in the wagon, the tinker. If you didn't know better, you'd think she was talking about her own children."

"Why do you hate Puerto Ricans?"

The question stopped me cold. Ricardo Collajo—pet student of Anatole Hafka. He must have been coached to disrupt my class.

I said, "The question is, Ricardo, why are you so ready to make false assumptions?"

He had the interview spread open on his desk—highlighted in yellow, no less. "You said right here that some students live in their parents' cars, and that's a problem, because they have to keep changing their address with the records office every day."

It had been an attempt at gallows humor. The sad thing was, it was true.

"Ricardo—I'm here to talk to you about the elements of short fiction, about plot, and character, and setting."

"And on page fourteen you say that Hispanic teachers can't teach English. It's right here in black and white. Why should we listen to anything a racist has to say?"

"I'm not a racist, Ricardo. My own son is Puerto Rican."

"Why do you hate your son?"

And I flipped. I flipped, was all. I ripped the newspaper out of his hands and said, "Get the fuck out—*now.*"

On his way out, he said, "I'm going to the principal. I'm going to tell him what you said." Then the door slammed and thirteen sleepy students looked at me, a little more attentively than they had when the subject had been "The Chrysanthemums."

I went to the blackboard, wrote *What change do we see in Elisa after she has spoken to the tinker?* I said, "I want a one-paragraph answer to that question before the class is over." I dropped the chalk in the chalk tray, stepped outside, and closed the door behind me. If this was the way it was going to be from now on, I didn't think I was going to be able to get through it.

Tracy came to see me on hall guard duty during fourth period. She was wearing a navy blue skirt suit with a striped tie and looked as though she should be checking airline tickets. She said, "How are you getting along?"

"Great, for a racist with a hangover."

There was a spare student desk next to mine, and she sat down in it, crossed her long legs. "You can't let them get to you, Johnny. This will blow over."

I tried to laugh, but nothing came out. "They're not going to let it blow over. They're getting too much mileage out of it."

She reached out and touched my shoulder. "Want to go to the shooting range after school?"

"Only if we use my head as a target."

I felt her studying my face. "You drank last night," she deduced.

"You must be clairvoyant."

"Under your eyes—you're all puffy. I can read you like a book, Johnny Spector."

"Oh, yeah? What am I thinking right now?"

"That you're the luckiest guy in the world to have someone like me care so much about you."

I didn't care if we were in the school or if anyone saw us. I kissed her. "That's true, but that's not what I was thinking."

"What were you thinking?"

Those young eyes, all that blond hair. Tracy Singer was a dream, a beautiful dream. "That it's all over."

"Don't be soft," she said. "You used to scold me whenever I was soft."

"I'm not being soft. It's just that they've got me, Tracy. Do you know I had a kid call me a racist in class today? Right in the middle of class."

"A kid called you a name, and so you fold? Come on."

"It's what that name *means*. I can't stand it that the people I've given my life to think that about me."

"Isabelle knows that. Don't you see? That's why she's using it against you. Stand up, Johnny. Don't let her do this to you."

It was a struggle just to get through a day at that school in the first place. I did not need the additional struggle of defending my reputation at every turn. "I just don't know if it's worth it anymore."

"Of course it is. Come out with me after school today. I'll buy you a drink. Hell—I'll buy you a whole bottle."

"Not today, sweetheart."

"What are you going to do, go home and sulk?"

"If I can get out of here in one piece, that's exactly what I'm going to do."

I would have given anything if she hadn't looked at me the way she did then, as if there was nothing to be done about me. I got up and squeezed her hand and then walked to the main office. A daring act of rebellion, leaving my hall guard post early.

I remembered my first day there, how excited I was to be a new teacher. The future looked pretty good back then, a wide-open vista of possibility. My father had bought me a new leather briefcase and I wore a navy blue suit. I was going to make a difference.

In my mailbox I found a memo announcing a meeting of the Committee Against Racial Hatred at Acosta High School. It invited the racist teacher who had given the recent interview so that he might explain his position and defend his remarks. I crumpled this up and shot it at the wastebasket in the corner. As I was walking out, Isabelle Villachez was walking in. When we passed one another, I heard her say, "*Estupido*," under her breath. I turned around and looked at her, but she kept walking toward her office as if she hadn't said anything.

By the end of the day I was ready to pack it all in and never come back. While riding the escalator just before sixth period, someone on the opposite escalator had leaned over and punched me in the face. It happened so fast, I didn't even see who had done it, and now there was a purple welt on my cheekbone. I ran cold water on it in the washroom, but it didn't help much.

Before leaving, I stopped in at Youth Services to see Marco Gonzalez. He was alone in his office writing case notes when I knocked on the glass partition. He looked up expectantly and then dropped his pen on his desk. "Jesus, what the hell happened to you?"

"I ran into one of my fans on the escalator. Can you talk, or is it better not to be seen with me in this lifetime?"

"Don't talk crazy. You're a friend, I told you that, and I'm as Puerto Rican as any of them. They can't do anything to me."

I sat in one of the two chairs set in front of his desk. He looked at me in much the same way that Tracy had, and I realized that this was the way it was going to be from now on. "May I ask you something?" I said.

"Of course."

I picked up a pencil that was lying on his desk and twirled it around. "You said you'd been hearing things about the spending of federal poverty funds. I was just wondering where you heard it."

Marco looked away, pushed his watchband further up his wrist. "Does it matter?"

I nodded. "Yeah, I think it might. I think there's a whole group of people in on it, and if I'm going to prove anything, I need to know where to look."

Marco stood up and walked over to his window. "Are you doing this to get back at them?"

"I told you about a scheme to divert funds even before the article was published. You know that."

He was looking below intently now. "I see the welcome committee is waiting for you again. It seems they've invited several hundred of their closest friends."

I stood up and joined him at the window. Sure enough, the front lobby was surrounded and the TV crews were back. "Must be a slow news day. How about it, Marco? Can you tell me who you heard it from?"

He had difficulty looking directly at me. "It won't get you out of this, Johnny."

"I know," I said. "Nothing's going to get me out of this."

He walked back over to his desk and began stacking some of the manila folders there. Each one had a student name and a homeroom number. All the sorrows of our kids in numerical order. "It was Elizabeth Mojica. We were riding up in the elevator, and I heard her tell a bilingual teacher that they had found a way to send money to the *Macheteros* on the island."

"Do you know who the bilingual teacher was?"

"No. I don't know her name. I'd recognize her if I saw her again, though."

I had guessed that Elizabeth was in on it. They operated as a clique. They must all know. I said, "Why would she talk about this in front of you?"

He shrugged. "Maybe she thinks I don't understand Spanish. Or maybe she assumes I approve. Or maybe she's just stupid."

Danny, Isabelle, Elizabeth, Murphy, Hafka, and Mike Parnell. Who'd think that six people could hijack a whole high school? Was it just six, or were there more?

I said, "Could this thing go beyond Danny? Maybe all the way to the downtown office?"

Marco shook his head. "I don't know." He put his hands in his pockets and strode over to the window again. "How are you going to get through that mob?"

"I'll leave through the auto shop. I'm parked just across the street."

He gazed absently down below and shook the loose change in his pocket. "Be careful," he said.

José DeLaTorre was working under the hood of a navy blue Cavalier when I entered the auto shop. There were pipes and parts scattered across the concrete floor, and just to José's left, on a table, his toolbox. He threw a wrench in the toolbox and wiped his hands on a rag which he'd pulled from his back pocket. "You want to hop in the back seat and I'll drive you out of here?"

I never knew which of my Latin friends would still speak to me. I was glad I could count on José.

I said, "Won't be necessary. I'm parked right across the street."

"They've got even more people than they did yesterday," he estimated.

I flicked the switch that raised the big garage door. "I know," I said. "I'm becoming a movement."

He stuck the rag back in his pocket and slammed the hood of the car shut. He had a kid's face, José did, and he looked at me kind of sadly. "What are you going to do, Johnny?"

That was the question of the week. "Go home and get drunk."

He said, "No—I meant about this whole thing."

"That's as far as I've gotten, José."

I walked out of the shop and crossed the street and leaned against my Jeep for a moment. Today the person with the bullhorn was a man I had never seen before. He had a receding hairline and wore a black overcoat that furled in the icy wind. I listened as he vehemently exhorted the huddled crowd, though I could not make out what he was saying at this distance. It didn't matter. You didn't need to know the words to grasp the general import. I opened the door and hopped in. The seats were cold and the engine ran hard as I watched the mob get smaller and smaller in my side view mirror.

221

Nothing tastes smoother than Smirnoff.
Created from the finest grain and filtered in a unique
charcoal process. Try an imaginative Smirnoff cocktail.

All right, I thought, *I will.* My idea of an imaginative cocktail was to pour it in a glass and drink it straight. I was at home, in a little room over a garage, reading liquor bottle labels at four-thirty in the afternoon. There was a warning sign there, somewhere. The TV was on with the sound turned down and I was watching footage of yellow dump trucks being loaded with salt in the yards of the city's sanitation department. Two missing people, a man and a small boy, looked up at me from the pile of mail that had been thrown on the coffee table.

After the yellow dump trucks there was a shot of the front steps of Acosta High School. I scrambled from the couch and turned up the sound in enough time to learn that the man with the receding hairline who was speaking through the bullhorn was an alderman. He was saying that there was no room for racial intolerance in the classrooms of Chicago, and he called for my immediate dismissal. The on-site reporter inverted my first and middle names, referring to me as Paul John Spector, a teacher who "recently made disparaging remarks about Hispanics in an interview given to Brian Podhorst for *Chicagoland Today.*" Then they showed a dog beauty pageant held in Aurora. The winner was a Dalmatian wearing a hat. He had mastered the feat of walking on his hind legs.

I snapped off the set and sat down right there on the floor. I wanted some ice for my drink, but I didn't have the wherewithal to get up and get it. What could be worse, I wondered, than being labeled a racist? It put you in league with George Wallace, David Duke, Himmler, Hitler. And what could you say in your own defense? *Some of my best friends . . . .*

So Brian got mentioned on TV. He was probably thrilled.

The phone rang. I stared at it distrustfully. There were very few people in the world that I cared to hear from at the moment.

"Hello?"

"I've been seeing more of you on TV lately than I used to at home." Marlyn. Her voice was like a warm Gulf tide. You could have swum in it.

"Yeah, well—you didn't actually see me. You just saw the people who were waiting for me."

"Somebody at work mentioned that you were in some kind of trouble. I didn't believe them at first. Then I turned on the TV today, and oh, my God. How did it happen, Johnny?"

"I don't know. It's like being run over. I never knew what hit me."

"I haven't read the interview, yet."

I said, "Spare yourself the ordeal."

"Let me guess. You were being a wise ass, and you stepped over the politically correct line."

"What in the world would ever give you that impression?"

"You have such a big mouth. I'm not even going to lecture you on silence and valor. You wouldn't listen to me anyway."

"I'm in a real jam, Marlyn."

"But how did it become all this so quickly?"

"Oh, Isabelle and her revolutionary pals needed a poster boy for Anglo intolerance, and there I was."

"You an Anglo. That's very funny."

"Unfortunately, none of this is very funny at all."

There were a few seconds of silence, and then Marlyn said, "No, I guess it isn't. How are you holding up?"

"I don't know that I am. What about Jason? The only thing worse than being a racist is being the son of one."

"He's all right. He knows you're not a racist, Johnny."

"Remind him, though, will you?"

"Of course."

"Tell him I love him."

"I will."

Then there was one of those gaps, one of those awkward pauses that always occurs between two people who have been out of touch for some time.

"Is there anything I can do for you?" she wanted to know.

Yes. Get rid of Bruce. Call off the divorce. Tell me you love me and you want me to come home. Tear off my clothes and throw me in bed. And fire that stupid lawyer with the cowboy boots.

"Johnny?"

"Uh—no. Thanks. Thanks just the same."

I placed the receiver in its cradle and picked up the snapshot of Marlyn as a little girl with her mother. Mrs. Valentin had stoic eyes.

She looked as though she'd never smiled a day in her life. I wished I could have met her, wondered what her absence had done to Marlyn. We all have our wounds.

And then I thought, *Marlyn*.

I got to school early enough so that I did not have to worry about getting through a crowd. I signed in and went to my office and hung up my coat, and then stopped in the boys room to comb my hair. What do you know. There on the hand drying machine was a little round green sticker. It said, *SPECTOR OUT*. On the mirror I found a red one, and out in the hallway they were stuck to windows, doors, walls. They were everywhere.

I went back to my office and sat in my chair and stared at my filing cabinet. Twenty-two years worth of manila folders—student essays, professional essays, tests, research papers. How the hell do you pack up and move an entire career? The pain from my cheekbone slowly merged with my headache. I had a bottle of aspirin somewhere, but I couldn't find it, so I lay my head down on my arms atop my desk and closed my eyes. Forty minutes later the period tone sounded and woke me. I had only intended to get a few moments' rest, and now I was late for class.

At the base of the escalator a tall man with gray hair and glasses stopped me. "Mr. Spector, may I have a word with you?"

I did not know how he knew me, as I didn't know him. I said, "What can I do for you?"

"Come into the conference room in the main office, please."

"Sorry," I said, "but I'm late for class."

"Your class has been covered, Mr. Spector. I'm Marshall Korman—the district superintendent. If you'll just come with me."

I had wondered when something like this was going to happen. I had no choice but to follow him into the main office, and then into the conference room. Behind the counter, Shirley gave me a mindful look.

Inside the conference room Danny Velez sat at a table, waiting for us. Marshall Korman closed the door and said, "Have a seat, Mr. Spector."

The three of us sat down, something like points on a triangle.

Danny had his hands folded before him, fingertips upon fingertips. "I suppose you know what this is about, Mr. Spector."

I said, "Well, let's don't make any hasty presuppositions. Why don't you go ahead and tell me."

224

Marshal Korman said, "Let me speak plainly. You have become a disruption at this school because of the interview you gave *Chicagoland Today*. As district superintendent, I cannot allow the daily routine of this educational institution to dissolve into chaos."

I rubbed my chin. I had forgotten to shave this morning. "Mr. Korman, if you'd like to end the chaos, then I suggest you talk to Isabelle Villachez. She's the one with the bullhorn and the mob. All I do is go home in the afternoon."

Danny said, "Mr. Spector, you must understand that Ms. Villachez is simply responding to the remarks you made to a reporter. She is not the problem. You are."

The pain in my head had reached alarming proportions. With my luck, it was probably a tumor. "Danny—don't make me recite the First Amendment for you."

Marshall Korman said, "This has nothing to do with your First Amendment rights, Mr. Spector."

I said, "The hell it doesn't."

Danny said, "You will please address me as Mr. Velez."

"The point of this meeting is to inform you that until further notice, Mr. Spector, you will be reassigned to the district office, where you will report from now on." Marshall Korman took a pen from his breast pocket and began writing something on a document that was placed in front of him on the table.

"Mr. Korman, let me recommend for your reading a copy of the faculty contract. You can start at the paragraph titled 'Due Process.'"

"You'll get your due process. In the meantime, you have been temporarily reassigned. This is my decision, and it's not a matter that's up for discussion."

Danny smirked and said, "I'm surprised you would care to remain where you are not wanted, Mr. Spector."

I said, "You're the one who doesn't want me, Danny. The kids do."

"I saw three hundred of them yesterday who want no part of you."

"You mean Isabelle's henchmen? Please. They don't represent student sentiment. They're just following orders."

Marshall Korman stood now, and handed me the paper that he had been writing upon. "This is your new assignment, Mr. Spector. I will expect you at the district office before eleven."

Just like that. No fanfare, not even a decent fight. Just a temporary transfer. I said, "Why don't you ask Mr. Velez here how he's been handing over public money to revolutionary forces on the island."

Danny jumped to his feet. "Do not say anything you may later regret, Mr. Spector."

"I can't help it, Danny. It's sort of become a habit with me."

Danny said, "That's insubordination."

"It can't be insubordination if I don't work here anymore."

He clenched his jaw, shoved open the conference room door, and stomped out. Marshall Korman reached for a camel's hair overcoat that had been draped over a chair back. He studied me a moment and then said, "It seems that everything I've heard about you is true."

I wanted to tell him that I really didn't give a good goddamn what he had heard about me, but that was probably what he expected. "I'd look into those poverty funds, if I were you. If a thing like that gets out to the papers, there's no telling how far the investigation will reach."

He lingered a moment or two, looking as though he were weighing something in his mind, then walked out into the main office.

Transferred. Son of a bitch.

I had forgotten to button my button-down collar. This I discovered absently as I left the conference room; I stood there trying to button it, but couldn't, and that's when I noticed Shirley beckoning me surreptitiously with her finger. I walked over to her desk and she placed a torn piece of paper in my hand.

I said, "Don' tell me. You want me to meet you in an out-of-the-way resort and this is your room number."

"That's the combination to the vault, and the vault is where you'll find the second set of accounting books." She nodded her head once toward the vault. "Left side—under a box of old student grade reports."

Shirley. When everything else in the world went wrong, there she was with her magic wand.

I put the combination to the safe in my pants pocket. "I take it you know I've just been transferred."

"I've called your union representative and she's in the process of filing a grievance right now."

I leaned over and kissed her cheek. "I've been wanting to do that for ages."

Shirley went crimson from the neck up. "It's about time. What took you so long?"

§

"What did they have you doing all day?"

I was out to dinner later that night with Tracy at Maggiano's and was having my third Stolichnaya. With one you felt a little better. Two and you had some of your self-respect back. Three—you could rule the world. I said, "I sat next to a filing cabinet and read the *Tribune*. All of it. Would you like to know your horoscope?"

"Did Jamel say how long the grievance would take?"

She meant Jamel Saunders—the union rep. "Maybe a week, maybe sooner. The problem is—what happens if I get reassigned? Walking through mobs every afternoon is getting a little old. She thinks maybe I should request that I be transferred to another school." Tracy had just had a sip of her Merlot and had a purple mustache. I folded my napkin and dabbed her lip. "Christ, I can't take you anywhere."

"You don't want to go to a different high school, Johnny."

I knew she was right. I didn't. "But I don't want to go back, either. Isn't that something? I think I've finally had enough."

"No more streethearts?"

I'd shared with her Marlyn's name for my kids. "It's just that—how long can I go on doing this? I'll be forty-five next year. I've been hanging out with teenagers since I *was* a teenager."

Angel hair pasta and shrimp. She had a fork full of it all spun around. "What *do* you want to do, then?"

"That college I teach at in the summer. I think I'd like to work there. Go in in the morning and talk about Keats and Shelley, and come home in the afternoon. Write stories, articles. How's that sound?"

"Sounds wonderful. Why don't you apply?"

My drink was empty. I asked the waitress for an Amstel Light and then said to Tracy—"Well, in case you've forgotten, every afternoon on TV they show the *Johnny Spector Racist Show*."

"It's not going to last, Johnny."

I said, "Nothing does."

Wasn't that the truth?

For a thin girl, she had quite an appetite. She had another piece of bread and nearly inhaled the pasta. Her mouth was still full when she said, "What are you going to do about the accounting books?"

"*We*. What are *we* going to do about the accounting books. You still work there, and I need you."

"I wondered when you were finally going to say that."

"What?"

"That you need me."

I took one of her hands in both of mine. "You're a hell of a pretty girl. You know that?"

She continued to eat with one hand as I held the other. "That's a very nice sentiment, but you could work a little on the delivery."

I was buzzed and she was pretty and I liked flirting with her. Such a nice kid. Such a sweet, nice kid. "We're going to break into the school and steal the books."

Tracy put her hand around the stem of her wineglass but did not lift it. "I have this sinking feeling you're not kidding."

"I'm not. It's the only way to prove that they've been robbing the Federal money. The books are in the vault, and I've got the vault's combination."

"And exactly how do we get in to the school?"

"The auto shop. I'll have José forget to lock the door."

She had finished her pasta and shrimp and was now eating my Caesar salad. "And what are we going to do with the books once we have them?"

"Take 'em to the FBI and get Danny's ass thrown in jail. Isabelle's too. Elizabeth's too. Anatole's too."

Tracy said, "That's a lot of jailing."

I said, "That's a lot of asses."

I had had too much to drink and Tracy insisted that she drive us back to her place for coffee. There was a slight snow flurry that night and I slipped while walking up the steps to her place, and she said I had better spend the night.

"Can't do that," I said.

A few cups of coffee later I stood up, grabbed my leather jacket, and called it a night. Tracy saw me to the door and put her arms around my neck. "Why don't you ever try to make love to me?" she asked.

I said, "I can't do that when I'm trying *not* to make love to you."

She kissed me, just a slight kiss, and said, "It's Marlyn, isn't it? You're still in love with her."

I wrapped my scarf around my neck and kissed her cheek. "Good night," I said.

I guessed I was sober enough to be driving—I kept the Jeep off the sidewalks, anyway. I pulled into the alleyway behind North Francisco, got out, opened the garage and backed in. It was a cold night and the wind numbed my ears as I climbed the rickety outdoor steps to my room. A sudden glint of headlights caught my attention. A car slowly made its way down the block, turned around, and idly headed back the other way. It did this several times. I stood on the landing watching it cut through the incessant sprinkle of snow, until it began to look familiar, a 1994 or 1995 gold Buick. It took a while before it dawned on me that it was Tito's car.

13

The next morning I drove halfway to the district office before hearing on the news that an asteroid would slam into earth in the year 2017. It figured. Just when the house would be paid off. I thought of having to sit next to that filing cabinet all day and became daunted just enough to turn the Jeep around and call in sick on my cell phone.

"I've been trying to get a hold of you for two days."
I said, "I've been out."
"Out where?"
"Passed out."
Tracy said, "I hope that isn't true. You sound terrible."
"If you think I *sound* bad, you should *see* me."
"It's almost one in the afternoon. Are you still in bed?"
"I never made it to the bed. I'm on the floor."
Tracy heaved a big sigh on the other end. "Johnny, Jamel Saunders has been trying to reach you. She got you transferred back to Acosta."
I did not know which was worse—having to report to the district office, or having to go back to Acosta. "She did? When do I start?"
"Tomorrow."
I got up and stepped over an empty Bombay Sapphire bottle. "To*morrow*? Isn't tomorrow Sunday?"
"Today is Sunday, Johnny."
"Oh." I'd lost a day there somewhere.
"That's it. I'm coming over."
"No," I said. "Please don't do that. I'll see you tomorrow at school."
"Are you sure? Are you all right?"
"I'm fine. I just need some time alone, is all."
There was a pause and then she said that I should take care of

myself, and I said I would. I hung up and rubbed my eyes. There was a funny feeling in my head, as though my brain was floating.

Then I remembered. Christ. I was supposed to have seen my kid the day before. I had forgotten all about it. I called and Marlyn answered. She was not pleased with me. This was one of the reasons she was divorcing me, she said. I didn't pay enough attention to Jason. She also said that the court date was set for February fifteenth. I did not have a chance to respond because the line went dead.

I crawled over to the bed and pulled myself up till I was sitting on it. I was still wearing Friday's clothes. It would be a good idea to shave, I thought, though I didn't know if I could make it to the bathroom. My wife and kid had had it with me, an entire community wanted me fired, and I wasn't so crazy about myself. *Try an imaginative cocktail. Drink it from the bottle wrapped in a brown paper bag while you're standing in the goddamn unemployment line.*

A knock at the door dismayed me. I didn't want to see anybody, and I certainly didn't want anybody to see me, not the way I looked.

"*Maestro.* Are you there?"

My father-in-law. I stood up uncertainly and held on to the wall while making my way to the door. It had been unlocked all this time. When I opened it, he looked troubled.

"I no see you for days. I wonder if you are all right."

The cold shot into the little room as I held out my arm to invite him in. He shut the door behind him and I stumbled back to the bed. His head pivoted slowly as he took in the debris scattered about. The gin bottle, several Corona empties, fast food wrappers, a blanket on the floor that should have been on the bed, my shoes, my tie.

"Why you do this to yourself?" he wanted to know.

Two days. I must have made Bela Lugosi look healthy by comparison. "I'll tell you, señor—I don't exactly know what I'm doing."

He picked up the blue gin bottle and took it over to the kitchen, set it on the counter. There were several unwashed plates and glasses in the sink. "No good, living like this. What is the problem, *maestro?*"

I tossed my hands up and let them fall in my lap. "I don't know what to say to you."

"You do not seem to know very much."

I had to turn slightly to see him as we spoke. "I know I'm not a racist, like everybody thinks."

"Are you sure of that?"

I think I just sat there and blinked at him a few times. He had caught me off guard. "What are you saying—that you think that I *am* a racist?"

"Only that you must look deep within to be sure what you are and what you are not, to know for yourself with certainty. You must do this."

It had never seemed to be an issue. I had never considered that maybe I was prejudiced, or had prejudices, had never considered it at all. A little soul searching, what could it hurt? "All right," I said. "I'll do that."

"That is all one has to do."

I said, "I wish somebody would tell the Acosta people that."

"Forget them. You know why they come after you. Make sure in your own heart that you are right, and all will be well."

He was a simple man, but he had such certainty. Faith, I suppose you would call it, something I lacked.

I nodded to him, and he said, "Come downstairs and have some soup or some chicken. You look terrible."

"Thank you," I said. "I'll just clean up a little first and then I'll be right down."

"Do not clean up a little, *maestro. Por favor,* clean up a *lot.*"

You've seen those milky, slushy winter days when the sky and the ground and everything in between are the same color; this was one of those. I parked the Jeep across the street from the auto shop and hiked uphill through the snow. When I got to the front entrance I looked up in disbelief. Strung from one lamppost to another across the Humboldt roadway was a giant yellow banner. It read: **JOHN SPECTOR MUST GO**. Once you become a political issue, it's kind of hard to be anything else.

Oscar stared at me evenly as I walked through the metal detector. He did not say a word. I rode the escalator up to the main office on the second floor and could not find my name on the sign-in sheet. Likewise in the mailroom, my name had been removed from the alphabetical sequencing and hastily scribbled on the last box under Tony Zannini's. When I tried to get into my office, I discovered the key was no longer on my ring. They were going to make this just as difficult for me as they could.

"Oh, Johnny—I'm sorry about all this."

Judy Santiago. I had been sitting in a student desk in front of the records office for a half hour because I had nowhere else to go.

"I take it you saw the banner out there."

"I'm going to call the park district and have it taken down. I'm so sorry." She inserted a key in the door, drew it open, and flicked on the stark fluorescent lights.

"It seems I haven't got the same office, mailbox or keys."

Judy took off her coat and hung it on a chrome coat rack. "You don't have the same program, either. When Jamel got you reinstated, Danny ordered all new classes for you."

I said, "My division, too?"

"Yeah. Your kids aren't going to like it."

She handed me a manila folder, which I opened and read. The son of a bitch had given me all freshman remedial reading classes. I was starting to miss my little chair next to the filing cabinet at the district office.

Judy said, "It's not just you, Johnny."

"What do you mean?"

"Don't say anything to anybody, but they've got Mike in a bind."

"What kind of a bind?"

She looked out the window to see if anyone was in the hallway. "Some funny things that are being done—they're making Mike do them. His name is on everything. Danny never signs a paper."

I said, "Or a check, right?"

She nodded gravely. "His ulcer has gotten worse. He was in the hospital emergency room last week."

"You know, Judy, no one's twisting Mike's arm."

Judy was loyal to Mike, and I understood that. "He's got kids, Johnny."

"I remember when he had ethics, too."

"Sometimes it's not all that easy."

"I guess," I said, and left the office.

For three hours I listened to kids trying to read aloud, struggling through sentences as if they were verbal jungles. I wrote phonetic translations on the blackboard. I broke up two fights and confiscated a joint. I tore four SPECTOR OUT stickers off of classroom windows. By eleven o'clock I thought I was going to lose my mind.

"Johnny, dude—where you been?"

Fernando caught up to me in the seventh floor lunchroom. "They transferred me. Then they transferred me back."

"How come you not back in division? Damn, man—we got this old white bitch gym teacher who won't let us breathe. It's fucked up."

"Who—you mean Anderson?"

"Yeah, man. The fat *puta*."

I said, "I can't do anything about it, Fernando. Danny and Isabelle are calling all the shots. They're trying to wear me down."

"Maybe it's time me and my boys have a talk with them."

I grabbed his shoulder. "Don't be crazy, Fernando. They've got all the power. They'd expel you and then where would you be? No, you listen to me. There's going to be an end to this."

"When? When's there gonna be an end to this?"

I said, "Fuck if I know."

Fernando cracked up. He loved to hear me swear. "You hang in there, Johnny. You face them—c*on gana*. Right?"

"*Con gana*, baby." I didn't tell him I was almost out of *gana*.

§

We stood in a dark so solid we could not see our own hands in front of our faces. Tracy clicked on her flashlight and waved it around the garage. The Cavalier was still in the service bay, and we followed the floor grating all the way to the hallway entrance.

It was one a.m. The door knob of the auto shop side entrance had given as soon as I'd turned it. José had come through.

Tracy said, "Are you sure there isn't a security guard at night?"

"I don't think so. The custodians work till ten and then leave through the park district doors. It's still kind of a good idea to be quiet, just in case."

I turned on my flashlight and shined it down the hallway. It's funny how a place you know so well in daylight can look so foreign and sinister at night. We tiptoed upon the linoleum, and when I reached the corner, I stood close to the brick wall and edged my head around to look down the next corridor.

"Keep your flashlight pointed down. We don't need to announce that we're here."

Tracy said, "I thought you said there wasn't a security guard."

"I don't *think* there's a security guard."

I guided her down the hall, my arm around her waist. We were both dressed in black, black leather jackets, jeans. Very stylish crooks we were. I kept wondering what we'd tell the cops if we got caught.

Uh—we left our lesson plans here.

We had no choice but to take the inner stairwell to the ground floor. It was the only route, except for the theater, and the theater doors were locked. When I climbed up to the first landing—I heard a click come from the wall above. A little red light went on.

"Shit," I said.

"What is it?"

"Motion detector."

"What happens now?"

"I don't know. I just hope it doesn't set off some kind of silent alarm." If the security system had been neglected as much as the daily running of the school, then we were safe.

We moved cautiously up the next flight of stairs, and the motion detector clicked once more. I pushed open the glass, wire-mesh door. We'd made it—the first floor. No flashlights now. There was enough light in the lobby from the street lamps in the park, and there was no telling who might see us from outside. The park had a nightlife, even in the winter. I hurried along the stainless steel side of the escalator, pulling Tracy along by her hand. Of course the escalator did not run at night, and we climbed it quickly, holding on to the rubber side rails. I was out of breath by the time we got to the second floor, though the run barely fazed Tracy. Youth.

Just today Shirley had slipped me a copy of the key for the main office doors. I pulled it out of my jeans pocket and inserted it in the lock. The tumblers turned smoothly, no problem—but when I opened the door, *click!* Another motion detector in the corner of the hallway. Its red light began blinking ominously.

"Son of a bitch," I said. "I've been working here years and I never noticed that damn thing before."

Tracy held my arm tightly. "Maybe we'd better get out of here."

"We've come this far. We can't stop now."

I moved through the maze of secretaries' desks to the windows on the far side. One by one I closed the mini blinds before turning on my flashlight again. From the rear pocket of my jeans I pulled the vault combination. L25-R13-L4-R7-L20. Tracy was waiting for me at the vault door. She held the glow of her flashlight on the dial, and I trained mine on the little scrap of paper. Slowly, I began turning the knob. I forgot if you were supposed to turn it all the way around in the opposite direction once you hit the number, or if you could just turn it directly to the next. The beam from Tracy's flashlight shook.

"Relax," I said.

I hit the last number and gave a tug on the release bar. Nothing.

"I think you went around one too many times in the last two sequences."

I spun the dial several times around and started all over again. Now my fingers were jittery. I tried to turn the knob as evenly as I could.

"Johnny?"

"What?"

"How do you feel about me?"

Jesus, I thought, *of all the times.* "I feel very good about you."

I had got as far as L4.

"Do you love me?"

"Tracy—I'm trying to break into a school vault, at the moment."

I could feel her pouting. Black turtleneck, black knit hat. The cutest cat burglar you ever saw.

"But do you love me? Or *did* you love me and then stop loving me?"

I'd messed it up again. I turned the dial around several times to the right. "You're asking me questions I haven't been able to answer myself. Did I love you? Yes. Do I love you? Yes. Am I trying not to love you? Yes. Do I still love Marlyn? Yes. Is that why I'm trying not to love you? Yes. Am I too old for you? Yes. Are you making me *meshugge*? Goddamn—*yes*."

"All right. Spin the dial. We'll talk about this later."

I'd done all the talking about this that I wanted. Right-left, right-left. Why wasn't this damned thing working? Was there some trick to it—something you were supposed to do before you began turning the knob? I went through the combination two more times, and then, just as I was about ready to give up, I pulled the release bar and the door

236

clicked open.

"Well, what do you know about that?"

We pulled the big door to and shined our flashlights inside. It was a big vault, the size of a room, and there were shelves and boxes and items stacked nearly to the ceiling.

I said, "We're going to have to turn on the light."

"Will anybody be able to see it from outside?"

That was a consideration. "I don't know. But we'll never find those books unless we do it."

I felt around for the light switch. It was about head level to my right. Fluorescent tubes—just what I needed. You could signal to Alaska with lights that bright. Where had Shirley said they'd be—to the left, under some boxes? I lifted every box in the vault—nothing. No sign of any accounting books.

"What do we do now?" Tracy asked.

"I don't understand it. Shirley said they'd be under a box, or on top of a box—but I don't see anything that looks like a check book, or a ledger. What the hell?"

"We can't have come all this way for nothing."

I whispered, "Shh—did you hear that?"

I snapped off the light. I don't know that I've ever done anything gingerly, but I tried right then to gingerly pull the big six-inch thick door, till it was almost shut. *Christ, wouldn't that be something*, I thought. *Locked in the vault all night and then the two of us being found in there by Danny in the morning.*

I pulled Tracy down on the floor next to me and held her tightly. Someone opened the office door—that much I could hear. Then the door closed, hard, and there was the unmistakable sound of a key turning in the lock.

Tracy whispered, "I'm going to pee in my pants."

I said, "Move over."

A few more moments of silence. Whoever it was had gone.

"No security guard, huh?"

"Well, he's not a very good one, anyway."

The way back was tricky. Now that we knew we had company, we couldn't afford to make any noise at all. I had to unlock the office door, and then once we were out, lock it again. We stopped and listened at the base of the escalator before proceeding, at the landing of the staircase, and in the lower hallway. We had almost made it to the auto shop when Tracy, out of sheer nervousness, I think, dropped her flashlight. It clattered and echoed throughout the bare, cinder block corridor. Neither of us took a step further, but waited, listened for a footfall, a voice. Nothing. The only sound was Tracy's labored breathing. I motioned with a flick of my head for her to pick up her flashlight, and then we ran. We ran through the darkened auto shop, with only the little circles of light to guide us, and then out the door into the cold, all the way to the Jeep. In the short time we had been in there, the windshield had glazed over with frost, so I scraped a little patch with my bare hands and we took off through the night.

It was fifteen after two by the time we got to her place, and I had to be up at five.

"Stay," she said. Though I thought it a poor idea, I slept on the floor beside her bed. It would make her feel better, she said; our night of espionage had made her jittery. When we woke in the morning her hair was all askew and in her face, and she looked lovely anyway. I realized that I would probably always love her, in a special kind of way, and that there was nothing much I could do about it. She said she had slept fine. I felt as though I needed back surgery.

The ball hit the alley, rolled wide, and knocked down two pins on the left. The rest remained standing. I had never been much of a bowler. Jason said, "You let go too late." I nodded and waited for my ball to return. It had been a last minute idea, to call and ask if he'd like to go bowling and have dinner. It's funny. After my parents divorced, my father and I used to go bowling too. Neither of us enjoyed it much. *Bowling: the divorce sport.*

I almost picked up the spare. That one stubborn goddamn nine pin. Jason got up and I sat down. "I'm sorry about last Saturday," I said.

"It's all right." He approached the line and held the ball before him. I could not believe how big he had gotten, not just in height, but in the musculature of his arms and chest. He moved in, swung back, and unleashed the ball smoothly. Strike. My kid.

"So your mom's still seeing this Bruce guy, I understand."

"This is just the way Zander Abrams said it would be."

I didn't understand this. "What way is that?"

Jason smiled to himself and shook his head. "He said that after your parents get divorced, your mother is always asking you about your dad, and your dad always asks you about your mother."

I remembered this too. "You have to understand about parents. We're all insane."

"That's the truth."

I marked his strike on the score sheet and felt Jason watching me. I looked up and said, "What is it?"

"They're giving you a pretty tough time at school, aren't they?"

If only I had gotten those accounting books. When I'd asked Shirley about them the other day, she told me she believed Danny had removed them and taken them home.

"The kids are all right. It's the adults who want me gone."

"What are you going to do?"

"I'm working on it."

He was quiet a moment. "You and Mom are really going to go through with this?"

I said, "I don't think either one of us knows what we're doing. Sometimes I think it's a game of chicken."

"I think you've got that right." The machine had gotten stuck. Jason pushed the button that resets the pins. Then he said, "There's no spark there, Dad. You don't have to worry."

"I beg your pardon?"

"With Bruce and Mom. He'd like it to lead to something serious, but Mom just goes out with him for company. He's a dufus."

Pretty amazing kid. "Thanks," I said.

"No problem. It's your turn. Hurry up so I can win."

The week wore on and each day was another personal struggle. Few teachers would speak to me or even acknowledge my existence. I had no office to go to other than the English book room—an enclave containing stacks of texts and a lone communal desk. I sat there during my free period and went through my mail. Four cut slips for some of my new division students whose names as of yet meant nothing to me. An ad for life insurance from some union affiliate. The daily bulletin with a message about new homeroom absence procedures. A flier from the Committee Against Racial Hatred at Acosta High School announcing a rally against the racist teacher in the park this afternoon. Why should today be any different?

I stood up and walked down the aisle between shelves of books. *1984, The Divine Comedy, The Great Gatsby, The Little Brown Handbook, For Whom the Bell Tolls, Down These Mean Streets, Of Mice and Men.* I wouldn't be teaching any of these anymore. I wondered what I could do for a living if I gave up teaching. I guessed I would probably be one of those guys you see selling ties at Macy's.

First the door burst open. "Johnny? Johnny—you here?"

I walked down the aisle to the doorway and Daisy was standing there, her book bag slung over her shoulder.

I said, "What's the matter?"

"Fernando's been shot. The D's shot him."

My worst nightmare. "Wait, slow down. Is he alive?"

"Yeah. They got him in intensive care."

"Where is he?"

"The Dragons sent him and Jorgé out to get rid of the Disciples in their hood and he got shot."

"*Daisy*—tell me where he is."

"Saint Mary's. They got him at Saint Mary's. Damn, Johnny—I been tryin' to call your cell phone since last night."

I said, "My Jeep is parked out back of the auto shop. Meet me there in two minutes, do you understand?"

"Johnny—the bullet went through his lung."

"Daisy, go!"

When Daisy was in her hysteria mode, all she could do was talk. She ran out the door and I picked up my jacket and took the stairwell down to the second floor. I would have taken the escalators, but guess in which direction they were all running? I signed out in the main office and Danny Velez caught me before I had a chance to leave.

"Mr. Spector—where do you think you're going?"

I said, "One of my students has been shot."

He put his hand on my arm. "This is a closed campus. Teachers are not permitted to leave at any time during the school day."

I pulled my arm away from him. He was a punk and a thief and I did not like him. I said, "Then why the fuck don't you fire me and get it over with? Afraid you won't have anybody to hold rallies against?"

I would have loved to have heard his comeback, but I was out the door and running down the stairs before he could get his jaw closed. Oh, well. There was always that tie counter at Macy's.

The Jeep was drafty and it took forever for that old heater to heat up. Daisy rattled off at the mouth a mile a minute, and as far as I could assimilate the information, the Dragon elders had sent Fernando and Jorgé out to get rid of the Disicples' dealers. They were both under seventeen and would not serve hard time if caught. I couldn't imagine that Chilo was behind such a decision; he was more responsible than that. It must have been someone under him—but Fernando. How many times had I told him about this sort of thing? I thought he had begun to grow up at last—grow away from this gang shit.

I think we hit every red light on Division Street, and all I could keep thinking was, *Somebody's going to pay.*

14

The nurse at the ICU desk would not let us in to see Fernando. She said only two people were allowed, and they must be family members. His mother was currently at his bedside.

I said, "We *are* family."

She dropped the clipboard she had been scribbling upon on the counter and looked at me severely over the rims of her glasses.

"I'm his sister," Daisy said.

"And I'm his uncle." She did not bat an eyelash. "His Uncle John."

"Sir—his mother is with him. When she comes out, then we'll see. All right—*Uncle John?*"

"Hold on—at least tell me his condition."

"I said, when his mother comes out." She turned from the desk and disappeared behind a door that read NO ADMITTANCE in large red letters.

Daisy looked at me hopelessly. I said, "Do you have a cigarette?"

She reached in her parka and pulled out a box of Newports. "You can't smoke here."

"Who said anything about smoking? I'm going to chew it."

We sat in the waiting room upon hard-backed plastic chairs. Newspaper sections and soft drink cans were scattered about. Every now and then some orderly or nurse would walk by, and in the corner a TV tuned to CNN droned softly. There had been a bombing in the Middle East. And they called that news. I let the cigarette dangle from my mouth and thought about praying for Fernando. It had been a long time since I had prayed. I didn't quite know how to go about it.

Please, don't let him die.

Well, that said it all. Now all we needed was someone to hear it.

I got up to pace. My back hurt and my shoulders hurt and my

head hurt too. Pretty much everything hurt. Nearly an hour later, Mrs. Morales, holding a wad of Kleenex to her eye, emerged from the ICU rooms. She was deep within herself and didn't know who I was at first. I said, "Mrs. Morales—"

She looked in my direction and then opened her arms and embraced me. "Oh, *señor* Spector. *Te doy las gracias por venir a visitar a mi hijo.*"

"I'm so sorry, señora. How is he?"

"No so good. The bullet—it went through. Go out his back. He bleed. From his liver he bleed, his lung. I pray to Jesus. You too—*por favor.*"

"Of course," I said.

Mrs. Morales let go of me and wiped stray tears away. "See him now."

"I will. Take care of yourself."

The nurse had returned and apparently this little scene had convinced her that Daisy and I, if not family members *per se*, were not strangers, either. She led us back to a series of closely spaced rooms, filled with equipment and some very sick looking patients. I saw an old man with white hair who looked like a ghost staring at the ceiling. The nurse stopped just outside of Fernando's room and said, "Please, keep it a short visit."

Daisy gasped and held both her hands to her face.

I whispered, "Let's not be doing any of that in front of him, okay?"

We entered the room. Fernando had two tubes up his nostrils, tubes in his arm, his chest. There was a machine that made a hissing sound. His face was sallow, his eyes closed. I walked to his side and pressed his shoulder slightly. His eyelids fluttered and lifted languidly. In a barely audible whisper he said my name.

I leaned over the rails. Quietly I said, "You stupid son of a bitch. The minute you get better, I'm going to kick your fucking ass."

He smiled, winced, and moved to hold his lower side. Soon he was trying to say something, and I lowered my ear near his mouth.

It took a while, but eventually he got out, "*Con gana.*"

Daisy approached the other side of the bed. She gently kissed his forehead and then ruffled his hair with her fingers. Fernando closed his eyes. He looked so tired and frail. Visiting here under these circumstances was not really visiting at all. It was hello and goodbye, and so we left the room, and I thanked the nurse on our way out.

She said, "Goodbye, Uncle John."

Outside, Daisy turned her head, thinking I wouldn't see that she was drying a tear. Toughness was her badge of honor.

"Give me a light," I said.

She looked distracted, and then fished around in her parka pocket for a book of matches. She tried to light my cigarette twice, but each time the wind blew the match out. Finally she said, "Give me that," and took the cigarette out of my mouth and put it in hers. She lit the cigarette herself and then extended it to me.

"Thanks," I said.

"Damn, Johnny. Did you see him? He looks like he's almost—"

"Don't say it." I took and drag and threw the cigarette to the ground, where I crushed it with my sneaker.

Daisy said, "What'd you do that for?"

I said, "What—you want me to get cancer?"

"From now on you're buying your own cigarettes."

"I don't smoke."

"That's what I'm gonna tell you the next time you ask for one."

St. Mary's Hospital was on Division Street between Western and Ashland, a tough neighborhood. The Jeep was parked in front of a joint that sold hot dogs. In the window was a sign that said *Jew Town Polish and Fries*. *Jew Town* was a reference to the old Maxwell Street merchant area where you used to be able to buy some of the best Polish sausages around. You would not find any pretenses of political correctness around here.

I unlocked the passenger door for Daisy. As she was getting in, she snapped her bubble gum and said, "Johnny, you think he's going to be all right?"

Her eyes were sweet and tender. "You care a lot about him, don't you?"

"Who, me?" She held a finger to her chest. "We're just friends. Besides, *you* know who I like."

I thought she had got past her Electra stage. She had a crush on her teacher, all right, but that's all it was, a crush. She'd soon outgrow it.

"He's a good boy, Daisy. You could do a lot worse than Fernando."

"You're a crazy white man, you know that?"

"So I've been told."

I took Daisy back to school and dropped her off near the loading dock. The last thing I needed was Danny seeing the two of us together in a car. I wrote her a pass and told her that if anybody asked, she had been making up a quiz.

The cigarette had made my mouth dry. Before she got out I said, "You wouldn't happen to have any more gum, would you?"

She looked directly into my eyes. Her fingers dipped into her mouth, and then wetly slipped the gum she had been chewing into mine. She hopped out, slammed the door, and gave me one final look over her shoulder as she strode up the walkway through the park.

We were going to have to have a talk.

§

It was the service desk of the Jewel supermarket on Chicago Avenue. The place was crowded and noisy and the poor clerk was working double time to keep up with refunds, rain checks and customer demands. When I had reached the first place in line, I said to her, "I'd like to talk to Chilo Fuentes, please."

The girl's face was pinched with uncertainty. "I think he's in back, somewhere."

"Could you please get him? This is kind of important. Tell him John Spector wants to see him."

She rolled her eyes, repeated my name to herself, and went out the service entrance. A few minutes later she came back with Chilo right behind her. Chilo—big grin, hand held out for me to shake.

"Johnny! Hey, *amigo*. What's up?"

I did not smile. "I take it you know that Fernando's been shot."

His face dropped. He took me by the arm and said, "Come in the back room, Johnny."

I walked around the counter and followed him to a small office that housed a desk, a computer, a chair and a few shelves. Chilo said, "I didn't have nothing to do with last night, Johnny. That was Blade's call."

"And you let him go ahead and do it—send young kids in against the Disciples because you older guys might serve hard time?"

"You don't understand. They been coming onto our turf, poisoning our kids with their fuckin' heroin. We got to take charge."

I said, "Why don't you really take charge? Go do your own

goddamn dirty work like a man, Chilo. That's what I thought you were."

There was an instant flicker of anger in his face as he lunged at me, grabbing the lapels of my leather jacket. I made no move to defend myself, just looked at him. Slowly he let go as he regained his composure. "I didn't know he was sending Fernando. You got to believe that, man. I only found out after it went down. You seen him?"

I nodded.

"How is he?"

I said, "He's doing pretty well for a kid who's nearly dead. He's got a hole clean through his body—through his liver, his lung."

Chilo slumped back against the wall and looked beyond me. "You don't live on these streets. You don't know the way it is. It's war. It ain't nothin' else than war."

The service door opened and for a moment the din of shoppers and checkers filled the little hall and fell away again. I said, "I helped you once."

"I remember."

"Now I need you to help me."

"Sure. Sure, Johnny."

I picked up a paper clip from the desk and played with it absently. "I want Fernando out."

"I just told you—I would never have sent him. He's off hood patrol. You have my word."

"No. I want him out of the Dragons for good."

Chilo wore a frown of incredulity. "No fuckin' way. You know the only way out is to take a *V*."

A *V* was a violation. Simply put, every other gang member beat the shit out of you at once. If you survived, you were out.

I said, "So change the rules."

"I can't do that."

"You owe me, man. Do it for me. If not for me, then do it for Fernando."

"I don't have that kind of authority. No one does. We got tradition, and we gotta respect it."

"Then start a new tradition. Let these kids grow up without gangs."

Chilo laughed quietly to himself and paced across the floor. "Without gangs, they won't have a chance to grow up." Gangs were like religions. Their members were willing to die for them. He stopped his pacing short, right in front of me. "I known you a long time, Johnny. As close as you are to bein' one of us, you still ain't. You'll never be one of us—no matter what you think."

He wasn't talking about the Dragons anymore. I knew what he was talking about. It was the same lesson that Isabelle and Danny had been trying to teach me the hard way. I thought I could come to Chilo, talk sense to him, because we had a history together. But that apparently wasn't the case. I dropped the twisted paper clip on the desk and saw myself out.

A few nights later, Tracy and I were together in her apartment. She was at her computer desk, assembling my curriculum vitae, and I was slumped in her big, green over-stuffed easy chair. Her nails were clear-coated. I watched them dance over the keyboard. She'd found a job ad from Forest College in the publication of the MLA—full-time assistant professor of English. It seemed like a waste of time to me. In the first place, I didn't have a Ph.D. And in the second, I'd been stuck in an inner-city high school for decades.

"What year did you get your master's degree?"

"They didn't have years back then. We just carved marks on the wall of the cave."

"I hope you understand I'm giving up a movie date for you."

That was interesting. "Who asked you out?"

Click-click-click-click. She continued typing before answering me. "Don't make it sound like it's such a stretch that somebody would want to go out with me. Donald Murray, for your information."

"Who the hell is Donald Murray?"

"My student teaching advisor. You met with him once to evaluate me. Remember?"

"Oh—that guy. He's got a hunched back."

The typing stopped. "He does not."

"Does too."

"Did you drink last night?"

This was her new crusade, to keep me healthy. We'd had carrot juice shakes tonight. I didn't think I'd be able to keep it down. "Why— are you going to list my cocktails on my vitae?"

"I'm just asking for myself. You've been drinking too much."

247

We might as well have been married.

She hit the tab button and then looked up and said, "What was the title of your first novel?"

"*Moby Dick.* I didn't think it would fly, but my agent—"

"Damn it, Johnny. I'm trying to help you here."

She was, and for that I was grateful, but something between us was changing, and even though at one level I knew it had to, on another level I was kind of sad about it. It had been a dream, the two of us, and it was dying now, which was the natural course of a dream, I supposed.

"Johnny?"

"Hm?"

"Are you worrying about Fernando?"

"I always worry about my kids, but at the moment I was just remembering a dream I had."

"Was it a good one?"

I nodded. "Yeah, it was a pretty good one."

"Tell me about it."

"Sometime," I said. "Sometime I will."

It was sunny and cold and you could see your own breath. I locked the Jeep inside the Waukegan municipal garage and crossed the street to the court building. February fifteenth—the day of our divorce. D Day. You could have picked me out in the crowd; I was the only one with a bouquet of flowers. I wondered what would happen if the judge was about to declare our marriage dissolved, and I were to stand up and say, "I object, your honor."

Up on the second floor, clients and attorneys sought each other out, couples were led into conference rooms—I knew that number by heart. I did not see Marlyn. I recalled a talk we'd had on a pier at Belmont Harbor back when she first applied to Loyola, and her future was at last in her own hands. We had wine to celebrate, Zinfandel, and we were in love.

A courtroom door opened and the baritone voice of an attorney said, ". . . irreconcilable differences, your honor."

"Mr. Spector?"

I turned around and found myself facing Arnold Gluck. He looked at the flowers and then he looked at me, baffled.

I said, "Have you seen my wife?"

He pointed to the courtroom. "She's inside. I've been waiting for you. You're late. Your case is about to be heard."

"Can you stall the judge?"

"Can I *what*?"

"Stall him—you know. Give me some time."

Arnold Gluck's face wrinkled with impatience. "Mr. Spector, when your case is called, that's it. I suggest we go inside—now."

We had sat on that pier most of the afternoon, feeling cut off from the rest of the city, in our own little world. An old fisherman let Marlyn hold his line and gave her fishing tips, and her bare feet dangled over the edge just above the water. We'd shared our wine with the fisherman and we were all happy.

I opened the courtroom door and walked inside. There were rows of chairs separated by a middle aisle, and several people turned around and stared at me. The bailiff was handing something to the judge as I scanned the faces of those seated, looking for Marlyn. She was in a back row to the left, seated beside Mitchell Arnoff. I walked over and sat down beside her on an aisle chair, resting the bouquet on my lap.

Arnold Gluck had followed me, and now he leaned down and whispered, "Mr. Spector, we should be sitting on the other side."

I said, "Well, you go over there and wait for me."

Marlyn looked at the flowers. "What's the occasion?"

I handed them to her. A lawyer was presenting to the judge a document about a property settlement involving joint ownership of a duplex in Lake Bluff. I said, "What do you say we stay hitched?"

Mitchell Arnoff appeared annoyed and whispered something to her that she seemed to ignore. "Is that the best you can do?"

"I love you," I said. "I've loved you from the first day I saw you."

Marlyn had a sphinx-like look she could turn on and you'd never know what she was thinking. She whispered, "What's in it for me?"

"Well, I'll spend more time at home than I used to."

Now she whispered something to Arnoff and he said, somewhat gruffly, "You can't do that."

"My attorney doesn't approve."

I said, "We'll do more things together."

"And?"

The bailiff, a man who had obviously once announced the arrival of passenger trains, wailed, "Spector versus Spector."

"The sex will be great."

She tilted her head toward the aisle and said, "Let's go."

Out in the hallway a distraught woman in her fifties in a blue dress was crying and telling a man in a striped suit that she could not take any more of this, not at all, she said. We found an unoccupied pocket of space near the stairs and held each other for some time. It was awkward, what with the flowers.

"What are you doing, Johnny Spector?"

I said, "I'm just doing what I do best."

"Yes," she said, "confusing the hell out of me." And then we stepped apart from one another and she said, "I'm glad you came. I kept hoping you would. I had a little daydream about you bursting in and saying, 'Stop these proceedings!' I'd just about given up on you when you walked in."

"I can come home, then?"

Marlyn looked at me sternly and shook her head. "It's not that easy, Johnny. You can't just come back with the same problems you had when you left. First of all, you're going to have to stop drinking."

"I did."

"When?"

"Two nights ago."

Marlyn laughed a sarcastic little laugh. "Oh, yeah? What happened—you ran out of gin?"

"Essentially, yes. But then I didn't run out and get any more."

"I'm talking about a program. You need a program."

Christ—she wanted me to go through 12-stepville. I'd never been any good at programs. "Can't I skip all that and just get a bumper sticker that says *One day at a time*?"

She said no, that I needed structure and direction, that I had needed both for quite some time. I did not respond to this. I hated structure and direction. They were foreign to my nature—but if it meant getting Marlyn back. . . .

I said, "What about Bruce?"

"What about him? He's just a friend."

"You always neck with your friends?"

She poked my chest with her finger. "That was a mistake. I admit it. But your detective has a tendency to overstate the circumstances. That's probably how he stays in business."

Arnold Gluck came out of the courtroom, looked left and then right, and then marched over to us. His pants cuffs were at least three inches too long.

"Would somebody mind telling me what's going on?"

I said, "We're calling off the divorce. We're absolute failures as single people."

He just shook his head and said, "That's great. That's just great. Clue somebody in, why don't you?" The last I saw of him, he was walking back into the courtroom, looking a little depressed. I think he had been looking forward to this divorce.

"And what about your little student teacher—Blondie, or whatever her name is?"

I made a face, a little twist of disregard. Just a friend, I told her, and she said, Uh-huh, that the day she'd seen her she had stars in her eyes whenever she looked at me. I said she must have been mistaken, that she was having trouble with her contact lenses.

Tracy didn't wear contact lenses.

We kissed goodbye on the courtroom steps and I remembered why I'd married her. I wondered aloud when I could come home. There would have to be changes, many changes, she said. She would let me know. I watched her walk away and for a moment I felt I had made the right decision, that we both had. And then I wondered if I was kidding myself, if it wasn't just too damn late for me to change.

After three remedial reading classes in a row, my brain was fried. I had tried phonics sheets, flash cards, a reading lab program, a machine that projected portions of sentences on a screen in timed sequences, and I didn't know if anyone's reading was improving, but I was ready to shoot myself. During my fourth period break I went into the faculty lunchroom and said hello to Betty Frycas and Fran Melnavicz. Fran stood first, then Betty after her, and they both walked out without saying a word to me.

Well, it had happened. I was a certifiable pariah. Dave Volmer had warned me. I guess I just didn't think that people I had known for so long would behave that way. It was as if they were afraid to be seen with me.

I took the stairs down to the second floor and found Jorgé smoking a cigarette on the landing. The second he saw me, he threw the butt on the floor and stamped it out, as if I gave a damn whether he was smoking or not.

"Yo, Johnny. Our homeboy got shot."

I grabbed his t-shirt in my fist and threw him up against the brick wall. "The fuck is wrong with you? You go out starting gun battles and think you and Fernando might not get killed? Haven't you got a fucking brain?"

"Cool it, Johnny. Le'go, man. It ain't like that. Me and Fernando had orders from the seniors, man. Ratman, Tony and Tito, they be sellin' dope to the peewees on our turf. We didn't shoot at 'em. We was just cappin', is all. We shot into the air, thinkin' they'd run."

"But they didn't." And now Tito, too. Had *he* shot Fernando? Jorgé hung his head and I let go of his shirt. "I don't give a shit what Blade tells you. Don't you ever go out looking for a gunfight, do you hear? And if you do—leave Fernando out of it."

"We gotta do what the seniors tell us, Johnny. It's what we be about."

"Don't give me that shit. What we *be* about, for Christ's sake. *Fuck* your gang. *Fuck* the Dragons. Start thinking about yourself, your future, or you won't have one."

He looked up at me out of dark, saddened eyes. I gave him a slight slap on the side of his face, and opened the fire door of the stairwell and went to the main office.

Inside, I asked Mary O'Hare if I could use her phone. Nothing. No word, no reaction. She just went off to use the photocopy machine. To hell with her. I picked up the phone and called the ICU unit at St. Mary's Hospital to see if there was any change in Fernando's condition. A nurse told me that he had been moved to a regular room and that he was listed as stable. I thanked her, and thought perhaps I would stop in and see him after school.

On top of a pile of papers on Mary's desk I saw an announcement about a meeting of faculty and staff regarding racism in the work environment. It was being sponsored by the Committee Against Racial Hatred at Acosta High. In other words, Isabelle Villachez.

"Oh Johnny—may I see you a moment?" Shirley. Mary looked over her shoulder and gave us both a dour look.

I walked to Shirley's desk and said, "What is it?"

She shoved a piece of paper toward me. It said, "*Guess what's back in the vault? Second shelf, against the wall.*"

I nodded, and she tore up the paper and let the scraps tumble into the wastebasket below her desk. I couldn't wait for another nighttime break in; Danny might take them home again. It had to be today. Now, how was I going to do this?

Tracy had Louise Denning's art program all week because Louise's mother was dying in Mansfield, Ohio. It was one of those cases that was supposed to be a blessing, as Louise had told me, though dying never sounded like such a hot deal to me. The art department was on the second floor just down the hall, and that's where I headed. The rooms were actually studios, with wide, room-length windows, and Tracy saw me even as I approached the door. She held her hand up to her students to signal a pause, and they all went "Oooh," as she opened the door and they saw us together.

"What's the matter?" she said.

I said, "The books are in the vault. We have to get them—now."

Tracy wrinkled her face, confounded. "How are we going to do that?"

Her big Abercrombie bag was leaning against her desk. This gave me an idea.

"There's going to be a fire drill in about three minutes."

"Fire drill? I didn't hear about any fire drill."

"I know. I just thought of it. Now, when the alarm goes off, open the door and let your kids out, but stay behind in the room. Wait a few minutes until the halls are cleared and meet me in the vault. And bring your bag."

"My bag?" Suddenly she understood. "Oh, Jesus, Johnny."

"You just keep the books in your bag all day. No one's going to go looking in it. After school, I'll meet you at your place. Instant evidence."

"You realize that if I get caught, I'll go to jail."

I said, "Honey, you're not going to get caught, and you're not the one who's going to jail."

She bit her lip and shook her head doubtfully. One girl in the back row nodded to another girl next to her. "They be rappin'," she surmised.

I'd always wanted to set off a fire alarm. The conventional assumption is that if you pull the handle, some kind of ink will spray your hand to enable the authorities to catch perpetrators of false alarms. I learned that this is not true.

I flipped the switch inside the second floor stairwell, triggering measured, earsplitting blasts. Classroom doors flew open, pouring hordes of kids and teachers out toward the escalators, both of which were running up. I fell in with the crowds, watched as Mike Parnell, walkie-talkie in hand, came racing from the records office and stooped at the base of an escalator, desperately trying to find the button that would stop it. Rather than head for the first floor, I entered the back door of the conference room. The opposite door led to the main office. I opened it just a crack and saw Danny ordering the secretaries out. His walkie-talkie squawked something indistinguishable while he held open the office door. I saw two blurs pass—which I took to be Mary and Shirley, and soon there was no more motion. A few moments later I pushed the door further—nothing. No one. The stampede had ended—there was just the blaring of the alarm. If it couldn't save you, it would deafen you.

I stepped across the main office and into the vault. Inside was a rack of room keys in numerical order, shelves filled with bond paper, the petty cash box—all the things you wouldn't need a vault for. And exactly where Shirley had instructed me to look were the books, two of them—a green ledger listing accounts and dollar amounts, and a big, hard-covered gray checkbook. I hadn't time to do more than open them up randomly and scan the contents. In fact I hadn't any time at all. In minutes, perhaps less, everyone would return to the building. Where the hell was Tracy?

I had to move quickly or the game would be up. I looked around for something in which to stow the books. A sack, perhaps, a bag. But there was no sack, no bag. The goddamn vault had everything but what I needed.

Tracy suddenly sprang inside and made me jump, and said, "Oh! You scared me half to death!"

I'd scared *her* half to death.

I grabbed her bag and tried to shove the books inside. There was barely room enough, with all the other contents.

"What is all this stuff?"

"I have to have lesson plans, don't I? And there are grammar exercises, and—"

"Well, empty some of it out when you get a chance. Go back to your room and stay there. Act as if you'd been outside and just returned."

"Did you find any—"

254

"Go," I said. *"Now."*

She ran out and I followed her as far as the escalator. Down in the lobby I heard walkie-talkie static and the clamor of students as they were herded back inside. I ran up the steps and stayed behind the stacks in the English book room until the all-clear tone went off. Except for the mind-dulling task of holding up flash cards in my next two remedial reading classes, the rest of the afternoon passed pleasantly enough. There were no rallies after school, and I wondered if this might be a sign that the controversy was growing cold.

"Here's one. It's made out to Pedro Cardoñas—ten thousand dollars. They have it listed as 'curriculum design.'"

Tracy and I were sitting on her living room floor, tallying up duplicate checks that were written against the general account. It wasn't as easy as it sounds, because we had to cross reference the expenses against the separate accounts that had been emptied.

I said, "That's a total of sixty thousand alone for the Cardoñases. Whose name is on the check?"

"Mike Parnell again."

So far, every check had been signed by Mike. No wonder he was having ulcer problems.

I stood up. "What've you got to drink?"

Tracy was punching numbers into a hand calculator. "There's cranberry juice in the refrigerator."

*Cran*berry juice. I could have used a nice scotch. I'd heard of alcoholics who drink hair spray when there's no other alternative. I couldn't imagine doing that. Wouldn't that make your tongue stick to the roof of your mouth?

I came back to the living room with a glass of juice on the rocks. Tracy was spread-eagle upon her oriental rug, jotting figures in a tablet when she abruptly threw down her pencil and said, "I've *got* it."

I said, "What—leg cramps?"

"This is the check for that revolutionary group of motivational speakers. Look at the name it was made out to."

I bent down and read over her shoulder. *Miguel Villachez.*

"You think he's related to Isabelle?"

"He has to be. And look at the amount," she directed. "Forty thousand dollars. Do you know of any motivational speakers who get forty thousand dollars for one appearance at a high school?"

The amount stolen from the general account totaled close to one hundred and eighty thousand dollars, most of which had come in as Federal poverty funds. It all went to individuals on the island. Tracy closed the books and sat up, her back against the front of the couch.

"Well, we've got them. We've got the proof right here."

She didn't get it. "Tracy, we haven't got them."

"What do you mean?"

I rattled the ice cubes in my glass and stretched out on the floor. "Every one of those checks was signed by Mike Parnell. He even signed off on the account transfers. If we turn over these books to the authorities, the only one going to prison will be Mike."

"But what about Isabelle? What if they find out that Miguel Villachez is related to her?"

"Then they'll go after him, not Isabelle."

Tracy was in black jeans and a red crew neck sweater. She pulled her legs in close to her, making her knees rise. She looked at me a long time without saying anything. Just that look, and it made me uncomfortable. I didn't need telepathy to know what she was thinking. We had gone through all that trouble to get those books. We had evidence of theft of public funds on a grand scale. To know and do nothing made us parties to the corruption. It was unethical, immoral.

But Mike had a boy, just a few years older than mine, a daughter, a wife. What would this do to them, and how in God's name would I live with myself afterward?

15

The morning did not start well. I found a hate letter in my mailbox accusing me of racial prejudice and the ongoing destruction of young Latino lives.

Only a white supremacist monster could have made the remarks that you did in that disgusting article. We will work to have you fired, and to assure that you will never again be allowed inside a public school classroom.

I was getting sick of this sort of thing. Of course, the letter was unsigned. I crumpled it up and threw it in a wastebasket, but then had second thoughts. You never knew when something like this might serve as some kind of evidence. I stooped and retrieved it from the wastebasket and uncrumpled it and put it in my pocket.

And the morning did not get better as it went along. I was inside the English book room, sport coat draped over my chair back, writing out cut slips, thinking how useless the process was, and someone knocked at the door.

"Come in," I said, and threw down my pen and rubbed my eyes. I couldn't get a single moment of peace around that place. Hair spray on the rocks sounded pretty good by now.

The door opened and Lico Pacheco walked in. I hadn't seen him in some time, and he seemed to have lost a little weight, gotten a little taller.

"Mr. Spector, may I—may I a-ask you something?"

His eyes shifted faster than a NASCAR driver. "Of course. What is it?"

He held his hands behind his back and struggled to get the words out. "W-w-why aren't you our teacher anymore?"

He fidgeted, put his hands in his pockets, took them out again. "Well, I'll tell you, Lico. They gave me a new assignment. Sometimes they do these things. I wish they hadn't. I liked my classes. I liked my students."

"They're saying—they're saying you *don't* like your students."

I said, "I know they are Lico, but that's not true."

He nodded, looked away. "I know it isn't. You helped me. I know you like me."

"I do, Lico. I like you very much. How have you been, by the way?"

Again, the nodding routine. "Good. I've been good. I'm getting an A in algebra. I'm studying hard. Sometimes I go to the math lab for help, and sometimes my mother helps me when she visits on the weekends."

I just stared at him. It had taken him all of thirty seconds to begin lying again.

"Lico—"

"I saw her this last weekend. Not the whole weekend. Just Saturday. She says she's going to make regular visits from now on. She told me so."

I sat back in my chair, folded my arms across my chest. "Lico, I talked to your counselor at the home, Jim Jarret."

His eyes cowered momentarily. "He's a nice man, a real nice man. I introduced him to my mother, and she—"

"He told me that you haven't seen your mother since you were six years old. He told me your mother never visits."

His eyes opened a little wider and he began wringing his hands. "But she *does* now. She does, and she bought me a new shirt. I'll show it to you sometime. And a key chain—she gave me a key chain, and—"

The poor boy wanted a mother so bad, he'd invented one. I stood up and walked around my desk. "Listen, buddy. You don't have to lie to me. I know the truth."

He backed away from me, broke into sudden tears. I'd never seen eyes fill up so quickly. "You'll see," he said, his voice quavering. "You'll see."

He bolted out the door and down the hall to the escalator. I ran after him a little way and called out, but he was gone.

Son of a bitch. Jim Jarret had instructed me to confront him with the truth whenever he began fabricating. Maybe I had been too direct.

I walked back to the book room, thinking that the truth had a better reputation than it deserved.

"Oh, *action*. Is right? Run. Jump. Is right?"

"That's right, Peter. A verb expresses action."

"What expresses means?"

"Tells. A verb *tells* action."

Peter was a Ukrainian kid in my second period reading class who was having an epiphany. I'd been trying to get him to write complete sentences by telling him he needed both a subject and a verb. The missing element was—he hadn't known what a verb was.

"Run," he said. "Jump. Hit." It was a small victory, but I'd take what I could get. "Build," he continued. "Wave. Write. Push."

Irritate. Drive insane.

In my peripheral vision I saw a movement outside the glass panel of the classroom door. Nydia. She did not appear happy. I walked out to the hall and semi-closed the door behind me. With her was Marco Gonzalez—black suit, starched white shirt. Their expressions looked something like Horatio's after he's seen Hamlet's father.

"I get the feeling the executioner sent you two for me."

Nydia said, "I was just downstairs in the main office and I saw the most peculiar thing."

"Really?" I said. "What was that?"

"First, Danny Velez came running out of the vault in a rage. He yelled at Mary O'Hare about where she had put something, and Mary crumpled up and cried and swore she hadn't touched anything. Then Danny stormed out of the office and returned a few minutes later with Mike Parnell. Mike ran in the vault, ran out, cursed up a storm, and said that he'd left the books on the shelf, but now they were gone. The two of them were going crazy."

I said, "That's a very interesting story. I would have paid money to see it. But I have a class just now. We're celebrating Verb Day."

Marco said, "Johnny, we know you have the books. We just want to make sure you do the right thing with them."

Friends were friends and pressure was pressure. I didn't like to get one from the other. "Slow down, Marco. Assuming I *did* have the books, what exactly do you mean by doing the *right thing* with them?"

"Turn them over to the authorities."

I said, "Which authorities?"

"Depending on where the money trail leads, either the State's Attorney's Office, or if the money has left the state, the FBI."

Nydia was looking in my classroom window. "Johnny, one boy is hitting another boy over the head with a textbook."

I said, "That's just the way they study." Then I turned to Marco and said, "And what if I found something in those books that made me decide not to do that?"

"What could you possibly find other than theft? Every school program is running at a deficit. They've scaled back the yearbook to soft covers, and Dan Finley's football program has been cancelled for next semester."

Nydia put her hand on my arm. "Johnny, what's wrong? You wanted to turn in Danny's regime as bad as any of us."

I looked at Nydia, at Marco. I said, "Listen—the money was sent to individuals on the island. Mike Parnell signed every account transfer and check. If I turn over the books, Mike is the only one going to prison, and I don't think I can do that to him."

Nydia slapped her forehead and then began to unleash on me. "What are you talking about? You won't be doing anything to Mike. Mike did this to *himself*. He's part of this mob, and if that's where we have to start, well then, that's where we start."

"Mr. Spector?" Someone was tugging at my sleeve from behind me. I turned around and there was Hilda. She was wearing a rust-colored dress with some kind of black splotches on it.

"Sweetheart, I'm a little busy right now."

"But I gotta tell you. It's about Tito."

Christ. Trouble in paradise. "What about Tito, Hilda?" She raised her eyebrows at Marco and Nydia. I said, "It's okay. These are my friends. You can talk in front of them."

"I broke up with him."

"Well, that's too bad, but—"

"He says he's gonna kill you." Now Marco raised *his* eyebrows at me. "He thinks you talked me into breaking up with him, and he thinks you had the Dragons send Jorgé and Fernando after him and Ratman and Tony."

That's about the level of thinking I expected from Tito. I said, "That's ridiculous. I don't tell people who to date, and I don't call shots for gang members."

"He thinks you *do*."

Jesus Christ, everybody was gunning for me today.

"All right, Hilda. Thanks for the warning. You go back to class now."

"Be careful Mr. Spector. Tito don't talk outta his ass. If he says he's gonna do something—"

"Okay. I get the idea. I'll be careful. Back to class, now."

She took a few tentative steps backwards and then turned and left. Marco and Nydia were openly glaring at me. I took a deep breath and sighed. "All right. What do you guys want from me?"

Marco pointed his index finger at me for emphasis. "I'm not going to give you the you-get-too-close-to-them lecture now, but I sure as hell will later. In the meantime, turn over those books. State's Attorney or FBI. I don't give a damn which."

I read Nydia's eyes and found something like angry disappointment there. "And what do I tell Mike's kids and wife when they haul him off to prison?"

Nydia said, "The same thing you'll tell Danny's family when they come for him—that administrators shouldn't steal."

"But they're not going to come for Danny. There's no documentation, no smoking gun with his prints on it."

"Use your head, Johnny. Don't you think Mike is going to cooperate so they can get to the top of the chain of command? They'll offer a plea bargain and he'll jump at it. And in the process they'll all tumble and fall—Murphy, Isabelle, Elizabeth, Anatole. All the bad apples."

I supposed she was right. No doubt Mike would talk to save his skin. And I guessed he was as guilty as any of them. I just wasn't used to thinking of him like that.

There was now general mayhem inside my classroom. A pencil went ricocheting off the window. "All right," I said. "I'll do it."

"When?" Marco wanted to know.

"Today," I told him, "after school."

He suggested I take the books to a photocopy center first, so that I would have a back-up set. Nydia patted my arm and winked at me.

My class had degenerated into a free-for-all. Tito wanted to kill me. And I wasn't all that sure I didn't want to kill myself.

It cost eighty-seven dollars and fifty-three cents to make copies of the documents at the copy shop on Elston Avenue, and it took most of

Tuesday afternoon. Tracy had been very helpful, splitting up the chores of duplicating the accounts book and the check ledger. We jumped back in the Jeep when we were finished. It was chilly and drafty and I couldn't wait for March. It was just a few weeks away.

"Do we go to the FBI now, or wait until tomorrow?"

I turned the heater up. "We? Why in the world would you want to get mixed up in this?"

She drew her coat collar to her neck and gave a little shiver. "I'm *already* mixed up in this—or did you happen to forget about the night we broke into the school together, or who carried the books out in a bag?"

"Yeah, but from here on it it gets scary. What if this little extremist mob decides to exact revenge once the Feds come after them? How far is Danny willing to go? His sister used Disciples to run bombs to New York. It's no secret that people died."

Tracy lowered her visor, I guess expecting that it had a mirror. She was in the wrong car. She opened her purse next and took out a compact, ran her tongue over her lips. "I hate it when you pull this chivalrous routine after I've already put my neck out. Don't worry, Johnny. I know it's over between us. I'm not trying to hang on."

She averted her eyes, pretended interest out the passenger window.

"It's not that. I didn't mean that. I care about you."

"Mm-hm."

"Honest, Tracy. And I appreciate what you've done."

"Did I tell you," she said, "that Woody is moving to Chicago?"

I just looked at her. "Can you really call him that and keep a straight face?"

"He's getting a seat on the Mercantile Exchange."

"Well, that's just great. Woodrow Wilson, the pork belly salesman."

"He'll make millions."

"I'm sure he will. You make sure you give Woody my best. In the meanwhile—what the hell do we do with these books? Maybe we could just call from a pay phone and leave an anonymous message."

"That won't work. You can't drop off a pile of evidence and say, 'Go get 'em.' They need to know the whole story."

That was true. The checkbook by itself didn't say anything about a plot to overthrow the government.

I said, "So what do we do? Just look in the phone book under FBI?"

"Why don't you call information on your cell phone?"

It was that simple. An operator answered and I said I wanted to speak to an agent about embezzlement. Soon a man with a voice as brassy as a trombone said he was Agent Daniels, and could he help me.

I said, "I'm a Chicago school teacher. What would you say if I told you a group of terrorists disguised as school administrators had taken control of a local high school and have stolen over one hundred and eighty thousand dollars of federal poverty funds to finance the independence movement in Puerto Rico?"

A few seonds went by and then he said, "Sounds like *West Side Story* meets *Conspiracy Theory*."

I said, "Yeah, except that it's true, and I've got the check book to prove it."

I heard the squeaking of a chair back being laid against. "And just how did you come to get this checkbook?"

"I took it."

"You stole a public document from a school?"

"I prefer to think of it as liberating it in the service of justice. If I'd wanted to steal it, I wouldn't have called you."

More chair squeaking. "How soon can you be here?"

The Chicago FBI office, it turned out, was located on South Dearborn Street. I told the agent that I could make it in fifteen minutes, and then he wanted to know my name. For just a moment I thought about saying *Vince Arcelli*. But it was a pretty safe bet that the FBI had caller ID, so I figured what the hell, and gave him my name. He said to be sure I brought the checkbook.

The inside of FBI headquarters looked exactly the way you would have expected. Walls with plaques on them, dark-suited men and women behind desks, offices sprouting other offices, crimped pile carpet. Agent Daniels was a man with swept-back, dirty-blond hair, in his late thirties. He worked in his shirt sleeves and had worry lines on his forehead and seemed weary from his day at work. He pulled Tracy's chair out for her when she sat down.

"You'll have to forgive my reaction to your claim when you first called, Mr. Spector, but we don't get many complaints about revolutionaries taking over high schools."

"Yeah, well, I don't blame you at all," I said. "We're a one-of-a-kind place. *I'm* still having trouble believing it."

"How did a thing like this get started?"

"Your organization has busted some of our teachers in the past—teachers with FALN ties. One gets in the system, he brings in others. Before you know it, they've established a secret base. You'd think someone would have done something about it sooner, but what's taken place at Acosta is what happens when political correctness overshadows public scrutiny."

"Believe me, we're familiar with the FALN. Have been since the seventies—even earlier."

"Yeah—but this incarnation of the network isn't limited by ethnicity. It's ideological and diverse. Some of the people involved in the scheme are Irish, Eastern European. And you'd be surprised how sloppy they are. They're drunk with power. They make mistakes."

"What kind of mistakes?"

I said, "Tracy—give him the checkbook."

She reached into her bag and produced the gray, hard-covered book and handed it to Agent Daniels, who smiled every time he set eyes on her. Today she was outfitted in a black sport coat over a Campbell tartan short skirt. I didn't know if my hands were shaking because of the lack of booze or the skirt.

Tracy said, "I've highlighted all the illegitimate expenses." Once more she dug into her bag, this time setting the accounts book down on the desk. "This ledger documents all the movements of funds from interior accounts. You can cross reference checks against withdrawals and deposits. I've highlighted these, too."

Agent Daniels said, "You two have been pretty busy."

He should only have known.

We were questioned for a good two-and-a-half hours, though pleasantly. They offered us coffee, rolls. We wrote lists of those teachers and administartors we believed to be involved, and were instructed not to tell anyone we'd had contact with the bureau. If it got back to Danny, to Murphy, or the others—they'd have time to clean house, delete evidence from computers, shred documents. Would we be available for further questioning, Daniels wanted to know, and naturally we said yes. And then the question I had been fearing: "Would you both be willing to testify against these individuals, should this case come to trial?"

I said, "Is this a case already?"

Daniels' lower lip protruded. "Not technically yet, but it's a fair bet it will be."

We both promised that we would testify, though that was something I looked forward to about as much as I did a proctoscope exam, appearing before the whole gang of them and their lawyers on some witness stand where I would be made out to be the racist once again. When we stood up, my legs ached and were numbly limp from having sat for so long. Agent Daniels escorted us out and held Tracy's cashmere overcoat (typically elegant) for her as she slid her arms into the green, satin-lined sleeves.

"One last thing," he said before we left. "How the devil did you manage to get these books out of the school?"

Tracy and I exchanged glances. "Fought fire with fire," I said.

Tracy just shook her head and rolled her eyes.

Out on the sidewalk of Dearborn Street the Chicago wind whistled through urban canyons and took icy jabs at my neck, and people walked past in the night.

"*Fought fire with fire*," Tracy repeated. "That's a line out of some cheesy detective novel."

"I might be cheesy, but I'm no detective. Sure could use a drink, though."

"Oh, no you don't. We're going to work out."

"After all that?"

"It'll be good for you," she said. "Man of your age ought to be looking out for himself. Especially if he thinks he's going to win his wife back."

The little shit.

I sat up with señor Valentin that night. He had prepared *lechon*, and the whole house smelled deliciously of ham, and we watched some television together, saying very little to one another, but I think we both enjoyed the company. I know *I* did. And I thought about what Chilo had said to me, about not being one of *them*. I had been close to Puerto Rican culture for so long that I had begun to assume it was part of who I was, that I could participate in it and comment freely about its matters. My son, my wife, my students—but not *me*? Was I really an outsider? And if so, why, and why didn't I feel like one?

§

Vince sat at his desk, fist beneath his chin, staring at his lone rocket launcher. A row of fluorescent lights mimicked itself in miniature upon

265

the lenses of his glasses, and his coffee mug rested on a ledge against the far wall. This one had a caption that read *Nuke the gay whales for Jesus*.

I said, "What the hell is that supposed to mean, Vince—'Nuke the gay whales for Jesus'?"

"Hell if I know. But it offends just about every politically correct organization out there." He went on comtemplating the launcher. "Maybe I could get a grant from the state—tell 'em I have a junior astronauts program."

I got up from my chair and walked over to the launcher and picked it up. It wasn't very complicated—a narrow steel rod surrounded by high-tech looking molded gray-and-blue plastic. It occurred to me that the plastic housing was entirely unnecessary—just aesthetic gilding.

"You don't even need this," I said.

Vince looked up, annoyed. "Spector—you can't launch rockets without some kind of guide. They'll go haywire. End up with a rocket up your wazoo."

"What I mean is, you go to a hobby shop and get two or three feet of copper tubing and stick it in the ground. Cost you about seventy cents."

He sat straight up and let his jaw hang open. He stayed that way for about half a minute. Then he said, "You know what? I think that might work."

I said, "Sure it will. And you call yourself a physics teacher."

"I should have thought of that."

"Yes, you should have."

He stood up, opened his thermos, and poured some coffee into his mug. "So how's the *gumad*?"

Gumad was Italian for *mistress*.

"She's not a *gumad*, Vince. She's a hell of a wonderful girl, and if I were fifteen years younger, and if there was no Marlyn . . . but I'm not, and there is."

"You and Marlyn getting back together?"

"Maybe, if I'm lucky. She's thinking about it."

"It's all up to her?"

"It's always been all up to her. I had to stop drinking."

He was screwing in the cap to his thermos, and when I said this, he just stopped, puzzled. "Really? You have a drinking problem?"

"Only for the past few years. Before that it wasn't a problem at all. I just drank."

Vince set his thermos beneath his desk. "Are you in some kind of program or something?"

I put the launcher down and returned to my chair and put my feet up on his desk. "Yes, yes I am, Vince. I call it *The Johnny Spector Twelve-Step Program to Stop Drinking and Feel Like Absolute Shit*."

"How do you feel when you *do* drink?"

"Like absolute shit."

"Then it's your age," he said. "The booze has nothing to do with it."

When I'd woken up that morning I had the certain knowledge that I could not keep coming to this place to work anymore. It had been ruined for me, and I'd had a hand in ruining it. So you lose your job—that's not the end of the world. I had even read the help wanted page of the *Tribune* over breakfast. There were openings at the phone company, and the Cape Cod Room in the Drake Hotel was looking for waiters. Communications and food services. The world was my goddamned oyster.

"You miss your boy?"

I said, "Sometimes I miss him so much I don't know how I stand it. It's funny, but all this trouble I've got myself into, it keeps my mind occupied, you know? It's almost like it's good for me."

"You must be pretty fucked up, because I don't see how *that* could be good for *anybody*."

"Oh, I am," I said. "I really am."

"Don't worry. We can always buy a six pack, pick up a few chicks, go down to the beach."

I was going to miss Vince.

I stood reading a flier taped to the stainless steel side of an escalator. It said that concerned students could sign a petition in the conference room on the second floor for the removal of John Spector from his teaching duties. Someone put a hand upon my shoulder. I turned around and found myself facing Jamel Saunders, my union representative.

"I hope you don't have anything planned for tomorrow morning. Your due process hearing has been scheduled for ten o'clock."

"Tomorrow? That's all I get—one day's notice?"

Jamel looked me dead center in the eyes and said, "Listen, Johnny. It'll be a cut and dried procedure. Korman is looking for an expedient way out of this mess. He'll probably offer you a position at a different school, and if you're smart, you'll take it."

I thought about that, about teaching at a different school. "I think I'd rather wait tables at the Cape Cod Room."

Jamel said, "What?"

"Never mind. You going to be there with me?"

"Yes, along with a union lawyer. But I'm telling you, it's just a formality. The decision has probably already been made."

"That's swell. Our public school system at work. It's kind of touching."

"At least there will be a job waiting for you."

And that was the point. When teaching becomes just a job, that's the time to get out. I remembered all the teachers I'd had who were just going through the motions, and I didn't want to be added to their ranks.

But that's all I was doing now, going through the motions. I wasn't leading young minds through Melville or introducing them to archetypes or existential philosophy. I was giving a scintillating lesson on syllables in remedial reading when a student aide called me out of class. She held a note out to me and I took it.

> *For John Spector*
> *Lico Pacheco never came home last night.*
> *Please call Jim Jarret.*

"When did this call come in?" I asked her.

"Just now. Shirley told me to bring it to you."

This was my fault. If I'd just listened to his fantasy and kept my mouth shut, everything would have been fine. Well, it wouldn't have been *fine*—but it wouldn't have been this, either.

"Go back to the main office and tell them to have the rest of my classes covered today. Tell them I took a sick day. Do you understand?"

"Yes, Mr. Spector."

I ran across the hall into the English offices and picked up the phone and called Jim Jarret. The phone rang about six times and I was afraid I would end up talking to a machine—but at the last second he answered.

"Jarret here."

"Mr. Jarret? John Spector. I'm afraid I'm responsible for Lico's having run away."

"How do you mean?"

I explained to him that Lico had begun spinning a tale about his mother visiting, and I had confronted him. "I thought I was doing the right thing," I said.

"You were. Lico's typical reaction to the truth is to hide. You can't blame yourself for this, Mr. Spector. He's done it before, and he always comes back. He disappears for a while and cools his heels. The police have been alerted."

I told him to please call me if Lico returned, and he said he would, certainly.

When I hung up the phone, I worried. It was a big city, this city, and not particularly a safe one. Then I thought of something—an essay Lico had handed in at the beginning of the school year. Sometimes, he'd written, when he missed his mother, he would go downtown to Union Station, to the Amtrak trains, and look at the passengers as they deboarded, hoping to see her face.

And didn't that say something about the nature of kids? You could beat them and you could neglect them and you could attempt to mutilate them, and they would still love you.

I got the Jeep up to about seventy-five on the Kennedy expressway and hit a jam at Ohio Street. I crawled the rest of the way to Jackson, and then headed east to Clinton Street. There was a parking lot there, and I told the attendant, a young, Middle-Eastern looking man, that I would only be twenty minutes. I paid in advance and he let me park up front near the exit.

Union Station in Chicago is really two different stations. First you had the old historical structure where they shot part of *The Untouchables*, and the newer building that was home to Amtrak and a bar and several restaurants. They connected with one another underground. As I passed the bar, I stopped for a moment, saw a bottle of Johnnie Walker Red, zeroed in on the label featuring him high stepping with his walking stick. He was a good man, Johnnie. We'd been through some tough campaigns together.

I walked into the Amtrak lounge area, crowded with midday travelers, people with rucksacks and compact suitcases on wheels, or else

269

shopping bags and boxes and luggage carts you could rent by the hour. There were expectant eyes and haunted eyes, and sad eyes and numb eyes. I saw a teenage girl in blue jeans sitting alone in the corner of the room, staring vacantly at the carpet. I wondered where her home was, and why she wasn't there. I combed the place, but there was no Lico.

Out in the corridor you could actually see the trains pull into the dark, cavernous enclosure, tracks snaking out in a maze of steel. The Empire Builder had just arrived from Portland. I watched weary looking passengers climb down the train car stairs onto the concourse, wobbling as they walked, used to the senation of constant movement. I turned around to find my way back out of the station, inspecting the sea of faces, people going this way and that, crowds of them. Where would I go if I were fifteen and I had no mother and no father? Pool hall? Not Lico. A church maybe—but they would call the police, and the police would call Jim Jarret. A woman's voice on the public address system echoed through the station, her words lost beneath the din and clatter of conversation and electric transport carts. Something about Cleveland.

Back out in the high-ceilinged historic station lobby, the throngs thinned out and quiet returned. The place had the look and feel of a dingy, stripped-down cathedral. There was a hot dog counter, a popcorn concession, and of all things between these, a dry cleaner. You could drop off your laundry on your way to work and pick it up when you went back home. I would have walked right past the wooden bench if it hadn't been for the splotch of red upon it that caught the corner of my eye. It was the sleeping form of a brown-skinned young man sitting up, his head reclined upon the bench back.

Lico. He wore a red snow parka that was one size too small, and black high top sneakers. His wrists stuck out of the cuffs of his sleeves, and there were scars there on the soft skin of the inner area. I could only guess the story behind those. His mouth was open and his lips were dry and chapped. He must have slept there like that all night. I sat down beside him, noticed the empty wrapper of a Hershey bar enfolded in the long narrow fingers of one hand. His dinner. His chest rose and fell in long even sleeper's breaths. He looked so peaceful. I hated to have to wake him up, bring him back to the world he had inherited.

I nudged his shoulder gently with my hand.

"Time to wake up, partner."

He woke with a start, one eye opening before the other. He glanced around to get his bearings, began to draw himself up when he saw who I was. He rubbed his face, squinted, eyes sensitive to the light. "How did you know?" he said. "How did you know where to find me?"

"I didn't. Lucky guess. You wrote something about the station in an essay last October."

He lowered his head. "Mr. Jarret told you about m-my mother."

"Yes."

"You know about all the things, all the things she—"

"Yes, I know, Lico. But that's over now."

He stared at nothing, dark eyes glassy, lost in an interior realm of his own. He played with the nylon zipper of his jacket, flipped it back and forth. "I'm sorry that I lied to you, Mr. Spector."

I reached out and ruffled his hair with my hand. "Well, I don't see it as a lie, so much. More like a wish. There's nothing wrong with wishing for a mother, Lico. Nothing wrong with that at all."

He looked up at me suddenly in quiet despair. "I'm so sorry," he said, and began weeping into his open hands. I put my arms around him and held him there on the bench as he struggled to catch his breath. Travelers strolled by, and some stared; others walked blindly past. Still I held him, occasionally patting his back. I thought of the undamaged boy he must have once been, the life he might have had, and I thought of Jason and Daisy and all the kids I had known throughout all the years, and the personal struggles they'd had to face.

At last I said, "Let's go, boy. Let's go home now."

16

I took Francisco Avenue to Augusta Boulevard and pulled into North Humboldt Drive. I parked the Jeep in my easy access spot by the auto shop, fully aware that this might be my last day at Acosta High , and that I might be leaving early, at a good clip, perhaps with a large, jeering crowd behind me. It was too early for the trees to be budding, but otherwise it looked almost like spring; the sky was trasparent blue, the air mild, and I was surprised to remember that it was possible to feel so alert and focused. After having been drunk for so long, being sober was a rush.

In my mailbox I found a scribbled note from Jamel Saunders. The hearing would be held in the conference room at ten o'clock sharp. This gave me enough time to go up to the seventh floor cafeteria and get a cup of coffee and sit around pondering the enigmatic nature of life. Trouble was, I was all pondered out. I figured someone else ought to have a shot at it. While I was paying the cashier, one of the other kitchen staff ladies said to her in Spanish that I was the bastard racist who had been in the newspaper.

She didn't even know me. Maybe a transfer wasn't such a bad idea.

"Anybody sitting here?"

I had taken my coffee to an out-of-the-way table in the corner of the lunchroom, so as not to appear conspicuous, and now Marco Gonzalez was standing over me, holding a cup of his own, making me conspicuous.

"Just us bastard racists."

Marco slid a chair out and sat down. "I hear today is your big day. I just wanted to stop by and add my vote of support, if it means anything."

I said, "It means a lot, Marco. Thank you."

He sipped his coffee and patted his mustache with a napkin. "You look good. Been working out?"

"Nope. Stopped drinking."

"That'll do it." He spun his cup around and then got to the heart of the matter. "I was wondering . . . those books."

"You sure are anxious about getting the Feds in here, aren't you?"

"I'll be honest with you, Johnny. If you go and Danny stays on, there's still going to be a rift in the powerbase here. It'll be Javier and Nydia and me against the revolutionaries, and that doesn't make anything better, know what I mean?"

"You mean, once they don't have Spector to kick around anymore, they might go looking to kick one of you around."

"Basically, yes. But don't say it like that, in Nixonese. Puts you in a bad light."

I had finished half my coffee before I realized it tasted like hell. "Tracy and I went to the FBI. We turned over the books and told them everything. Named names. Dates. The whole bit."

Marco nodded solemnly at the news. "That took courage."

"No, it didn't. I had nothing left to lose, Marco. This year alone I've lost my wife, my son, my home, the respect of the community, now my position. I just couldn't stand to see Danny walk away a winner in this thing."

"I didn't mean you. I meant Tracy." It was a little way Marco had of pulling the conversationl rug out from under you. "Still," he continued, "something good will come of it. They didn't say when?"

"They didn't say when, or *if*, for that matter. I have no idea."

He put his hand on my arm and just kept it there for a moment or two. "I'm going to hate to see you go. You're a hell of a good teacher."

I said, "I just get too close, right?"

"Way too close. You just don't know any other way to do it, I guess."

"I guess," I said.

I watched as he got up and walked away from the table. Tall, lean, dark-suited. One of the finest counselors I'd ever known, and the biggest pain in the ass.

I ran across Tracy in the third floor stairwell on my way down. Her arms were laden with books and she had on a beige cardigan and matching skirt. She beamed at me, and my heart fell when I thought of our school year together, and how I was going to miss her.

"Oh—I'm so glad I found you. They're picketing in front of the conference room."

I said, "Who is?"

"Anatole and Elizabeth."

"For Christ sake. A two-person picket line?"

She shifted her books around in her arms. "Just don't do anything rash, anything that they can use against you in the hearing."

"You know me. Mr. Cool."

She smirked and said, "I know you, all right." She looked down at her books and then back up at me. "If they transfer you, will you be leaving right away?"

"I don't know, Tracy. I don't know what to expect."

"You'll come by, though. I mean, you won't just leave without saying—"

I pressed her arm and then continued down the stairs.

I'd seen a lot of things in my day, but nothing like Anatole and Elizabeth marching back and forth in the corridor with big placards. One said *Spector Out* and the other, *Racist Must Go*. As I approached the room, Anatole blocked the entrance and held his placcard directly in front of me.

He said, "There is no room for bigots in Acosta High ."

I said, "Well, apparently there's room for crazy twits, or else you wouldn't be here. Get out of my way, Anatole."

He skittered off to the side in that funny diagonal way of walking he had, and Elizabeth called after me, "Oppressor!"

It happened like this:

As I entered the room, everyone was already seated. They all looked up at me in solemn embarrassment, as if this were a wake, and I had the starring role. There was a heavy man with slick black hair and a pencil-thin mustache. Beside him was Jamel Saunders in a black pinstripe suit. Across from her was Danny with his indelible sneer, and next to him, a tiny woman who had a laptop computer opened before her on the rectangular table, a stenographer. And just to the right of the chair I presumed had been left open for me, Marshall Korman—gray suit, gray hair, gold-rimmed glasses. He looked as though he'd just been shipped from Bureaucrats, Inc.

I took my seat.

"Mr. Spector?" said the portly man to my left. "I'm Stan Wojehowski , your union attorney. I'll be monitoring your hearing for procedural purposes, and to ensure that your contractural rights are not violated."

I got up and shook his hand, and he took in my sneakers, my jeans, clearly with an air of disapproval. I sat back down and wondered what we were waiting for, but I did not want to ask. Marshall Korman was busy pretending I wasn't in the room. His eyes remained in a neutral spot on the table, upon a series of documnets.

At last Korman said that the hearing was called to order. Then he flipped over a page of the documents and began enumerating my offenses.

"Mr. Spector, according to the documentation assembled by the administration of Acosta High School, you have a chronic history of behaving in an undignified and unprofessional manner."

Stan Wojehowski stretched his arm across the table and said, "May I see that please?" In profile, Stan had three chins.

Korman slid the paper across the table toward him while the tiny stenographer stared straight ahead at her laptop monitor fiercely, as though she had blinders on.

He continued. "You refuse to turn in lesson plans and outcomes assessments, you have left the school premises on several occasions without permission, sometimes in the company of teenage girls."

At the mention of the girls, I thought Stan was going to fall through the floor, chins, chair and all.

"You additionally gave an interview to a Chicago newspaper in which you made inflamatory and derogatory remarks about this high school, and now the daily running of Acosta High has been disrupted." He then turned to me for the first time during the procedings and asked, "Do you deny any of those charges, Mr. Spector?"

"Yes. Yes, I do. I did not make inflamatory or derogatory remarks about this high school in that interview."

"Perhaps my wording was off—but certainly you cannot refute the fact that your comments were at the very least insensitive."

Stan Wojehowski rubbed his jowl with his hand and looked worried.

"They were *deliberately* insensitive. That's called satire, Mr. Korman. It ridicules painful truths to underscore their tragedy."

"I don't understand that at all."

"I'm sure you don't."

He tapped his knuckles against the table and looked at me as though I were a puzzle to him. "And what about the teenage girls?"

"What about the teenage boys, for that matter? They're in my car, they visit my apartment. I'm their teacher. I live in their neighborhood."

Marshall Korman laced his fingers together on the table. "Mr. Spector, you cannot remain at this high school. Your presence alone is a hindrance to the orderly running of business." He took a small black journal from the breast pocket of his suit coat, turned several pages, and ran his finger down the margin. "I have an opening at Lakeview High School. You will be transferred there, effective tomorrow. You will retain your tenure and seniority, and no punitive actions will be taken against you. Please gather up your belongings and be off the school grounds by the end of the school day. Your classes will be covered. This hearing is adjourned."

And that was that. Danny and Korman got up.

I said, "That gets you out of the fire, doesn't it, Mr. Korman?"

He halted and looked down at me, holding his manilla folder at his side. "What do you mean?"

"You know what I mean. Place me someplace else and you can tell the community that you are responsive to their needs. In the meantime, the controversy disappears and none of the problems I talked about in that interview will be addressed. Kids will graduate without the skills they need, the books still won't be balanced, programs remain underfunded, but what the hell. You did your job."

Korman just looked at me with that confused look of his, then turned around and walked out the door with Danny at his side.

The little typist lady closed her computer and backed away from the table, her eyes trained on me as though she thought I might get up and mug her. Jamel came over and put her hand on my shoulder. "You know," she said, "there is life after Acosta. Lakeview is a good school."

Stan Wojehowski slid his chair back from the table. "There was nothing I could do, Mr. Spector."

I got to my feet and said, "Yeah, I noticed that, Stan."

Word traveled quickly. It was what I had been hoping to avoid—a formal departure ceremony. I'd been in the English department book room getting my things together, and the kids began dropping in on me to say goodbye. First Wanda and Hilda. Hilda was still whining about Tito.

"He's gonna kill you, Mr. Spector."

"Yeah. I know he is. Thanks."

I had twenty years of stuff—files, books, magazines. I didn't know how I was going to get it all down to the Jeep. Some of it could be tossed, I guessed.

Nelson bounded in the room, and Phil sleepily followed him. Phil wore a backwards White Sox cap and an oversized sweatshirt, the sleeves of which concealed his hands.

Nelson said, "They can't do this to you, man. Don't you got a union or somethin'?"

I said, "The union just makes sure you keep a job. They can't do anything about a transfer, Nelsito. It's not the end of the world. I'll still see you guys once in a while."

Nelson slouched against the long narrow window next to the doorway. "Yeah, but it ain't gonna be the same."

"Nothing stays the same for long." It was one of those truths about life that I more or less hated.

Then I had an idea, one in the vein of Tom Sawyer and white washing a fence. "Hey—you guys want to give me a hand? I need some help getting these boxes down to my car."

Nelson said sure, and I gave him my car keys—but Phil stayed behind, moping. When I asked him what the problem was, he said, "Mrs. Anderson. She not call me Phil. She call me Phuoc. She say my name not Phil."

"Look—get a note from your parents in Vietnamese. Tell her it says they want you to be called Phil. She won't know the difference."

He shook his head. "She say Phuoc anyway."

"Well, say *fuck* back to her. If she complains to an assistant principal, just say you were explaining how to pronounce your name."

"Say fuck her?"

"That's right. Fuck her, Phil."

Soon the room filled up. Nydia and Marco came by with a tray of soft drinks, and all my Flying Bagel baseball team—Chico Martinez, Pedro Ruiz, and of course fiery, intense old Jorgé. "We're gonna slash Danny's tires after school, man. That dude'll be drivin' on rims."

277

I didn't even tell him not to. Flat tires were the least Danny deserved.

I wondered where Daisy was. Out of all the others, I would have expected her to be here first.

Vince, who seldomly left the rarified air of the science labs on the eighth floor, stopped in. He had a present for me. It was a navy blue coffee mug that had printed on it a little poem:

> *Roses are red,*
> *Violets are blue.*
> *I'm schizophrenic,*
> *And so am I.*

Vince said, "I figured you ought to have it," he said. "The faculty of that new joint they're sending you to is going to find out you're crazy anyway."

It had turned into a party. I picked up a plastic cup of soda and moved to a corner, looking at all the people who had touched my life, and who I would no longer see. It's funny. You complain about your job and begrudge it, and the moment it's gone, you miss it.

"We'll stay in touch, you and I."

Marco. He appeared at my side and put his hand on my shoulder. When we had first gotten to Acosta High School, back when it was Freddie Prinze High, we were going to be journalists, a team. He was a photographer, and I was going to write the articles. Somewhere along the line, we got too busy. All those streethearts, all those years. We'd been so young.

I said, "That's what people always say, Marco, but they never do."

This is why I disliked goodbyes. No one really knew what to say.

Marco said, "Lakeview's a good school."

"I keep hearing that. It's not the school that bothers me. I just wish I'd had some say in this. When they just pick you up and put you somewhere, it makes you feel a little like a chess piece."

Marco considered this. "In a way, you are."

I put my cup of soda down on a bookshelf. "That does it. If you're going to start getting metaphorical, I'm leaving."

Tracy walked in the room, her arm around the shoulder of Kirk Douglas Perez. The kid looked great. Only now in contrast could you see how stoned he'd been before. But what a letdown. Here I'd been appointed to lead his community service project—and now the transfer.

"Look who I found in the records office," Tracy said.

Kirk high-fived me. "Johnny—whattup?"

"You look good, kid. You been behaving yourself?"

"Clean for nine weeks. And I been stayin' away from my brother. My ma kicked him out of the house."

"Time he grew up," I said.

"They gonna tear up my record if I stay outta trouble for a year. All I gotta do is that community thing."

Christ. Talk about cutting to the chase. "Look, Kirk—I don't know if Ms. Singer has said anything about this or not—"

Tracy said, "I've already told him, Johnny. I'll be mentoring him for his project. We're going to put together a bibliography of teen novels for the English department."

"I wish I could be here to see that." Kirk may have lost a semester of school, but he'd gained so much more. The two of them, Tracy and he, were going to have some great times, working together. I envied them both. It couldn't have been made more clearly to me than at that moment. It was time for me to go—figuratively, literally.

It's difficult to explain to people what happens to you inside when you teach kids in the inner city. You fail more than you succeed. You blame yourself for the failures. There are no rules because no one is watching, and so you do what you have to do. You take shortcuts, you improvise, anything in order to get a success, or sometimes just to get by. The kids are hungry for someone to love them, and so you love them. Maybe it's a mistake to love them, but when it comes so naturally, you don't question it. And then when they leave, they take part of you with them. They stay young; you get old. And you remember, and half of remembering is regret.

"Weren't you even going to say goodbye to me?"

I was carrying a box of lessons and had my coat slung over my shoulder as I looked up at Tracy, standing on the landing of the second floor stairwell, arms crossed in front of her. I'd nearly made a clean break of it.

I said, "Well, I'll tell you, Tracy. This isn't exactly the way I wanted you to see me leave—sneaking out the back entrance, all my worldly goods in a cardboard box, like the town leper."

She walked down the stairs to my landing. I set the box down on the floor, my coat on top of it.

"When I first got here, I hated you."

"I think they have a club you can join here for that now."

She reached out and touched my arm lightly with her fingers. "I was soft. I was green. You taught me everything I know."

I said, "You taught me plenty, too."

Her lips stretched in a bemused smile. "Oh, yeah? Like what?"

I put my arms around her and held her close. "How to feel. You taught me how to feel again. I'd been numb for so long, I'd forgotten what it was like."

We stood like that a little while, and then she pulled back to face me. "Will you remember me, Johnny?"

"Are you kidding? That's going to be half the problem." I kissed her cheek, and then stooped to pick up the box, my overcoat. I began walking down the stairs again and did not dare look back. Saying goodbye to Tracy was like having open heart surgery—without the anesthetic.

I had to wait for Nelson for fifteen minutes out on the street—locked out of my Jeep. We had made no plans about where or when to meet. The sun upon the park grounds had awakened dormant life. You could smell it in the air, see it in the faces of the kids as they smoked in clannish circles around benches. Once Nelson returned and tossed me my keys, I handled my goodbye to José Julián Acosta High School in the same manner I had with Tracy. I said so long, and did not look back. You look back, you could get daunted.

My garage apartment scowled down at me with familiar disdain as I carried boxes of folders, papers, pens, erasers, yearbooks. Funny about yearbooks, how I never looked through them.

"So you ain't comin' back, I hear."

Daisy. She came swaggering through the stubbled garden in her blue parka, blowing a bubble nonchalantly, like she owned the place. Hair pulled back to rest on her shoulders in careless curls, snug Levis, silver hoops in pierced earlobes—queen of the homegirls.

I knew that if I kept putting boxes down, I'd never finish moving, so I began climbing the stairs to my apartment and talked to her over my shoulder. "Kind of missed you at my going away party."

"I didn't wanna say goodbye there in front of everybody. Especially one somebody."

I got my keys out and had the storm door open and fumbled with the lock. Daisy had followed me up. She pulled the keys from my hand, snapped a gum bubble in my ear, and said, "Here."

The door swung open. The place was sunny and bright because there was a northern exposure—more evidence of spring in the offing. I left the box on the floor, turned around, and Daisy was right beside me, like my shadow.

"I said, "Come in, why don't you?"

She chewed on her gum and said, "Thanks, I will."

I shut the door and took off my coat and walked to the kitchen. Actually—it was all part of the same room. I walked to the kitchen side of the room. "What can I get you, Daisy? Coke? Milk?"

"Milk? What—you think I'm a kid?"

I slapped my forehead. "What was I thinking? A woman of your distinction. Coke it is."

She had escorted me to the kitchenette. It was as though we were attached. "Anyway," she said, "it's not like we gotta really say goodbye. I mean, I live right down the street and all. We'll be seeing each other."

I found a glass in a cabinet and set it on the sink. She had unzipped her jacket and was wearing only a halter top beneath it. "Daisy, things are changing in my life."

"We'll do things together. You know, hang out."

"I've got a new school now, and—"

"Do you think I'm pretty, Johnny?"

Uh-oh, I thought. "You don't need me to tell you you're pretty. You know it already."

"Do you think I'm prettier than Ms. Singer?"

I opened the freezer and took out a tray of ice cubes. "Look, Daisy—it's not a contest."

"Don't be doin' me that way, brother. Who do you think is prettier, me or Ms. Singer?"

I pulled the tab on the can of Coke. It erupted.

I said, "I told you. It's not a compettion. You're both of you very—"

"Didja ever kiss her?"

I poured the Coke over the ice cubes in the glass, watched it foam upward toward the rim. "Daisy, what the hell has gotten into you? What are we playing—twenty questions?"

She smiled secretly to herself. "You did, didn't you?"

I said nothing to this.

"Do you think she could kiss you like this?"

And the next thing I knew, she grabbed the back of my head with both of her hands and pressed her mouth fiercely against mine. Just that one moment, her breath hot against my face, and the dissonance of feelings that followed.

I got hold of her forearms and wrenched her away with all the force I could muster. She nearly fell over before she looked up at me, wounded.

"No," I said sternly. "Not like that. Not like that, Daisy."

If the tears were not immediate, they were imminent. You could see the hurt on her face, and the attendant rage brewing. She backed up a few steps, then turned and lunged toward the door. She did not bother to shut it—just kicked open the storm door and scrambled down the wooden stairs, making a frantic racket.

I held on to the kitchen counter, suspending mysef over the sink, and spit out the bubble gum. The pink wad sat upon the stainless steel. I touched the back of my hand to my lips. *Not like that, Daisy,* I thought.

17

I looked out one of my two windows. Six-thirty—the sun had already come up and it was just light enough to see how tattered the neighborhood was. I had on my boxers and an Ivy League shirt and was looking through my ties. I figured I ought to wear a tie on my first day at a new school, set some standard from which I could work my way down. Ten minutes later I still had no pants on and had decided to hell with the tie. Then the phone rang and it was Marlyn.

"I was just wondering if you'd like to have dinner tonight," she said.

I did not know if this was my call to come back home, but thought I ought not to rush things.

"Sure," I said. "It's kind of a busy day, but I'd like that very much."

"If you have some school activity, we can always make it another time."

"No, tonight's fine. Did you have any place in mind?"

Marlyn said, "No, not really."

"How about Rico's at six? I can pick you up, if you'd like."

"That'll be fine. We haven't been to Rico's in ages."

I said, "We haven't been *anywhere* in ages." I sat down on the bed for a moment and looked at the old photo of Marlyn with her mother, looking at the world as if anything that might come around the corner could not be all that good.

"That's true," Marlyn said. "Have you taken any time to consider whether we still have a future together or not?"

"I thought you'd never ask."

"I didn't. I was just wondering if you still had that in mind. You haven't said a word about it. In fact, you haven't said anything at all."

"I was waiting for you to bring it up."

This was an interesting form of torture. I didn't want to sound too eager, and I also couldn't sound too disinterested, and it was almost impossible not to be at least one of these.

Marlyn said, "Make a girl wait too long and she might think you don't care."

"On the other hand, it's always more polite to wait for an invitation."

"And you're polite, now?"

I said, "I'm trying."

She gave a little laugh and then said, "Are you still on the wagon?"

"Honey, I'm *hitched* to the wagon. I'm pulling the goddamn thing."

"How long has it been?"

"I don't know. Sobriety. It's impaired my ability to count."

She said six o'clock then, and I said all right, and then I hung up the phone and sat there looking at it. *What was that all about?* I wondered.

§

Lakeview High School was an older building on Ashland Avenue, set right there in the urban sprawl, next to banks and laundromats and restaurants. There were *up* stairways and *down* stairways and no escalators. I had a squeamish feeling in my stomach. Everything and everyone looked utterly unfamiliar. It made me want to call my mother. My mother died in 1992.

I was introduced to the principal and an assistant principal and the head of the English department, and I forgot all of their names instantly. They were very nice and very superfluous and seemed as interchangeable as pieces of office furniture.

My program was a good one—two freshman comps and three junior lit classes. I had free time at eleven and was given a little cubicle in the English office that featured a computer with Internet access and my own printer. Luxuries. I sat at my computer and discovered I had an email address. In my account were three mortgage ads, one adult site ad, and a newsletter from the principal. I didn't get as far as the newsletter.

But I did get to study hall. It was on the second floor—a big, wooden-floored room with very tall windows covered by green canvas shades. An Asian student, a girl in a green fuzzy sweatshirt, walked up to my desk and asked for the washroom pass.

I looked on the desk, moved a paper tray, but couldn't find it.

The Asian girl rolled her eyes and said, "Right side, second drawer."

And that's exactly where it was. It must have been made in shop class—in 1937. It was an artifact, a long, flat piece of wood, like a spatula, and it had a worn handle. Burned into its oak-brown surface were the words **washroom pass**.

I took attendance. I broke up a card game in the corner of the room, and told a white kid who looked like a skateboarder what *serendipity* meant. He held out a paperback novel to me, his finger targeting the word.

"Then how come they don't just say *good fortune?*" he wanted to know.

I said, "Writers just like to confuse kids. It's the only fun they get."

Now here is what I should have done. When Daisy followed me into my apartment, I should have stopped her immediately, and told her to wait for me outside. It would have sounded rude, and she might have complained or laughed at me, because she was well aware of the allure of her own sexuality, and my attempts to ignore it—but even so. That's what I should have done. That would have taken care of it. Or perhaps not. She might have kissed me right there on the steps—either way, I shouldn't have pushed her away. I ought not to have yelled at her. That look on her face.

The tone of the intercom sounded. A woman's static-ridden voice said, "Will Mr. John Spector please report to the main office? Mr. John Spector—a parent is here to see you."

It was my first day. I didn't know any students. What would a parent want to talk to me about?

I couldn't very well leave a full study hall unattended. I stood up, paced behind my desk, looked out a window at a Blues Club on Belmont Avenue. A sign announced that Big Time Sarah was playing there this week. Drinks were $3.50.

A young, husky man in a white and navy polo shirt strode in the door. He had biceps that looked like cannon balls, and short, black hair. "Mr. Spector?" he said, extending his hand. "Micky Alverno, PE. The office sent me up to watch your study hall for you."

I said, "You wouldn't happen to know what this is about, would you?"

Micky Alverno shook his head, his lower lip protruding a little. "Nope. Mr. Davis just asked me to sit in for you."

"Mr. Davis?"

"The assistant principal."

"Oh—of course. The assistant principal."

I gathered up my attendance book as he swung his arms, as if performing calisthenics to kill the time. "First day?"

I nodded. "Yeah."

"Don't worry. You'll get the hang of it. Teaching is like riding a bike."

For Christ's sake. He couldn't have been out of his twenties and he was going to show *me* the ropes. I thought, *Micky, why don't you just go nuke the gay whales for Jesus?*

Inside the main office secretaries buzzed around behind the counter, stooping over desks, searching through file cabinets. There was a man in his fifties in a burgundy sport coat sitting in one of a row of chairs along the wall, obviously a substitute. He had the air of a milquetoast. His slacks cuffs did not quite reach the tops of his socks, and a good inch of dull, white shin was exposed. Three chairs down was a Latin man in a gray-hooded sweatshirt and Levis, dark brown skin, tight curly hair. A bird-like secretary with thick, corrective lenses said to me—"Oh—Mr. Spector. Mr. Morales is waiting to see you."

She indicated the man in the sweatshirt. He stood, smiling, worrying the inside rim of a baseball cap between two very nervous hands. "Mr. Morales?" I said, holding out my hand to him.

He nodded several times. "*Si, si. Señor* Spector. Good to meet you. I am Fernando's father."

I still had his hand in mine when he said that. I pumped his hand vigorously now.

"It's very good to meet you, too," I said. "Fernando is a good boy. I feel like he's my own son."

When I said that, the son of a bitch clasped his solid arms around me in a bear hug, pulled me to him, and patted my back, right there in the office. "*Gracias, señor. Gracias.*" Then he grasped my forearms and forced me back, the better to address me.

I said, "Is he all right, Fernando?"

"Oh, *si. Bien, bien.* He tell me about you and your son. You been good to him. He home from hospital now. He back with his mother, resting. The doctors, they say he start therapy this week. Two hour only, after school. His nerve got a damage, in his right side. No move so good. The bullet, it hit a nerve."

"I'm sorry to hear that," I said. "Is there anything I can do for you—or for your son?"

Mr. Morales looked around the offfice suspiciously. "We maybe talk somewhere?"

I did not know my way around the school, but the hallway was fairly vacant, and so I extended my hand toward the office door. We walked out into the hallway, toward a barred emergency exit. I stood and looked at him, waiting to hear what this was about. He glanced back and forth down the hall toward the main office. "My boy, he no live with me. Sometimes, yes, sometimes no. I have a girlfriend."

"I know," I said. "I'm aware of the situation."

"Fernando—he in a gang."

"The Dragons."

"*Si*, the Dragons. They say they protect the neighborhood, but they almost get him killed. He is my only son."

There was another shoe, someplace. It had to drop sometime.

I said, "I know all of this, señor."

He nodded, his eyes cast downward. He swallowed with difficulty. "I work construction. Fernando's mother, she work too. He has to get— how you say? *Rehab*. But it not safe in the streets. I worry."

"Is that what this is about? Fernando needs a ride? I'd be happy to drive him after school."

"*Gracias, señ*or Spector, but that is not what this is about."

A male student with a pink hall pass slouched by, looking as though he was half asleep. A radiator at the end of the hall began to hiss. I waited for Mr. Morales to continue and had to struggle against the urge to shake it out of him.

"The Disciples want to kill my son. I see them when I drop him off. They come in the neighborhood, hide in alleys, waiting, always waiting. Is because of the gunfight. Is because he is a Dragon. I tell him get out, but he no want to listen. He say he cannot get out. You have a son, señor."

I said, "Yes."

"You know how it is I feel."

"Yes, señor. I know how you feel. But I don't know what you want from me."

He looked up at me—big, dolorous brown eyes. "Please, you talk to him. Talk to the other members. You get him out—out of Dragons. You do this for me, *por favor*."

"Señor, I've tried. You don't understand—"

"Please. Please do not tell me that. I understand. My boy will die. You can help me. Fernando, he tells me about you. They all know you—for years. The Dragons, they will listen. They will do this for you."

Work another miracle, Johnny. Promise your wife you'll give up this sort of thing and see if you can have it done before dinner.

I had not had a good night's sleep since I quit drinking. Night sweats, anxiety, waking every hour on the hour. Do-it-yourself detox. It was little situations like this that provided an excuse to have just one more.

I said, "I'll drive Fernando home from rehab whenever you need me to. I'll make sure he gets home safely."

"*Gracias, señor.* You have made me very happy."

"But I can't get him out of the Dragons."

Mr. Morales took my hand in his and smiled broadly. "You will try again. I know you will try again. You have a boy too. I know you will."

He put on his baseball hat, and walked slowly down the darkened corridor, the walk of a laboring man, sore from aches and pains of inflamed joints and muscles.

Just one drink. That's all I needed.

§

Rico's was tiny and dark inside, and the tables were all set too close together. It was like being at a party in a cramped apartment. There was too much red in the decor—*Early Elvis Mediterranean.* The patrons were wealthy and had gray hair and had all left their Mercedes and Jaguars and Cadillacs with the valet attendant. The maitre d' had ambushed me at the door with the news that I would not be permitted entrance in my leather jacket. Marlyn reddened, looked up at the ceiling as if she wished she could fly up there and disappear. I was led to a closet where I was encouraged to select one or another ugly sport coat that was either too big or too small, but ugly nonetheless. I chose a black one with a felt collar, and the waiter seated us at a round table that was pushed against the far wall next to the kitchen entrance. Several times I was almost squashed by a swinging kitchen door as busboys and waiters shot by, as if out of a mortar.

Marlyn said, "You might have wanted to check the dress code, dear, when you made reservations."

I buttered a piece of bread and said, "I didn't make reservations. Besides, it's the twenty-first century. Who knew there were still dress codes?"

She sighed and turned her water glass, and I knew she was thinking that I was a hopeless case, that I would never change. This was not exactly the foot I had wanted to get off on.

The waiter, a young man with an olive complexion and eyebrows that met at the bridge of his nose, took our drink orders.

Marlyn said, "Cabernet—Louis Martini."

The waiter looked at me next. "Iced tea," I said.

He nodded and jotted something down. "Very impressive. I hope that wasn't for my sake," Marlyn said.

The couple seated next to us held hands across the table. What was remarkable about this was their age; they were easily in their eighties, yet they clung to one another as if they might have been in their teens. The man had light blue watery eyes that sparkled in the candlelight. I wondered why that happened to old men, why their eyes always looked as though they were leaking.

Marlyn said, "Look," and tilted her head in their direction.

"I know."

"Isn't that wonderful?"

It was, I suppose—but something about it just didn't ring true, not with everything I'd learned about the world. "You never know," I said. "He might just be demented and think he's out with another woman."

She kicked me under the table. "You're about as romantic as a boulder."

It seemed to me that if you're seeing to the things you're supposed to see to, you have just enough time to survive from day to day. I did not see how romance entered into it, but I did not say this, either.

The waiter appeared with a round tray and our drinks. He placed the iced tea in front of me. It had a lemon slice. Iced tea, for Christ's sake.

The old couple were gazing into one another's eyes. They were drinking water. I supposed they had a lot of pills they had to take. The waiter presented menus to us with an embarrassing flourish, as if to imply, *Voila.*

"They're a charming old couple, and I'll bet they love each other deeply. He probably brings her flowers, and leaves her little love notes around the house, and makes her breakfast in bed on the weekends."

I said, "If he does all that, he's been hired. She's out with the butler."

Marlyn abruptly lowered her butter knife to her plate. "What is it you want, Johnny? Why are we even here?"

"Don't you remember? You asked if I'd like to have dinner."

"But what is it you *want* from me—someone to do the laundry? A familiar face around the house so you don't get lonely?"

Six months later and whatever had gone wrong was still wrong. It was like cable TV programming difficulty. We wanted to appear on the same screen, but were stuck on different channels.

"I do my own laundry, Marlyn. I also cook my own meals and clean my own apartment. I go to my job, and I come home. I pay the bills—my own, and yours. I do it gladly. And yes, a familiar face around the house would be nice, if it were yours. Nobody else's—just yours."

She sipped her wine and looked at me over the rim of her glass. Then she set the wineglass down, and propped her chin upon two joined hands, elbows rested upon the table top. "What I meant was, don't you have any passion for me anymore? When we first started going out, you couldn't be with me enough. I had a sense that you really loved me, that I came first in your life."

The old couple were served their dessert. The gentleman rearranged the placement of the plates for his wife, for her convenience. From time to time he would cut a little piece of his dessert and set it on her plate for her.

"When we first started going out, I was twenty-nine. You were eighteen. It was us against the world. Now we have a mortgage, a car payment, insurance, income tax, a boy to send to college, a boy we'll have to soon learn to live without. And my job got suddenly complicated."

"*You're* the one who complicated it."

"You're right; I am. I'm the one who complicated it, because I stumble, I make mistakes. I'm trying to correct my mistakes. I shouldn't have given the interview, and I should have checked the dress code. In the meantime, I'm a guy in an ugly coat who's trying to tell his wife he still loves her, in his awkward, passionless way. But wait till I get you home."

Marlyn pressed her napkin to her lips and reached her hand across the table to mine, gave it a squeeze. "Johnny?"

"Hm?"

"It really *is* an ugly coat."

We continued to hold hands. At last the old man signed the check, folded his napkin, and rose from his place. He walked around the table to his wife, and I believed he was going to pull her chair back for her, because he had been so gallant all evening, but instead he grasped what I saw now were handles, and rolled her first backward, and then toward the door. She was wheelchair-bound. Her wrap, a knitted thing with flowers on it, had covered the hand grips, and so I had believed it was nothing other than a high-backed chair. As he pushed her down the crowded aisle, navigating the straits of chairs and dinner stands, he paused to lean over and kiss her cheek.

Marlyn unclenched her hand from mine, opened her purse. A tear raced down her cheek while she worked her way through all the standard purse contents, lipstick, compact, coin purse. She pulled some Kleenex out and brought it to her face. "Wasn't that beautiful?" she asked me. It was that. It was also terribly sad. "Just think, that could be us someday."

I said, "I don't want that to be us. I want *this* to be us." I reached across the table and pulled her to me, kissing her firmly upon the mouth. She made a little *umph* sound of surprise, and I heard a woman at the table next to us gasp and drop her silverware. When we came out of the clench, our waiter with the eyebrows was standing there, pen and paper in hand.

"Would you care for a little more time?" he said.

§

"Maybe I could sleep over," I suggested. The sun was setting later every day, and there was still a thin ribbon of orange along the western horizon as we drove down Route 41.

"That would confuse Jason. Besides, I think I know what you have in mind, and we wouldn't have enough privacy. We'd need a hotel for that—a hotel with a very discreet staff."

"And you said I was passionless."

"*You* said that." She pushed my arm playfully. "It's just been a long time, is all. You probably only get this way once a year."

"Only one way to find out."

291

"Not tonight."

I merged into traffic on the Deerfield Road overpass, and this ruined the life of the driver behind me. He strobed his brights at me and leaned on his horn.

"When, then?" I asked. "I've done everything you wanted me to. I've quit drinking, I've left my kids behind."

Marlyn turned toward me. I saw the silhouette of her face in the darkened interior of the car. "Have you, Johnny? Have you really?"

I thought of Fernando, of Daisy. "Well, there might be a little unfinished business."

"Finish it, then. Finish it before you come back home."

"All right," I said. "I will."

In the shadows of the oak trees along the edge of our yard, I made out two figures standing beside a car parked in the "L" portion of the drive. I pulled the car in, the headlight beams illuminating a Dodge Neon. Next to it, Jason was pointing out the mouth of the drive, apparently telling the other figure—who could only have been Bruce—to leave.

I said, "Your boyfriend's back."

"I told him I'd be out tonight."

"Looks like you need to tell him again."

I put the car in park, but left the headlights on. Marlyn opened her passenger door and said, "Johnny, let *me* take care of this."

"I never said a word."

There were the thuds of car doors closing, the susurration of Marlyn saying something under her breath to Bruce—either asking him a question, or telling him to leave. I could not tell which. I heard Jason say, "I told him you weren't here," and then there was an undisguised catcall, evidently intended for me.

"Well, if it isn't the neighborhood racist, Mr. Johnny Spector. What's the matter, the Klan closed for the night?"

I took a few steps toward him. It was chilly, and as he spoke, steam came out of his mouth, his nose. Reminded me of one of those carriage horses you see on Michigan Avenue near Lake Shore Drive.

I put my arm around Jason and said, "You get inside, buddy. You haven't even got a coat on."

Jason refused to budge. "Not until he leaves," he insisted.

Marlyn stepped up to Bruce. She spoke the way you would to a child. "Bruce, I want you out of here, right now. Do you hear me?"

"The great Johnny Spector," he bellowed on. I wondered if he'd been drinking. "Haven't seen you on the news lately. Didja run out of minorities to insult? Huh? Who's next—the Japs?"

Jason tilted his head toward me and said, "Dad, what are you waiting for?"

Marlyn called out, "*No.* I'll take care of this. Bruce—get in your car and go home, this minute."

"Fucking racist bastard. Your wife doesn't want you. She *never* wanted you. Don't you get it?" He stepped around Marlyn until his face was in mine. "What's the matter—you scared? You scared of me?"

I looked at Marlyn. She said, "Oh, hell. Let him have it."

And so I did. I socked him in the jaw with everything I had. There was a crack—either my hand or his chin, and he went down. My knuckles were first numb, but within a few seconds they throbbed like nobody's business.

To no one in particular I said, "I think my hand is broken."

Bruce lifted himself off the pavement until he was sitting up. There was blood, slick on his lower lip, which shone in the beams of the Camry's headlights. "I'm gonna *sue* you, Spector."

I said, "No you won't."

"Oh, yeah? Why not?"

"Because if you sue me, I'll hit you again."

It was not a happily-ever-after kind of ending. You've probably guessed that. Life is too messy for happy endings. Besides, no one really wants things to end. We just want them to get *better*. We keep hoping they will, anyway. We keep waiting.

My first week at Lakeview was not a failure. I actually received some pretty good student essays on Blake's "The Tyger." (I no longer judge the quality of my teaching by successes. I just try to avoid defeat.) One kid wrote that Blake saw God as a sort of "cosmic blacksmith", and added that if he were alive today and tried to write a similar poem, he'd probably see Him as a software design specialist. His conclusion was that technology ruins poetry. I thought the kid was on to something.

And so I made it safely through till Thursday at one o'clock, which is when I received a call in my cubicle.

"You get a little exiled and I never hear from you again."

293

Tracy. One of life's prettier complications.

I said, "How's my favorite substitute?"

"That's really what I was to you, wasn't I?"

I had never thought of it that way. "What do you say you leave the irony alone and tell me how the hell you've been? Has Woody moved here yet?"

"No. Woody isn't coming until April. Why, are you jealous?"

"Of course. I'll always be jealous."

"And how's the wife?"

"Fine. We had dinner the other night. Why—are *you* jealous?"

"No."

"Liar."

"All right. I am a liar. Listen, I've got someone here who needs to ask a favor. Hold on a minute."

There was some fumbling with the phone, and the next thing I heard was, "Yo—whattup?"

"Fernando? Where have you been? Why haven't you called me?"

"I got all this homework and shit to make up. You know how it is. The neighborhood's hot, and I'm just trying to keep from gettin' killed. Listen—my old man, he said he talked to you, and maybe I could get a ride to rehab. What you doin' tomorrow?"

"Tomorrow? Tomorrow's good. Where's the rehab center?"

"Northwestern Hospital—all the way downtown."

"Not a problem. Pick you up at school around three-fifteen?"

There was a muffled exchange on the other end. When he was back on he said, "Oh—I almost forgot. Ms. Singer says she wants to come with."

I closed my eyes and rubbed my eyelids with my fingers. A faint headache was growing at the base of my neck. I asked Fernando to please put her back on the line.

"Hello?"

I said, "Tracy—what are you trying to do to me?"

"I'm sorry. Am I doing something to you?"

I had a little postcard portrait of Jonathan Swift tacked to the bulletin board fabric of my cubicle. The Dean looked askance at me, and I thought of his Stella.

"We'll talk tomorrow."

There was a letter from Forest College waiting for me back at my digs. I set my briefcase down on the first step of the outdoor staircase and tore one end of the envelope away. The English hiring committee wrote that they were pleased to inform me that I had been selected for an on-campus interview for the position of assistant professor. *Now, how the hell do you like that?* I thought. The first thing that came to mind was that I should have a drink. But I didn't drink anymore. Just as well. Get your hopes up and you'll be disappointed every time. I folded the letter back up and put it in the breast pocket of my leather jacket.

It occurred to me that there was something different about señor Valentin's place, but I didn't know exactly what it was. I glanced around slowly. The garden was the same, the walkway—*the sundial.* That was it. It had been moved to the center of the yard where it caught the afternoon sunshine, producing a shadow near the Roman numeral four. The damn thing worked. You didn't even have to wind it up, and it worked. I looked up at the windows of my apartment and must have caught them off guard. They no longer seemed to be scowling. I wondered if it was spring that was responsible for this change, or if I was simply imagining it.

And for a change I felt good. I did, at least, until I remembered about Daisy. Then whatever lightness of heart I'd had vanished. I needed to see her.

I brought my briefcase upstairs and splashed some water on my face and combed my hair. Daisy lived right down the street. As I approached her house—a little single story brick bungalow—I had misgivings, wondered what her mother might think of a teacher calling on her daughter. I thought of explanations I might offer. *I have a program change I forgot to give her.* But I wasn't her teacher anymore. *I wanted to apologize for pushing her away after we made out.* The truth was definitely not the way to go.

On the front porch lay a little blue mat that read *Bienvenido.* I took off my sunglasses, brushed a hand over my hair. The doorbell had been painted over. I pushed it twice. No answer. I heard no movement inside. I thought perhaps no one was home. There was a brass door knocker on the front door. I opened the storm door and grabbed hold of it, just as the door swept open, pulling me up and a good foot or so into the house. I stumbled, felt foolish. A plump woman with black hair gave me a stern, questioning look.

"I'm sorry," I said, taking a step back onto the porch. "I had my hand on your knocker. I mean—" I pointed to the front door. "The door knocker." *Shut up!* I thought to myself.

"What can I do for you?" she demanded, stepping slightly behind the door.

"I'm John Spector. I used to be Daisy's homeroom teacher. I live down the street, and. . ."

She gave a long, drawn out, "Ohhh," and then said, "señor Spector" in a canny way that made me even more nervous than I had been. She might as well have said, *"So you're the bastard who tried to rape my daughter."*

Though it was cold outside, she left the door open as she loudly bellowed Daisy's name. I heard Daisy screech back.

"What do you want?"

"Your teacher's here, señor Spector."

"Tell him to go to hell!"

Mrs. Rosario ran off to wherever Daisy was and I was left standing on the porch, holding the storm door open. I peeked inside at the living room—dark wooden furniture, console TV. Framed quotations in Spanish from the New Testament, but not a crucifix in sight. Puerto Rican families in Chicago were pretty evenly split between the Catholic Church and The Church of God—Pentecostals. Pentecostals didn't believe in icons of any sort, and so I guessed that that was Daisy's family's religious orientation. They were also extremely conservative when it came to dress, and I gathered that Mrs. Rosario must have had a heart attack every time she saw her daughter in those tight jeans. Then again, in those jeans, Daisy could give *anybody* a heart attack.

"¡No hables de tu maestro así!"

"He's not my teacher anymore. Let go!"

There was some scuffling and heated whispers and suddenly Daisy appeared at the door. She was chewing gum and wearing a short-sleeve top. It's not that I stared, but it was kind of hard to ignore. It was electric blue. It was Spandex. It was Daisy. She would not look at me.

"What do *you* want?" she said.

I could sense Mrs. Rosario just behind the door. "I came to apologize."

"So go ahead. Apologize."

I said, "I'm sorry, Daisy—"

And she said, "Whatever," and began to close the door on me.

I put my hand out against it to hold it open. "Would you just listen to me for a second?"

"Why? You apologized already. There's nothing else to say."

"I think there is."

"Well, then you better say it, 'cause it ain't coming from me."

From behind the door I could hear Mrs. Rosario whisper fiercely, "Use your manners when you talk to a teacher!"

This wasn't working. "Can't you just put a jacket on and come out and talk to me?"

She made eye contact with me now, though you would have thought she had just stepped in dog shit. "I told you. I got nothin' to say to you."

"Daisy, please. Come walk with me. We can have a cigarette."

She was twirling a little hair curl around her finger. "You're buying."

"Fine, I'm buying."

She disappeared inside and I heard more heated whispers.

"¿Adónde vas? ¿Qué te está diciendo?"

"Please, ma. It's between me and him."

"¿Qué pasa aquí? ¡Es un hombre hecho y derecho!"

"Let go of my jacket, please."

She pulled her jacket on and slammed the door behind her as she hopped down the porch steps. I saw Mrs. Rosario's face pushed against the front window as she struggled to keep us in sight.

I said, "Well, that should get me arrested."

"It would serve you right." She two-fingered a Newport from a box and extended it to me. "There's a gas station up the street. You can buy me a pack there."

What a great teacher. One day I'm trying to get her tongue out of my mouth, the next I'm buying her smokes. She clicked a red butane lighter and I hunched over it, cupping the flame to protect it against the wind. She lighted hers next, and our eyes met, and then we sort of aimlessly walked down the block. There was a hubcap in somebody's front yard. I took a big drag off my cigarette. It was so good.

I said, "It's my fault, what happened the other day. I didn't handle anything right."

"You sure didn't."

I watched her French inhale. She was showing off. "Look,

297

Daisy—we're friends. That is, I want to *be* your friend."

"You got a funny way to treat your friends."

"So do you."

She stopped, right there on the sidewalk. Magenta eyeshadow. Black mascara. She exhaled a gray stream of smoke and said, "What do you mean?"

"Well, you don't go around kissing all your friends, do you?"

"You're not supposed to kiss your students, either."

"I didn't kiss you. You know it didn't happen like that."

"I *know* how it happened. You pushed me away. Was I so terrible, Johnny? Is it so awful to kiss me? Is it?"

She was crying now, not vocally, but the tears, the irreversible frown.

"No—not at all. Quite the contrary, and that's the problem. You freaked me out. I'm too old for you."

"So what? You're older than your wife too, and she was your student."

"That's different, Daisy."

"Is it? How's it different?"

I wanted to comfort her, to hold her—but that would have only worsened the situation, and we'd be right back where we'd started. "Don't cry. Listen to me. Please don't cry."

"I'm not *crying*."

But of course she was crying. "All right. Do the math. I'm twenty-nine years older than you are. You're fifteen. *Fifteen*, Daisy. You're supposed to be going to slumber parties, and—you know, talk about boys, and polish your toenails. Girl stuff."

"Fifteen's just a number." She threw her cigarette to the sidewalk and stomped it out with one of her Pumas while wiping a tear away with the back of her hand.

"It's not just a number. It's youth, dreams, possibility. You've got your whole future to think about."

"I thought I knew about my future."

I had smoked my cigarette right down to the filter and burned my fingers. "I was never your future." I dropped the filter to the ground. It rolled a little way and then fell into a storm drain.

Daisy fished in her jacket pocket and brought out the box again. "I was so stupid. I thought you loved me." She extracted a cigarette, handed it to me, and then put another between her lips. "I didn't know any better."

"I do love you—as a friend. Not in that other way."

She lighted our cigarettes, mine first. I held my hands around hers. They were cold to the touch. "You love Ms. Singer," she said.

"No. I love my wife."

She took half a drag, stopped, exhaled. "You do?"

"Yes."

We began walking again. The smoke filled my lungs and smoothed everything over. The afternoon was waning, but the edges were gone— the uncomforatble emotional edges. I felt that we were connecting.

"You guys gonna get back together?"

"We're going to try."

Daisy tipped her cigarette ash and let the wind carry it away. "That's good. You belong with a Rican girl. Rican girls know how to take care of you."

I said, "You think so?"

She smiled, and let the smoke out of her nostrils this time. "I know so."

At the gas station I bought a package of Newports and a bottle of water for each of us. Daisy had a sudden craving for Twinkies, so we had some of those, too. The man behind the bulletproof glass gave us a wary look and I knew what he was thinking.

The walk back was much easier. The wind numbed my ears, but the Twinkies were good, and the smokes were fantastic—and to think I'd have to give them up all over again.

Daisy said, "Tell me something."

"What?" I said.

"Am I a good kisser?"

I pulled on my cigarette and held the smoke in a long time.

She popped the last of her Twinkie in her mouth, made smacking sounds with her lips, and then wiped the crums off her hands on the sleeve of my jacket. "Well, am I?"

I gave her a veiled, peripheral look and smiled. "Eat your Twinkie," I said.

She laughed all the way home.

§

Someone had left a newspaper on a table in the teachers lunchroom and it was right on the front page. **"High School Principal under Arrest—Grand Jury Hands Down Indictment."**

Danny Velez, prinicpal of José Julián Acosta High School in Chicago's Humboldt Park, was arrested Wednesday afternoon by Federal authorities on charges that he approved of a plan to embezzle over one hundred thousand dollars of taxpayer funds earmarked for poverty programs. Additional charges of conspiracy to aid and abet a terrorist group were also filed against Velez, and faculty members Michael Parnell, Elizabeth Mojica, Isabelle Villachez, Patrick Murphy, and others.

The photo above the text could have been an album cover. Covering two-thirds of the page, it was a wide-angle, floor-to-roof shot of the Acosta structure in the middle of the park. In the foreground students looked on in little groups of twos, threes and fours as FBI agents left the building carrying confiscated computers and office records. The caption read: **"Federal agents impound evidence in connection with the case against the Acosta 6."**

The Acosta 6. Sounded like a salsa band.

I let the paper drop upon the table and sat back in the uncomfortable plastic salmon-colored cafeteria chair. All this time and they had finally got them. I had believed it would never happen, thought that Danny was so powerfully connected that even the Feds would look the other way—and so I was wrong again. I didn't mind being wrong like this.

I pulled up in front of Acosta High that afternoon right in the open. No more hiding near the rear entrance for me. There were television crews in their vans with those absurdly tall antennae reaching for the sky, and reporters with microphones, and cameramen adjusting their lenses. It was a wonderful feeling not to be the lead story.

After the first upsurge of students had exited and thinned out across the park, I searched faces, found some I knew, others I didn't. It was something like returning to the scene of the crime. Shortly, Tracy exited the big main doors, Fernando right behind her. She visored her eyes with her hand, spotted me, and pointed in my direction. I saw that Fernando moved in a herky-jerky fashion, and it pained me to think that a bullet had done that to him, had ripped through his young body.

Tracy pulled open the old rusty passenger door of the Jeep, making it squeak harshly. She handed me a folded newspaper.

"I have a surprise for you," she said.

"I know," I said, taking the paper from her. "I saw it."

Fernando climbed in the back seat and slapped his hand on mine, giving me the Dragon handshake. "Folks to the end," he said.

"How are you doing, buddy?"

"One day at a time, you know what I mean?"

"Yeah, I'm familiar with that routine."

Tracy hopped in and shut the door and gave me a kiss on the cheek. She was wearing a tan trench coat and a black pinstripe skirt, beneath the hem of which two long legs poured out, crossed, one prettily over the other. The girl had it, and there was no use pretending she didn't, only now things were different, and it was almost beside the point.

Almost.

"Hello, Johnny. And now you see why I wanted to come along with you and Fernando."

"I read about it this morning in the lunchroom. I thought I was seeing things."

"That's probably the way Danny's feeling right now. But you have to let me tell you all about it. It was unbelieveable."

Fernando hunched between us. "The Feds stormed the joint. Damn, Johnny— you missed somethin' cool."

"Sit back," I said. "Fasten your seatbelt."

Fernando snickered to himself.

"What is it?"

"Johnny—you sat in your back seat lately?"

I looked at him through the rearview mirror. He was holding up two broken ends of what had formerly been seatbelts.

"Oh. Well, just sit back, then."

I pulled away from the curb and sped down Humboldt Drive. It was a warm day, the first day I'd worn my khaki jacket. The sunlight was fresh and liquidy and the air was fresh too, and I thought of Marlyn and Jason, and what it would be like to have a home again.

Tracy gave the blow-by-blow of the raid. "At first no one knew what was going on—all these people running up the escaltor, some wearing holsters, you know, the way they do under their suit coats." She indicated where the gun would be by using her hand. "They went straight into the main office—they didn't ask or anything, just went single file, straight into Danny's office, and made him stand up against the wall. I was handing in outcomes assessments to Shirley, and I saw the whole thing. It was unbelieveable."

"Yeah, you said that, that it was unbelievable. You should use specific details in a report."

"Go to hell. Where was I?"

Fernando said, "Damn, dude. She slammed you cold."

"You were giving outcomes assesments to Shirley."

"Oh, yeah. Next thing you know, they're asking everyone to leave the main office as they haul in Mike Parnell and Elizabeth and Murphy. They had them in handcuffs already, agents with walkie-talkies on either side, pushing them around by their forearms—that enough detail for you?"

"Make it colorful."

"But isn't this unbelievable, Johnny?"

"I'm going to have to buy you a thesaurus."

"Go to hell again. So by now there's a huge crowd outside the main office, and still *more* agents are coming up the escalator. There were all these black cars and vans parked in the main turnaround, and it was like the place was under seige. Well, it *was*, I guess. And as I was watching from out in the hallway, the look on Elizabeth's face was like nothing I'd ever seen before. She was stupefied, as if she were in a dream, as if something like this could never happen to her."

"Unbelievable." I said.

"Exactly."

I guided the Jeep down Division Street, shook my head as we passed *Jew Town Polish and Fries,* and took the Kennedy to Ohio Street. The Magnificent Mile was just that today as we crossed Michigan Avenue into Streeterville. There was construction everywhere, and I was surprised there was still any land to build on in such a crowded part of the city. I found a parking lot off of St. Clair Street and took a ticket stub from the attendant, an old African-American man with gray hair and a warm smile.

Walking was a bit of a struggle for Fernando, though he didn't complain. I said, "Maybe I should have dropped you off in front before I parked."

"No. Doctor says walkin's s'posed to be good for me."

302

Tracy said, "He's getting better every day. I can see it already." The lake breeze played with her hair and reflections of quick clouds skidded across the mirror-like windows of skycrapers. I remembered the way it had been with us, Tracy and me, how it had come on like a spell and then ended. "I love this part of the city in spring. It's as though everything is new and beginning all over again."

I guess we weren't meant to be. Or maybe that wasn't true. Maybe *nothing* was meant to be. Maybe we just go through this world encountering accidents that change the course of our lives. Anyway, it didn't do any good to think about it. And so then I tried not thinking about it.

We followed Fernando into the hospital and down several long hallways to the outpatient clinic. While he was signing in, Tracy said, "I'm going to find the little girls room."

She hadn't really changed since I'd first met her. She still couldn't say *toilet*.

I sat down in a green vinyl chair and wondered why every medical waiting room in the world subscribed to *Highlights for Children* and *The New Yorker*.

"I didn't want to say nothin' in front of Ms. Singer, but she shouldn't've come." Fernando sat down stiffly next to me and made a little grunting noise. "You got to take her home before you drop me at my crib."

"Oh? And why is that?"

He unzipped his jacket and hoisted it off. "One of our boys was run over last night—only twelve years old, a peewee. He was just fuckin' crossing the street, and a car run him down. He's in St. Elizabeth's. D's did it. Shit, the neighborhood's so hot, even *I'm* afraid to be there. Chilo says it's gonna happen any time now."

"What is?"

"A war—D's against the Dragons. We can't have them fuckin' with our kids."

I thought of when I had gone to high school and how the only thing I'd had to worry about on the way home was if I could carry Cindy Ballard's books. Fernando gazed at nothing, deep in some private reverie. I imagined how it had happened, the bullet piercing his skin, slicing the nerves, exiting through his back, how that might alter your perspective on things, like ever having a chance to live peacefully.

303

I said, "Can't you stay at your dad's place?"

Fernando squinted, tipped his his head to one side. "That's not such a good idea right now."

"Why not? I know he cares about you."

"Yeah, he cares. It's just that when I'm around, things don't go so good between him and his his new O.G. She didn't count on no kids when they hooked up."

I wondered what the hell was wrong with some people, the way they treated kids. I said, "Fernando, you can't stay in that gang."

"Johnny, don't go there."

"Your dad's worried about you."

"If he was so worried, he wouldn't've left us."

"It's not that simple. Don't hang the rap on him."

"I'm just sayin'."

It's never easy—talking to kids, reaching them. You would have thought I'd be better at it by now. I could see it in his face, how he was nonplused by worry, didn't understand himself what to do.

"There's going to be a day when it's not cool anymore, being in a gang, not the way it was when you were thirteen. And one day there might not be any more days at *all* for you, if you know what I mean."

He looked at me as if he were imagining that day. "Dragons are all I got."

"They don't give a shit about you. If they did, Blade wouldn't have sent you out to get Tony, Ratman, or Tito. Did Blade come to see you when you were laid up in the hospital?"

"Don't be talkin about my boys."

"They're not your *boys.* Blade's a fucking adult. Doesn't act like one, but he is."

"I gotta have backup. I gotta do whatever it takes to protect me and my ma."

"Like what—shoot someone?"

"Shit, man—if I have to, yeah."

A woman with a little girl walked into the waiting room. The woman draped a purple coat across a chair back, and the little girl took a *Highlights for Children* from the magazine rack.

I said, "You can't go through life thinking you have to kill people."

The receptionist behind the window called out Fernnando's name.

He stood up awkwardly and shook his head. "Johnny, man—you just don't get it."

Tracy sat down next to me as Fernando followed a nurse back to the treatment rooms. "What is it you don't get?" she asked.

The little girl was swinging her legs alternately as she turned the pages, humming "The Happy Wanderer."

"Life on the streets. Fernando thinks it would kind of be a good idea if we didn't bring you into the neighborhood. The way I get it, there's been some trouble lately."

"I'm a big girl, Johnny. I don't need to be taken care of, thank you very much."

"Still, there's no reason to live dangerously."

"That doesn't sound like the Johnny Spector I know. Besides, we have to go out for our last drink together."

"What last drink? I've had my last drink."

"For closure. You can have a club soda."

Closure? Was she kidding?

I tried to picture her with Woody, and the picture just didn't fit. Of course, I didn't know what he looked like. I didn't know anything about him at all, except what he did for a living, and his preposterous name. Still, an East-Coast guy with a seat on the commodities exchange didn't seem like a match for Tracy. There was something too horn-rimmed about him. Woody was the kind of guy who would own a Saab. I hated guys like that.

I found myself suddenly asking, "What kind of car does Woody drive?"

"Where did that come from?"

"I don't know. I was just wondering."

"An Audi. Why?"

Close enough. "Does he wear glasses?"

"Yes. How did you know?"

He shopped at L.L. Bean and played golf. Put me out of my misery. "Lucky guess."

And then it occurred to me that she was probably right, that we did need closure, and that I had never been able to achieve closure with any relationship. If I had, I wouldn't have been sitting in a hospital waiting room thirty years later thinking about Cindy Ballard and her books. All I wanted was to be able to set the direction of Tracy's future, and to be sure that nothing bad would happen to her, that no one would hurt her, ever. That was not a likely option, however, things going the way they do, all those accidents happening, sending us spinning off in different directions.

"I guess you'll move back in with your wife and son."

I wondered if she was thinking the same kinds of things that I was. "Yeah, I guess I will."

"Good. You belong with them."

I pictured the moving truck returning to the suburbs, recalled with a stab of horror that baby pigeon being pecked to death. "Yes."

"And I'll stay at Acosta and hold down the fort."

I nodded. "Good. That's a good thing to do."

"They say that the superintendant is going to make Javier the new principal."

"Javier's the right man for the job."

"And you'll go on with your life."

"And you with yours."

Her hand patted mine and then squeezed it, and then remained on top of it. "I'm going to need that drink," she said.

It was a strangely moving moment. Our relationship had turned on its axis, had shifted again. Now we were something else to each other, but damned if I knew what. Every time I thought I understood it, I was bewildered again.

§

"So Rico decides he wants a picture of the boys, you know, have it framed, hang it on the wall of his crib. So he asks his neighbor, Mr. Sanchez, 'cause Mr. Sanchez is into photography and shit. Develops his own pictures."

Fernando was leaning against the back of Tracy's seat, telling stories. It was rush hour, and I had decided to take Chicago Avenue back to the neighborhood. There was a mild breeze that made crests in the water, and the shadows were long as we drove across a bridge over the river.

"So we all lined up in the front yard wearing our sweaters. You seen them, right Ms. Singer? They're cool."

Tracy looked at me and smiled. "They're very cool, Fernando."

306

"Yeah. So we're all in Dragon sweaters, except for Turtle, who's wearing a long leather coat. You remember Turtle, from the initiation?"

"Hard to forget Turtle," I said. "Kind of a slow guy? Green shell?"

"I'm ignoring you, Johnny. So Mr. Sanchez was about to snap the picture, when Turtle pulls a sawed-off shotgun out of his leather coat and points it at the camera. You know, just to pose with it. Mr. Sanchez was so scared, lookin' down the barrel of that gun, he fell over backwards on his ass, like in slow motion. Thought Turtle was gonna shoot him. We had to all go over and lift him off the ground. He'd peed his pants."

Fernando burst into an explosion of laughter and could not stop. Tracy said, "That poor man."

You probably had to be there.

We crossed Western Avenue and passed the Jewel-Osco and several storefront churches. The sidewalks were crowded, people getting off work, tired people walking to bus stops, making their way around racks of clothes that merchants had set up outside. This part of town always saddened me in a way I found difficult to express, even to myself. There was a hopelessness about it, as if the very bricks of the old neglected buildings had absorbed the sorrow and defeat of the dwellers within.

"There used to be a Goldblatt's back on that corner," Fernando said. "My ma used to buy me my church clothes there."

Tracy scanned the dilapidated structures, the second story apartments above the shops, chipped paint on splintered window frames. She tucked a few strands of blond hair behind her ear, in the lobe of which was a simple diamond stud.

"There used to be a restauraunt in that building," Fernando said, continuing his tour. "An old man sold Italian beef sandwiches and sno-cones. My old man, he used to walk me up here in the summertime for those sno-cones. They were cold and sweet—you could get cherry, grape or lime. Man, I used to love them sno-cones."

I couldn't help but think that it wasn't the sno-cones he remembered so well as the walk with his father.

"Yo, Johnny. Maybe Ms. Singer and I better change places, so I can just run out of the car to my crib."

I said, "We're not going to do that again. I'll make sure you get to your front door safely. Besides, you couldn't run right now if you wanted to."

I cruised slowly down Sacramento, remembering those years I used to hang out here when I first started teaching. My students weren't much younger than I was. They were eighteen; I was twenty-two. After school we'd go to the old Walgreens on North Avenue, near the Armory. We'd have hamburgers at the lunch counter, and afterward we'd smoke cigarettes in the park, along the grassy shore of the lagoon in Humboldt Park. Somebody would come by with a reefer and we'd get high. The line between teacher and students grew fuzzy. I became an honorary Dragon. A few years later, I met Marlyn.

I pulled the Jeep up alongside the curb in front of Fernando's place. At first I couldn't tell what had happened. It sounded like *pop-pop-pop*; shattered safety glass from the windshiled was strewn across the dashboard and front seat, got in my hair.

"Down!" Fernando shouted. "Get *down*."

We all dove for the floor. The reality that we were under attack did not come as a fully developed thought, but just a clutch of panic as the popping sounds continued, and then the clink-clank of metal—a volley of bullets piercing the hood. There was little room up front; Tracy was lying somewhat below me, and red droplets wetted my hand. I saw that there was a thin slice across her temple, and I didn't know if she'd been grazed, or if the splintered glass had cut her.

"Here," I said, pressing the sleeve of her trench coat against the cut. "You're bleeding. Just hold this here."

She looked dazed. I reached across her, opening the glove box. Inside a doctored VHS video case was my Decocker, my gun. I didn't remember how many rounds I'd left in the clip, and now all I could do was hope it was full.

One more blast and the entire windshield blew out—tiny greenish-blue pellets rained everywhere. Tracy screamed one continuous high-pitched note.

"Fernando—are you okay?"

"Man, can't you get us out of here? They're gonna kill us. I told you, Johnny. I *told* you."

"If I sit up, they'll shoot my head off."

"You gotta get us the fuck outta here."

"I can't drive from the floor. Tell me you've got your gun, Fernando."

"Are you kidding? You're the one who told me not to carry."

"Of all the goddamn times, *now* you listen to me?"

I moved over Tracy, helped lay her down on the floor, around the gearshift. Her trench coat sleeve was saturated, a ruby stain. If I could get the passenger door open, I knew I'd have a position from which to fire. All at once there was a crack, and then another, and a soft thud sounded as the car lurched over to the left.

Fernando said, "They got your front tire."

I thought, *Fuck*, and then I thought, *God, please save us*. And then I thought *Fuck* again.

With a click of the handle, I pushed against the door and swung it open. I crawled out of the car to the curb, crouched behind the cover of the door and the hood. Two figures stooped behind a gold-colored sedan, maybe seven cars ahead. One of them appeared to be Tony, and I wondered, *How the hell am I supposed to shoot a former student?* I fired one warning shot in the air and they both hit the ground. They hadn't expected that we'd fire back.

"Did you get 'em?" Fernando asked.

"No."

"Oh, man. It's Ratman and Tony. I'm telling you, Johnny, they're gonna kill us if you don't kill them."

If it was Guiso and Tony, why would they be firing at me?

My cell phone—where was my cell phone? I always kept it in the breast pocket of my leather jacket. My leather jacket was back at the apartment.

"Tracy—your cell phone. Tracy?"

She was sprawled upon the floor, unresponsive. Her eyes were open, but she didn't move.

Three shots came in rapid succession—one of them hitting the windshield of the car in front of us, either a Nissan or a Toyota. I don't really recall.

"Shoot 'em, Johnny! Goodamn it, *shoot 'em*."

I steadied my arm against the side of the door and fired a shot into one of the cars parked along the roadside. I knew I wouldn't be able to shoot them. I tried to force myself, but it was no use. I couldn't kill kids. I couldn't kill anybody.

Fernando cried, "Did you get 'em?"

I heard myself exhale the word "No."

"Shit, man—you ain't even even *trying*."

Now the two shooters separated, one running long to the right, the other across the street behind another row of cars. I fired another shot into the air, but this time the gun made an empty clicking sound. No more bullets.

I jumped headlong across the front passenger seat of the car, searching for Tracy's purse. It was not between the seats. I said, "Tracy? Are you all right?"

Her eyes fluttered as I reached down to lift the sleeve from her temple. She was bleeding profusely, but I pressed the wound, and it didn't appear deep. Head wounds, I knew, tended to look worse than they really were.

I took off my jacket and made a pillow for her head. "You're going to be fine, sweetheart. It's just a scratch."

"I'm shivering, Johnny."

Those were the first words she'd said. I'd been afraid she was already in shock. "Your purse, Tracy." Her left hand felt around the floor of the Jeep. "I think I'm on top of it."

I reached beneath her, touched something leather, and lifted her slightly to ease the purse out. I considered for a moment simply jumping back into the driver's seat, starting the car, and running it in reverse. But there wasn't enough time, especially with one tire gone.

Tracy's purse was a mess. There were moisturizer tubes and lipstick and nail polish and pens, an address book. "Jesus Christ. How do you ever find anything?"

"If you don't mind, I'm bleeding at the moment."

"Is the phone even in here?"

"I don't know. Try the side pocket."

I ripped the zipper open and there it was.

And then a voice behind me said: "Put the fuckin' phone down."

I dropped the cell phone and turned around. Right outside the open door of the Jeep was Tito, pointing what looked like a nine millimeter automatic at my head. Might as well have been a cannon. He held the gun in both hands, arms extended military style, the way he had the first time he'd tried to shoot us at the bus stop.

"Remember me, *maestro*?"

I should have listened to Hilda. He really *was* going to kill me. His arms shook as he spoke, and you could see he was several steps over the edge. I figured I had nothing to lose.

"I remember you beat up your girlfriend."

"You fucked me up with my lady and you fucked me up with the cops. Now I'm gonna fuck you up, motherfucker."

When your number is up, I think you have just that one second to understand, and then it's all over. I was half reclined against Tracy, and all I could think was, *Maybe he won't hurt her or Fernando after he kills me.*

Like something out of a nightmare, with no warning whatsoever, the top of his head splattered into pulp, went flying into the air. Following came four staccato gun blasts, a pause between the first and the following three. But it couldn't have been. The shots must have been fired first, the sound traveling more slowly than the bullets. I can still see it, his eyes wide open but already lifeless, as he staggered forward, falling face-first upon the parkway, one hand twitching upon the ground, and then finally still.

I heard Fernando say from the back seat, "Holy *fuck*."

No sign of the second shooter. Perhaps he had run off. There were clots of bloody matter sprayed upon the door of the Jeep, the sidewalk, my jeans. I leaned over and got sick at the side of the curb.

"Johnny?" Tracy asked. "Johnny, what is it?"

I lifted my head back. From a second story window of Fernando's building, I saw Chilo leaning out, clad in a white sleeveless t-shirt, a gun in one hand, cigarette dangling from his lip. Tito hadn't been hit from the front, as it had first appeared, but from behind. What I had seen was the bullet exiting. It had been Chilo who had shot him, and I, I guessed that now we were even.

18

In the early mornings, with the coming of dawn, I run. I run no fewer than four and a half miles, and I do it because I have to. I push myself to my limits and I push myself beyond, afraid that if I don't, I'll slide backward. The secret of progress, I've discovered, is not to look back.

I pass the tennis courts in the late summer under canopies of maple boughs, and beyond these the eastern sky opens up in dabbles of subtle colors before the sunlight scorches them away. I'd never noticed the complexity of change the sky undergoes in as little time as an hour, hue, texture, depth—never noticed because I wasn't looking.

I had coffee with señor Valentin the morning I moved out of the loft. I sat on the steps of the outdoor stairway near the sundial while he stood and appraised his garden, an overly delicate looking china coffee cup in his hand. We'd had something of a heat spell, and already the sun was oppressive. At times he would remove a checkered handkerchief from the rear pocket of his trousers and dab his forehead with it.

"Is better to give the vegetables a good soak, not many small ones."

"Why is that?" I asked.

He sipped his coffee sparingly, his Adam's apple bobbing. "A long soak get to the root. Short ones dry too soon. I water early before the sun, she rob the water."

The sun, that old thief.

The Bustelo was strong and acrid and was the beverage equivalent to a kick in the head. It was funny about señor, how he seemed to converse without conversing, his silences as salient as his spoken words. I would miss these moments with him, the feeling of sharing that came from something as simple as observing a garden on a Tuesday morning. I wondered if he had always been this strong, this wise, or if those were things he grew into. I couldn't ask him such a thing because it would have embarrassed him deeply. He was implicitly unselfconscious.

"You go where you belong now."

I did not know if that was an order, or simply an understanding. "Yes."

"You had to leave before you could know."

I said, "I'm a slow learner."

He clasped his free hand on my shoulder and squeezed it. I think it may have been the first time he had ever touched me demonstratively. I'm certain, in fact. "Everything in time, *maestro*, like I tell you. Everything in good time."

Sometimes I wonder what would have become of me were it not for Miguel Valentin.

There was nothing to move except for my clothing and a gift for Marlyn; I'd left the few furnishings I had in the apartment. It was only a matter of jumping in my new Jeep—the old one having been destroyed in the gunfight—and saying a mental goodbye to the old house, North Francisco in general, and Daisy, my old neighbor. This Jeep was a convertible, and I drove home with the top down, the world of the city falling away from me, disappearing behind suburban lawns, shopping centers, the Chicago Botanical Garden. This time I would stay, I knew. I was home again.

When I pulled into the driveway, a few neighbors across the street stood on their parkways, openly staring as I hopped out of the Jeep. I wondered what they were thinking.

Here we go again.

I have a take on nosy neighbors. It goes something like this: To hell with them.

It was May. Jason was still at school, and Marlyn and I had the house to ourselves. Warm breezes through open windows, leafy afternoon shadows swaying, the flutter of gauze curtains. Movement upon satin sheets, whole again, half again, the toil and rewards of love, never quite understanding the mystery of life, the need for one another. We lay still upon the bed, the scent of fresh mown grass coming in the window.

I said, "I have something for you."

"I know. We just finished."

"No, I mean a gift."

I freshened up and dressed in the master bathroom, splashed water on my face and dried it upon a turquoise towel that I remembered. Everything looked new and familiar at the same time. Outside the walkway was cold upon my bare feet and I heard the sizzle of lawn sprinklers, the jangle of a bicycle bell. I felt numbly drowsy as I lifted the wrapped frame from the back seat of the Jeep. To the west there was a wall of purple clouds and I wondered if we would have a storm.

I set the package against a chair in the living room, beside the sliding glass doors. Marlyn came downstairs in a white terry cloth robe. She asked, "What is it?"

I told her to open it and find out. She gave me a quirky look, then kneeled down before the picture. Slipping a fingernail beneath a flap of brown paper, she eased the tape up, opened the layers of folded paper, and pulled them away. It was a framed enlargement of the photograph of her and her mother. She gazed and gazed, shook her head in wonder.

"Where did you get this?"

"I found it at your father's house. Or actually, I think it found me."

She sat back upon her calves. "What made you think of it?"

"It just seemed like something you ought to have."

She stared at it for several minutes without saying anything. Then, visibly overcome, Marlyn left the room. I don't know who took that picture—obviously someone who knew how to focus on the soul. I wish I had been there to tell Sra. Valentin to smile, to please smile for her lovely daughter.

On that first day back there was the wonderful sound of Jason coming through the front door. I think being away from him was the worst part of my exile. He had stayed late to work out in the weight room. He tells me the coach has made him a starting wide receiver on the varsity team this season, which gives me a whole semester worth of worry over possible injuries, along with bragging rights. When he found me unpacking my bags in the living room, he came over and draped a big, beefed-up arm around my shoulders and said, "Nice to have you home, Pop."

It meant everything to hear him say it.

§

"Mr. Spector, did Mr. Velez order English classes to attend a

314

program in the auditorium featuring a group of speakers called the Comrades of Liberation?"

Even before I moved back home, I was subpoenaed to testify in a preliminary Federal hearing involving charges against the Acosta 6. Just behind where the prosecutor stood, Danny Velez, Isabelle, Elizabeth, Murphy, Anatole and Mike Parnell were all seated with their attorneys. Mike looked down at the table, but the others scowled at me.

"Yes," I responded.

"You had no choice in the matter? It wasn't voluntary?"

"No."

"And what was the gist of the presentation, Mr. Spector?"

This was a closed hearing, in a rather small room, and now and then a chair back would squeak and punctuate the silence between question and response.

I said, "Well, there were a few points. One was that the United States and its policies had done harm to the Puerto Rican culture."

"And the others?"

"That the island should be given independent status, that statehood should not be an option on the next referendum."

The prosecutor, a Mr. Feldon, approached the witness stand and looked me directly in the eye. "And did they advocate the violent overthrow of the United States government?"

"They did."

The judge looked out at the defendants and then picked up a pen and made a little note in his records.

"They said this to high school students, that the government of the United States should be overthrown?"

"Yes."

"And are you aware of how much the Comrades of Liberation were compensated for their presentation."

"Yes. Forty thousand dollars."

"And may I ask you how you know that?"

This is something I will never forget—the expectant looks from every one of them. I suppose they had suspected as much, but now I confirmed it for them. "Because I was the one who turned over the school's financial records to the Federal Bureau of Investigation."

Danny's fist came down hard on the table, and the judge rebuked him.

"Counsel, advise your client not to disrupt these proceedings."

I was kept on the stand for over an hour. I was asked about dates, contents of classroom curriculum, statements made during assemblies. At one point Danny's attorney stood and objected to something I'd said on the basis that my testimony was worthless since I was a racist. The judge overruled the objection and warned that if any other accusations of that sort were made, he would recommend that I sue him and his client for defamation. I could feel a quiet fury just below the surface of the hearing. When I was discharged, I walked down the center aisle. As I passed Danny, he leaned over and whispered to me, "I'll get you for this, you son of a bitch."

Danny Velez was convicted of embezzlement. He received ten to fifteen years in a federal prison, though with good behavior (something I'm not sure he is capable of) he could be out in eight. There are rumors that he conducts clandestine revolutionary activity from his cell, though knowing Danny's level of competence, he shouldn't be much of a threat. Before his conviction, when he was still free to walk the streets, he was arrested for pumping and fleeing from an Amoco station in the south suburbs. He almost got away with $37.50 worth of high test gasoline. Some principal.

Mike Parnell received a three-year suspended sentence and was dismissed from the school system. I don't know what happened to him. It's as though he has disappeared. I still feel bad for him and his family. His name was besmirched, his likeness plastered on newspaper front pages under degrading headlines. It's not likely that he is working as an educator these days, so thoroughly was his reputation ruined. I hope his family is all right.

As for the others—Isabelle Villachez, Elizabeth Mojica, Anatole Hafka and good old Murphy, no charges were filed against them; however the school superintendent transferred them to widely scattered, obscure school sites. I spoke to Ira Hirsch recently, and he tells me he has a friend who teaches at Anatole's new school, and according to this friend, Anatole has already been written up twice for ineffectual classroom control. It seems he's swimming downstream in the educational hierarchy. It won't be long before he is given an innocuous post at the downtown headquarters where he won't be able to do any more damage.

Happily, José Julián Acosta High School is presently being run under the highly proficient supervision of Javier Acosta and newly appointed assistant principal Marco Gonzalez. Sedition 101 has been eliminated from the curriculum, and the gym has been opened to students for dances every Friday night. (It was my idea. I called Marco about it and volunteered Vince as a chaperon.)

I'd had the interview at the college in early June, and it had gone poorly, I thought, though I was offered the position. The way they went about informing me was somewhat unorthodox, and I was unprepared for it. After a two-hour grilling I'd received at the hands of the hiring committee (*"Give us your reflections on Yeats's phases of the moon, Mr. Spector"*), Elaine Carver, a full professor of English, took me for a stroll through the gardens. Elaine was a bright, endearing, motherly woman who found phallic symbols in every passage of every poem or novel she'd ever read. We eventually came to a bench overlooking two man-made lakes, and we sat down, and she'd said, "You seem a little on edge, Mr. Spector."

She'd just given me her interpretation of Agamemnon's betrayal, and what she thought his tower represented. I wanted to suggest that perhaps it was only a tower, after all, but I did not say anything. She was so certain.

I said, "Well, I'll tell you, Elaine. It's just that the interview was a little rougher than I had expected."

"Oh," she said, "that wasn't an interview. The department just wanted to get to know you. We decided to hire you last week."

And I'd said, "How's that?"

"Welcome to the English Department, Mr. Spector. Or should I say, *Assistant Professor* Spector?"

I was taken aback, stumbled while I thanked her. She informed me that next I must meet with the dean of Liberal Arts, and I asked her if I might have a moment first to myself, and she said of course. She left me there on the bench in the gardens, where there were milkweed and daffodils, even cacti in tiered levels, hundreds of them. Canadian geese floated restively upon the lake waters. Stretching out in long rows, pine trees grew as far as the eye could see. It was as though someone had spread a blanket of quiet calm over the entire campus. I thought of where I had just come from, the grim streets and territorial lines. All at once I saw Tito's head blown off again in front of me. Directly afterward, Chilo had come down. I could still see him, black hair wet from a recent shower, shiny and combed straight back, dark brooding eyes. He examined the corpse by pushing one of the legs with the toe of his shoe, as if to make sure he was finished. He needn't have bothered.

I said, "How'd you know?"

He turned his head, spat on the ground. "I promised his ma I'd watch out for him."

Most likely I would have been dead but for the shots he had fired, perhaps Tracy too, and Fernando. But I couldn't find it within myself to say thank you. You don't thank someone for what I witnessed. When I'd pulled Tracy from the car, we took her straight to Fernando's apartment. I didn't want her to have to see the mess on the sidewalk. I called the police and soon the neighborhood was overrun with squad cars. A little later the ambulance arrived, and I rode with Tracy to St. Mary's Hospital.

Chilo was taken into custody, but freed after Tracy and I gave an account of what had transpired. I think he was given a fine for unlawful discharge of a weapon within the city limits—something ridiculous, given the situation, but that's just par for the course when it comes to justice, or a lack thereof on the city streets. It's life and death. Chilo was right. Even though I had believed otherwise, I didn't really understand. Not really.

Tito's death has prompted threats of another gang war. However there is no new leadership within the Disciples to step up, to organize. Ratman was busted with a hundred thousand dollars' worth of heroin. He is over twenty-one, and there will be no deals cut with the prosecution. I've talked to my old student Gilberto Marquez, and he has made sure of it.

In any case, I've washed my hands of it all. I've promised Marlyn. Twenty-two years. I've paid my dues.

About halfway into my morning run I come to a bridge that spans the north branch of the Chicago River. When we first moved out to the suburbs, when Jason was no older than five, I used to take him on nature hikes. We'd bring along our cameras, and when we reached this spot, he loved to climb down below the bridge and photograph ducks, or turtles. On one occasion we were fortunate enough to have spotted a fully grown doe, drinking at the banks of the river. She tarried, looked at us calmly for a few moments as though posing, before she ambled along into the deepest part of the woods.

I stopped there the other day and remembered this, my son so young, and then tripping the way the mind does, I thought about what it was like to live without him, back when Tracy filled so many voids. Tracy Singer.

When I think of Tracy, I do so obliquely, the way you look at the sun, or the headlights of oncoming cars. It's too complicated to sort out—who she is, how I feel toward her, what she has meant to me. I don't think it diminishes my love for Marlyn in the least to say that Tracy will always occupy a corner of my heart in some recondite, albeit remarkable fashion. I remember Tracy in her pajamas, bringing me warmed milk—a substance I craved about as much as a nice cup of ammonia. I see her still, firing her Ruger Decocker, scoring more bull's-eye hits than I ever could. And I think back to that day she first came through the lunchroom door, green as a cucumber, with that sappy Abercrombie bag, to complicate my life and her own, and I'm eternally grateful for the complication, and greatly in her debt.

Did you know—she took five stitches to the scalp that day of the shooting? It was a glass shard that had cut her, just above the right ear. She wouldn't allow the emergency room physician to do the sewing, either. She made me wait there at the hospital for *three hours* before the staff could locate a plastic surgeon. She kept removing the gauze that the emergency room team had taped to her scalp, asking me, "How does it look?" And I kept saying, "It looks like a cut, for Christ's sake, Tracy," to which she rejoined, "But does it look ugly?" "No," I told her. "It's a perfectly *adorable* cut."

I took the rest of the school year off to use up some of my sick days before beginning the summer term at the college. Marlyn urged me to begin writing again, and that's what I was doing one night when Vince called. He said he wanted me to stop by the school the next day.

I said, "Vince, why in God's name would I want to do a thing like that?"

"Victory lap," he said.

"What are you talking about?"

"You're in the clear. Come back and show 'em you're in the clear."

And I said that I didn't know, that I'd to have to give it some thought. I slept on it that night, and the next morning I told Marlyn that I had to go back one last time. She was upset with my decision, at first.

"Why, Johnny? Why go back after you've just gotten out?"

319

"Vince calls it a victory lap. I don't know. I think it's just a way of putting my seal on it."

I could see the worry in her eyes. I think she was afraid that I'd break into a sprint and head to the inner city and not come back. But she surprised me.

"I love you," she said, "and you know that, and you love me too, don't you?"

I said, "I've always loved you."

"Of course you have, and I know it, and things will be different now that you'll be at the college. You go back. Go back for one last goodbye."

She kissed me, and I thought about that, about how things really would be different now. My life was changing, and it was going to call for an adjustment.

I got off the Kennedy Expressway at North Avenue and passed that restaurant where I used to pick up doughnuts. I wondered how that little waitress was doing, and if she'd be all right. The Armory, Punto-Frio (an air conditioning service), the park. Just off the school grounds the gangsters hung out, showing off their colors, black and blue, black and green—D's, snakes. I drove up Humboldt Parkway, past pockets of students signing yearbooks, blasting boomboxes, others in the school yard shooting hoops. Javier had obviously relaxed the closed-door policy—a good decision. The kids deserved this. It was the second-to-the-last day of the school year, and there was a vibe in the air—celebration. It was almost all over.

I pulled the Jeep right up to the front entrance and killed the engine and jerked the emergency brake up. As soon as I hopped out, Jorgé came running out the main entrance as if he'd been waiting for me. "Johnny!" He high-fived me, grinning widely, eyes sparkling. "Where you been, dude?"

I said, "What are you—the lookout?"

Good old Jorgé, as hyper and intense as ever. "Man, it's great to see you. Hold on—I'm just gonna tell the boys you're here."

He ran off before I could get another word out, and that's when I spotted Oscar, the security guard. He came at me, a squawking walkie-talkie in his hand.

"No parking here. You move car now."

I said, "It's nice to see you again too, Oscar."

"You get ticket."

"That's fine. Go ahead and give me a ticket. It'll give me something to remember you by."

I walked around the building, through the park. The girls soccer team was practicing. Mona Anderson blew furiously on her whistle and yelled at some poor kid who'd blown a play. Some things never change. On the other side of the athletic field, Ed Faber had his boys PE class doing push ups. I walked down the sidewalk, past strutting, cooing pigeons to the south part of the park where Vince and his physics class had set up dozens upon dozens of rockets, aligned to copper rods that stuck out of the earth. He was down on one knee adjusting a blast-off angle and he wore a t-shirt that said *Whatever goes up, must come down, except for my wife's credit card balance.*

I said, "There he is, the Wernher von Braun of Humboldt Park."

He looked up distractedly. "Hey—the old college prof himself! Did you bring the coeds?"

"No. I brought the six pack. I figured you'd have the coeds."

He stood up and shook my hand. "Take a look at what we got here. You think Cape Canaveral is going to be jealous or what?"

He led me around command central. It was really quite an operation. He had split his class into guidance crews who adjusted the launcher tubing, take-off techs who wired the rockets, and recovery specialists who would gather the rockets upon their return. High schools needed teachers like Vince—if for no other reason than the entertainment value of their coffee mugs and t-shirts.

"What I've done is, I've eliminated the need for individual igniters. Every row you see here is hooked up to its own Delco car battery. I can launch twenty rockets by pressing one button."

I said, "Vince, leave it to you to reach outer space with used car parts."

It was a beautiful June day—mild breeze, sunshine. We walked down a worn path between rows of trees, exchanged pleasantries.

"How's it going on the home front?" he asked me.

I nodded. "It's good, Vince. It's very good."

He stopped short and I circled around to face him. He said, "So have you seen her yet?"

He meant Tracy. "I don't think I'm going inside."

"Oh?"

"Leave the past in the past, you know."

"It's the present, and look where you are."

I didn't understand what his slant was. "I'm here because you asked me to be. I just don't think it's a good idea, is all."

"It may not be a good idea, but it's the right thing. She thinks the world of you, and she's got some news."

Get a load of this guy, I thought. "All right, Vince, if you say so. I'll stop in on her."

I wondered what news Tracy could have for me, but then realized it probably had to do with Woody. I hoped she wasn't making snap decisions, rebounding. But as she would have been the first to tell me, she was a big girl, and she could take care of herself.

Woody. Don't get me started.

I took a walk down one of the lagoon paths along a curved stretch of fence. When I first began teaching I was required to attend a week-long in-service meeting across the street, at the district office. Those sessions were long and boring, and when they let out for lunch, I would walk here and have a smoke. I was befriended by another teacher, a dark Puerto Rican man named Huascar who was new to Chicago, and as homesick as a man can be. He showed me photographs of his wife and children, and we ate hot dogs that we bought at one of the food service concession trucks that are set up in the park in the summertime. He said to me, "Someday, after we have become successful teachers, we will remember when we were brand new, and I will remember when you were my only friend."

Huascar was killed in front of his house a few years later—crossfire from a gang fight. He was right. I remembered, and now he was gone, sweet man.

"Johnny! Damn, dude. Where'd you go?"

Jorgé had caught up to me, and he had Nelson and Phil in tow. Phil had a newly pierced earlobe, and he kept turning his head to the side to see if I would notice. We traded high fives all around—*down low—too slow.* The old hand-jive routines.

Nelson said, "I knew you'd be back, Johnny. I be tellin' the boys—'Johnny's comin' back.'"

"It's just a visit, Nelson. I've got a new job."

He looked downcast. "Yeah? What—you givin' up teaching?"

I said, "No. I'm at a college now."

"No fuckin' way. A college? What—you a professor?"

"Yes."

"Yeah—you gonna teach Shakespeare and shit?"

I told him yes, Shakespeare and shit. Maybe a little Milton and shit.

Phil was standing so that his ear was practically in my face. "Phil?" I said. "Is there something in your ear?"

"It pierced. You like?"

"Yeah. Cool ear gear. What is that—a diamond?"

"Zir-zir-zirconia."

Jorgé said, "Bet you can't say that ten times real fast."

We walked clear around the park back to the front steps. Nydia Velazquez had her dance troupe performing out in the front courtyard. When they finished their number, she ran over and hugged me, dressed in black leotards and a short, wrap-around skirt, ever the artsy dance instructor.

"Lover! You're back."

"Just to say goodbye."

"It's a new place around here, Johnny. You just wouldn't believe it. The reign of terror is over."

I said, "I'm glad to hear it."

"And how about you?" she said. "Things going well?"

I put my arm around her, "Sweetheart, everything's fine." Lico sidled up to Nydia. He was one of her dancers, and very apparently quite attached to her. Good old Lico. I'll always think of him asleep on that bench in Union Station. He told me he was getting an A in English, and for a moment the hurt in his eyes was overshadowed by a glow of pride.

Lucy and Hilda came by to see me, and there was Kirk, and even Marco Gonzalez came out. He was wearing a taupe suit with a gold handkerchief fluffed in the pocket. I said, "Marco, you look like you're about to give the weather on TV."

He shook my hand. "The same lack of respect we've come to expect from you. How do they put up with you at home?"

"They're keeping me in the back yard until I'm housebroken."

Nydia pinched my arm, and in a hushed voice said, "Here comes somebody I bet you remember."

I saw her coming out of the building from a distance, walking directly toward us, even before Nydia spoke up—Tracy. Behind her were Fernando and Daisy, holding hands, by the way. It was about time.

Tracy walked assuredly, her hair tied back, eyes straight ahead. She wore a white, short-sleeved blouse and a summery flower-print skirt, just above the knees. The sun danced upon her hair, but what you noticed were the cheekbones, pink and prominent. Marco had been saying something to Nydia, but suddenly his eyes looked out beyond her, because he had seen Tracy too. Everyone fell silent.

In a tone a little too full of equanimity, Tracy said, "Hello, Johnny. Daisy said she saw you from the second floor. How nice to see you again."

She held out her hand to me, and I shook it, formally. The morning seemed to have come to a halt. I said, "Hello, Tracy. Nice to see you, too."

There was an awkward moment the size of an iceberg during which I believe we both tried to find something else to focus upon. Did I remember the name of the handbook we used in class last semester, she wanted to know. I kept waiting for Nydia to jump in and rescue me, but at the moment her mouth was slightly ajar as if she were watching the aftermath of a car accident.

Writing Research Papers, I said. I said that I thought that was the one. Slowly, the conversation began to resuscitate. *There is a new class schedule. Is that so? Our baseball team has made the playoffs. Isn't that wonderful?*

Fernando was walking better, and I was relieved to see it. The therapy had worked. And he had news. He and his mother would be moving to Wheeling this summer. She had gotten a new job and signed a lease on an apartment. I knew that that would keep him clear of the Dragons and any more gunfights.

Fernando said, "I'm happy and everything, don't get me wrong. But I ain't so crazy about leaving Acosta."

I knew Daisy would miss him too, but kids work these things out. I said, "Fernando—this will be good for you. Trust me. Your life will change."

"I know," he said. "That's what I'm not so crazy about."

"You can't avoid change, buddy. Change is what brings you tomorrow." And then I'd heard what I'd just said.

Out of the blue someone said, "Ms. Singer is engaged." There was

324

a sudden explosion of congratulations.

Nydia said, "We'll have to give you a shower!"

Tracy blushed and answered questions as quickly as they came. "He's from New York. His name is Woody. No, we haven't set a date."

Daisy nudged my ribs with her elbow. "Johnny, sign my yearbook."

She opened it to the faculty section and handed it to me. I saw my photo among all the others, those people I had known and worked with for so long.

John Spector—English

I wrote, "Dear Daisy—There are some kids who walk in and out of my life and are gone forever. Then there are the other kind, the ones who make an indelible impression, kids with souls and hearts as big as the world. You're the first among that second group. Love—Johnny."

Someone was talking to me. I looked up and said, "Pardon?"

It was Marco. "I asked what brings you back today."

I said, "It's got something to do with closure."

Tracy's eyes found mine.

A tremendous hissing sound, clouds of smoke, and soon the sky was filled with Vince's rockets, a hundred of them at once, some arcing wildly, others racing for the moon. Then colorful parachutes played upon the breeze, descending gently. Whatever goes up . . . .

And so I teach Shelley and Keats now, and I write my stories and essays, and take walks along the college's gardens, the lake's shore. It's good and it's healthy, a wonderful way to live, really. But on some days like today, there are moments when the years compress, familiar faces slide across the memory lens, in scenes of gangways or alleys, among the soft yellow glow of lampposts in Humboldt Park at twilight, and I find myself suspended in time once again with my young, wild streethearts. How I miss them.

Greg Herriges's books include six novels, a memoir, and a collection of short stories. *The Chicago Tribune* has called his fiction, "Story of [the] first order" and *Pif Magazine* proclaims that it portrays "the grim story of teen survival against the odds." The nonfiction *JD: A Memoir of a Time and a Journey* (Wordcraft) depicts how he literally set out to meet J. D. Salinger (a great influence on his writing) and how against all odds he succeeded, as well as experiencing surprising, entertaining and enlightening adventures throughout the journey. His novel *The Winter Dance Party Murders* (Wordcraft) is a combination of postmodern-mystery-satire-conspiracy theory and belly-laugh funny, in which Buddy Holly is not killed on that tragic plane flight in February 1959, but... Well, no spoilers here. His other novels include *Secondary Attachments* (Morrow), *Someplace Safe* (St. Martin's, Avon), *Lennon and Me*, and *A Song of Innocence*. His recently published collection of stories *The Bay of Marseilles and Other Stories* is also a Serving House Book.

Herriges's short stories and essays have appeared in a variety of literary periodicals including, inter alia, *Story Quarterly*, *The South Carolina Review*, *The Literary Review*—as well as commercial magazines such as *The Chicago Tribune Magazine* and the reference book *The Encyclopedia of Beat Literature*.

Among his many activities, Herriges produces and writes literary documentary films studying the work of writers such as T. C. Boyle. He is professor of English at William Rainey Harper College in Palatine, Illinois, and divides his time between domiciles in Deerfield, Illinois and Lake Geneva, Wisconsin.